WHEN THE
WICKED
SING

S.L. DeBois

WHEN THE WICKED SING

Cover Art by Tyli Jura

Cover Design by S.L. DeBois

Map Designed by S.L. DeBois

Paperback ISBN: 979-8-9929360-0-1

Hardcover ISBN: 979-8-9929360-1-8

To the writers who fear their words will never be enough,

Your story matters.

Your voice deserves to be heard.

Be brave. Keep writing.

The world is waiting.

VARASOV

KYTHERA

THE CROSSING

ANDROS ISLANDS

TASSOS

EGAN VILLAGE

THE MORTAL REALM

THE SOUTHERN CONTINENT

THE KINGDOM
OF AURELIA

MOUNTAINS

AURELIA ◇

◇ SAMOS

THE FAE REALM

SIRENIA ◇

SALUS
◇

THE
LERUNA SEA

PROLOGUE

SCREAMS PIERCED THE MORNING air, echoes of agony and betrayal reverberating through the palace halls.

The fae king cradled his dead son, his trembling hands stained with blood. Hot tears streamed down his cheeks, burning like fire. The world around him dimmed, his vision narrowing to the lifeless face of Helios, his only son, his hope, his future. A silent wail tore through his soul, a chasm of pain that swallowed everything.

Chaos erupted as the siren queen's pleas for mercy were drowned out by the roar of enraged guards.

King Stavros lifted his bloodshot eyes. Queen Cybele's crown atop her head glinted mockingly in the early sunlight. Her once vibrant and glowing green skin seemed ashen under the weight of her shackles. He met her wide amethyst eyes and knew in that silent exchange that she saw the fury he would unleash upon her people.

"You," the king rasped, his voice trembling with rage, and she stilled. "You took my son—my heir—"

She shook her head, her long magenta hair falling over her shoulders. Lifting her hands toward him, she pleaded, "Stavros, listen to me—"

"How could you?" His voice cracked, each word a blade slicing through the air. Cybele flinched, beginning to tremble.

"Please," she whispered, "you don't understand."

But her words were lost as the king rose to his feet, Helios limp in his arms. He barked orders to his guards, his voice cold and detached, commanding them to kill any siren on sight. His realm would be purged of them. Any civilian who turned in a siren's tail would be rewarded.

He carried his son to the healers, placing the boy's body on the bed with a tenderness that belied the storm brewing within him. The healers' downcast eyes, the way they avoided his gaze, told him everything. Helios was beyond saving.

Stavros pressed his lips to his son's cold forehead, his breath hitching. A memory flashed: Helios's laughter echoing through the halls, his eyes bright with mischief.

Gripping the bed rail, he leaned back to hide the flood of tears and caught a glimpse of his reflection in the polished marble floor—a ghastly face, drained of the once rich brown color, stared back at him.

His son ... his son was gone. What was he going to do? How would he move on?

The king's heart twisted, the pain almost unbearable. But in the next breath, it hardened into something else. Something dark. As he turned to leave, a servant presented him with the crown he'd discarded. He hesitated, staring at it as if seeing it for the first time. Snatching it, he placed its weight upon his head and walked out, his steps echoing with cold determination.

The king boarded his warship. The chilled autumn breeze did nothing to cool the fire raging within him. The queen's desperate screams faded into the distance, muffled by the wind of an impending storm as they departed from the harbor. He kept his eyes fixed on the horizon, ignoring the growing ache in his chest, which felt like it might tear him apart.

After two relentless days, the queen's voice was reduced to a whisper, her pleas weak and rasping. Stavros approached her, the wind lashing at his face. She looked up, her eyes wide with terror, her lips cracked and dry.

He stooped low, bringing his face close to hers. "Do you understand what you've done? What you've taken from me? From my kingdom's future?"

"Stavros," she gasped, her voice a mere thread. "Please … don't …"

"My son. My heir. My everything. You stole that from me." He straightened, turning away from her as a massive glass dome surrounded by towering mountains loomed ahead. His gaze darkened, his grief twisting into something colder, more dangerous. "Now, I will take it all from you."

Despite the raw, festering wound in his chest, he lifted his chin, his resolve steeling. The Queendom of Sirenia would fall.

"Please," he heard the queen whisper, the word a soft prayer, a breath of horror.

The sirens in the bay watched anxiously at the approaching fleet of warships, confusion and fear etched on their faces. The cannons roared, and the world turned to chaos. Screams, blood, smoke—death filled the once sweet floral air that carried on a sea breeze. The sirens who couldn't escape were ensnared in nets, their desperate cries cut short by the sharp thrust of spears. The river that flowed from the glass dome ran red with their blood.

On board his ship, Stavros watched the carnage unfold. When the glass dome finally shattered under the relentless bombardment, shards rained down, slicing through everything in their path. The sky above darkened, and rain began to pour, drenching the dying. Lightning split the heavens, and thunder rumbled like the growl of an angry god.

The king stood still, drenched by the storm, his eyes fixed on the destruction he had wrought. He had expected to feel satisfaction, maybe even a measure of peace. But all he felt was a hollow ache, and something else—guilt, creeping in like a slow poison, tainting his victory.

He turned his gaze to the waterfall that fed the bay, its waters cascading into the pool below. With a wave of his hand, he called upon his power, tearing trees from the earth and hurling boulders into the river. The waterfall slowed, then stopped altogether. The bay began to empty, and the bodies of the dead sirens—eyes wide, mouths open in silent screams—floated lifelessly down the river into the sea.

King Stavros stared at the scene, waiting for the relief he so desperately sought. But there was none. Only a deep, gnawing void.

Behind him, the siren queen's hoarse voice broke through the silence. "Please! Please stop! No more!"

He barely recognized his voice when he spoke, the words low and rough. "Let her go."

The guards released her, and she collapsed onto the deck, her crown tumbling from her head. She stared at it with tear-filled eyes, broken.

"Never come back here," he said, each word heavy with grief that threatened to choke him. "Your kind isn't welcome in my kingdom. If I catch you trying to rebuild, I'll slaughter every last one of you. Now go."

He wasn't sure she'd heard him. But then she slowly rose to her feet, clutching the crown to her chest.

"The agony you've inflicted upon my sisters will haunt your dark soul for the rest of your eternal life," she whispered, her voice filled with a sorrow that mirrored his own. "I promise you."

Then she was gone, disappearing into the rain-soaked night.

Stavros stood alone amidst the ruins, surrounded by death and destruction. All that remained was silence.

CHAPTER 1

ALTHOUGH IT WAS MIDDAY, the trench at the bottom of the sea was cloaked in eternal darkness, reeking of death. The only light source came from the scorching violet fire billowing out from a crack in the earth. It did little to keep the cold from sinking deep into Mariana's bones.

Ethereal voices echoed through the stone cavern.

The sacred cremation ceremony had begun.

The gathered sirens sang their enchanting song about life, death, love, and family in perfect harmony. The sad melody slithered and crept across Mariana's skin, giving her chills. It was the only song that haunted her dreams.

Three sisters were dead, and one was missing. It was a dark and ominous reminder of how precious life was when you were part of an endangered species. A despairing shadow was cast over the underwater caverns of Salus as, once again, hope for peace and safety became a desperate, tragic dream.

Mariana's eyes were locked on the corpses before her, each wrapped in black, metallic fiber.

Astra, her eldest blood sister, was gone. No one knew where she was or what had happened to her.

As if in a trance, Mariana felt her lips move along with the chorus. She felt hollow, like the sea reaper had slithered out from these black depths and carved out her broken heart. She could envision Astra's ivory hair woven with pearls into thin dreadlocks, her tail blending in with the kelp forest's mossy depths. With pale blue eyes and a delicate voice, Astra could capture anyone in a story like no other. She was compassionate, gentle, and caring, always making everyone around her feel special. Her determination was admirable, as was her bravery.

Mariana was furious with the siren queen. She had kept Mariana in the dark about crucial details regarding Astra's mission to the fae realm. She cast her eyes at her mother.

Queen Cybele appeared regal with a shimmering, translucent top wrapped around her waist and long billowing sleeves that brushed halfway down her tail. Glinting underneath was her fitted white armor that closely matched Mariana's. The scales on her arms gleamed the colors of the sea, and her tail was as black as midnight yet sparkled with the light of a thousand stars. The ends of her fins faded into her hair's magenta hue, which was braided and pinned back with black diamonds beneath her deadly crown. It was meant to inspire and intimidate. It was also a weapon in battle. It had five diamonds carved into sharp, twisted points reaching upward, with a row of rough blue sapphires sitting above the queen's arched brow. More diamonds were woven across the top and back of the head as a shield. It was a warrior's crown, a symbol of power and death.

Mariana hated it.

She'd held the heavy crown before and even felt it upon her small head as a youngling when she and her mother played. She couldn't wait to be queen then. But that was a very long time ago.

The song faded away, and silence settled over the cave. The sirens all watched as their queen approached the three bodies lying in wait on woven kelp pallets. Mariana could hear the quiet sound of her mother scraping her long, sharp nails against the staff she held tightly in her left hand. Cybele gestured for Luna, Astra's only daughter, to come forward.

Although every siren was a sister, the protective nature of sisters connected by blood was fierce. Astra, Aurora, and Mariana had all been born from Cybele. Like many sirens, Luna was single-born, and her kin were her closest companions.

Mariana breathed deeply and kept her arms locked at her sides despite the urge to reach out and comfort her.

Luna approached the queen as the crowd parted for her. She was the spitting image of Astra, though her scales were ivory and shimmered a violet hue instead of green. Although considered small for a siren, Luna was much older than Mariana. She appeared even smaller now, hunched protectively over the marble box that housed Astra's memorabilia.

The queen gave a soft smile and held her free hand out to Luna, who took it lightly.

Mariana watched Cybele face the audience with Luna. The blazing violet furnace behind them cast their faces into dark shadows while outlining their bodies in a purple glow.

"This never gets easier. These ceremonies have become habitual for us, and I dread them," the queen admitted, her velvety voice thick with grief. "And telling you that we're here to mourn more of our fallen sisters ... it breaks my heart." She shook her head slightly. "Today, we're here to remember four truly beloved sisters who risked and dedicated their lives to help create a better future for us all. One where there is no fear of exploring, growing old, or finding a mate. That is the future they believed in, and that is the future I still believe in.

"I promise you all that I will never stop trying to find a solution for us to return to Sirenia, our home. For Telesia, for Hella, for Iris, and"—she gazed down at Luna, who peered up at her with swollen eyes—"for Astra, we will all persevere. From ruin, we rise."

Conflicting thoughts rattled Mariana as she scrutinized her mother.

A century ago, all sirens had been banished from the fae realm. Thousands of their sisters were brutally killed, all because of the death of one fae.

Prince Helios.

The Kingdom of Aurelia, once a place of wonder and enchantment, became a symbol of treachery. King Stavros had been known as an honorable leader. Yet, everything changed the day he found Queen Cybele standing over his son's dead body.

The truth of what happened that fateful day remained shrouded in mystery. Some said Cybele had slain the heir, while others whispered that she had tried to save him. Whatever the case, the fae king's wrath knew no bounds. Without trial or evidence, he banished all sirens from the fae realm, condemning them to an existence of suffering and exile. He razed the siren queendom to the ground, forcing the survivors to flee for their lives.

The bitter, imaginary taste of death and smoke formed on Mariana's tongue, and she hardly noticed when someone sidled up next to her. The Siren Witch touched Mariana's arm, startling her from her clouded thoughts.

The witch's hands were stained black from the ritual of wrapping the bodies before cremation. Her polished claws were long and so sharp that they could easily slice open a vein in the blink of an eye. Mariana shook her head to immediately cut off the dark thought. She lifted her eyes and caught her mother's intimidating stare. She realized her role in the ceremony was next.

After giving her a curt nod, the witch retreated behind Cybele. With a steadying breath to calm her heart, Mariana slowly raised her hands as her power came forth with its familiar buzz. Carefully, she commanded the surrounding water to gently lift all three pallets to eye level.

Just as they'd done hundreds of times before, the sirens behind her started to sing their final song as the queen used the staff she held to push each pallet forward. The purple flames enveloped the bodies, and the flaring heat blasted Mariana's skin. Her voice cracked as she sang goodbye to her fallen sisters, imagining their journey to the afterlife.

The song faded, and Luna's muffled sobs replaced the sad melody.

"Luna." Mariana gently grabbed her sister's hand and pulled her into an embrace. They held each other with the stone box clutched tightly between their bodies.

"She's not dead. She can't be. My heart knows she's still out there," Luna whispered, her voice quivering.

Mariana rested her head on Luna's and held her tighter. "She could still be alive. We don't know for sure, but—"

"But I do know!" Luna cried out. "I do. She's alive. She has to be. Please, find her."

Mariana softly hushed Luna's wailing and unfolded her arms to put her hands on Luna's shoulders. She held her gaze, and when she tucked Luna's silvery hair behind her pointed ear, she saw the gills on her neck inhaling and exhaling rapidly. Unable to look into the sad eyes of her sister any longer, Mariana fixed her gaze instead on the tattooed moon phases on Luna's forehead. Like all their tattoos, they glowed gently when in contact with the sea.

"Luna, if she's still alive, then I will find her. If she isn't—" Mariana gently halted the start of Luna's protesting. "If her soul is wandering, we have to say goodbye. Amphitrite needs to guide Astra on her journey to peace. We can't delay it any longer. And if she is alive, Amphitrite will hear us and ..." Mariana choked and breathed deeply to steady herself. "And she will guide Astra back home." She gave an encouraging nod to Luna, then placed her hand over the box's lid, right on top of Astra's carved name.

Cybele's right hand settled over Mariana's, and their eyes met briefly before the Siren Witch placed a hand on Cybele's right shoulder. When the comforting hands of her blood sister, Aurora, rested on both her shoulders, Mariana closed her eyes. She silently prayed to the Goddess to guide Astra to peace and herself to find justice for her sister.

She listened to Luna weep and opened her eyes to watch as the free hands of every remaining siren alive were placed on each other's shoulders, encircling Astra's unopened box.

CHAPTER 2

THE SUN SOARED ACROSS the sky like a falling star until twilight descended, quieting the crashing waves and seabirds. From one shade of darkness to another, Mariana lifted herself from the sea onto a line of rocks not far from the beach ahead of her. Her nails sank deep into the slick algae to keep herself from falling before she settled onto her elbows. Crabs skittered across the rocks, making Mariana scrunch her nose as she flicked one of them away.

Her gaze homed in on the dark waves crashing against the sand. It was the mortal island of Tassos, one of many within the Andros Islands. The village was settled beside a river where they grew crops, herbs, and spices for trade. Lanterns surrounded by mesmerized insects hung on wooden posts around the village paths, casting a soft glow through the fog.

No sign of them yet, she thought to herself.

Aurora appeared beside her so quietly that Mariana didn't notice until they were shoulder to shoulder. The skittering crabs made more noise than her, but Mariana expected nothing less. After all, her sister was a lethal warrior.

She glanced at her, at their touching shoulders. Where Mariana's pale blue skin blended into the sea, Aurora's brushed brass skin stood out. But under the cloudy night, she could hardly tell the difference between their shoulders, except that Mariana's was covered in tattoos.

Their hair whipped gently in the wind, mingling the dark teal and blood red strands. Mariana lifted a finger to her sister's golden cuff, tracing the geometric pattern carved within. Mariana's bracelet—a fiber cord threaded with colorful shells and beads—was a cheap comparison to the beautiful cuff. Aurora had made it herself; she loved gold jewelry and made everything she wore, from the several earrings piercing her ears to the necklaces around her neck. She said it made her happy, and she deserved it after everything she'd gone through. Happiness was a rarity in Salus.

After the Banishment, Salus became a haven for the last remaining sirens. It was a long-forgotten ruin at the bottom of the Leruna Sea. It was deep enough that any creature without the ability to breathe underwater would drown or be crushed by the pressure before they could reach it.

The few siren survivors, many of whom were skilled architects, engineers, sculptors, and designers, rebuilt Salus into a fortress that would stand the test of time. Queen Cybele called it their sanctuary; Mariana called it their grave.

The only way sirens could reproduce was with male fae. When sirens were suddenly forced out of the fae realm, reproduction plummeted. Their numbers had dropped steadily for years as the old grew weary and frail, eventually dying.

"They're here," Aurora whispered, and Mariana snapped her eyes up to the dark, lapping water ahead of them.

Cursed sirens approached the beach slowly, their heads peeking out of the water, their tails lapping gently in the waves.

They began to sing. A soft, eerie melody sent chills over Mariana's skin.

"We shouldn't be here," she heard Aurora mutter.

Mariana's gaze hardened. She had to see this. She wanted to understand what happened during the culling. But when she turned her head and saw the concern in her older sister's golden eyes, she understood.

The culling was forbidden to watch or partake in by anyone who wasn't cursed or ready to accept the Scourge. But no matter what Cybele said, Mariana was the heir; she had to know. And Aurora wouldn't let her do this alone. Together, they would watch the darkness unfold.

Mariana turned her eyes back to the beach. Mortals shuffled out of the fog toward their fate. Her breath hitched when she saw their glazed eyes and slack hands, enchanted by the haunting melody.

The mortals of these islands were taught to believe that if they heard the song of the sea under a full moon, they were worthy sacrifices to the underwater goddesses. In return, the sirens would keep their fish ecosystems thriving and the reefs clear of unwanted predators. They had no idea it was cursed sirens falling victim to the Scourge and its promise of eternal life.

The instinct to protect them unexpectedly overwhelmed Mariana.

This was what Astra wanted to stop.

Astra had advocated for the end of the culling.

Under intense scrutiny, Astra decided not to accept the Scourge, to live forever. Mariana had always admired her eldest sister's decision and knew the queen did too. Astra was Cybele's firstborn, and as Astra began to feel her body change, with slight wrinkles near her eyes and wisps of gray in her hair, she pushed heavily for a peace mission to the fae realm as an emissary to restore Sirenia. Cybele only allowed it because it was Astra's final wish. Astra would have lost her ability to transform her tail into legs and walk on land in a few years. She'd felt that if she didn't die trying to save their people, she had failed in life.

A siren would reach her life's third and final stage at around five hundred years. This was when they had to choose between the path leading to death or the Scourge's path to immortality. The Queen of the Sea was an exception to this rule. Cybele would not begin her descent into the final stage of life until Mariana, who had inherited the power of the sea, had matured. If a queen chose to put off producing an heir, she could live for hundreds of years before her instincts gave her no choice but to reproduce. Cybele had witnessed two generations of sirens being born and dying before finally giving birth to Mariana. Now, her mother would soon begin to grow old.

The first sign of an aging siren was the fading of her magic, when the power to control mortals with her voice would weaken. Her body would wrinkle, and her scales would turn gray. Half a century later, the Goddess, Amphitrite, would guide the siren's soul on their journey to peace. This was a siren's inevitable ending—before immortality became essential to survival.

Before the Banishment, the Scourge was considered evil, for all it did was take away a sister everyone loved, replacing them with a husk, a ghost of who they were.

Despite Queen Cybele's firm disdain for the Scourge, she allowed the cullings to keep the siren population from declining. The fewer warriors they had, the less protection they had.

The Scourge offered a path to eternal youth and strength for any siren willing to endure its curse. By accepting this fate, a sister's soul would gradually decay, her organs and eyes would turn black, and she would lose not only her ability to walk on land but also to reproduce. Stripped of her very identity, she would become a neurotic, soulless creature, confined to the sea for all eternity—all for the sake of immortality.

The Siren Witch's head bobbed up from the waves, her headdress dripping seawater. Renowned as the most powerful cursed siren alive, she alone had been permitted to study and practice the dark magic unlocked by the Scourge, despite Astra's objections. As the queen's only blood sister and most trusted advisor, her growing power commanded profound respect from all cursed sirens and ensured their obedience.

Astra had always made it clear that she did not believe in how sirens changed their views on the Scourge, even as a survival aid. She rejected that excuse, claiming that the Goddess would have shown them the way to a safer world, but instead, sirens have lost their way. She'd once said that sirens were created out of love and sacrifice and that to steal anyone's life, anyone's soul, to achieve immortality was reprehensible.

The Siren Witch strongly disagreed with Astra, insisting it was the path to unlocking a siren's true potential.

Why did it feel so wrong if it was that easy to justify the culling?

Shivers danced along her spine as Mariana watched the scene ahead. She could feel the sinister energy radiating from the song.

A dozen mortals entered the water. Then clawed hands reached up and gently pulled them down into the waves.

"Calliope," Mariana breathed, recognizing the sister who had guarded her when she was young. "What is she doing here?"

Aurora gripped her hand in support as they watched Calliope kiss a man with a heavily bandaged stomach. They looked like two lovers lost in their own world. Then, a white glow formed within the chest of the mortal man and slowly transferred itself through their locked lips and into Calliope.

Every embraced mortal within the pack began to slacken, their hands and legs no longer working to keep close to the siren kissing them.

They were dead.

Mariana's vision began to blur as her eyes unexpectedly filled with tears.

When the glow faded, each siren released the lips of their mortal and pulled their lifeless body down into the darkness of the sea.

"Where are they taking them?" Mariana whispered in alarm when they all disappeared underwater. "They don't let their families bury them?"

Aurora shook her head, fear in her eyes. Mariana found it hard to believe Aurora was afraid of anything. She was their best warrior. She was known in the fae realm as an assassin, the Scarlet Serpent.

Aurora hated that name.

After the Banishment, she'd worked tirelessly to forget it. She took a vow to never kill ever again except under the direst circumstances. Instead, she devoted her time to becoming an armorer, choosing to protect her fellow siren sisters with nearly indestructible armor made from scavenged basilisk bones. It was her legacy.

"We have to go. The sun will rise soon, and I want to find out what happened to Astra's Guardians. The witch said she'd give a report after the culling." The hitch in Aurora's voice as she slid down the rocks made Mariana pause. Guardians had been wearing sun-protected armor when they were discovered dead near the entrance to Salus.

"Rora?" she said gently, causing her sister to go still and meet her gaze. Mariana wanted to tell her it would all be okay, but she knew that was a lie. None of this was okay. "Thank you for coming with me."

What Aurora had done by being there for her in that difficult moment was worth more than just a thank you. Still, by the slight tilt of Aurora's lips, she knew her sister appreciated it.

"I'll be there before sunrise, but I need a moment alone."

Aurora gave her a nod before slipping into the waves.

As soon as she was gone, Mariana left the rocks and approached the beach. The waves flowed through her hair, and she wished they could wash away the sick, shameful feeling coursing through her at what she had just witnessed.

A dozen mortals were dead because *they* didn't have a solution to *their* problem with the fae. No mortal deserved this.

The cursed were ordered never to take more than one soul per siren at a time, once a month. They were only allowed to call on the weak-minded adults who were no longer in their prime, dying, or sometimes an assaulter in need of penance, as though that made up for all the deaths. As the number of sirens who chose the immortal path grew, so did the number of mortals required to die month after month.

Mariana glared at the silent dark sky and wanted to shout at how unfair it all was. She let her head dip under the water and was about to leave when a flicker of light rippling above the waves caught her attention.

She peeked her head out of the water. A weeping child wrapped in a blue sleeping robe with a lit torch in her hand stood alone on the beach. Her crying eyes were locked on the dark water before her.

Mariana swallowed the painful lump forming in her throat as she wondered who the girl mourned.

Who was taken from her? Who heard the siren song and disappeared under the moonlight into the sea forever?

With her heavy breaths clouding the air in front of her, the little girl sniffled and peered down at her bare feet, taking a nervous step toward the waves. They greeted her with a sweep of salty water. The girl dropped her torch on the sand, the water snuffing out its light, and began walking into the water.

Mariana's blood ran cold.

Just as the sea grazed the little girl's stomach and the ends of her curly hair, Mariana quickly lifted her hands and pulled the water away from the child.

The girl stopped, gawking at the churning barrier surrounding her. She lifted her eyes straight into Mariana's and gasped.

Not knowing what to do, they stared at each other for a long moment before Mariana lifted her hand and gestured for the girl to leave. The child continued to stare at her with puffy eyes.

Guilt washed over Mariana at the thought of what she was about to do. She opened her mouth and began to sing to the little mortal.

Her lips moved carefully, words about hope and love slithering into the child's ears. Mariana sang softly, as a mother would sing her baby to sleep, influencing the child to return home to her bed and dream of only the best memories. The girl's mouth lifted into a little smile, and her body obeyed the song.

Mariana finally sank back into the sea when the little girl disappeared through the dense fog and into town. Her heart was a heavy weight in her chest. It dragged her down and settled her on the sandy bottom.

The kisses of a thousand tiny fish began pecking her skin clean of impurities, and she let the lonely bitterness crash down upon her.

CHAPTER 3

EGAN VILLAGE WAS THE largest mortal settlement in the Andros Islands, a fishing port nestled at the base of craggy cliffs, where pine trees loomed tall and dark like sentinels. The bay stretched out in calm shades of steel blue. Its surface rippled with the morning tide, swaying boats gently as their mooring lines creaked. Smoke curled faintly from scattered chimneys, a sign that a few villagers were beginning their day. Beyond the woods was the Crossing—a land bridge connecting the mortal realm to the fae realm. However, the fae never ventured into the mortal realm; they hated mortals and their scent.

The village itself smelled of dead fish, brine, and musky earth. Mariana wrinkled her nose as she rose from the waves just beyond the port, stepping onto the coarse sand with the water lapping at her legs. She adjusted her white linen dress, the fabric clinging to her form before she expelled the water from her body in one smooth motion, letting it puddle and sink into the sand at her feet. Finger-combing her now-dry hair, she approached a small wooden cabin hidden between the trees.

She knocked on the chipped yellow door, casting a glance at the other silent cabins around her. Most of the villagers were still asleep, but Mariana knew, without a doubt, who would already be awake.

As the sun began to lift from its slumber beneath the horizon, the door creaked open. Celeste's familiar face appeared, wrinkled and warm, framed by a curtain of soft white hair.

"Morning, sleepyhead!" Mariana greeted, her lips lifting into a genuine smile as she leaned in for a hug.

"I was wondering what time you'd get here today," Celeste said, wrapping her willowy arms tightly around Mariana in the way that only Celeste could. Lavender wafted from her skin, the scent comforting.

Even with all the storm clouds that loomed in Mariana's life, Celeste always managed to make her feel safe.

"I'm not *that* late," Mariana said with mock defensiveness as she stepped back. "The sun isn't even fully up yet."

Celeste chuckled, her laugh light and warm as a spring breeze. "If the sky has a touch of light, it's time to prepare," she teased, motioning Mariana inside.

The cabin's interior welcomed her with a burst of color and scents. Herbs and flowers hung in bundles from the ceiling beams, their fragrant oils infusing the air with earthy sweetness. Jars of dried petals and powders lined every available shelf, each labeled with Celeste's elegant handwriting. And the round table at the center of the room overflowed with more herbs, wax, cloth bags, and strings for bundling.

Mariana often thought of this cabin as a sanctuary. It was a world apart from the cold, dark waters of Salus, where everything tasted of salt and decay. Here, she could *smell*. She could breathe deeply and savor the richness of the air, her senses delighting in things she could never find underwater.

She stooped to pick up a bundle of mint that had fallen to the floor, inhaling its sharp, refreshing aroma as she set it on the table. "I suppose you're right," she said, eyeing the piles of herbs still waiting to be chopped. Two mugs of steaming chamomile tea sat waiting on the table, their golden liquid catching the light.

Mariana smiled faintly but found her gaze lingering on the tea bags, her thoughts drifting. *Astra.* The name surfaced unbidden, cutting through the moment like a jagged blade. Her sister would've loved this. She was the only one who knew about her visits to Celeste, so why hadn't she brought Astra to meet her?

Now, with the very real possibility that she might never see her eldest sister again, regret hit her like a wave. Why had she kept this part of her life separate? Why had she never shared this haven, this safe place, with the sister she loved so dearly? There was still so much she wanted to tell her, so much she wanted to *show* her.

"Dear," Celeste's soft voice broke through her thoughts with a touch to Mariana's elbow, her brown eyes filled with concern. "Are you alright?"

Mariana blinked, her vision suddenly blurring with unshed tears. She stared at Celeste, at the lines etched into her face, at the gentle strength in her gaze, and for a fleeting moment, she considered lying. She didn't want to burden her friend with the dark storm that had settled over her life. Celeste lived in the light, and Mariana didn't want to drag her into the darkness.

Mariana's eyes skated over Celeste's wrinkled features and saw the young female beneath that had found her on a beach nearly fifty years ago.

Celeste always had a knack for understanding plants. She knew where to find even the most elusive, insignificant sapling and how to nurture it in the wild. This turned out to be true for sirens. The night they met, she had found Mariana flopping around on the sand with freshly transformed legs, trying to get the damn things to work. She thought Mariana was a mortal child having a seizure at first and rushed to help her. Of course, Mariana screamed in surprise, making Celeste scream too, and they'd been friends ever since.

Truthfully, Mariana was never supposed to be on that beach. Cybele wouldn't have allowed her to practice walking until she was older, but Mariana refused to wait. Learning to walk meant adventures where she could escape the dark confines of Salus. Back then, she had been innocent to all the harm that could be inflicted on a young siren if she left the sea, but she was desperate—desperate to listen to the sky, desperate to be free. So, she'd defied her mother's orders, escaped her Guardians, and found the quiet, empty beach, determined to walk. After many days of practice, Celeste taught her how, taught her the mortal language, taught her their culture.

But most importantly, Celeste treated her like an equal. Not like a *sea goddess*. The title was like acid in the back of her throat.

The memory of the culling bombarded her thoughts, and though it deeply bothered her, she couldn't bring herself to tell Celeste what she saw. Egan Village was off-limits for the cullings, a rule Mariana had fiercely enforced to protect her friend and the people there, one Cybele only agreed to because of the importance of the mortal population's stability. Still, the image of those mortals—sacrificed under the ruse of honor but prey for cursed sirens—lingered in her mind.

Mariana realized she hadn't said anything for a few minutes. Celeste was waiting patiently, a concerned look in her brown eyes that said she was ready to listen when Mariana was ready to speak.

That was when Mariana decided she couldn't lie to her. She may have been growing old, having only lived a tiny portion of the life Mariana would live, but Celeste was the strongest person she'd ever met.

Reaching down for one of her friend's hands, she held it in her own, noticing how different they were. Mariana's skin was pale blue, covered in an array of delicate tattoos, which Celeste always said were the stanzas in the poem of Mariana's life. Celeste's hands were withered with age and scarred from whatever had happened to her before she made it to Egan Village—a part of her life she never discussed. Perhaps that made them respect each other: They were both physically marked by their pasts and refused to let it control their futures.

Clearing her tight throat, Mariana admitted, "My sister, Astra, has been missing for several weeks now." She swallowed hard. Celeste rested her other hand on top of hers, gripping it tight. It was the encouragement she needed to keep talking. "There's a chance she's..." Mariana swallowed again, then took a deep breath. "Dead." The word was so heavy on her tongue that she barely got it out.

Celeste gasped, her eyes wide. "Oh dear, what's happened to her?" Her voice cracked, and she pressed a hand to her heart. Mariana felt a pang of guilt for bringing her grief into this peaceful little cabin, but she couldn't stop now.

Lifting a shoulder, Mariana pulled out a chair and sighed as she sat. Celeste sat beside her but still gripped her hand. She squeezed it affectionately, making a corner of Mariana's mouth lift briefly.

"She was on a peace mission to the fae realm. She wanted to meet with the king and negotiate for the safety of Salus. I don't know what she planned on bargaining with. My mother is keeping me in the dark about it all," she admitted with a scowl. "I just know that her Guardians returned, but all died before they could tell us what happened, and now we have no idea where Astra is or whether she's even alive."

Mariana let out a shaky breath, thoughts of Astra locked up in a dungeon or hanging by her tail in front of the fae palace gates haunting her. She shivered.

Without saying anything, Celeste pulled her into her arms and held her.

"I'm so sorry, love, that's terrifying," Celeste whispered as she rubbed her back gently in soothing circles. Mariana sank into her embrace, wishing to stay there until everything got better. She expected herself to start crying, but it felt like she was dried out, desperate for a drop of water, yet knowing nothing would satisfy.

The look on Luna's face as she begged Mariana to find her mother made her chest ache. "I have to find her, Celeste. I have to bring her home."

Celeste gently pulled back and cupped Mariana's cheeks with warm, soft hands. "I know you do," she admitted, yet tears still filled her eyes. "But that scares me. What if something happens to you too?"

The question echoed in her mind, and she couldn't figure out how to deal with it. Instead, she covered her friend's hands with her own and slowly pulled away. She chewed on the inside of her cheek. "You've always told me to be brave." She tried to smile, knowing it was weak, and yet it somehow gave her the strength she needed. "We don't let anything stand in our way, right?"

Celeste smiled back and sniffed. "I suppose you're right. I know what it's like to lose someone. But sometimes, the best way to honor them is to fight for the ones who are still here." She sighed, her smile fading, her expression turning grim and serious. "The fae realm is dangerous—"

"Let's not talk about that right now," Mariana objected gently, knowing it would only upset Celeste if they talked about the dangers that infected that place beyond the Crossing. "In all honesty," she said with a shrug, "I have no idea if I'll even be allowed to go—"

"Hah!" Celeste chuckled. "Like that would stop you."

Mariana rolled her eyes, hiding her smile. "But I want you to know that if I do, I will come back here first."

Celeste's smile dropped. "To say goodbye," she murmured.

Mariana shook her head. "No, to help you prepare for the market and say I'll see you soon." She gave her a wink, making her friend chuckle and wipe her eyes. "Thank you for listening to me," Mariana said.

Celeste gave her a sad smile. "I will always listen, you know that." Pinching Mariana's chin with her thumb and forefinger, she added, "I sincerely hope you find your sister. Thank you for trusting me with this."

Mariana returned the gesture, making both of them release a sad, short chuckle. But Mariana didn't want her news to ruin their morning. She wanted to run away from the darkness, just for a little bit, and straight into the light.

Standing, she said, "Now." She grabbed a few bundles of herbs to take over to the tiny kitchen. "Let's hurry up and get you ready for the market. The sun's already up, and we're running out of time."

Celeste waved her hands. "Bah, it's fine. We have all the time in the world. They'll always wait for my potions," she said with a twinkle in her eye as she began stuffing tea bags.

A sudden knock on the door startled them both.

Mariana's hands froze mid-pluck of the mint leaves. Celeste stiffened, her smile faltering as her gaze darted toward the door. For a fleeting moment, there was something unreadable in her expression—a shadow of unease that Mariana had never seen before.

"I'll get it," Celeste blurted. Her voice was calm, but its slight tremor in it wasn't lost on Mariana. Her friend rose from her chair, her jaw tightening as she crossed the room with hurried steps.

Mariana tilted her head, her brows knitting together. "Do you want me to—?"

"No, no," Celeste interrupted, already at the door. She paused with her hand on the knob, her body momentarily still as if steeling herself. Then, with a deep breath, she opened it.

A raggedy middle-aged fisherman stood on the other side, the smell of salt, sweat, and stale fish wafting in like a noxious tide. Mariana wrinkled her nose and stepped away, trying to subtly cover her face as the man began speaking in a gruff, hesitant tone.

"Good morning, Miss Celeste," he said, pulling off his battered hat and twisting it nervously. "We checked out that island you asked about—"

"Just a moment," Celeste interrupted sharply, holding up a hand. She glanced back over her shoulder, her brown eyes meeting Mariana's. The unease in her gaze hadn't faded, but her lips curved into a strained smile that didn't quite reach her eyes. "I'll be right back," she said softly before slipping outside and shutting the door firmly behind her.

Mariana blinked, caught off guard.

Her curiosity sparked, and though she knew she shouldn't, she couldn't resist stepping quietly toward the window. She peeked through the colorful curtains, her heart beating a little faster as she strained to catch their conversation.

"What do you mean it was empty?" Celeste's voice quivered, the heartbreak in her tone slicing through the air like a blade.

"I mean, there was nobody there," the fisherman replied with a helpless shrug. "Not a single person around. The place was deserted."

"You were certain?" Celeste pressed, her hands clasped so tightly that her knuckles turned white. "You looked *everywhere*?"

"We searched the whole island, just like you asked," the fisherman said, gesturing with his weathered hands. His gray dreadlocks swung slightly as he adjusted his stained hat, clearly uncomfortable. "I know this was important to you, but ... there wasn't anyone there. No signs of life. No footprints. Nothing."

Mariana's frown deepened as she studied her friend. Celeste's shoulders slumped, her head dipping as if the man's words had stolen the strength right out of her.

The fisherman hesitated before placing a hand on Celeste's shoulder, giving it a small, reassuring squeeze. "I'm sorry," he muttered. Then, with a tip of his hat, he turned and trudged away.

Mariana stepped back from the window just as Celeste opened the door and reentered the cabin. Her smile had returned, but it was weaker now—and forced as if stitched together by fraying threads.

"Sorry about that, dear," she said brightly, shutting the door with a soft click. Her voice carried its usual warmth, but her eyes were distant as she hobbled back to her chair.

Mariana watched her, chewing the inside of her cheek. "What was that about?" she asked casually, plucking a few mint leaves and pretending she hadn't just been eavesdropping.

"Oh," Celeste said, waving a hand in the air, "don't worry about it. It turns out it was nothing, so..." She shrugged, her forced smile returning. "Nothing to worry about."

But her gaze flickered away, lingering briefly on the door before dropping to the table. Mariana caught it, and the knot of unease in her chest tightened. Whatever Celeste was hiding, it clearly *wasn't* nothing.

Mariana hesitated, then cleared her throat. "You know," she started carefully, "if something's going on and you need my help—"

"No."

The firmness of Celeste's voice startled Mariana. Her friend met her gaze, her expression softening almost immediately as if to ease the sting of her words. Celeste swallowed hard, her eyes scanning the cluttered table for something to busy her hands with. "No, thank you, dear," she said more gently, shaking her head. "Let's just focus on getting ready for the market. The people will need their potions and brews."

Her smile was warm again, but the tension that had rippled through the room hadn't gone unnoticed.

Mariana's hands paused over the mint leaves, her gaze lingering on Celeste's face. She didn't like being shut out. Celeste had always been the one with whom she could share her burdens. It felt wrong to know her friend was struggling with something but wouldn't let her in.

Her thoughts drifted to a memory—one that had been tucked away for years but now resurfaced with startling clarity.

She had been so young, so angry, standing in this very cabin and shouting at Celeste for telling her she couldn't explore Egan Village. *"You're not my mother!"* she had spat, her voice sharp and full of venom she hadn't meant.

Celeste hadn't shouted back. She hadn't scolded her. She just stood there, silent tears slipping down her withered cheeks as she whispered, *"I know you're not mine, but you're the closest I will ever get to having one. And I want to protect you. Please, just let me protect you."*

Mariana's heart squeezed as the memory faded. Now, standing here years later, she understood what Celeste had meant. She hadn't known it back then, but that was when she realized Celeste wasn't just her mentor or friend. She was family.

Celeste glanced up and caught her staring, tilting her head in amusement. "Come on, now, time's wasting!" she said, holding up a stuffed tea bag and wiggling it like a prize. "The people need their potions!"

Mariana forced a laugh, shaking her head. "Okay, okay." She turned back to the mint leaves, but the knot of unease in her chest remained.

The question still lingered in her mind, refusing to let go:

What is Celeste searching for?

CHAPTER 4

"Sorry I'm late," Mariana said as she sat at the round stone table where Queen Cybele, Aurora, and the Siren Witch waited.

"It would be wise to arrive on time, Mariana," Cybele replied, her gaze as sharp as a blade. The queen's lifted eyebrow communicated more than her words—a silent warning.

Mariana lowered her eyes, her mother's scrutiny heavy on her shoulders. "Apologies, Your Majesty."

"Let us begin," Cybele declared, her voice cold and commanding.

Mariana's eyes caught on the Siren Witch's razor-sharp black claws tapping against the table in a rhythmic click. Her mind conjured an image of those claws digging into mortal flesh, scraping away blood and bone. The rumors of what the Siren Witch did to those sacrificed mortals lingered, unspoken but ever-present.

Her stomach twisted.

"Zafiria," Cybele addressed the Siren Witch beside her. The name seemed to sting the witch, her lips tightening in displeasure. After the Banishment, she had cast off that name, considering it a remnant of a weaker self. "What do you have on the cause of death for Telesia, Hella, and Iris?" Cybele's voice softened, just barely, as she spoke.

The Siren Witch leaned back in her chair, her black cape draping around her like a shadow. A golden scorpion fish brooch pinned the cape at her breast, its ruby eyes gleaming, almost as if it were watching Mariana. The witch's ink-stained lips pressed into a thin line as her obsidian eyes dropped to her lap.

"It was sun poisoning, Majesty."

The words hit Mariana like a punch to the gut. Air left her lungs, and her thoughts scattered. Across the table, Cybele's face drained of color, her pale green skin turning an alarming shade of white.

"No ... there's no way," Cybele murmured, her spine snapping straight. "I enchanted their armor to protect them from the sun, and they returned wearing it."

Mariana's pulse quickened. The enchantments—powerful, ancient magic—were supposed to shield sirens from the sun's deadly rays. Cybele's magic had always been strong enough, and yet ...

"Sun poisoning without visible burns suggests indirect exposure over several days," Aurora interjected, her brow furrowed. "They must have been without their armor at some point, even if the enchantment held."

"Actually," the Siren Witch began, her gaze flickering to Cybele, "the armor was only enchanted for three full moon cycles—the duration this journey should have taken. Once those lunation periods passed, the armor would have been useless."

Mariana frowned, despite the urge to grin at the witch's use of the old terminology for time, her thoughts swirling. She had been told Cybele's enchantments lasted for decades, not mere months.

What had changed?

A tense, silent exchange passed between the queen and her advisor. Mariana's unease deepened.

"I don't understand why they would forget something so crucial," Aurora continued, confusion lacing her voice. "Why risk sun exposure if they knew their protection was failing?"

Cybele opened her mouth to respond, but Mariana's voice cut through the air before she could speak.

"What did Astra trade with the fae king?" Mariana's eyes locked onto her mother's stern expression.

"That's none of your concern."

"Isn't it?" Mariana leaned forward, her arms crossing over her chest. "Why did her Guardians rush back here only to die before delivering any message? Where is Astra? Luna is going mad waiting to hear how you plan to get her mother—your daughter— back." She rested her elbows on the table, staring her mother down. "Let me go find her."

The silence that followed felt thick and heavy, like the weight of the ocean pressing down on them. Above, the coral chandelier flickered, the glowing algae dimming as if it too sensed the tension in the room.

"Absolutely not."

"Why?" Aurora's voice startled Mariana, breaking the electric tension between her and Cybele. "I'll go with her. Together, we can find out what happened and get Astra back."

Cybele's head shook slowly, deliberately. "I refuse to send any more of my daughters to the fae realm. This is not up for discussion."

"Mother, please—" Aurora's tone was pleading, her gaze unyielding.

"No."

Mariana fought to keep her voice steady, though frustration simmered beneath the surface. "How can we help her if we do nothing? You promised to stop at nothing to find a way back to Sirenia. Astra might know how to do that. We need to know what she knew and why she was so determined to meet with the king. Then we can form a plan to rescue—"

"We know why she went!" Cybele's outburst cut through Mariana's words, startling her into silence. "She wanted to be our emissary, to find a solution to end this conflict between us and the fae. She dreamed of seeing Sirenia restored, just as we all do." The fire in her eyes dimmed, replaced by a deep, weary sorrow. "I'm the one who let her go. She's either dead or captured because of me."

Cybele's gaze dropped to her hands, her fingers trembling ever so slightly, and Mariana knew her mother saw blood all over them.

"So, let us rescue her," Aurora urged, her voice soft but firm. Mariana admired her sister's persistence, but she could see the finality in Cybele's posture.

"I think they should go," the Siren Witch muttered, drawing all eyes to her. "Astra is a sister. If we refuse to rescue one of our princesses, what message does that send to the others? That we've grown weak? That our fighting spirit has died? Besides," she added with a sly wink at Mariana, "this could be the perfect opportunity for Mariana to prove herself as your heir."

Mariana's heart swelled with a flicker of hope. The witch had always believed in her, teaching her to trust her instincts and respecting her in ways her mother never had. Despite her curse, Mariana knew she could always count on the witch's support.

Cybele's frown deepened, her face set in a hard line. "Everyone out," she commanded, her voice leaving no room for argument. "I want to speak to Mariana alone."

The hope she felt was quickly replaced with dread, weighing her down in her chair. Aurora and the witch both glanced her way before getting up from their seats and leaving the room.

When the door shut softly behind them, Mariana let out a slow breath as she lifted her eyes.

Cybele's gaze was icy, piercing. "Why do you do this?"

Mariana blinked, confused. "Do what?"

"You enjoy turning everyone against me," Cybele spat, her voice dripping with bitterness.

For a moment, Mariana was too stunned to respond. *That's what she thinks?*

A short, bitter laugh escaped her. "No disrespect, but you're doing a fine job of that on your own." She regretted the words the instant they left her mouth. Cybele's eyes darkened like an approaching storm; the room growing cold. "Mother," Mariana tried again, her tone softening, "I didn't tell either of them to advocate for a rescue mission."

"And you expect me to believe that?" Cybele's voice was sharp, but underneath it, Mariana heard something else: hurt.

The realization hit her like a wave crashing against the shore. "Yes, I do."

"Hmm." Cybele turned her face away to stare out the massive stained glass windows depicting the rise of Salus. Sisters helping sisters. *From ruin, we rise.*

"Why don't you want to rescue her?" Mariana asked, her voice barely above a whisper.

Cybele stayed silent for a long while, her gills flaring as though she was struggling with her composure.

"Mother—"

"You've always been like this. So quick to assume the worst of me." The queen turned to face her, and Mariana couldn't help the fear that shivered down her spine at what she saw. "I am not just your mother; I am your queen. And when I say you are not stepping foot in the fae realm, I mean it."

Mariana's frustration boiled over. "I *will* save my sister. I *will* bring her home. No matter the cost, no matter the price I have to pay. She needs me, and I *refuse* to let her suffer alone!"

"You are not going anywhere!"

Mariana released a harsh breath and shook her head. "Why is it so hard for you to believe in me?"

"Believe in you?" Cybele scoffed, her gaze raking over Mariana's body. "Do you even see yourself? The scars you've suffered because death never frightened you?" She gestured to Mariana's face and the terrible sun scar that stretched from the left portion of her forehead down her temple.

Mariana's breath caught in her throat. The memory of herself as a youngling venturing close to the surface, the sun's harsh rays searing her skin as she desperately tried to listen to a song that only she could hear, surged to the forefront of her mind. She had been devastated when the sky went silent once she became an adult. It had been a constant in her life, a melody that lulled her to sleep, soothed her nightmares, and chased away her darkest doubts. It was a constant reminder that she was never alone, even in the darkness, despite the mystery of who or what was singing to her. But now, the song was muted and difficult to recall.

As much as Mariana wished for the sun scars to heal away like the beatings she received for her disobedience, they stayed on her body as permanent reminders of her stupidity. She had been reckless, desperate to find the source of that haunting melody, only to be punished with scars that would never heal. Scars that her mother saw as nothing but evidence of her foolishness. Which was why she'd covered them with tattoos. Except the one on her face.

"I can't trust that you won't do something reckless," Cybele continued, her voice cracking ever so slightly. "I've already lost one daughter I love dearly. I will not risk losing you too."

Mariana's chest clenched. She forced herself to meet Cybele's gaze, the words she had long held back finally spilling out. "You know I've changed. I take my responsibilities seriously. And since when have you ever shown me that you loved me? You've never cared about me beyond my role as your heir."

"That's not true—"

"If you loved me, you'd understand how important this is to me," Mariana pressed, her voice rising louder with every word. "Our cursed sisters have never respected me. How can I become their queen if I'm sheltered in a cave all my life? I have a duty to restore Sirenia just as much as you do, and I believe Astra knows how."

Cybele raised a hand, silencing her. "I want to find a solution as much as you do. I wanted Astra to succeed. I want to go back to Sirenia before I die, but I can't do anything that would jeopardize the future of our people by risking your life. I don't care what the others say. Protecting you and our people is all that matters."

Mariana's frustration surged, her voice trembling with the effort to keep her emotions in check. "There won't be anyone left to protect if we all die or fall to the Scourge. We have to act now!"

"No!" Cybele's refusal was as sharp as a knife.

Mariana threw her hands up in exasperation. "You've given up! Are we supposed to just stay here in these caves forever? This is a tomb, a grave for us all, if we don't do something! Let me go out there and find a solution—"

"I will *not* send my heir to her death!" Cybele's voice cracked like thunder, and for the first time, Mariana noticed the deep lines of worry etched into her mother's face. "Don't you see? I'm trying to save you."

Mariana froze, the words sinking in. "Save me?" she echoed, her tone bitter. "How heroic of you, Mother. Why don't you focus on saving Astra?"

She turned to leave, her heart pounding, but Cybele's voice stopped her cold.

"My power is fading, Mari." Cybele's confession was barely a whisper, laced with a heartache that made Mariana turn back around. "You heard the report. They had sun poisoning. I enchanted their armor to protect them, and ... my magic failed."

Mariana's heart skipped a beat. She could hear the unspoken words, the guilt that weighed down every syllable.

"You think you killed them," Mariana said softly.

Cybele didn't respond. Her silence confirmed Mariana's worst fears.

"Why did she lie?" Mariana asked, referring to the Siren Witch's claim about the enchantment's duration.

"I don't know," Cybele whispered, her shoulders slumping. "Maybe she thought she was protecting me."

Mariana studied her mother, the queen who had always seemed so invincible, now sitting before her with a vulnerability she had never shown before.

"That seems to be going around lately," Mariana muttered, suddenly exhausted as she sank back into her chair.

Cybele rested her elbows on the table, her clasped hands trembling as she brought them to her face. "You have to stay here, as my heir. If I can't even manage simple enchantments, you need to be here for your people. I've already begun to age." She lifted her hands into the light, and Mariana noticed the fine lines that had begun to etch across her mother's once-smooth skin.

A wave of dread washed over her, tightening her chest. The thought of becoming queen—of carrying that burden—made her feel like she was suffocating.

I'm not ready, she whispered desperately into the darkness of her mind.

"If you want me to stay," Mariana said after a long pause, her voice steady despite the turmoil within her, "I need to know something."

Cybele narrowed her eyes but said nothing.

"No more secrets," Mariana continued, refusing to back down. "Tell me what Astra was planning to trade with the fae king."

For a moment, Cybele remained silent, her gaze fixed on Mariana, as if weighing whether to trust her with the truth. The tension in the room was palpable, each second stretching into an eternity.

"Come with me."

CHAPTER 5

MARIANA STRUGGLED TO STEADY her breathing as she followed her mother deeper into the palace's underbelly. The winding path ahead was so dark that Mariana could barely make out the queen's silhouette, even with her vision attuned to the blackest depths of the sea.

They were heading toward the Athenaeum—the forbidden archives where scholars safeguarded history by infusing glass orbs with magic from their voices. Mariana had never been allowed inside before. Astra, who'd been a scholar her whole life, used to bring up orbs to teach her siren and fae history. Prior to the Siren Witch falling into the Scourge's clutches, she had been a scholar and the only cursed siren allowed inside.

A pale glow seeped into the tunnel's end, and the queen's crown glinted with the approaching light. Mariana's chest tightened as the cavern opened before her, and her mouth fell open.

Rows upon rows of glowing orbs stretched along stone shelves as far as she could see. A millennium of knowledge was preserved here, seen by no more than ten sirens in all of history.

Now, Mariana understood why her mother had always forbidden anyone outside the appointed scholars from entering.

Cybele's serious gaze caught the dim light, casting harsh shadows over her regal features. The sight sent a wave of unease curling through Mariana's stomach.

Clearing her throat, Mariana looked away and followed her mother through the maze of shelves.

"Astra was determined to find something that would give us the upper hand in restoring Sirenia," Cybele said over her shoulder, stopping at a row of orbs that gave no hint of their contents. "What she found made me realize that if we ever want to escape this shadowed existence, we must accept the consequences of what comes next."

"What do you mean?" Mariana asked, her voice barely above a whisper.

Cybele handed her an orb with a slight crack on its surface. It fit snugly in Mariana's palm, heavy with the knowledge sealed inside.

Mariana met her mother's somber expression, sensing the weight of the secret her mother felt compelled to keep. Her eyes drifted back to the orb's faint glow. Was she ready to uncover its truth? Would the orb even work, damaged as it was?

Gathering her courage, she lifted the orb to her face and whispered, "*Revelare.*"

To her surprise, words spilled forth.

It was the origin of sirens.

Seraphina descended on wings of feathered stars from the celestial city in the sky, escaping her malicious betrothed. Whilst wandering the fae realm, she became enamored with a fae male named Erasmus. He was mesmerized by her ethereal singing voice, enchanted by her beauty, and fell in love with her kindness. When Seraphina conceived a youngling, Erasmus bestowed upon her an amulet of pure golden light.

Upon discovering their surreptitious affair, her betrothed bound Erasmus to an anchor and sank him into the sea's abyss. Fearless, Seraphina dived after him, forfeiting her glorious wings in exchange for a strong swimming tail in place of her legs. Pulling her beloved from the dark depths, she enchanted the gifted amulet with the power to recall his soul from the shadowed Veil. Death released its grip upon Erasmus at the cost of binding Seraphina and her unborn to the sea.

Enraged, her betrothed cursed Seraphina and the fruit of her womb to be scorched by the sun should they ever attempt to seek solace on land and forewarned of an ominous descent into darkness should she dare defy mortality alongside Erasmus.

In her final act of maternal grace, Seraphina birthed a daughter of unparalleled beauty and granted her the power of the sea for protection and the gift to transform her tail into limbs so that she might forge a lineage of her own, saving her from eternal isolation. Seraphina's remaining days were spent serenading Erasmus from beneath the moon's silent watch, her melodies a bittersweet lament of love everlasting.

"Seraphina," Mariana whispered, her throat tight as she tried to swallow.

It was the amulet—the one capable of bringing back the dead.

Mariana's breath caught as her mind began to race.

Astra planned to tell King Stavros she could bring his son back to life.

"No ... this ..." Mariana quickly set the orb back down on its small pedestal as though it was scorching hot. "This is madness. Astra would never allow this to happen."

Cybele's lips pressed into a thin line. "She brought the orb to me."

"Why? Why would she do that? She knows if Prince Helios were ever revived, he'd seek his revenge on us!"

"Lower your voice, now." The queen's tone silenced Mariana, though her mind continued shouting. "We can't be certain he would want revenge or that the amulet would even work. Besides, no one knows where the amulet is. It's been missing since before my own mother was queen."

Mariana ran her fingers through her hair, shaking her head. "Then why would Astra suggest telling the king about it?"

"She believed the knowledge of the amulet would be enough. I suspect it wasn't."

Mariana clenched her jaw, her hands dropping to her sides as she fixed her mother with a glare. "Why did you keep this from me?"

"It wasn't your concern."

"You thought I couldn't handle it."

Cybele's gaze hardened. "I knew you wouldn't accept it."

"That's not fair. You should have given me the chance to—"

"To what? Try to stop Astra? Convince me it was a terrible plan?" The queen's eyes blazed. "I know you, Mariana. Nothing you could've said back then would've changed a thing."

Because she was the queen, not Mariana.

Swallowing her pride, Mariana clasped her hands together. "Please, let me rescue Astra. She needs our help, and if something terrible happened, we all deserve to know—especially Luna."

The cold finality in Cybele's eyes gave Mariana the answer she'd dreaded.

"Mother, please!" she pleaded, her voice breaking under the weight of grief at the thought of never seeing her sister again.

"I'm going to say this one last time. No. And don't ask me again."

With that, the queen turned and swam into the darkness, leaving Mariana with a heart that felt as though it had been torn apart.

CHAPTER 6

THE CAVE SYSTEM WHERE the Siren Witch and the other cursed sirens lived extended deep into the earth, a labyrinth of shadows and secrets. It was a place where few dared to venture, yet Mariana entered without hesitation.

She navigated the twisting paths with ease, the soft glowing sconces cast enough light to guide her. The deeper she went, the quieter it became, until all she could hear was the swish of her tail and the steady thrum of her heartbeat. The water grew colder, biting into her skin, and the faint taste of rotten blood tinged her senses. She grimaced but pressed on, her fists clenched.

Don't think about it. Just go.

She'd visited the witch countless times before, but today the caves felt different—eerie, as though something was watching her from the shadows.

Rounding a corner, she was abruptly stopped by two cursed sirens, spears in hand.

"Stop. What business do you have here?"

Mariana recognized Madea; she used to maintain the bio-luminescent garden at the palace but gave up that task when she realized she wasn't concerned whether the garden lived or died. Her once-bright blue eyes were now pitch-black voids, a reflection of who she'd become.

"I'm here to see the Siren Witch. Move aside." Mariana moved forward, but the other cursed siren's spear blocked her path.

Mariana scrutinized the revolting siren, unable to recognize her given how deep she was in the Scourge's clutches. Her stringy hair, sallow skin, and decaying scales made Mariana wrinkle her nose in disgust. She looked like a swimming corpse, riddled with disease.

"Careful, princess," the siren hissed through a mouth of missing teeth. "This is our territory. You enter if we say you can."

"I don't have time for your games," Mariana snapped. "You're soiling my water. Move aside, or I'll make you."

The cursed sisters exchanged a glance before cackling, the sound grating on Mariana's nerves, turning her vision red.

With a flick of her hand, the two sirens slammed against the cave wall. Their spears clattered to the ground as they screeched, pinned by the force of her magic. The water churned around them, pushing them harder into the jagged rock.

"You should have listened." Mariana's voice was cold as she watched them writhe, the sharp stone cutting their bodies. "Next time, you'll move aside the moment you see me."

Madea bared her teeth in a feral snarl, her eyes gleaming with hatred. Mariana narrowed her gaze, sending a silent command. Tiny crabs swarmed from the cracks in the cave walls, covering the sirens and tearing at their flesh. Their screams filled the tunnel, echoing in Mariana's ears.

"Your territory is my territory," she said, her voice low and dangerous. "Next time, think twice before crossing me."

She dropped her hand, and the sirens slid to the ground, crabs scattering as the water calmed. Turning away from the pitiful sight, Mariana continued toward the witch's dwelling.

The Siren Witch waited at her door, a small smile playing on her lips. "Hello, little one. I see you made some friends."

Mariana shot a glance over her shoulder at the cursed sirens, their wounds already beginning to heal. "You could say that."

Swimming inside, she was hit with a wave of nostalgia. The witch's home was cluttered, filled with objects whose origins and purposes were a mystery to Mariana. She remembered curling up in the corner with a pile of orbs, lost in the histories Astra had brought her from the Athenaeum. Back then, the witch's home had been a sanctuary, a place where she wasn't judged for her scars. But now, the tunnels outside were filled with the cursed—a far cry from the adventures she once had.

A pile of bones in the corner caught her eye, and she went still, only releasing a breath when she realized they were just fish bones.

She grimaced at the thought of eating any sort of creature.

Passing the bones, she entered the main room. It was large but crowded, the black stone table littered with scraps of ingredients. It felt like a lifetime ago when she'd sat there, learning about dark magic and siren history.

"Am I interrupting?" Mariana asked, eyeing the dead squid on the table and the jar filling with shimmering black liquid.

"No, just refilling the stock of stygian oil," the witch replied, her hands stained as she worked.

"Isn't that lethal to touch?"

"Only if inhaled. Or if it enters the bloodstream."

Mariana leaned on the table, watching the dark liquid fill the jar from the tube stuck inside the squid.

"What happens if it does?"

"The toxin blackens your veins, and they would need to be cleansed. It's terribly taxing on the body. I recommend avoiding it if you can. Otherwise, you'll be wishing for death."

Mariana frowned, the thought unsettling. She glanced down at her hands, still trembling from her earlier confrontation with her mother. Although, teaching those cursed sirens to back off had helped ease the tension slightly.

"Did you know?" she asked, lifting her gaze. "Astra planned to trade knowledge of Seraphina's amulet to the fae king in exchange for Sirenia."

The witch tilted her head, unfazed. "Yes, I knew. What of it?"

Mariana stared at her, incredulous. "Why didn't you tell me?"

"Because Cybele would, eventually. And she has, hasn't she?" she said while removing the tubes.

Mariana scoffed, biting back the arguments on the tip of her tongue. The witch had always been loyal to Cybele. If her mother had decided to keep something from her, the witch would have respected that.

With a sigh, she rested her elbows on the table and buried her face in her hands.

"You seem conflicted," the witch observed, her claws tapping rhythmically on the stone.

Mariana dropped her hands, exclaiming, "Of course I'm conflicted! How can I help Astra if I'm kept in the dark? And how am I supposed to convince Cybele to let me go to Aurelia?"

"She won't."

Mariana shook her head, frustration boiling over. "Why? She let Astra go, why not me?"

The witch regarded Mariana with a steady gaze. "The fae realm is dangerous for a siren. Astra had top-tier Guardians, and even they couldn't prevent what happened. Aurelia is the fae capital. They'd cut off your tail and sell it to the highest bidder. Your scales would be ripped from you and used as currency. Do you understand?"

Mariana stiffened, holding back the urge to roll her eyes. "You think I can't defend myself."

"I think you don't have it in you to *kill* them. You've been trained as a warrior, but you've never faced a fae opponent. Hesitation will cost you—not only your life but Astra's as well."

The witch's words were a punch to the gut. She stared at her mentor, feeling like her eyes were about to swallow Mariana down into an endless black hole. Glancing away, she imagined killing someone, driving a blade through their chest. The thought made her stomach sour instantly.

"You're brave, little one, but you've not seen death the way some of us have."

Grabbing the dead squid off the table, she moved toward a curtained wall and pulled it aside to reveal a cage of slithering, red-eyed serpents. Mariana recoiled as the witch tossed the dead squid into the cage, the serpents devouring it in seconds. The witch let the curtain fall.

"Why do you keep those things in here?"

"The sound of them puts me at ease."

Mariana was baffled, unable to comprehend how the hissing, slithering creatures could be comforting to anyone.

"Look, I know you came down here to ask me to convince Cybele to let you go to the fae realm. Unfortunately, I cannot," the witch said, scrubbing her hands with a gritty gray paste.

"We've lost so many," Mariana whispered, her gaze fixed on the swirling stygian oil. "I don't want to lose Astra too. Not like this, hiding away in the darkness." She looked up, her voice trembling. "If you won't talk to Cybele, then why did you support my plan to rescue Astra during the meeting?"

The witch was silent for a moment before she sighed. "Because ... despite everything, I believe *you* need to be the one to find the amulet."

"Why?"

"The amulet is a powerful source of raw magic. Only a siren can wield it, but that doesn't mean Astra wouldn't bring back the fae king's son if he demanded it. We need the amulet safe in Salus. And you, as the heir to the sea, should be the one to possess it."

Mariana nodded slowly. "Astra would know where it is," she said. "I have to find her. I have to stop all of this." The weight of responsibility pressed down on her, threatening to crush her. "I have to prove myself. What happened out there"—she gestured toward the door leading to the tunnels—"can't happen when I'm queen. I need their respect."

"They respect no one."

"They respect you."

The witch shook her head and wiped away the paste from her hands. "That's different. You don't need to earn anything. Whether they respect you or not, you will be queen." She sat across from Mariana, leveling her with a look.

Mariana shook her head, determination hardening her voice. "I know I have to do this."

The witch's eyes lit with a hint of mischief. "Then it sounds like you know what you have to do."

Mariana's breath caught in her throat as she understood the witch's unspoken suggestion. "I can't," she stammered. "That would be treason!"

The witch shrugged, expression unreadable. "I have no idea what you're talking about," she said, rising from her stool. "But remember, you will be our queen soon. Consider each outcome carefully, then decide which path leads to the future you desire."

"How am I supposed to know which is the right path?"

For a fleeting moment, the witch looked almost … normal. As if the Scourge had never tainted her.

Then she said, "I'd prefer the path that doesn't lead to Helios returning and killing us all, but the choice is yours." She turned away, her figure blending into the shadows once more.

CHAPTER 7

"I CAN'T BELIEVE IT'S been three weeks, and we still haven't heard anything," Aurora muttered, her voice barely cutting through the rhythmic sound of waves crashing overhead. She lay beside Mariana on the sand, their bodies bathed in the moon's silvery light, which filtered through the water, casting them in a shifting, rippling glow.

No word had come from the fae king after Astra had vanished without a trace. Each day without news wound Mariana tighter, coiling tension through her muscles like a predator ready to strike.

"We need to do something," she admitted softly.

She'd told Aurora everything she'd learned—everything except the conversation with the witch. Since leaving the witch's dwelling after their talk, Mariana couldn't stop thinking about what the witch had implied. The thought of adventuring into the fae realm without permission haunted her, a shadow she couldn't shake. She could go, she knew that, but it would mean crossing a line she didn't think she could ever come back from. That thought scared her more than she cared to admit.

"We can't," Aurora replied, her voice firm. "Cybele made herself very clear. We wait until the king sends word of a trade."

"And if he doesn't send word?" Mariana turned to her sister, their eyes locking in a silent exchange of fear. Astra's fate hung between them, a fragile thread that could snap at any moment. Luna claimed she could still feel their mother's soul, but how long would that last? How long until they were too late?

"We'll think of something. Somehow, we'll convince the queen to let us go. I know it."

Mariana exhaled slowly, her breath stirring the sand as she turned her gaze back to the moon. Tonight, more sirens than ever would take part in another culling, five new souls pledged to sacrifice themselves to the Scourge to keep their sisters safe—a noble choice in the queen's eyes, but to Mariana, it was abhorrent. She couldn't bear to be near them, to witness such barbarity. The thought of anyone accepting the Scourge as an honor made her skin crawl. Each day, the cursed sirens grew stronger, more wicked, and she felt powerless to stop them.

But was she truly powerless?

The witch's unspoken suggestion echoed in her mind: *Go. Take matters into your own hands.* So, why hadn't she?

She cleared her throat, glancing at Aurora. "What if we just went to Aurelia to rescue Astra?"

Aurora's head snapped toward her, concern etched in her eyes. "What?"

Mariana pushed herself up, pulling Aurora up with her so they were face to face. "Hear me out. The witch would defend us if we left on our own. Together, we could find Astra and secure the amulet before the king gets *close* to resurrecting his dead son."

Aurora scoffed, pulling her hands free from Mariana's grasp. "And you think the queen wouldn't punish us for defying her? You're living in a dream if you believe that," she said, turning away.

"If we succeed, she wouldn't dare!" Mariana quickly swam around to block her sister's path. "Rora, we have to do something. You know it—"

"Of course I know it, Mari! But I don't want to make a stupid choice that'll get us both killed!"

"We won't! We'll protect each other, just like we planned during the meeting," Mariana argued, desperation edging into her voice. But Aurora's tail shifted her away, her eyes dark with turmoil.

"No. What you're suggesting is treason. You can't just march into enemy territory against the queen's orders to prove a point. We all want Astra back but not at the cost of losing you."

"And what about Astra?" Mariana's voice trembled with raw emotion. "Are we so willing to lose her?"

Aurora's expression was a battlefield, rage and fear warring beneath the surface. The silence between them grew heavy, fraught with unspoken fears and the weight of impossible decisions.

"I need to think," Aurora finally whispered, her voice strained.

Mariana watched her sister swim back toward Salus, her auburn hair vanishing into the swaying kelp like a fading ember. Mariana's fists tightened, nails digging into her palms until she felt the sting and her blood seeping out. She stared at the half-moon marks in her skin and the slow tendrils of crimson swirling in the current as the wounds healed.

More blood would stain the sea if she did nothing. No, it couldn't end here.

Glancing back in the direction Aurora had gone, Mariana shot after her, weaving through the kelp and descending into the dark tunnel that led into the heart of Salus. She emerged in the bioluminescent garden where Aurora sat among the glowing flora.

Vines twisted around marble columns, their violet blossoms glowing softly in the cavern's eternal night. Brightly colored fish swam lazily through the coral, weaving in and out of Aurora's long hair, while crustaceans scuttled across the sand, tending to the vibrant display.

"This was her favorite spot to think," Aurora murmured, fingers trailing through a delicate anemone. Its soft, stinging tendrils curled around her thumb, turning it a dark shade of pink. Mariana could feel the weight of her sister's grief, a shared ache that pressed down on her heart.

Mariana settled beside her on the sand, careful to avoid the coral. She gently pulled Aurora's hand away from the anemone, holding her fingers lightly as the pink hue faded to its natural bronze color.

"I miss her," Aurora whispered, her voice breaking.

"Me too," Mariana replied, meeting her sister's sad gaze. She swallowed, then cleared her throat. "I'm sorry I suggested going against the queen's orders. It wasn't fair of me."

"I want to do it."

S.L. DEBOIS

Mariana's heart skipped a beat. "You want to?"

"Yes." Aurora's expression was suddenly resolute, her eyes burning with determination. "You're right, Mari. Astra needs us; and the amulet can't fall into the wrong hands." She squeezed Mariana's hands, her grip firm. "I need to gather supplies, and we need to rest. Tomorrow, midday, while all of Salus is asleep, we'll meet here. Then, we'll swim for Aurelia."

Mariana's breath caught in her throat. They were going to do this. "Together," she whispered, her voice trembling with a mix of fear and excitement.

Aurora nodded. "Together."

CHAPTER 8

MARIANA LIFTED HER HEAD from the violent waves and used her power to shift the unruly water out of the way, creating a path up to the beach. She expelled the water from her body and glanced up. A storm was brewing. Its wicked and wild head roared a short distance away. Soon, rain would fall from the dark clouds filling the early morning sky.

No market today, Mariana silently noted as she trudged through the sand toward Celeste's home.

Aurora had everything prepared for their journey. It would take a few days to swim all the way to the fae capital city, assuming the currents didn't shift, but Mariana was ready. This was the right choice; it had to be. Everything hinged on their success. Once they got Astra out, together, they would find the amulet and take it back home to Salus. Simple.

Mariana glanced over her shoulder as thunder cracked overhead. It wasn't a good omen—if she believed in those things like Celeste did. Hopefully, her friend wouldn't overthink it.

She knocked on the door and was surprised when Celeste didn't answer.

"Hello? Celeste?" Knocking again, Mariana said in a joking tone, "Are you still sleeping?" She knocked harder, and the door swung open with a *bang*, jolting her.

Taking a hesitant step inside, she halted. The bed was empty and rumpled, and fear gripped her heart.

"Celeste?" she whispered, her throat tightening as she inspected the small room. The table didn't have fresh herbs scattered all over it, which meant Celeste didn't go picking before dawn.

Mariana's heart began to race, taking ragged breaths. She hurried outside and checked the usual spots where Celeste might be. She searched the herb garden behind the house, the rocky cliff where she liked to meditate, and even the old willow tree by the creek. But Celeste was nowhere to be found.

Panic settled in as she returned to the empty cabin, the storm's first droplets beginning to fall. The room felt colder, more desolate without Celeste's presence. Mariana's eyes darted around, searching for a clue.

The bed was unmade as if her friend had left in a hurry. Her heart pounded louder with each passing second. Then a paper's edge, stuck under a pile of books on the table, caught her eye.

Pulling it free, Mariana frowned. It was a hand-drawn map of what looked like the Andros Islands. Several islands had circles with x's drawn through them, except one near the end of the chain closest to the Southern Continent. She didn't recognize it, but there were plenty of islands in the chain that she hadn't explored. Was this the one Celeste had asked that fisherman to look into?

The sound of a door closing outside drew her attention, and Mariana dropped the map. Maybe someone knew where Celeste had gone.

Stepping outside, Mariana saw a little boy with curly black hair atop his head putting his boots on.

"Hey there," she called softly, startling him.

The child stared up at her, eyes wide.

Clearing her throat, she asked, "The lady who lives here, have you seen her?"

He nodded.

"Do you know where she went?"

"She's gone," he murmured. "The ones from across the sea took her." Mariana's stomach dropped, her eyes going wide. Then he lifted a golden-brown hand up to his rounded ear. "They had pointed ears like yours."

Mariana's body went ice cold. She lifted her shaky hands to her mouth, muffling a gasp.

The culling.

"No," she whispered.

The culling was last night.

"Are you a sea goddess?" the boy asked, and Mariana squeezed her blurring eyes shut, shaking her head.

Without another word, she turned around and ran toward the beach, unable to believe her mother would betray her that way. How could Cybele allow the culling to take place at Egan Village? Had she found out Mariana had been visiting Celeste?

Was this all because of her?

Tears flooded her eyes, spilling down her cheeks as she stumbled. Her knees hit the sand, and a sob escaped her chest.

She couldn't be gone. She—

"Wait! Storm's coming! You shouldn't be out there," the boy shouted from behind her. The innocent concern twisted the knife already lodged in her chest.

"Let the lightning come," she whispered, pulling her knees to her chest, resting her chin on them as she stared out at the dark, churning sea, praying to the Goddess that Celeste hadn't felt a thing.

A gust of chilled wind blew her hair over her shoulder, making Mariana shiver.

How did this happen? She shook her head, wiping her eyes, but the tears kept coming.

Celeste was gone, and she could've stopped it. Her friend, her confidant, her—

Mariana swallowed, her throat tight and painful.

Celeste was the one person who understood Mariana, who accepted her without question. She was kind and loving, never judging or accusing. She had a light about her that could pierce even the deepest, darkest parts of Mariana's life. And now, she was gone.

The truth sent a fresh wave of grief through her body. It tightened her muscles and strangled her soul so hard that she barely noticed the sting of something piercing the side of her neck.

Lifting her hand, she felt a small dart and pulled it out with a hiss. It was a small wooden needle tipped with her blood.

Her eyes shot upward as everything began to blur. Then it dawned on her that as the wound healed, the poison—now coursing through her veins—was being sealed inside her.

Shit.

She tried and failed to get up off the sand, stumbling and rolling onto her back. The poison that infected her blood was weakening her. Mariana gasped, clawing at the sand as a dark-hooded figure loomed over her. A reaper ready to take a life.

Mariana silently prayed for it to be quick as darkness swept her away.

CHAPTER 9

Darkness wrapped around Mariana like a shroud, muting her senses as whispered words brushed against her ears, barely more than a breath on the wind. She strained to open her eyes, but the voices grew louder, more insistent, as if someone was racing past her, their hot breath grazing her skin.

"*Listen.*"

"*Unleash it.*"

"*Feel it within you.*"

Mariana shook her head, fighting the fog that clung to her thoughts, and forced her eyes open. A thick, swirling mist clung to her skin, wrapping around her like a living thing. She struggled to catch her breath, her pulse quickening as a figure slowly emerged from the haze, moving toward her with deliberate steps. The closer the figure came, the harder it was for her to remain still, her heart thundering in her chest.

"Who are you?" she whispered, her voice trembling with uncertainty.

A strange sense of detachment washed over her, as if she were floating outside her body. Her limbs felt numb, and a chill had seeped into her bones. Was this the afterlife? Was the figure approaching her the Goddess Amphitrite?

Tears welled in her eyes, her throat tightening painfully. Confusion, anger, and a bittersweet happiness crashed over her, overwhelming her as the figure drew nearer. Panic clawed at her soul, the thought of never seeing her family again threatening to break her. But a voice deep within urged her to stay strong, to pull herself together.

She wiped her eyes, trying to focus, but the figure remained blurred, its edges fading into the fog.

"*The time has come. You must listen,*" the figure said, its voice distant yet soothing, a melody she couldn't place but felt she had heard before.

Mariana struggled to make sense of the words. "Listen?" Her voice echoed strangely into the surrounding mist.

"*Let it guide you. Listen, and you will be free.*"

Suddenly, a blinding white light seared her eyes, forcing them shut as her body began to fall into a vast emptiness.

Then, gradually, the world came back into focus. The cold, damp air filled her lungs as she opened her eyes, blinking up at a canopy of trees. Moonlight filtered through the swaying branches, casting shifting shadows on the forest floor.

What in the blazing sun ...?

She tried to lift her hands to shield her eyes, only to find them bound tightly at the wrists. Her pulse quickened, a sharp, suffocating pressure tightening in her chest as she strained against the ropes, her breaths shallow and uneven.

This wasn't a dream.

She lay on a bed of pine needles and damp moss, the chill of the forest floor seeping into her bones. She struggled to sit up but found her ankles bound. A warm hand pressed against her back, helping her rise. The hooded figure she had seen before she lost consciousness loomed over her, its presence as ominous as the darkness surrounding them.

"What ... what did you do to me?" Mariana stammered, her voice weak as nausea roiled in her stomach. She turned away, gagging as she emptied what little was in her stomach onto the ground. When she was finished, she wiped her mouth with the back of her bound hands, grimacing at the mess.

Settling against a tree, she surveyed her surroundings with wary eyes. They were in a forest, that much she was sure. The air carried a slight chill that suggested they were farther north than she had expected. The moon was dipping below the horizon, a sign that she had been unconscious for hours.

Glancing down, she inspected the ropes binding her wrists and ankles as her captor rummaged through a leather bag. She dug her nails into the silky white rope around her ankles, but it held firm, resisting her attempts to loosen it.

"Don't touch that," the hooded figure demanded, his deep voice startling her. He held out a waterskin, but his face remained hidden beneath his hood. All she could see was the stubble on his jaw. "Here, drink."

She hesitated. Her throat was parched, but fear kept her from accepting the offer. The memory of the drug he had used to knock her out was still fresh.

With an irritated sigh, he took a long swig from the waterskin himself, the moonlight briefly illuminating a strong, shadowed jaw, before he held it out to her again. Reluctantly, Mariana snatched it from his hand, drinking deeply until he took it back.

"Who are you?" she asked softly, water dripping from her chin.

He said nothing, pulling a piece of cured meat from his bag and offering it to her.

"I can't eat that." She shook her head, frustration bubbling beneath her fear. "I'm a siren. We don't eat meat—*usually*," she added under her breath.

The stranger grunted in response, returning to his bag and pulling out a piece of bread. She reached out, taking the offering from his outstretched hand, her fingers brushing against his. He watched her for a long moment, his hooded face inscrutable.

As she tore off small chunks of bread, eating slowly, she kept a cautious eye on him. His silence was unnerving, and the chill in the air crept deeper into her bones, making her shiver despite herself. The thin dress she wore did little to protect her from the cold, but it was the one Celeste had made for her, a small comfort.

She couldn't let her thoughts drift to Celeste, not now. She needed to stay present and figure out who this male was and why he had taken her. His large size alone suggested he was fae. She couldn't sense any magic emanating from her captor, but that didn't mean he wasn't *Blessed*. The fae who wielded power were at the top of their society, their immortality making them nearly impossible to kill by conventional means.

Her eyes darted to the dagger at his waist, catching the glint of metal in the dim light. She noticed the faint etchings of a royal seal on the hilt—a symbol she recognized all too well.

"Did King Stavros send you?"

She noticed the fae still for a split second.

"If the king wants to negotiate—"

The fae raised a hand. "I'm not here for diplomacy." His voice was deep and smooth, gliding over her skin like a soft touch of his fingertips.

Shivering, she glared at him. "Then why are you here? Why have you taken me?"

He continued eating, his silence making her jaw clench and her eyes narrow on the dagger at his waist once more. If she could grab it and cut the ropes at her ankles, then she might have a chance of escaping him. Or if she could fight her way out of this, she could get to the coast and call for help. The fae wouldn't kill her. If that had been his objective, he would've done so by now. She suspected his orders were to bring her to the king. But why? Was it to discuss Astra's mission or negotiate for her life? Or something else entirely?

Either way, she couldn't let the fae king control whether she lived or died. She had to escape before they reached the fae realm. Once there, she would lose her connection to the sea and her ability to call for help. Fae lands were mountainous and frigid in winter, and though spring was on its way, the chill in the air was a constant reminder of how far from home she was.

Her captor closed his bag and stood, his full height towering above her. Mariana's breath caught as she realized how tall he was, his broad shoulders filling her vision. He wore a dark shirt beneath leather armor, a long black leather cloak, and mud-splattered boots. The bow and arrows on his back glinted gently under the moonlight, and she wondered how trained he was with them. If she ran, would one of those arrows find its way into her back? As he turned to survey their surroundings, his back briefly facing her, she didn't waste time with the what-ifs. This was her chance.

Thrusting out her feet, she kicked the back of his knees. The fae shouted as she snatched the dagger at his waist as he fell.

Slicing through the ropes around her ankles, she scrambled to her feet and bolted into the trees, the smell of the sea guiding her.

Her heart pounded in her chest, each beat echoing in her ears as she ran, her eyes locked on the barely visible trail ahead. She leaped over a large branch, her bare feet landing on a pile of broken twigs, making her stumble. Cursing under her breath, she pushed herself up, the sounds of the fae crashing through the underbrush behind her.

Damn, he's fast.

She pushed herself harder, her legs burning with the effort, but the weight of gravity dragged her down, slowing her with every step. Just as she thought she might outrun him, a powerful arm wrapped around her waist, lifting her off the ground.

Mariana screamed, kicking with all her might, catching a glimpse of the shimmering sea through the trees before he spun her back toward the forest and threw her to the ground.

The impact knocked the wind from her lungs, and she lost her grip on the dagger. The fae was on her, turning her over and pinning her wrists to the ground above her head.

"Stop!" he shouted as she struggled, trying to claw at his face. "Stop this now! I don't want to hurt you!"

His words drew a bitter laugh from her. She leaned closer, her breath mingling with his. "You're abducting me! Taking me away from my home! Don't act like you're not hurting me!" she hissed, snapping her teeth at his face, forcing him to jerk his head back.

Breathless and spent, Mariana went still, her head resting against the cool, damp moss beneath her. For the first time, she could see his face clearly, and she was immediately repulsed by the instinctive attraction she felt. His features were handsome but held a menacing edge, his dark eyes promising retaliation for her defiance. His strong jaw, covered in stubble, clenched tight as he held her down.

She wanted to punch his teeth straight into his throat.

He released a low growl. "Listen to me." His voice was commanding, eyes locking onto hers. She became acutely aware of the warmth of his body, his weight pressing down on her. Confusion swept through her as a flutter of something else—something she didn't want to acknowledge—stirred in her stomach.

What is wrong with me?

The fae let out a frustrated breath. "I understand you want to go home, but I can't let you do that. You're coming with me. Are you going to make me knock you out again, or will you listen to what I say?"

Mariana glared at him. Her jaw clenched so hard it sent a sharp ache to her temples. She wanted to spit in his face, to scream at him, but something held her back.

As dawn started to creep through the trees, she summoned her magic to shield her from the sun. The light chased the shadows away from the male's face, and Mariana stilled.

Beneath thick black brows were striking emerald eyes. She could even see flecks of copper deep within the iris. They reminded her of a hidden enchanted forest filled with secrets, and perhaps the monster that plagued his nightmares and caused the dark circles beneath.

Wait ... Mariana blinked as realization flooded her mind. His skin ... it was the color of stone. She thought the darkness was playing tricks on her, but she could now see the truth. The fae race had been created in the image of mortals with similar skin tones. But this man's skin was different. Astra used to bring orbs up from the Athenaeum to show her the images of fae and the fae realm stored within. This male's skin looked nothing like what she had seen in those images. Some creatures, like sirens, could mate with fae and produce colorful fae offspring. Still, society often considered them outcasts as they were not *true fae*. With those prejudices in mind, she wondered how the king employed someone like him.

"Who are you?" she asked in bewilderment.

His mouth tightened, and his eyes narrowed.

"No one," he grunted, lifting her to her feet.

"You're—" Her words were cut off as he snatched up his dagger and sheathed it, his movements swift and practiced.

"I'm done talking. Now, let's go." He bound her wrists again, leaving her ankles free this time. He ran a hand over his short black hair, brushing off dried leaves. The remnants of their fight.

He peered down at where he held her wrists. "You're shaking. Are you cold?"

"No." She was, a little, but she wasn't about to admit it. "I haven't been on land this long before. Your kind has no idea how painful gravity is to someone who lives in the sea," she spat back at him.

The fae male glared down at her, but she refused to feel small as she shot daggers right back, hoping they pierced his soul.

"The solution to that is simple," he stated as he lifted a small glass bottle from a pouch secured on his waist.

Mariana leaned in close to his face. "I *refuse* to be drugged again. Just try. You'll regret it."

He shook his head, slipping the bottle back into his pouch. Without another word, he swept her up into his arms. She protested at first, but as the tension left her muscles, she realized how much she needed the relief.

"Trust me not to murder you now?" His voice was tinged with sarcasm, but she refused to give him the satisfaction of a response. She was too tired, her muscles too sore to argue.

The fae frowned, his steps light and cautious as he carried her through the forest, as if fearing to wake a sleeping giant. His eyes remained alert, scanning the trees and foliage for anything that might pose a threat.

"I don't trust you at all," she muttered, her gaze fixed on the path ahead.

"Then, why aren't you fighting me?"

"Because I will defeat you," she said, her voice low but fierce. "And when I do"—she turned her steely gaze toward him—"you'll never see daylight again."

A brief silence hung between them before he spoke again, his tone maddeningly calm. "Even if you manage to beat me, you won't escape me, siren."

Mariana scoffed. "What makes you so sure?"

He smirked, staring straight ahead. "I know your scent."

She stilled, a shiver running down her spine. Their eyes locked, and she could see the certainty in his gaze, the confidence that unnerved her more than anything else.

"There's no hiding from me. Even in the sea."

Mariana swallowed hard, her nerves tightening as she stared at the hand gripping her knees, holding her securely against him.

Their eyes caught, and her breath stilled.

"Fresh flowers and sea salt," he murmured.

She couldn't stop the way her heart stuttered in her chest. She quickly averted her gaze, focusing on the path ahead.

"Can all fae track scents?" she asked, worried that she had underestimated the fae.

"No."

"What makes you so different?" she pressed, her curiosity piqued.

Silence was her answer, leaving no room for further questions.

Mariana didn't know what to make of his cryptic response. If he could track her scent, there was no point in attempting to escape—at least not yet.

He was a skilled fighter, and as much as she hated to admit it, she was beginning to realize that if he truly was employed by King Stavros, he might lead her directly to Astra. But what about Aurora? She had to be worried sick by now.

Her stomach twisted with guilt as the truth settled over her like a heavy fog. She wasn't going anywhere, not anytime soon.

The Siren Witch had once taught her about the power of tactical diplomacy, the strength in making allies, even among enemies. It was a lesson she couldn't afford to forget.

Clearing her throat, she tried to push down the heat rising in her cheeks. "My name is Mariana," she offered quietly. "Everyone calls me Mari."

She kept her gaze on the path ahead, refusing to let him see how nervous she was, hoping the small offering would earn her some information in return. But he remained silent, expression unreadable.

Minutes passed before she heard a sigh escape him; it was so soft she almost missed it.

"Dax," he finally said, his voice low and hesitant, as if revealing his name was an act of trust.

They shared a brief glance, and Mariana found herself at a loss for words for the first time since she had woken up.

Time slipped by in a blur, exhaustion weighing down her eyelids. She fought to stay awake, scrubbing her hands over her face, but the warmth of his chest against her cheek was a comfort she couldn't resist.

"I recommend you sleep while you can," he said quietly.

"No," she murmured, stubbornness lacing her voice. "It's just as bad as being knocked out."

"I'm not going to murder you or leave you to die," he reassured her, his voice oddly gentle. "Sleep so you have the energy to walk when we stop next."

"Where are you taking me?" she asked, her voice fading as sleep began to claim her.

He hesitated before answering, his jaw working as he considered what to say. Finally, he sighed. "We're going to the Crossing. Once we're out of the mortal realm, I'll tell you more. Until then, sleep."

Mariana squeezed her clasped hands, her mind racing with questions, but the exhaustion was too strong. He'd confirmed they were headed toward the fae realm, but she still needed to know if Astra was alive. That had to wait. The fae didn't seem to be in the mood for more conversation, so she focused on the path as he carried her, her thoughts drifting as her head settled against his chest.

Within moments, her vision faded to black, and she slipped into a deep, dreamless sleep.

CHAPTER 10

THERE WAS VERY LITTLE in the world that bewildered Dax anymore. Still, a siren with a vixen's mouth and was as beautiful as the rising dawn unnerved him more than he'd ever care to admit.

Her turquoise eyes reminded him of the sea she'd come from. Mysterious, endless, and full of storms. Even her tattoos intrigued him; the subtle black lines and soft swirls caressing her body formed images of nature, notes of songs, and reflections of her life under the waves.

The scar on her face was a reminder that life, although it felt endless, was fragile. It did nothing to dissuade him from believing she was a deadly, beautiful foe. Turning his back to her, even for that second, could've cost him everything if she'd escaped.

She was a force to be reckoned with, a hurricane on the brink of destruction, yet he found himself drawn to her in every way—like a moth flirting with the edge of a flame.

This wasn't what he'd expected, and he knew he needed to get her back to Aurelia as fast as possible.

Dax glanced over at her sleeping form covered with a blanket as he wiped his chest and neck clean with a wet rag. She was going to be so pissed when she woke up. A bucket was beside the bed, awaiting the fate that would befall her when the drug wore off.

He yawned, shaking his head. Sleep was a luxury he couldn't afford with her around, and he needed the silence as he walked to maintain his energy, so he'd knocked her out. The longest he'd ever gone without sleep was five days, and it would take at least seven to get to Aurelia. They were only on day two, and he already felt his body reacting in subtle ways.

Dropping the rag, he dumped the bowl of water out the window of the hunter's cabin they occupied. It was a stop for anyone who needed rest, but it was apparent no one had stopped there in years. Dust coated every surface; windows and doors hung off broken hinges that creaked in the wind. Thankfully, the cots left on the wooden floors were decent enough. At least the siren wouldn't have mold infecting her pores.

Mariana.

Even her name did something to him he couldn't explain. He didn't want to call her anything, but he knew she would cut him up like a knife if he didn't call her by her name. Mari. It was simple enough.

Sighing, he scrubbed his face with his hands and rubbed his aching neck before donning his shirt and armor again.

"What in the silver stars have you done to me?" The venomous question was followed by heavy retching.

Dax glanced over at her, watching her struggle not to get any bile in her long hair. Taking two strides, he lifted the bucket closer to her face. When she was done, she slumped back onto the bed, breathing hard.

"Don't ever do that to me again!"

Dax couldn't help the smirk that lifted his lips, hiding it as he dumped the bucket out the window. "I won't unless I have to."

A blaze of fury glowed in her eyes.

He retrieved the waterskin he'd just refilled and a piece of bread, holding them out as offerings to her. When she didn't take them, he dropped them in her lap. Turning back to his bag, he pulled out a small pair of brown boots he'd procured for her along their journey from a traveling mortal merchant. The whole exchange made Dax want to laugh. The old man had been so terrified, he pissed himself, yet he couldn't turn down the coin Dax offered.

Glancing over at her, he was surprised to find her taking small, angry bites of the bread. Her wrists were still tied together, but her ankles were free.

He set the boots by the bed, and she gazed at them with pure repulsion.

"Um ... what are those?"

"Boots. I suspect they'll fit you well enough to walk in."

Her eyes shot up to his. "Walk?"

"Yes," he said, putting on his hooded cloak. "I am not a horse. I cannot carry you the whole way."

"I'm not putting those things on."

"Yes, you are."

"No, I'm not," she argued. Dax felt bad for the bread she crushed in her hand. "I don't wear shoes. I'm a siren. Don't you know anything about us?"

"That excuse won't get you far, Little Tempest, especially as it gets colder the farther north we go. Speaking of ..." He tossed a leather coat at her, and she snatched it out of the air with a scowl.

"Don't call me that," she growled, her sharp glare meeting his.

Dax tilted his head, a faint smirk tugging at his lips as he stepped closer, towering over her. "Don't like it, Little Tempest?" He dropped his voice to a low murmur and leaned close to her face. "Then stop kicking up a storm over every damn thing and put on the boots."

Her head slammed into his face with such force that he stumbled backward. Dax clutched his nose, cursing loudly as Mari shot out of the bed.

Dropping a hand from his throbbing nose, he reached out to grab her, but she slipped through his fingers like water.

Reaching the door, she struggled to open it, not realizing it was locked. Dax smirked as he stepped behind her and forcefully turned her around by her shoulders.

One thing he could count on about Mari was that she was a fighter. And she liked to fight dirty.

Claws reached for his throat, scratching his skin. He grabbed her tied wrists before her nails had the chance to rip out his larynx. She kicked and screamed as he slammed her wrists above her head against the wooden door. It groaned under the weight of their thrashing.

"Calm down!" he shouted and trapped her body with his. She tried biting him, her sharp canines on display, but she was too short to reach anything important.

"Just stop! You're not going anywhere!"

She hissed at him, tried biting him again, then gave up and let her head fall back against the door, their heaving chests brushing slightly together. Dax couldn't stop himself from staring down at her. She was wild, stunning chaos. And somehow, he had to tame it.

He took a small step back, creating space between their bodies so he could think clearly, but her eyes threatened to drown all sensible thoughts.

Releasing a sigh, he said softly, "Shit, you're not going to make this easy on me, are you?" He shook his head. "I don't want to be your enemy. I just want to get you safely to Aurelia."

"To do what with me? Hand me over to the king so he can chop off my tail and stick my head on the pike at the palace gates? Make an example out of my kind?" He detected fear beneath her viscous tone.

He opened his mouth to reassure her that wouldn't happen, but he knew it would mean nothing to her. She couldn't trust him and had no idea what awaited her. Escape seemed like her only option. "Death isn't what awaits you in Aurelia."

Mari stilled, her eyes searching his, probing for lies. He held her gaze, steady and unyielding. He needed her to believe him, if only just enough to cooperate.

He drew a short knife from his thigh, and her eyes narrowed on the sheathed dagger there. The same one he had taken from her when he first found her.

"You want it back?" he asked softly, drawing her hateful gaze up to him. "Then earn it." The knife sliced through her wrist bonds. He knew it was a risk, but she deserved the chance to prove—

Within half a second of her being free, she snatched her dagger back and had it pointed at his throat. Moving quickly, he dropped his knife, slammed her right wrist against the door, and gripped the other, holding back the dagger.

"Let's get one thing straight, *fae*," she hissed through her teeth. "I don't have to earn anything. This is *mine!*"

Dax smirked down at her, half tempted to laugh. Settling his knee between her thighs, he pushed her into the door and got close to her face.

"Your hatred for me won't help you save your sister." Her eyes widened, her jaw dropping slightly. "Now, give me the dagger."

"You know where Astra is?" she breathed.

He didn't say anything. Instead, he released her wrists and took the dagger from her weak grip to sheath it back at his thigh. He stepped back, finally breathing easier, and snatched the boots.

"Put on the damn boots. Now." He pushed them toward her and was surprised when she took them. She shoved them onto her feet with such aggression that she nearly toppled over.

"Fit?" he asked.

"How am I supposed to know?" she snapped.

He glanced down at them. They were a bit too big, but they'd have to do.

"Tell me about Astra. Have you seen her?"

He held up the coat and motioned for her to put it on.

With a huff, she shrugged the coat on, grimacing at the faint odor of sheep.

"I'm not telling you anything else until we get to the Crossing." He grabbed her wrists again and began gently wrapping them with the white silk.

"What is this stuff?" she asked.

"It's spider silk. You've never seen it before?"

"No."

He secured it with a tight knot. "It's everywhere in the fae realm."

"Well, clearly, I've never *been* to the fae realm."

They glanced at each other, and Dax realized she must've been born after the sirens were banished.

He hardly knew anything about sirens; he had been employed by the royal family shortly after the terrible event that forced their exodus from the fae realm.

Dropping her wrists, he secured his bag around his shoulders.

"Well, *siren*, now's your chance."

Dax unlocked the door and pushed her through.

CHAPTER 11

"So, WHAT'S THE PLAN here? Are we walking until my feet fall apart, or will we stop somewhere with running water?" Mariana stumbled over loose rocks and held back a curse as pain radiated up her feet into her knees and thighs.

"Why? Tough siren can't handle a little walking?" Dax teased, and she glared at the back of his head.

"No, you stink," she snapped, hoping the blatant lie offended him. "I'm about to choke to death from your stench."

"Wow, thanks for the brutal honesty. I appreciate it. Now, stop talking."

Ignoring him, she said, "How about we talk about *you?* Tell me all about yourself. I can barely speak without getting nauseated from all the smells—"

"Then you should shut your trap and keep walking," he barked over his shoulder, tugging her hard by her leash. Her wrists ached in protest, but she yanked back, causing him to stop and turn around.

They held each other's firm, disdainful stares.

Blazes, she wanted to fight him. But she knew she wouldn't win if she did, and that fact deeply bothered her. "Fine," she snapped. "I'll shut my trap like a good little captive," she taunted in an overly sweet tone and batted her eyelashes up at him.

She would follow the intolerable fae as long as she needed to, but that didn't mean she had to make it easy on him.

Her feet stung with each step inside the torture devices they called *shoes*; her natural healing unable to keep up with the blisters ripping her skin open over and over again. And quite frankly, she was pissed, hungry, and tired—there was no room in her heart to care how the fae felt about her constant annoyances. In fact, each time he growled at her or ordered her to stop talking, the pain eased just the slightest bit.

"Let's get one thing straight, princess. You and I have to tolerate each other until we get to Aurelia. Save your energy for walking instead of intentionally trying to annoy me so we get there faster. Once we're there, we can go our separate ways. Agreed?"

Mariana's fists tightened, and the silk dug into her skin, threatening to slice her wrists apart. But her anger couldn't overshadow the fact that he had called her princess.

"You know who I am," she said in a deadly calm tone, noticing how his jaw clenched in response. He wasn't just a mercenary for hire; the king had told him about her, and the only way the king would've known anything was if he had spoken to Astra.

"Is my sister still alive?" she blurted.

His face didn't move a muscle as his emerald gaze stared her down.

Instead of responding, he turned around and continued walking, forcing her to follow.

She let out a low growl. "Just tell me if she's alive, that's all I ask."

"I won't tell you anything unless you stop talking and we enter the fae realm."

Her nails dug into her skin as she gripped her fists tight, wanting to throw something at his head.

The water in the air coating her skin and misting the trees called to her again now that the drug had completely worn off. She let herself answer the call, pulling droplets into her hand. Glancing up, she contemplated throwing the ball of water at the fae's head. Maybe drowning him just a little ... Instead, she formed shapes of sea creatures in her palms as she walked. The light from the sun glinted off their little forms, casting small rainbows against her skin. She smiled, finally enjoying herself with youngling tricks. It killed the time, and before she knew it, Dax had stopped.

She slammed into his back, the tiny water octopus in her hand splashing to the ground. Moaning, she stumbled back and lifted her hands to her face.

"*Good Goddess!* You can't just stop like tha—" Her words dropped away with her hands when she saw what he was looking at.

Through the dense trees at the edge of a cliff stood a pillared arch covered in overgrowth. Ivy spiraled up the columns, and moss covered the cobblestone ramp leading up to a glittering door.

"What is that?" she asked softly. She'd never seen anything like it.

"The Crossing," Dax replied and began walking toward the archway.

"*That* is the Crossing? Everyone always talked about it like it was a land bridge."

"It was," he said to her, then turned to face the strange, colorful window. "Before the Infernal Wars."

Before the fae all wanted to kill each other over power.

"Huh." She stepped up next to him, staring at it in wonder. It didn't show what was on the other side, just an array of glittering colors.

"Why would the fae build this and then never use it?"

"They did use it when mortals didn't inhabit the islands, before the Southern Continent decided all fae were—"

"Demons?" she chuckled. "Yeah, I've heard that before."

"Back then, these islands didn't have much value, so the fae left, and mortals moved in."

"The vultures," she joked. The sound of the sea crashing drifted to her ears, and she stepped to the side of the arch, tugging on the rope that connected her to Dax. He huffed but let her look over the edge.

"Damn," she breathed as she stared down at how far the sea was from where they stood. Violent waves crashed against the rocks jutting out from the sea and up the side of the cliff. Her gaze lifted to the other side of the chasm, where another archway stood, far enough away to appear twice as small. The salty wind blew her hair around her face, stinging her eyes.

Dax let out a low whistle over her shoulder. "Yeah, there's no jumping that. You'll die instantly."

Mariana lifted an eyebrow at him. "So would you."

He had the nerve to smirk at her, then pulled her back toward the strange doorway.

"If this thing doesn't work, we'll both fall to our deaths. That's nice," she muttered.

"The only way it wouldn't work was if you and I were mortals."

She squinted. "How's that?"

"Mortal blood can't use the Crossing. Only fae blood can pass through."

Taking a hesitant step back, she said, "But I'm not fae, I'm a siren."

He placed his hand against her back, stopping her. "Every siren has fae blood; that much I know. You'll be fine."

She hated the worried look he must've seen across her face and quickly schooled her features.

"Fine. Bastards first," she said politely and gestured for him to go. The smirk never left his eyes as he shook his head and shoved her through.

Mariana's lungs seized. She closed her eyes, fearing the worst, and expected to feel herself falling to her death, straight into the place she called home, when her feet stumbled.

Rocks crunched beneath her boots, and she realized she wasn't falling.

Releasing a shaky breath, she smiled and opened her eyes just as a pair of rough hands grabbed her arms and sneering copper eyes inspected her.

A gravelly voice from chapped lips said, "Who do we have here?"

CHAPTER 12

DAX TOOK A DEEP breath, enjoying the moment of peace and quiet. As he slowly exhaled, he reminded himself why he was doing this and why he had to follow through with his orders.

Then the silk string connecting him to Mari yanked him right out of his relaxed state and through the archway.

"Look what we have here at the other end of the leash!" a rough voice he didn't recognize shouted.

Dax's body tensed as he inspected the three male fae surrounding him.

One with long, black hair was holding Mari by the throat as she tried kicking him in the shins with zero luck getting free. The male was tall and built like a brick wall. He sneered in her face before turning that scornful gaze at Dax as if he were proud of his shiny new stolen toy.

But Mari was no toy. She seethed, glaring at the lowlife like she couldn't wait to rip *his* throat out.

The one who'd shouted at him held a long steel blade in his weathered hand. Dax could tell from where he stood a few steps away that it hadn't been sharpened in quite some time. They weren't typical marauders then, so why were they staking out the archway?

"A *gray-skin* trackin' down a *blue-skin*. Hah! Come to collect yourself a bounty, have you?" The knave's dirty brown hair blew in stringy strands around his face, and he kept shaking his head to clear his eyes. One of them was swollen and bruised.

Dax made a silent promise that by the time he was finished with these idiots, he would make sure both eyes were even.

"Oi! How much is a siren worth these days?" the greasy brute asked the black-haired male holding Mari, who laughed and sneered.

"Plenty," he seethed in her face.

The greasy fae laughed, then lifted the spider silk connecting Dax to Mari with a sausage-like finger. "Well, this won't do! Let me get that for you." He sliced the silk with a vicious swipe of his blade. "You're welcome," he mocked in a deep tone as he bowed.

Dax stayed quiet, scanning the last male who stood out like a peacock among pigeons.

His leather armor was polished and well-maintained, and the blond hair tucked behind his ears appeared clean. But despite the obvious differences between this male and the other two, his pale gray eyes scrutinized Dax as though he were an old foe.

"Do I know you?" Dax asked, and the male's lips lifted into a sly smile, showing off a row of perfectly white, straight teeth.

"You'd remember me if we did, I assure you," he replied in a rich, deep voice.

Dax regarded the male carefully, noticing the confident way he held himself, resting his hands on the sword sheathed at

his waist. He knew Dax. That meant they had something—or *someone*—in common.

Dax clenched his jaw hard, instantly irritated as he de-
duced who that someone might be.

"You a hunter, then, is that it?" the greasy brute asked,
shaking the hair from his eyes again.

"What's it to you?" Dax muttered.

"Oh, I think you know, eh? We plan on takin' this pretty
one back to Aurelia and makin' ourselves rich." He laughed.
The tall, sneering one joined him.

Mari dug her long, sharp nails deep into the fae's hand at
her throat, and in one swift move, she ripped it open.

Blood gushed from the screaming male's hand, and he let
her go, cradling it to his chest.

Dax used the opportunity to punch the shocked, greasy
brute hard in his good eye. He howled and stumbled back,
one hand still gripping his weapon and the other covering
his face. Dax's lips lifted in satisfaction as he pulled out both
his daggers.

"Don't!" the blond one shouted at his comrades. Dax
elbowed him in the head. He stumbled, falling flat on his
back with a groan.

Dax turned to the howling idiot still gripping his eye and
stabbed him in the stomach. The howling turned to screams
as Dax ripped the dagger free.

Lifting his gaze, he flung the other straight into the neck
of the black-haired male fighting off Mari.

He couldn't stop himself from admiring her at that moment.
With her hands still tied together, she managed to hold the male

hostage in a way that made him look like he was gasping for air without even touching him.

Water and blood sputtered from the male's mouth and leaked from the dagger's wound. Droplets from the damp ground rolled over moss and rocks up the convulsing fae, filling every orifice.

She was drowning him.

A sharp, sudden pain speared Dax's side. He shouted, pulled back into his own fight. The greasy shithead had rammed his blade into the softest part of Dax's armor. It might have been dull, but it was coated in widow toxin. He could feel its familiar burning sting as it streamed into his bloodstream.

These were no random marauders looking for their next score. This was a trap set up as a deadly warning.

Shifting his bloodthirsty gaze to swollen, grinning eyes, Dax growled, "You're next." Then he stabbed the brute in the wrist. The male squealed like a pig and let go of the blade. Dax removed it from his side as the crying male gripped his bleeding wrist. Taking the cheap blade's handle, Dax slammed it straight into its owner's heart.

The greasy brute collapsed, falling silent.

Dax swung around and plunged his daggers into the drowning male's stomach, slicing it open with a swipe of his hands. The male collapsed, bright cobalt eyes rolling to the back of his head as the last of his blood spilled to the ground.

Mari gasped, letting her power go, and fell to the grass as she struggled to breathe. She stared in horror at the dead fae before her, letting out a slightly strangled sound as she tore her eyes away to stare at her hands.

Dax took a step toward her as he heard the blond male whisper, "Gods be damned..."

His sun-kissed skin had turned pallid, lips drained of color.

Dax turned toward him and lifted him by his white linen collar.

"Please, don't hurt me! I was sent—"

"I know why you're here. Shut your trap," Dax growled in his face. "Now, be a good little puppet and run home to your master. I've got everything under control."

Dropping the male to the ground, Dax watched him scramble away toward a huddle of horses.

As soon as the male's form had disappeared through the trees and the clopping of the horse's hooves went silent, Dax sighed.

Then, burning pain consumed him. He gasped and groaned. The toxin was spreading through him like wildfire, searing every vein and nerve until his knees gave out.

"Dax!" he heard Mari shout as his face collided with the dirt.

CHAPTER 13

SHE KILLED SOMEONE. SHE killed—

No. Stop. Mariana shook her head, trying to banish thoughts of the dead fae she'd left behind at the Crossing. *There's nothing you can do for him now. But you can still save this stupid, inconsiderate bastard*, she told herself, huffing as she hauled Dax onto a cement slab, using it as a table.

She had followed the horses, which had bolted after the released fae galloped into the forest. They led her to an abandoned village, overrun with vines and decay. Only a few buildings remained standing, and this one, where she'd dragged Dax's heavy body, seemed the least likely to collapse.

Mariana stared down at him, unsure what was wrong. She peeled his eyes open and saw that his pupils were completely dilated. *That's not good.* She let his eyes drift shut again and tore open his shirt, exposing the still-bleeding wound.

He wasn't healing. That wound should've been gone by now.

Leaning closer, she noticed the skin around the gash was turning an alarming shade of black.

She speared her fingers through her hair and closed her eyes, trying to think.

Astra had taught her how to treat infections that their bodies couldn't heal on their own, but this ... this was different. Fae poison. She had never flushed a fae's body before—would it kill him?

Does it matter? He's dying anyway.

Opening her eyes and dropping her hands, Mariana stared down at Dax, wondering why she was even considering saving his sorry ass. Her lips tightened, arms crossing over her chest.

He'd stolen her away from her family, ripped her from everything she loved. He expected her to just follow his orders, to be his *good little siren?*

"No," she whispered darkly, turning away.

She made it all the way to the grazing horses before her conscience screamed at her to stop. To turn around. To save that ridiculous male.

She looked back, something deep inside tugging her toward him. *This isn't who you are,* a small voice whispered. Her shoulders sagged.

With a groan of frustration, she stomped back toward Dax. The moment she got close, she slapped her hands over his bleeding wound and channeled her power.

Water from the air, droplets clinging to the vines, rushed up and out of her palm.

Dax screamed. His body convulsed, thrashing under her hands.

Mariana focused, steadying the water's path. *Careful. Keep it away from his heart.* She focused her energy, guiding the water carefully through his veins.

The moment she sensed the sinister poison, the water wrapped around it and pulled.

Slowly, she lifted her hand, her breathing growing heavy as she coaxed the tainted water out of his body. Dax's thrashing stilled. Her heart stuttered, fearing she'd killed him—but then his pulse fluttered weakly at his throat. He'd only passed out.

Hissing under her breath, Mariana yanked the last of the poison free, the blackened liquid dripping onto the ground at her feet. She stepped back, chest heaving.

She hadn't practiced that technique enough to know if she'd gotten every last bit of it, but as she watched the wound slowly close, she let out a shaky breath.

"Thank the goddess," she whispered.

She grabbed his pack from where she'd thrown it earlier, rifling through it until she found a pouch of medical supplies. Quickly, she patched the healing gash with gauze and tape.

As she smoothed the last piece of tape over the bandage, Dax's hand drifted over hers.

Mariana stilled, glancing up to find his eyes barely open, half-lidded, and unfocused.

She leaned over him. "Dax?" she asked softly, unsure if he was even fully conscious.

His eyes fluttered closed again, but his hand tugged hers closer, pressing it over his heart.

Mariana didn't know what to make of the gesture. She was exhausted, her body aching from using so much power in such a short span. Blaming it on the weariness, she sat beside him on the table, leaning back against a wall covered in soft vines.

She glanced down at him. He was still clutching her hand. His skin was warm. His calloused fingers, though rough, felt surprisingly gentle.

Lifting her free hand, she brushed her fingers across his forehead, smoothing the crease there. His face relaxed, tension fading from his brow.

Curiosity stirred. Her fingers trailed over his sharp cheekbones, tracing the line of his temple, his nose, and his lips. His facial hair was growing in, and she dragged her fingers against the roughness, enjoying the sensation.

She held her breath as his head shifted toward her touch, but his eyes never opened. Instead, he settled his head in her lap, her right arm resting on his shoulder as he continued to hold her hand.

She exhaled softly, a strange warmth spreading in her chest. Gently, she settled her other hand over his head and stroked his short, soft hair. His breathing slowed, steadying as his body relaxed completely against her thighs.

Mariana glanced down at the dirty dress barely covering where his head now rested. If he woke up like this ... would he be embarrassed? Angry? Or ...

Her lower belly tightened at the thought, and she quickly closed her eyes, resting her head back against the wall.

It didn't matter. She honestly should have left already. Her sister was counting on her, and her family was looking for her. So why hadn't she? Dax was the enemy, and yet ...

She couldn't bring herself to pull away.

Instead, her breathing evened out, her heartbeat calming as she stayed with the sleeping male.

CHAPTER 14

DAX GROANED; HIS WHOLE body felt like it had been through a meat grinder and then sewn back together.

Movement to his right had him instinctively snatching the dagger strapped to his thigh and bringing it up to the siren's throat.

"You're alive," Mari breathed. "What a surprise."

Glancing down, Dax realized she, too, held a short blade to his throat. Pale light glinted off the sharpened bone in her hand.

It only took him a second to realize she had been about to change the bandage on his side. Pulling the dagger back, he sheathed it and waited for her to do the same. She hesitated before setting her blade down. He eyed it wearily. It was the same one he'd taken from her during their first encounter. He knew he should take it back, but was too tired for another fight.

Dax scrubbed his face with his hands. "What happened? Where are we?"

They appeared to be in some sort of ruin. Crumbling stone walls covered in moss surrounded them. Above was half a wooden ceiling with a broken skylight that provided little shelter. Dax eyed the rotted beams with caution. The last thing he wanted was to have a shoddy ceiling collapse and bury them alive.

"This place looks like a tomb waiting to happen."

"Yeah, well, it was the only building in this destroyed village with a roof. I dragged you all the way out here after the fight. You're welcome." She helped him sit up, and he swung his legs over the side of the slab of stone she must've laid him out on. Cracking his back, he rolled his neck and heard a series of pops.

"Let me see," she demanded. Dax tensed as she crouched between his legs to inspect the wound. His eyes studied her carefully while she peeled away the bandage to reveal a red slice. The skin that had touched the tainted blade was dark. "It's looking better."

"How ... That was widow toxin. Without an antidote, I should be dead right now," he muttered, his voice thick and drowsy. He'd come close to death so many times over the course of his long life that it felt like any other day by this point. How he'd managed to survive this one, he had no idea.

Widow toxin was incredibly rare and difficult to come by. He hadn't expected anyone to have it, much less attack him with it, so he never kept the antidote on hand. A stupid mistake.

"I had to flush the wound," she replied, then let out an irritated sigh when he stared at her in confusion. "I drowned your veins until the toxin spilled free. You were asleep for ... *most* of it."

"Most of it?" A hiss slipped between his gritted teeth as the sting intensified. She was wiping the wound clean with the disinfectant he kept in his bag.

"You don't remember anything?" she asked, avoiding his gaze.

"No," he groaned.

Her eyes met his briefly before she focused back on cleaning the wound. "That's probably for the best."

"What makes you say that?" he ground out.

What Mari did next surprised him. She gently blew on the inflamed area until the sting faded, then brought her stormy gaze up to his.

"You were screaming," she murmured.

He couldn't describe what he felt then, staring into the sea trapped within her eyes. The softness in her gaze countered the tension in her shoulders and mouth.

"Why did you save me?" He had to know. It made no sense for her to stick around. He was grateful to be alive but couldn't forget that she was a dangerous enemy—one that clearly had a hidden agenda.

Mari shrugged. "I just killed a fae, and I wasn't about to watch another die."

Dax studied her as she patched him back up. "Why would that matter to you?"

"Because"—she slapped the tape on, making him grunt—"I'd never killed anyone before, and I didn't like the feeling. Don't make me think otherwise."

They glared at each other for a solid minute before Mari finally looked away.

"How long was I out for?"

Mari shrugged as she began cleaning up the bloody patches. "Since last night. Your body needed time to recover."

No shit, he almost said. Instead, his eye caught on the dagger she'd set on the ground beside her. "What kind of blade is that?"

Picking it up, she turned it over in her hands. "Basilisk bone. My sister, Aurora, makes armor and weapons out of it."

Dax's eyebrows shot up. "Impressive. How in the blazes did she find a basilisk?" *And survive?*

"She found a carcass in an underwater cave, brought back what she could, and discovered that the bone bent under extreme heat and pressure. As it cooled, it hardened." Mari flipped the blade in her hand. "Harder than steel." Her gaze flitted to his. "Ever seen one before?"

Dax swallowed. "Yeah, a long time ago." He tried not to recall the memory long stowed away in his mind, but he couldn't stop his body from growing tense as the bloody battle filled his thoughts.

He dragged his eyes away from the bone blade to study the creeping vines that climbed up the stone wall in front of him.

Mari sheathed the dagger at her hip and stood up. "Best to let that scab so you'll heal faster."

He glanced down at the wound. He could feel his skin knitting itself back together. It was going much slower than usual, but at least he was healing.

"How did you find this place?"

"I followed the horses. They seemed to know where they were going when that fae let them loose. I assume this was where the scumbags were staying, awaiting the moment we came through the Crossing." Mari turned her head toward him. Dax kept his gaze steady, unflinching under her scrutinizing stare. "I think you know who they were. And why they were waiting for us."

"I had no idea they'd be there."

She tilted her head. "You wouldn't have let that last one go if you didn't know who he was."

He stayed silent, watching her calculating and cynical gaze inspect him. He didn't like where this was going; he needed to turn it around.

"Thank you," he said softly and cleared his throat. "I'm grateful for what you did."

"Yes, well ..." She brushed her hands together before settling them on her hips. "Don't thank me yet. You're still on my bad side. Plus, you owe me."

Dax's brows pulled together, instantly frowning at the idea. "What do you want?"

"A swim," she stated firmly.

He scoffed, "I don't think so."

She crossed her arms and took a defiant stance. "I could've let you die, your face smothered in the dirt. By the time I even dragged your ass here, you weren't breathing. I'm the only reason you're alive. So, I'm going to have a swim."

Why did she save me? She could've escaped, so why is she still here?

Dax turned the cynical, inspecting look on her. She wasn't leaving until she found what she wanted to know. That much was clear.

"Fine, have at it. I'm sure there's a river nearby," he said. It was a ballsy risk, one he really couldn't afford if she decided to leave, but something about her sudden need to swim made him want to test her.

"Great, let's go."

"What?" he asked, confused. "Why do I need to go?"

"Why do you think? You stink."

Dax shook his head. "Not this again."

"And you're covered in blood."

"I'll wipe it off."

"Or you could wash your body," she said slowly, like he was a total idiot. He glared at her. "What? A tough fae like you can't handle a little cold water?"

He ground his teeth together, hating the idea of getting caught in her trap. She would completely control his fate if he stepped foot into water. Yet her challenge made his decision spill from his lips without a second thought.

"Fine." Standing, he swiped his bloody shirt off the ground and slipped it on before grabbing his cloak. "Now seems like a great time to risk dying of hypothermia. Why not?"

"Sirens don't get hypothermia from water; we're only sensitive to cold air. So don't worry," she said, her voice soft as she met his gaze. "I'll keep you from dying." Then, she turned on her bare feet and muttered, "Just don't make me regret it."

"Wait," he said, stopping her. "Give me your dagger." He held out his hand, and she scoffed.

"Why? It's mine."

"Want me to trust you?" Dax saw a look of uncertainty pass over her face. "Then give it to me."

"Fine," she gritted and slammed the dagger into his palm. "But you already know I don't need it to kill you."

CHAPTER 15

MARIANA BREATHED THE COOL air deep into her lungs as she navigated toward the river. She could feel it calling to her. Its sweet song lured her toward its welcoming embrace, teasing her with the promise of relief.

Dax was silent behind her, somehow making far less noise than she did as they stepped through the remnants of autumn and winter. The dried leaves crunched beneath her bare feet, and she curled her toes against the cold bite of the ground.

She'd been stupid for saying she didn't need the dagger to kill him. She was supposed to be earning his trust, not putting his guard up! But she couldn't take back the words now. He had to have known she was a worthy opponent already, so why did he ask for the dagger? Was it some kind of test? Or maybe ...

Biting the inside of her cheeks, she realized the answer. *Trust goes both ways.*

Her legs ached painfully, ready to transform the second she was in the water. Her whole body itched to let her tail free, to feel the rush of water through her hair and saturate her scales. They felt dry and flaky, frantic for hydration that drinking water couldn't fix. The gnawing sensation overwhelmed her the moment her eyes landed on the flowing river.

Moss-covered rocks interrupted the heavy current farther upstream, allowing the river to calm substantially into an easy, steady flow. The sight of it made her sigh in relief. *Almost there.*

Glancing back at Dax, she caught him eyeing the river cautiously, like it might swallow him whole if he dared step into it. She knew what she had to do. She'd insisted he come with her because she needed to gain the upper hand. Trust was her goal. Control was her weapon. And he had no idea what she was capable of.

She let her coat fall to the ground, then with deliberate slowness, she lifted her hands to the knot at her neck and untied her dress.

"Do you have to undress before you transform?" Dax asked, his expression tight and unyielding.

"No," she muttered, not offering anything else. It was true she could slip her clothing into the *fold*, making it disappear as she transformed, but that took energy she didn't want to waste.

Turning toward the river with her back to Dax, she let the dress fall to her feet and stepped into the water. Her tail splashed through the rippling waves, and she smiled, letting out a deep sigh. Tilting her head back, she floated. Her tail moved slowly, keeping her from going downstream.

She gazed up at the sky. The sun was approaching the horizon, casting long, dark shadows through the trees. Turning her head toward Dax, she found him still clothed, his hood covering his head and shrouding his eyes in darkness.

"What are you waiting for?" she asked, spreading her arms wide. "It's not that cold."

"It's not that warm either."

She slapped her tail, splashing water at him, and he quickly sidestepped.

"Oh, come on, get in! You'll get used to it."

The fae continued staring at her. Good. *Let him look. Let him think I trust him. The closer he gets, the more careless he'll be.*

"Your tattoos ..." he said carefully, "they're glowing."

Mariana glanced down at her arms and saw the pale glow from the tattoos embedded in her skin. "They are," she said, tilting her gaze back at him, unable to see his shadowed eyes. "It tells me that this river connects to the sea."

Dax remained silent for a long moment, and she began to worry. "Mari," he started softly, "I need to ask you something."

His serious tone sobered her, her euphoria fading as her body grew tense. Shifting so she was facing him, she gave him an equally concerned look. "What?"

"If I enter that river, am I in danger?"

He was as tense as a coiled snake, believing she was dangerous. *Good.*

She forced her gaze to soften. "No, Dax. I just saved your life, why would I hurt you now?"

It was the truth. Mariana didn't plan on killing him, but she wanted him to understand that she *could* if he crossed her. Power needed to stay on her side.

"Just this morning, you tried ripping my throat out with your teeth."

Mariana smiled faintly at the memory. "That was all in good fun. Besides, watching you fight earlier, the way you killed those fae, it reminded me that I need an ally. My only concern is finding my sister. I think you can help me save her."

A long, drawn-out moment of silence made her doubt everything she'd revealed. But then Dax lifted his hands and pushed back his hood, revealing his cautious gaze.

"You're telling the truth."

She rolled her eyes. "Just get in the water, Dax."

He sighed before dropping his cloak. As he lifted his shirt over his head, her eyes trailed his toned chest and abs, and she quickly glanced away as soon as he began taking off his pants.

Focus on anything else. Not the naked fae just a short distance away.

Mariana's cheeks burned with shame. Her core tightened, and something inside her began to ache. It was a sensation she'd never felt before. She shoved it aside. *This isn't about him.*

When Dax stepped into the river, his cautious gaze inspected her like he was trying to solve a riddle.

"Why were you crying the morning I found you?"

The question made her heart skip a beat. "You mean the morning you drugged me?"

He shrugged, and Mariana tilted her head back, letting the water cascade through her hair. She tried to steady herself as the pain of that morning came rushing back—Celeste's face, the sound of her voice, the crushing emptiness left in her absence.

"Are you asking or demanding to know?" she said softly, silently begging him to let the matter drop.

"I'll listen, but only if you wish to tell me."

With an aching heart, she sank into the water briefly, taking a few steadying moments before resurfacing. Wiping the water—and the tears—from her eyes, she wrapped her arms around herself.

"Someone I care about died. She ..." Mariana paused, gathering her composure. "She was like a mother to me."

"She was mortal," he stated.

"Yes. And despite how you fae feel about them, they are an intelligent, caring species. They may not have electricity or much care for proper hygiene," she said with a faint smirk at his expression, "but at least they take care of each other."

Dax tilted his head, his gaze steady. "Not all fae hate mortals."

"And yet, for all I've seen of your kind, the lot of you have proven to be selfish, hostile brutes."

A corner of his mouth lifted. "Your mouth is going to get you killed someday."

"Or it'll save my life." Her eyes roamed his face. "Why did you take me, Dax? Why bring me back to a king who wants to destroy my people? You don't seem like the sadistic type."

His smirk faded. "Just following orders."

"That's it?"

He shrugged. "You have all the power to kill me. Right now. And yet, all you do is cut me with your sharp tongue. So, why did you save my life?"

"Because you're the only hope I have of finding my sister."

Dax didn't respond, yet his eyes never left hers.

"Do you have any siblings?" she asked suddenly, the question slipping out before she could stop it.

His silence unnerved her until he muttered, "I have a younger sister."

"What's her name?"

"Kenna," he said, his tone flat, distant.

Mariana frowned. "Do you miss her?"

Dax's jaw tightened. His answer came a moment too late. "Always."

Her heart clenched at the truth she saw in his expression.

"Is she in Aurelia?"

His glare made any lingering questions die on her lips.

She stopped before him, suddenly taken back by the painful look he was trying to hide behind a mask of indifference.

This fae, with his dark shadowed eyes and silent demeanor ... was haunted. By what, Mariana couldn't tell, but it clearly had something to do with his family.

Her heart seized as she lifted an unsteady hand to his cheek. When he sharply pulled back, she swallowed hard. *What am I doing? I don't need to touch him to get answers.* But her hand moved anyway, almost against her will.

His cheek was prickly to the touch, and strangely, she liked it. Dax only stared at her with mistrust in his darkening eyes.

"It's alright to miss those you love, Dax. I miss my sister more than I can tell you," she whispered.

He snatched her wrist, pulling it away from his cheek, startling her. His grip was tight and unrelenting—a warning.

His gaze traveled to her lips, then back to her eyes. Their breath mingled, and she wondered if he'd close the distance.

The idea was like ice sliding down her spine, and she tried to yank her arm back, but Dax held her wrist firm.

"I know what you're doing," he growled.

"You know nothing," she said, trying to sound strong, but the shake in her voice gave her away.

Pulling her closer, he put a firm hand on her lower back, and she shivered despite her body growing warm. Her free hand landed on his chest, pushing him back slightly with her nails digging into his gray skin.

Her breath came out in short pants, fear slithering through her insides. But it wasn't him she feared, it was what she'd do if he came any closer.

His brows lowered. "You want me to open up, reveal all my secrets."

Her voice shook despite herself. "Wouldn't you do everything you could if your sister was in danger?"

His grip loosened. "Without a doubt."

"Then tell me she's alive. Tell me why you came after me. Did Astra send you? No one else would've known about my presence at Egan Village. So I know she told you something."

Dax closed his eyes briefly, his face tightening as if in pain. When he opened them, his resolve was clear.

He dropped his hands and waded slowly toward the edge of the river. "Your sister's alive. But don't think for a second that I'm your ally."

Mariana watched in stunned silence as he moved toward the edge of the river, put on his clothes, and disappeared into the darkened forest.

CHAPTER 16

NIGHT FELL, SMOTHERING THE world in darkness, but Mariana stayed in the river, her body suspended in the cool water like a leaf caught in a current. The gentle lapping of the waves against her skin did little to soothe her nerves. Every instinct told her something was wrong, and she had to return home, but an invisible weight kept her anchored.

The way Dax had evaded her after she asked about her sister made her anxious.

Mariana's thoughts spiraled, her mind a whirlwind of doubts and fears. Astra was the only one who knew about Mariana's visits to Celeste, the only one who knew how close she was to the mortals of Egan Village. But Astra was fiercely loyal, always putting her sisters' safety above her own. Would she really tell Stavros about Mariana, risking her life?

She should leave. Going any further with Dax meant more uncertainty. More trouble.

Lifting her right wrist, Mariana brushed her fingers over the charms that dangled there, each a memory from her days as a youngling. She found the one the Siren Witch had given her long ago: a dark-spotted, spiraled shell with a large opening at the bottom. The shell was no larger than the pad of her thumb, yet it pulsed with a latent power that thrummed beneath her fingertips.

She had to speak with her mother. Cybele would know what to do. She could formulate a plan with the council if she could return to Salus. Perhaps Cybele would be more open to the idea of Mariana and Aurora traveling to Aurelia to rescue Astra, considering she'd have been able to escape her fae abductor. Or ... perhaps Cybele would lock her up forever.

Mariana hesitated, holding that tiny charm with the power to call for help and staring at it as though it could tell her what to do.

Taking a steady breath, she knew it was time. She had to go back home. If Astra truly needed help, Mariana couldn't do it all on her own. And if it were a trap ... then at least she'd thwart the king's plans. Now was her only shot at escaping while Dax was stomping around in the forest.

Dipping below the surface, she began to sing. The melodic tune drifted downstream, carrying her message with it. The notes were a plea, a call for aid that only those attuned to the sea's magic could hear. Her song echoed through the water, a haunting melody that resonated with the ancient spirits that dwelled within, carrying her message.

She rose to the surface and waited, her heart pounding. The seconds stretched into what felt like an eternity, the silence pressing in on her. Then, swirling lights appeared before her near the shore. The witch had heard her message.

"Mari?" she heard Dax shout behind her. She glanced over her shoulder just as he came into view between the trees, his silhouette framed by the moonlight. His expression tight with confusion.

Mariana hesitated for the slightest moment. His boots neared the edge of the river, and their eyes met.

Dax's hand twitched at his side, like he was fighting the urge to reach for her. "Don't," he said, the single word heavy with something she couldn't name. His jaw clenched, and though his voice was soft, his gaze was hard, unyielding.

Her throat tightened. "I have to."

Thrusting herself forward, she dove into the portal before he could say any more, the water closing over her head like a shroud. Breathing hard, she watched the portal spin into nothing behind her, disappearing when she entered Salus.

Strong hands gripped her shoulders, pulling her from the depths.

"Mariana." Her mother's typically cold voice sounded relieved to see her. Queen Cybele appeared before her, regal and imposing. "What happened? Where have you been?"

Wearing her typical midnight-black cape, the witch came into view behind her, the beady red eyes of the scorpion fish brooch staring into her soul.

"I was taken," she said quickly, averting her gaze to notice they were alone. The familiar surroundings of the council chamber, with its walls lined with ancient carvings and artifacts, brought a small measure of comfort.

"Who would dare?" the witch questioned in a tone so deadly that Mariana had to remind herself that it wasn't her the witch was angry with.

"A fae that works for King Stavros."

"What? What did he want?" the witch asked, her tone turned calm and measured, her eyes dark and piercing as they bore into Mariana's, demanding answers.

"I don't know what he wants, but this was the first moment I had alone to send a message for help." Mariana's voice trembled slightly, the weight of her ordeal pressing down on her.

The Siren Witch drew near, scanning her for wounds. "I'm glad you did."

"Are you alright?" her mother asked. The concern in her expression unsettled Mariana. It wasn't something she had ever been familiar with. Queen Cybele was known for her stoicism, a trait that had earned her the respect and fear of her people.

"I'm fine. He didn't hurt me. Listen," Mariana said, shaking off her mother's hands. "The fae said that Astra is alive but that she didn't send for me. He wouldn't tell me any more, but the way he was behaving—"

"Astra is in Aurelia? You're certain?" her mother interrupted, eyes narrowing.

"I can only assume so, but—"

"If she's there, she needs help," the witch said.

Mariana let out an irritated breath. "Something is wrong," she stated firmly. "I think it's a trap."

Cybele's expression darkened. "What do you mean?"

"The way he evaded my questions, the look in his eyes, I don't know ... I just have a hunch." She hated the doubt she felt as her mother continued to scrutinize her. The queen's gaze was like a blade, cutting through her defenses.

"A hunch?" The witch's face remained composed, but her voice carried a note of skepticism. "Mariana, the fae could've led you right to Astra. They could've gotten you where you needed to go in order to stop the king from getting ahold of Seraphina's amulet. Have you forgotten what's at stake here?" she scolded, and Mariana's mind began to spin.

"I haven't forgotten—" she started, but the witch held up a hand to stop her, then turned toward Queen Cybele.

"Your Majesty, she must go back. The fate of our people rests in her hands. She must find the amulet." The witch's face was stern, unable to accept any other answer.

Cybele paused, glancing between the two of them. Mariana could practically see her mother weighing her options. "If it is a trap, you must be prepared. Malea!"

The queen's lady-in-waiting popped inside, keeping her hands locked in front of her and her eyes cast down. "Yes, Your Majesty?"

"Fetch Mariana's armor."

"What?" Mariana breathed with wide eyes.

"Right away." Malea exited the chamber, returning only a moment later with the armor. The sight of it glinting in the dim light made Mariana's heart skip.

She couldn't believe what was happening as Malea strapped the custom armor Aurora had made for her onto her chest and back. The armor was a masterpiece, crafted from basilisk bones and imbued with protective enchantments.

"You want me to go back?" she asked her mother softly. The way Cybele's eyes narrowed made Mariana regret asking.

"You don't want to find Astra? Rescue your people? I thought this was what you wanted all along?"

"No, I know, of course it is, I just—*ah!*" Agony pierced her skull, her eyes shutting out the sudden tears as her skin began to vibrate. She gripped her head tightly. Voices screeched between her ears like nails, scraping against her brain, ripping it apart.

It was like her whole body was begging, *Go back! GO BACK!*

"Mariana? What's wrong?"

Cybele's words sounded far away, as if she were falling into a black hole of nothing. Hands gripped her arms and pushed her hair from her face. She couldn't see anything. All she could do was scream.

The arguing voices of the witch and the queen were like pounding drums, breaking her apart. Their words blurred together, an unintelligible cacophony that made her head throb.

"What's happening to me?" She felt her lips move but had no idea if the words even left her mouth.

"She has to go back! She'll die!" The statement from the witch broke through the chaos for a split second before her mother's lips landed on her forehead.

Searing pain burst to life as Mariana's mind exploded. She let out a guttural scream, desperately clawing at her mother's hands that gripped her cheeks. The pain was unbearable, a white-hot fire that consumed her.

As she opened her eyes, her mother's somber expression filled her vision, and her lungs burned. It felt like the sea, the home she loved, was killing her.

"You can do more than you know, my love." That was the last thing Mariana heard before she was pushed back through the reopened portal into the river.

CHAPTER 17

Freezing water enveloped her, the pain searing her flesh. Mariana screamed in agony as imaginary flames scorched her skin, searing deeper with each passing second. She squeezed her eyes tight, the world around her dissolving into a chaotic blend of pain and confusion.

She fought against the river's icy flow, commanding it to leave her be. But the relentless current swallowed her words, and terror spiked through her heart when nothing happened. What was happening to her body? Why was her magic failing her now when she needed it most?

The painfully cold water pushed her below, crashing over her head and drowning her cries for help. It was as if her power was trapped in a glass box, banging its fists and tearing at the shackles, pleading to be set free but finding no release.

Water filled her throat, and her gills, usually a source of comfort and life, burned with the intrusion. She couldn't breathe, couldn't think beyond the primal urge to survive. Summoning every ounce of strength, she pushed herself up, her head bursting through the surface. She gasped for air, each breath a desperate fight. Coughing up water, she dragged herself to the river's edge. Tears slid down her face, blurring her vision and mixing with the river's icy grip.

Her whole body was on fire despite the lack of a single flame. Each movement was a new wave of torment. Her body began to transform. Her legs felt blistered, red, and aching, as if they were being flayed alive. Grinding her teeth together, she shoved her bleeding hands beneath her chest and pushed herself out of the water. Her muscles ached painfully, but she refused to fall. The wind thrashed against her mercilessly, making her sensitive skin sting. Her wet hair whipped against her face and neck, adding to her torment.

Kneeling, she sat on her legs and allowed her eyes to dip down to her body. She shouldn't have looked. Her once pale blue skin was peeling away, revealing inflamed warm tones under the haunting moonlight. Each flake that fell was a piece of her identity, a shard of her soul ripped away.

Her fingers slipped against the wet buckles of her chest armor, struggling to get it off. When the protective shell finally fell away, panic poisoned her veins. Fear danced in her stomach as her whole body, mind, and soul refused to accept what she saw. Slowly, she brought a shaky hand up to her chest. As she dragged it down, her beautiful scales fell to the ground. She lifted a handful up to her face and stared in horror at their bright hues fading before her eyes, turning to lifeless ash.

Her heart shattered, and the world began to spin. The trees around her swirled like the raging storm inside her. The sound of the river at her back became an agonizing melody of a cruel truth that squeezed her chest. She begged the Goddess to tell her what was happening, but deep down beneath a thick layer of hope, she knew.

As the truth wound its way around her destroyed, broken body, Mariana looked up at the night sky and screamed. She was trapped. Trapped in a foreign skin. Trapped in her turbulent, violent thoughts, and all she could think was, why? Why would her mother do this to her with so much at stake?

Why, why, WHY?!

Only when her throat was raw and hoarse did she finally fall silent, a sob escaping from her lips. The night air was thick with her despair, echoing her unanswered questions.

Dax appeared in front of her, his face a blur through the tears. His mouth moved like he was trying to speak to her, but she heard nothing. She was lost in her world, drowning beneath the weight of what her mother had done. His warm, calloused hands, grounded her against the storm raging inside. "Mari, look at me," he said, his voice cutting through the haze. She clung to the sound, to the solidity of him.

"Why did she do this to me?" she whispered, then turned her gaze back down to her chest. The pain was so unbearable; she swore she could feel her mother's claws tearing her apart. Each breath was a struggle, each heartbeat a reminder of her transformation.

Mariana knew it then, the undeniable truth she couldn't ignore. She was no longer a siren. The realization crawled through her mind like a parasite, spreading tendrils of despair through every thought. Her scales—the essence of her people, her power, her very soul—were gone, and in their place, only fragility remained. She felt hollow, foreign in her own skin.

Her vision darkened, and she prayed for her Goddess to take her away. To end this suffering, this living nightmare. But the Goddess remained silent, leaving her to face this new reality alone.

CHAPTER 18

DARKNESS HAD SETTLED OVER the forest like a suffocating shroud, broken only by the faint sliver of moonlight filtering through the canopy. Dax crouched beside Mari's limp form, her hair a damp curtain splayed across the cool earth. Her breathing was shallow, each rise and fall of her chest fainter than the last. She looked so small, so fragile—words he'd never thought to associate with her until now.

"Mari," he murmured, his voice taut with worry as he gently shook her shoulder. "Wake up."

Nothing.

His jaw tightened as he pressed two fingers to her neck, searching for the stuttering pulse beneath her feverish skin. It was there, only in rapid little bursts, as though it was struggling to keep up. Her body burned with unnatural heat, trembling as if caught in the grip of a nightmare she couldn't escape.

Dax scrubbed a hand over his face, his breath coming in sharp bursts. *Did I do this?*

The thought clawed at him, dragging his mind back to the serum.

Back at the traveler's cabin before they went through the Crossing, while Mari was still knocked out, Dax had given her shackle serum. A precaution, he told himself, in case she tried to run again.

The crone he'd bought from said it would last three days and assured him it would make any captive "turn back." That's all she'd said in her raspy, withered voice. And now, with Mari crumpled and unresponsive at his feet, he wondered if the damned potion had done more than he'd bargained for.

He grabbed her discarded dress and coat before gently putting them back on her so she wasn't exposed to the cold air sweeping through the trees. Then, he lifted her to rest against the trunk of an old oak. "Mari, wake up," he urged again as he cupped her cheeks and shook her slightly. Her skin was damp, almost slick, shedding faint layers of pale blue like flakes of ash. Colorless scales fell from her legs and chest, littering the ground like remnants of something broken beyond repair.

Dax's stomach churned. *What in the Gods is happening to you?* he asked silently.

Pressing his hands against her face, he stilled. There it was. An energy pulsing beneath her skin, strange and unnatural. He closed his eyes, letting himself feel it. The magic throbbed in waves, foreign and wrong. This wasn't her power. It belonged to someone else.

Realization struck like a hammer. His serum hadn't done this. One of her people had. Something had happened to her on the other side of that portal, something that was ripping the siren from her body, piece by piece.

A curse hissed through his teeth, and Dax dropped his hands, standing so abruptly that the world around him seemed to sway. He paced in frantic strides, the weight of his failure pressing down on him.

He couldn't deliver her like this. His mission was to keep her alive, protect her, and bring her to Aurelia intact. Not ... not like *this*.

And yet, the truth gnawed at the edges of his mind. *She never would've gone through that portal if I'd just kept my mouth shut.*

He'd pushed her too far. She could have left him at the river, could have drowned him if she wanted. She didn't owe him her loyalty, but she'd stayed. She'd looked him in the eye and asked for his help to save her sister. And what had he done? Pushed her away with half-truths and pointed barbs, making sure she didn't see the cracks she'd carved into his walls.

He should have lied. He should have told her whatever she wanted to hear. But at that moment, he couldn't. Not with her.

Dax crouched before her again, his hands trembling as he reached for her neck, but his reach faltered. Her gills were sealed. The sight made his breath hitch. Whatever was happening to her was stripping away the very thing that made her a siren. She was losing herself, and he could do nothing to stop it.

Her pulse was weaker now, fading like a dying ember. "No," he whispered, pressing his fingers to her neck. Panic clawed at his chest, his breathing coming fast and uneven.

Desperation surged through him as he released another curse and tilted her head, prying her eyelids open. Her gaze was unfocused, distant, as if slipping deeper into the void with every passing second. She was still breathing—but barely. Adrenaline gripped his heart, and fear of her dying made his lungs seize.

She couldn't die. He wouldn't let her.

Grabbing her armor from where it had been discarded on the ground, he held it up to her chest and began strapping it on. She looked impossibly small as he worked the buckles.

He had to get her out of here, get her somewhere warm—

A whimper escaped her lips, and Dax's hands stilled on the last strap. The silence that followed was so thick, he could only hear his heart beating erratically.

"Mari?" Lifting a hand, he cupped her cheek, and her eyes opened slightly. Glazed, unseeing.

She moaned, "I can't." Her breath was tight, gasping as she squeezed her eyes shut, and her whole body began to shake.

"Mari," he said, hoping to get her eyes to open again. "You're going to be okay."

"Please, just ... don't leave me," she whispered. Then her whole body went limp as though she was descending into the darkness of her mind.

Dax stared at her for a moment. He knew it then, the place he had to go to save her. "I won't leave you," he replied softly, lifting her into his arms.

Where he had to go, where he had to take her to heal, was a risk. It would be considered a betrayal after years of protection, of secrecy. Was he really willing to risk all of that for this one siren?

Mari shifted weakly in his arms, her body curling into his warmth. Her face pressed against his chest, her breathing faint but steady.

She had no one else. No one to pull her back from the brink. The thought of leaving her or watching the life drain from her body was unbearable. No, she didn't deserve that. She had saved his life; now, it was time for him to repay the favor.

Dax glanced in the direction he had to go, his chest tightening as doubt clawed at him. But as he took his first step, the forest answered, moving on an unnatural wind to part the path ahead. Branches swayed, leaves whispering softly as though urging him forward. He adjusted Mari in his arms, her faint breaths brushing against his neck, and pressed on.

~

The hours blurred together. Each step he took was measured as he carefully navigated the forest. The towering trees watched him silently, their shadows twisted under the pale moonlight. He paid attention to every sound—the distant sound of owls, the crunch of his boots over dried leaves—listening to the chorus of night as he ignored the ache building in his arms. Several times, he considered stopping to rest, but each time he glanced down at the sweat gathering on Mari's brow or felt her faint pulse, he knew there was no time.

When the first red poppies appeared beneath his boots, vibrant and startling against the dark forest floor, he froze. For the first time in hours, it was a sign. His eyes traced their bright petals, every one a sign of home.

Relief and unease warred in his chest, the weight of his choice pressing harder than ever.

His eyes trailed up the massive trunk of a nearby redwood, its gnarled bark twisting upward into the darkness. Somewhere high in the canopy, hidden among the towering branches, was the lookout. He knew it was there, even if his eyes couldn't find it.

A low hum filled the air, subtle and steady, like the forest itself was breathing. He wasn't alone anymore.

Dax shifted Mari's weight, her head lolling against his shoulder as her breath fluttered faintly against his collarbone. He tightened his hold, his gaze lifting to the unseen watcher above.

"Either someone is getting lazy, or they're shocked to see me," he shouted toward the lookout.

"Or they're already waiting for you," a smooth, feminine voice said from behind him.

The corners of Dax's lips tilted upward. He turned his head just as a tall female with a black braid draped over one shoulder stepped out from the shadows, a bow slung casually across her back. The moon's pale light shone over the streaks of white in her braid, revealing her heritage.

"And maybe a little shocked," she added, her voice cracking as her eyes glistened with unshed tears.

Dax stared at her for a long second, her familiar presence tugging at something deep in his chest. Finally, he exhaled softly.

"Hey, Kenna."

CHAPTER 19

DAX STARED AHEAD AT his sister's form as she led him through the darkness toward the village. He hadn't been home in years, yet he knew this part of the forest like the back of his hand. The way the wind rustled the branches, the way even a sliver of moonlight could illuminate the smallest forest secrets, the way the sweet scent of charred wood and fresh pine filled his lungs—it all seemed to restore something inside him.

And yet, the weight in his arms refused to let him feel any peace.

The pale lanterns began lighting their path as the red petals dotting the forest floor like drops of blood gave way to dirt. Ahead, a set of wooden stairs loomed, climbing toward the treetops.

Dax glanced up, his gaze settling on the village nestled among the branches. Kythera was a sanctuary, a place of peace that had kept his people hidden from war for generations. He could only hope that bringing Mari here wouldn't undo everything they'd worked to protect.

Kenna paused, glancing over her shoulder when she noticed he'd stopped. The soft glow of the lanterns above lit her stone-gray skin, so much like his own, and her pale green eyes studied him intently. For a moment, she looked as though she couldn't quite believe he was there.

Lifting a brow, Dax stepped closer. "What?"

Kenna shrugged. "It's just strange seeing you here after all this time," she said softly. "With hair." She chuckled, making a corner of his mouth lift. Then, her smile faltered as her gaze shifted to Mari's unconscious form. "And with her, no less."

Dax's jaw tightened. He didn't want to talk about it. Instead, he moved around his sister and started up the stairs. Kenna trailed behind him.

"What's going on, Dax? What happened to her?" Her voice was quiet but tinged with worry, each word squeezing his chest.

"I don't have time to explain right now. I just need to get her to Spiro."

The staircase stretched high into the trees; from above, he could hear the faint murmur of voices—the sounds of home. His throat tightened at the familiarity of it.

Kythera hadn't changed. The treehouses still nestled among the branches as though they'd grown from the trees themselves, the A-frame cabins covered in moss. Ivy coiled around railings and beams, and soft golden light spilled from the windows, illuminating the bridges that crisscrossed the canopy. It was beautiful, serene. Untouched.

Dax could feel the magic humming in the air, warm and welcoming, as though the village was alive. His jaw tightened as he slammed an iron grip on the energy stirring in his chest.

There were two reasons he rarely set foot in Kythera. The first was for the safety of the village. The second was to avoid the gnawing feeling that something inside him wanted to be set free.

The higher they climbed, the heavier the pressure grew until each step felt louder than the last.

Kenna brushed against his shoulder as she went ahead of him. "Could you be any louder?" she hissed before urging a few villagers peeking out to return to their homes for the night.

"Daxon," a low, familiar voice called from the top of the stairs. Spiro came into view, their tall figure illuminated by the golden glow of the lanterns.

Relief coursed through Dax the moment their emerald-green eyes connected. "I need your help," he said, his voice rough as he adjusted Mari's weight in his arms. "She's dying."

Spiro's gaze softened as they quickly descended the stairs, placing a hand on Mari's fevered forehead. Their lips pressed into a thin line, and they gave a short nod. "Let's get her inside."

Without another word, Dax and Kenna followed the village leader into the clinic.

The cabin was small and unassuming, its entrance covered in thick moss. Yet, inside, it was immaculately clean. Shelves lined the walls, filled with bottles of liquid, bundles of herbs, and strange objects that faintly glowed in the dim light. The air was rich with the sharp scents of medicinal salves and musty, dried flowers.

A wooden table sat on one side of the room, its surface scarred and stained from years of use. Dax felt a twinge of familiarity as he glanced at it—he'd sat there more than once, being stitched up by Spiro after some accident or another.

"Lay her down over there," Spiro instructed, motioning toward a low cot near the fireplace.

Dax carefully set Mari down, brushing a hand against her cheek as her head lolled to the side. Her skin was still feverish, her breaths were shallow, and she murmured faintly, the words too soft to make out.

Kenna lingered in the doorway, crossing her arms. "She doesn't look good," she said softly.

Spiro glanced up. "Kenna, fill the tub with warm water," they said, gesturing toward the large wooden tub in the corner.

"Got it."

"Let's get her armor off," Spiro instructed, kneeling beside the cot to help unbuckle the chest armor. As the last piece came away, a few of the scales Mari was shedding fell onto the fur blankets. Spiro picked one up, their shrewd gaze inspecting the colorless fragment before glancing at Dax.

"Siren?"

Dax gave a short nod, crossing his arms.

Spiro's jaw tightened slightly, but they said nothing. Instead, they lowered themselves to the floor, placing their hands over Mari's chest and closing their eyes. Their gray hands, covered in silver rings, stood out starkly against Mari's inflamed skin.

Dax watched her chest rise and fall in shallow, uneven breaths. The sight coiled something tight and uncomfortable in his chest. He hated it—the helplessness, the ache.

"What's happening to her?" he asked, his voice darker than he intended.

Spiro's white brows furrowed, their lips tightening as though they were concentrating deeply. "She's shifting. Her body is battling the change."

"The change?" Kenna asked, returning to stand beside Dax.

Spiro opened their eyes, their expression grim as they pressed a hand to Mari's forehead. "She's been turned into a fae."

Dax's hands clenched at his sides. "Can you heal her?"

Spiro sighed. "I don't know. Her fever is gone now, but her body is weakened. It will take time to accept what's already been done."

The village leader's touch was gentle as they brushed a few strands of hair away from Mari's sweaty face. Then their head turned toward Dax. "Who did this to her?"

Dax swallowed beneath the intimidating stare. "I don't know."

"How'd you end up with her, anyway?" Kenna asked, one brow arched in curiosity.

Dax's jaw tightened. He was unwilling to meet her gaze. "It's complicated."

"Everything with you is complicated," she muttered, annoyance clear in her tone. "Does she have anything to do with why you've been gone for so long?"

Dax glared at her briefly but said nothing.

"Kenna," Spiro said gently with a tired look on their face. "Leave him be and go get some food."

With a deep sigh, Kenna left the clinic.

Alone, Dax met Spiro's curious gaze and waited for the inevitable slew of questions. But none came. Instead, the leader stood and dipped their fingers into the tub, feeling the temperature of the water.

"I can't imagine what it felt like," Spiro murmured as they stared into the steaming water. "The transition ... it must have been excruciating."

Dax glanced out the stained glass window, the dark sway of branches the only thing visible. But that was not what he saw. Instead, he saw a frightened, screaming siren kneeling on the edge of a river.

"It was awful," he finally admitted softly. "She kept screaming until her voice gave out."

A hand gently gripped his forearm as his eyes flickered back to Spiro's. An unspoken understanding passed between them.

"C'mon, let's get her in the tub. The warm water will help soothe her."

Dax removed his cloak and rolled up the sleeves of his shirt. Then, together, they removed Mari's dirty dress and set her gently in the tub.

"Hold her up so she doesn't drown," Spiro instructed, moving his hands so one was beneath Mari's neck and the other under her back. "If she wakes, take it slow. She'll be frightened and in pain. Be kind, Dax."

Spiro held his gaze, and Dax nodded as the door opened, revealing Kenna holding a steaming plate of food.

"I brought all they had left in the kitchens at this time of night." She set it down on the table as Spiro stood.

"Thank you," Dax said, and Kenna gave him a slight nod.

"If she doesn't wake in an hour, pull her out and let her rest on the cot," Spiro instructed, their voice soft but firm. They gave Dax's shoulder a reassuring squeeze. "Try to eat. I'll check on you both in the morning."

The door closed softly behind them, leaving Dax alone with Mari.

Releasing a deep sigh, Dax glanced at Mari's face. Her brows were tight and her mouth slightly open. It looked like she was concentrating on whatever was happening inside her mind.

"C'mon, Little Tempest," he whispered, his voice barely audible as rain began softly pattering the roof. "Wake up."

CHAPTER 20

DEATH HAD ALWAYS FELT like a distant concept to Mariana—something inevitable yet unknowable. She had never dared to imagine what might come after. Would it be silence? Light? The comforting embrace of Amphitrite, leading her somewhere beyond the waves?

This wasn't what she'd expected: floating weightlessly through a sea of stars, their soft glow brushing against her like whispered secrets. Millions of tiny, sparkling stars surrounded her, each pulsing with a soft, otherworldly light. They shimmered and danced, casting a kaleidoscope of colors across the void. Unable to feel anything, her mind devoid of all thoughts, she was completely weightless in mind, body, and soul.

Then that weightlessness shifted as the stars began to blur, melting into streams of light that twisted and intertwined like ribbons in the wind. The sensation of falling, yet not falling, enveloped her.

Mariana blinked, and she was standing on a beach. One that was all too familiar. The moon hung low in the starry sky, casting a silvery glow over the sands. The horizon was a deep indigo where the sky met the sea, blending into an infinite expanse.

Waves washed over her feet, startling her as her senses all flooded back. The water was cool against her skin, the salt air sharp in her lungs. She was wearing a gown of flowing blue fabric that seemed to ripple like water in the breeze. She ran her fingers over the pristine fabric, feeling its delicate texture.

"Mari?" a soft voice called from behind her as gentle as the breeze. She turned to find Celeste standing under the moonlight near her small home, which looked different than before. It looked like a quaint cottage made of driftwood and sea glass, glowing faintly in the lunar light.

Blinking past the confusion, she gazed at Celeste. Mariana couldn't believe it was her.

"Celeste?" she murmured, her voice catching in her throat before she bolted up the beach toward her friend, her heart pounding in her chest.

Celeste opened her arms wide and embraced Mariana. The scent of lavender coated her lungs, mingling with the salty tang of the sea, and tears sprang into her eyes. "You're here, you're here," she whispered over and over as Celeste softly laughed, a sound like wind chimes in a gentle breeze.

"Of course I am! Where else would I be?"

Mariana pulled back, her face dropping as she stared into her friend's pale eyes, which now seemed to reflect the depths of the ocean, endless and ancient.

"You're ..." *dead*. She couldn't bring herself to say the word out loud, as it appeared Mariana, too, may very well be dead.

"Tongue tied up, my dear? You know, I have a potion for that," Celeste said with a wink and a glimmer in her eye. She tugged Mariana toward the cabin, their feet leaving no prints in the sand, and a few moments later, they were sitting at her round table with steaming mugs in their hands. The cabin's interior was cozy, filled with the warm glow of candlelight, casting flickering shadows on the walls adorned with shells and dried herbs.

It wasn't the same as the cabin Celeste had in Egan Village. There were hints of things Mariana remembered from before—like the table she sat at was still chipping white paint, and her bed quilt was still the same colorful weave—yet everything felt ... different.

She shook her head and glanced down at the warm mug.

"I don't understand," Mariana whispered, watching the steam curling up from her tea turn into intricate patterns that hung in the air. The fragrant aroma of chamomile and honey filled the room.

Mariana's eyes shot up to her friend. "Are we both ...?"

"Dead?"

Mariana shuddered as the word clanged through the room. Her chest tightened with a storm of tormented emotions.

Celeste reached out and gripped Mariana's hand, her touch warm and grounding. "No, darling. We're not dead. We're *free*."

Mariana's brows pulled together, and she glanced between their hands and Celeste's sincere expression. "Free?" she asked softly. "I don't understand. You were gone. I looked everywhere for you. The little boy on the beach, he said—"

"*The ones from across the sea took her*," Celeste finished, mimicking the boy's voice with a strange clarity, and then gave Mariana a small, wistful smile. "Yes, I know. But I'm here now, with you, that's all that matters."

Mariana stared at her, unsure what to say. She was hardly able to believe she was holding her dear friend's hand to begin with, drinking tea at her table in the middle of the night, and the familiar yet otherworldly surroundings made her feel both comforted and disoriented.

Her grip on the mug tightened, her fingers trembling. She didn't understand why she was here, sitting across from Celeste. She couldn't believe this moment was real, and yet, it *felt* real.

"Celeste," Mariana whispered, her voice breaking. "I—" Her words faltered as a storm of emotions churned inside her chest. "I looked everywhere for you."

"I know," Celeste said kindly, her pale eyes watching Mariana with infinite patience.

"I thought you were—" The word caught in her throat like jagged glass. Her lips trembled as tears sprang into her eyes. "I thought you were dead."

Celeste smiled gently, the kind of smile that used to make everything feel okay. "Oh, my dear girl," she said. "You don't need to carry that burden. You don't need to carry any of it."

Mariana pulled her hand back, shaking her head as a sob rose unbidden in her throat. "How can you say that? You're *gone,* Celeste. You just—disappeared. You left me. You left me when I—" She choked on the words, her voice cracking. "When I needed you." The moment the words spilled from her lips, she regretted them. Celeste didn't leave her; she had been taken from her. Taken by her own people.

Celeste's expression softened, and for the first time, she looked sad. "Oh, Mari," she murmured, her tone heavy with regret. "I never meant to leave you. I never would have if it were up to me."

Mariana squeezed her eyes shut, tears streaking down her cheeks. Her chest felt heavy, like the grief she'd kept buried was finally clawing its way to the surface. She had tried to ignore it, push it away, distract herself with everything else. But now, in this strange and quiet dream, there was nothing to stop it.

She gripped the edge of the table, her knuckles turning white. "It's not fair," she whispered, her voice trembling. "You were the only one who ... who listened to me, who let me be myself. You treated me like *me*. And now you're gone, and I—" She broke off, sobbing.

Celeste stood and moved around the table, pulling Mariana into her arms. Mariana clung to her like she was afraid to let go, her body trembling with the weight of everything she'd held in. Celeste's embrace was warm and steady, her hands running soothingly over Mariana's back as she whispered, "Let it out, my girl. Let it all out."

For what felt like an eternity, Mariana cried, her tears soaking into Celeste's shoulder. She cried for the loss of her friend, for the loss of her siren self, for the loss of everything she'd ever known.

Finally, her sobs began to quiet, though her chest still ached with the rawness of it all. Celeste pulled back just enough to cup Mariana's face in her hands, her thumbs brushing away the tears. "You've been so strong for so long," she said. "But even the strongest need to let themselves feel, Mariana. It's not a weakness. It's what makes us mortal—or siren, or fae, or whatever else you might be."

Mariana let out a shaky laugh, her lips trembling. "I don't even know what I am anymore," she admitted.

Celeste tilted her head, her eyes sparkling faintly like the sea under moonlight. "You're you," she said simply. "And that's enough."

Mariana blinked, her tears slowing as she stared at her friend. She wanted to believe those words and cling to them, but doubt still gnawed at the edges of her mind. "I don't feel like enough," she whispered.

"You will," Celeste said with a small, knowing smile. She reached out and tapped Mariana's chest, right over her heart. "You've always had everything you need right here. The rest ... well, that will come in time."

Mariana frowned slightly, her mind spinning with questions. But before she could speak, the air around them began to change. The cozy glow of the cabin's candles flickered, their light dimming as shadows began to creep across the walls.

"Wait," Mariana said, panic rising in her chest. She clutched Celeste's arm, her fingers digging into the fabric of her sleeve. "Don't go. Please—don't leave me again."

Celeste smiled sadly, her form beginning to blur at the edges like sea foam dissolving into the tide. "I'm not leaving you, my dear. I'll always be with you, just as I've always been. In the light. In the waves. In the wind."

Mariana shook her head, her heart aching as Celeste's figure grew fainter. "I'm not ready," she whispered.

Celeste's voice was soft, echoing faintly as the dream began to fade. "You're stronger than you think, Mari. You always have been."

The cabin dissolved into starlight, the scent of lavender lingering in the air.

Mariana felt herself falling, weightless and untethered. Then she detected something warm soothing her head. The sensation was comforting, like someone was running their fingers through her hair and pouring warm water over her scalp. She floated like that until—like the snap of someone's fingers—she woke up.

CHAPTER 21

MARIANA GASPED, SHOOTING UPWARD, water splashing around her.

"Shit," a deep voice muttered. Mariana spun to find Dax crouched beside her. One of his hands gripped her arm, steadying her, while the other rested firmly on the rim of the large wooden basin she was submerged in.

Breathing deep, she lowered her eyebrows as her eyes shifted frantically over the foreign space.

"Where am I?" she gasped. Lifting a hand to her chest, she felt her heart beating its loud drum against her hand and willed it to calm. Her whole body throbbed, like someone had beaten her with a hammer.

"It's okay, you're alright," Dax replied softly. When he brushed his thumb against her tender skin, she yanked her arm from his grip and shifted to the other side of the tub, far from his touch.

"Where are we, Dax?" she growled. Looking around again, she detected the familiar, sharp scent of arnica and traces of herbs. The space was warmly lit by a fireplace crackling on one end of the room, casting shadows and flickering light across shelves full of jars and tiny glass bottles.

Dax lifted his hands, water dripping down his arms. "You're in a clinic. I brought you here to heal."

"A clinic," she muttered softly, then lifted her eyes toward the skylight above them. The stars peeked through branches swaying above them. Her gaze drifted back down to where Dax rested his elbows against the tub, his clasped hands barely touching the water's surface. His concerned eyes studied her, making her cross her arms protectively over her chest.

"How long have I been asleep?"

Dax regarded her carefully. "Two days."

Two days. Mariana blinked, unable to comprehend how she'd slept that long.

"Are you okay?" he asked, his voice barely above a whisper.

Then, everything came flooding back. The dream. Celeste. The river. Her mother's kiss.

Gripping her head, she winced. Her heart was too loud in her ears, her skin was too sensitive, her ears too tender to touch. Every part of her was in pain—as if a poisonous phantom's touch was sliding across her body, wreaking havoc on her nerves. A whimper escaped her lips. The moment her eyes saw her reflection in the water, they began to blur with tears.

Feeling the urge to escape, Mariana dipped beneath the water, letting its warmth embrace her. When water began to fill her nose, her throat—

She shot up, coughing and clutching her neck, squeezing her burning eyes. She couldn't breathe. Why couldn't she breathe?

She felt around her neck.

No, she thought as her eyes widened in horror.

Her gills were gone.

Taking a ragged breath, she reached out into the *fold* for her tail, but there was nothing. Her tail, her beautiful tail ... it was gone.

A strangled sound escaped her throat as her mind reeled, grasping for comprehension.

"This can't be real," she murmured, glancing around frantically, searching for a sign that she was still in a dreamland.

"Mari," Dax started softly, his eyes sad. "This is real."

Mariana shook her head, groaning at a phantom pain she didn't expect. Then it dawned on her ...

"My mother did this to me," she whispered darkly.

Out of the corner of her eye, she saw Dax's brows lift, and she slowly looked up to peer at him through dripping lashes.

"She's punishing me," she said, the anger in her voice echoing through the small space. "Why, why is she punishing me?" She knew Dax didn't have the answers but watching him struggle to form one fractured some part of her deep down.

Lifting her shaky hands, she noticed her usually sharp nails were now blunted, the skin around them splotches of dark pink and honey. She didn't recognize the color leeching into her normally pale blue skin. The tattoos on her hands and arms were faded, but she could still make out the swirl of waves. Confusion spread through her, unable to understand whether she was still herself or someone pretending to be who she was before.

"Nothing feels right. My body is—"

Broken.

A darkness taut with tension and torment consumed her. She wanted to scream. Wanted to cry. Wanted to beg for forgiveness if it meant she could go back. She was a siren whose soul *knew* she was a siren, and yet nothing physical said she was, not anymore.

Droplets fell from her cheeks as she cried. Sobs broke from her mouth while her shaking hands fisted her hair and her whole body began to shake.

Her mother's kiss—her mother had done this to her.

The pain ripped her apart again, her heart aching as though she was experiencing the same moment by the river all over again.

"*My tail, my tail,*" she wailed. Squeezing her eyes shut, she begged for the Goddess to give her back her siren form. Give her back the part of her that made her whole.

She couldn't stay like this. She couldn't survive it.

Then, warm hands were pulling her forward, forcing her to let go of her hair, and a warm chest met her cheek as she sobbed.

Mariana gripped Dax's shirt tight, and something inside her said she was safe. Safe to feel the betrayal. Safe to feel the heartbreak.

Her mind was a savage hurricane beating at every vulnerable part of her, leaving her ruined, destroyed.

Celeste's comforting smile broke through the storm, and yet it did nothing to dampen the violent waves of agony drowning her.

"Celeste," she whispered. Hot tears streamed down her cheeks, blurring her vision, she could see her friend as clear as day in her mind.

The crushing heartbreak of losing someone who had been a part of her family, someone who had cared for her through it all, who taught her how to walk, who listened and always pushed her to be the best version of herself—it was killing her. Celeste had been the mother she never knew she needed until that day on the beach when they found each other. And now she was gone.

Mariana pushed her face into her fists, willing her sobs to stop. But she missed her home, she missed her sisters, and seeing Celeste in that dream only made the terrible truth that much harder to accept.

"Shh, you're alright. It's okay, you're safe," Dax said softly in her ear, and her heartbeat began to slow along with her tears.

Breathing deep, she felt herself calming down. After a moment, she pulled back, wiping her face. She couldn't believe she'd lost control of herself like that. Dropping her hands, she looked anywhere but at the fae beside her, embarrassment heating her already warm cheeks.

"Umm," she started, peeking at his soaked chest, "sorry about that."

Dax shrugged. "Nothing to be sorry for."

They sat in silence long enough that Mariana began to fidget uncomfortably.

Then, Dax cleared his throat and stood. "I'm sure you'd appreciate some space. When you're ready to get out, you can wear the robe beside the tub, and the bed is yours. There's food on the table if you're hungry."

Mariana glanced up at him, and all she could bring herself to do was nod.

"I'll be right outside if you need me," Dax said over his stiff shoulder as he approached the door.

"Why are you being so nice to me?"

Her question made him pause with his hand on the knob and turn around.

He smirked, leaning a shoulder against the door frame and folding his arms over his chest. "Why? Miss being tied up and called Little Tempest?"

Mariana glowered at him, letting her eyes answer that insulting question.

Dax shrugged, looking anywhere but at her. "I don't like seeing people in pain. With lives as long as ours, horrors are inevitable, things our minds can barely understand." He shifted his weight and cleared his throat. "Watching you drown in those horrors ... It bothered me."

Her gaze softened. "Because you couldn't stop it?"

"Because no one should have to go through it alone."

Mariana bit the inside of her cheek and had to look away, either to keep herself from smiling or because she was afraid to say something she'd regret.

Dax confused her. He wasn't like anyone she'd ever met before, and the way her body seemed to gravitate toward him bothered her. She didn't want to like him, but some part of her did.

She sighed. "Please don't leave." Peeking up through her lashes at him, she met his eyes and decided to be honest. "You're right; I don't want to be alone."

CHAPTER 22

DAX LINGERED IN THE doorway, hands flexing at his sides, unsure what to do. For two days, he'd been caught in the same rhythm—moving Mari between the warm tub and the bed, just as Spiro instructed. The healer checked in periodically, ensuring Mari was stable and Dax had eaten. Even Kenna had made a few appearances—once with fresh clothes for Mari, and twice to give Dax grief. Not that he'd ever admit he'd missed her sharp tongue.

Now that Mari was awake, he felt completely uncertain. What was he supposed to do? What was he supposed to say? She'd been through something horrifying—something that had torn her apart from the inside out, nearly killing her. And learning it had been her own mother who'd done this to her ... that was a cruelty Dax couldn't begin to wrap his head around.

What Mari needed was a friend. Someone to help her carry the weight of this nightmare. But he wasn't that guy. Couldn't be. He was here to keep her alive, get her on her feet, and get her to Aurelia as fast as possible.

"Please sit down," Mari whispered, her voice soft and frayed at the edges, like it hurt to speak. The sound sent an ache straight through his chest.

Clearing his throat, Dax walked back over to the stool beside the tub and dropped onto it. His hands dangled between his knees as he stared down at them, searching for something—anything—to say.

"There's, ah ..." He gestured awkwardly toward a small dish on the tub's edge, where a sponge and a few soap petals rested. "Soap and stuff, if you want to, you know ... wash."

Mari turned her head, her eyes finding the petals. She dipped her fingers in, gathering a few, and rubbed them together. Foam bubbled and dripped from her hands into the water.

"Thank you," she murmured, her voice barely audible. She ran the soap across her arms, then her neck and chest, in slow, mechanical movements, as though her body was moving on autopilot. He didn't miss how she slightly winced with each swipe.

"Does it hurt?" he asked gently.

Mariana didn't look at him. Instead, she gave a subtle nod.

Dax shifted uncomfortably, then rubbed at the tension in his neck, forcing himself to glance away.

"I'm surprised your tattoos stayed," he said, trying to fill the heavy silence. His eyes flicked briefly to her hands, where her tattoos glimmered faintly in the low light.

Mari froze, staring down at the swirling ink on her arms. "Me too," she said after a long moment. Her voice was brittle, distant. "I don't know what I would've done if I'd lost those too."

The sadness in her eyes hollowed something out inside him. He swallowed against the tightness in his throat, feeling the weight of her loss like a stone in his chest. Dax knew what it meant to lose something—or someone—but to lose yourself the way Mari had? He couldn't imagine it.

"You know," he began, his voice lighter, trying to shift the mood. "Being a fae does have its perks."

Mari looked up at him, waiting, her expression unreadable.

He shrugged. "There's the immortality thing, the fact that you'll blend in—"

"Is that what you think I want? To live forever and to be just like everyone else?" Her words were laced with venom, her anger cutting through his reassurances.

"No, Mari. That's not what I meant—"

"That's exactly what you just said."

Dammit. Dax exhaled, dragging a hand through his hair. "Okay, fine. You're right. But we both have to face the truth here."

Her laugh was bitter, hollow. "Oh, you want me to face the truth? I have no power, Dax." The words spilled out of her like poison, each one twisting her features with anguish. "I can't feel the water's energy. I can't sense the sea. I am powerless. A siren trapped in a fae body. Is that what you wanted me to say? Well, there it is. The truth is out."

She scrubbed at her arms, desperate, like she could wash away her admission—or the reality of it. Her movements grew frantic as she clawed at the last stubborn scales still clinging to her back.

Dax winced as he watched her struggle, his chest tightening with every shallow breath she took, every soft whimper that escaped her lips. When he couldn't take it anymore, he reached out and rested a hand on her shoulder.

Mari froze beneath his touch, her breathing sharp and uneven. Her hair, damp and tangled, clung to her shoulders like a curtain.

"Let me help you," he said softly, his voice barely more than a whisper.

She blinked, and for a moment, he thought she might tell him to leave. But instead, she nodded ever so slightly and turned, exposing her back. "I can't reach the scales on my spine," she admitted, her voice small.

Dax carefully swept her hair over her shoulder, revealing the pale curve of her back. The water lapped gently around her, making it hard to see the jagged patches of scales clinging stubbornly to her skin.

"Can you stand?" he asked.

Mari shifted on the submerged bench and rose to her feet, her legs unsteady. The water rippled around her, still too high for him to get a clear view.

"Uh." He hesitated, groaning inwardly. "I think ... you're going to have to get out."

Mari glanced over her shoulder, brows furrowed. "What? Why?"

"Because I can't see through the water. It's too dark."

Her lips parted like she wanted to argue, but then she sighed. "Just get in."

Dax blinked. "What?"

"I said, get in." Her tone left no room for argument. "You're already wet. Might as well."

He just stared at her, unsure if he'd heard her correctly.

Mari rolled her eyes and groaned. "Look, I'm not ready to get out, and this tub is big enough for four people. So, if you can't help me from out there, you can help me from in here."

Dax opened his mouth, but the glare she leveled at him silenced his objections.

"Get in the water, Dax."

A slow, incredulous smile tugged at his lips as he stood. "You know, I remember the last time you told me that."

"Yeah, and I didn't kill you then, and I won't kill you now. So, what are you waiting for?"

Fine. Dax kicked off his boots and socks, peeled off his shirt, and stepped cautiously into the warm water, careful not to splash.

"What?" he asked when he noticed Mari staring at him, a faint, amused grin playing at her lips.

She shrugged. "Nothing."

Turning away, she kneeled on the submerged bench, lifting herself just enough for the water to fall to her lower back.

"Is this better?"

Dax swallowed hard, his resolve beginning to fray. Why had he agreed to get into a tub with a naked, gorgeous female? Rubbing a hand over the back of his neck, he tried to focus.

"Yup."

CHAPTER 23

I CAN'T TRUST HIM, I can't trust him, Mariana chanted silently to herself, hoping it would drown out the instant desire that rose as their skin touched. *It's your emotional response to the horror you just experienced, that's it.*

Soft hands worked to peel away stubborn scales as the water lapped around her hips. Every touch was methodical, careful.

Her body burned beneath his touch; the sensation magnified by the quiet intimacy of the moment. The water rippled gently around them, and every time his fingers brushed her skin, they left a trail of warmth she couldn't ignore.

She bit her lip hard, fighting to contain the emotions swirling inside her. Some of the scales were harder to remove, clinging to her like a second skin, as though they knew they belonged and didn't want to leave.

Every scale gave a soft plop before disappearing beneath the surface, and a small piece of her chipped away with it. She tightened her grip on the tub's edge until her knuckles turned white, trying to focus on the discomfort instead of the growing awareness of Dax's closeness.

Her traitorous mind flashed to the memory of his lips, and she silently cursed herself. She needed to think of something else. Anything else.

"You know," she said, her voice slightly strained, "you never answered my question."

Dax paused, his hands stilling for a moment before resuming their careful work. She peeked over her shoulder at his serious expression, meeting his gaze.

"Where are we, Dax?"

He sighed, looking away. "We're in Kythera."

Her brows knitted together. "I've never heard of it before."

"You wouldn't have." His hands moved to rub soap over her back. His palms against her sensitive skin sent a shiver through her body. She bit her bottom lip to keep from making a sound.

"You won't find it on a map," he continued. "This place ... it's special. You were dying, and I knew you could heal here."

He rinsed her back with handfuls of water, the warm cascade soothing and intoxicating. She fought every instinct to turn and kiss him.

Mariana's mouth tightened.

Dax leaned forward, gripping the edge of the tub. His hands settled beside hers, caging her in. "I need you to do something for me," he murmured, his voice so close, she could feel his breath against her ear.

Her pulse quickened as his bare chest brushed against her damp back. She turned her head, realizing how close his face was to hers. "What?"

He lowered his lips to her ear. "I need you to keep this place a secret. You can't tell anyone about it. Kythera has to remain hidden."

She blinked in confusion. "Why?"

His thumb brushed lightly over her hand, and she ached to lace her fingers with his. "So, history doesn't repeat itself."

The words sparked something in her mind. "This is your home, isn't it?"

Dax hesitated, then gave a small nod, his chin brushing against her forehead.

Storing the valuable information away, she turned between the arms that trapped her. His green eyes were deep wells of emotion that she couldn't read. She needed him to trust her, so she placed her hands on his chest.

"Homes are the sacred places we hold closest to our hearts," she said softly. "I understand your need to keep it safe. You saved my life, and in return, I'll keep your secret."

His chest rose and fell only inches from hers, and for a fleeting moment, she wondered if he could feel the erratic rhythm of her heartbeat. His green eyes dipped to her lips, and her breath caught.

When he leaned forward, resting his forehead against hers, her mouth parted involuntarily. Their breaths mingled, the air between them taut and electric.

It would be so easy to close the space. So simple.

But she didn't.

And neither did he.

She could feel it: the tension, the desire twisting and pulling between them, the cord stretched too tight. But she refused to give in and cross the invisible line between them. Not when so much was at stake.

He's the enemy.

Dax sighed, pulling back just enough to let the moment pass. But before he stepped away completely, his thumb brushed her bottom lip, a touch so gentle it made her shiver.

"C'mon, you're starting to prune. It's time to get out."

Mariana's brows lifted. "I'm what?"

"You've been in the water too long," he answered, the statement confusing her.

Disappointment tightened her chest as she watched him step out of the tub, dripping water all over the hardwood floor. He grabbed a thick, dark robe and held it out for her.

Mariana stared at him for a moment, needing to hate him, to feel nothing but anger toward him. But as his gaze softened, she knew she couldn't.

He was still the enemy. That much hadn't changed.

But the connection between them was something she couldn't explain—something her heart refused to ignore. It was like a wire wrapped around her ribs, pulling tighter and tighter every time he looked at her like that.

She hated how it made her feel. How it made her want him.

Clearing her throat, she stepped out of the tub slowly, the heat of his hands steadying her as he helped her into the robe. He lingered for just a moment longer than necessary, his fingers brushing the edge of her collar as he held the lapels together.

"I know you think you're powerless, but that isn't true," he said, his voice low and certain.

Mariana struggled to take a breath. "My mother took away everything that made me strong."

Dax lifted one of her hands into his, inspecting it. "These fingers nearly took out my eyes just the other day."

She shrugged. "My nails aren't even sharp anymore."

Their eyes met, and the world seemed to fade away.

"You don't need claws—or your magic—to be a weapon." He curled her hand into a fist. "You, yourself, are a weapon. A warrior. A deadly one, at that."

A small smile tugged at her lips as she glanced between him and her fist. "Still afraid of me?"

Dax didn't smile back. Instead, he brushed a strand of hair behind her ear and whispered, "Terrified."

Before she could respond, a wave of cold air burst through the room as the front door opened, making them pull away from each other.

CHAPTER 24

THEIR HEADS TURNED, AND Mariana saw two people standing in the doorway. The glaring bright light of dawn in the background cast them in shadows.

The tallest one cleared their throat. "Sorry for the interruption. I wanted to see how you were doing." Their deep voice, rich and smooth, like silk brushing along weathered river rocks, resonated with a soothing melody. It was soft, yet low and full of life.

As they stepped inside and closed the door, Dax tugged on his shirt and shoes.

"Mari, this is Spiro, the village leader."

Spiro smiled warmly at her. "I'm so happy to see you're awake, Mariana." Their bright emerald eyes, tender and mesmerizing, seemed almost familiar. Framed by white lashes and arched eyebrows, those striking eyes stood out against the gray hue of their skin.

Spiro waited patiently for a response, gaze unwavering as Mariana observed the leader. Their black and white dreadlocks were half tied back, revealing high cheekbones and a strong jaw.

Mariana crossed her arms, burying her hands into the cozy robe. "Hello," she greeted nervously, unsure what else to say to the stranger.

The second person, standing behind the leader, poked their head around and smiled brightly.

"Hi, I'm Kenna," she said, then glanced at Dax with an arched brow. "Thanks for the intro, Dax, so nice of you."

Dax scowled. "Mari, this is my impatient sister, Kenna. There, happy?"

Kenna continued smiling. Her high cheekbones and the curve of her lips were similar to Dax's, but her eyes were more like spring green. Her thick black braid was draped over one shoulder, streaks of white woven between. White and black hair, just like Spiro's ...

It clicked that all three of them were family, yet Mariana couldn't quite discern whether Spiro was their mother or father. Their facial features had a blend of both masculine and feminine traits.

"May I touch your hand, my dear?" Spiro asked gently, extending their hand toward her with a delicate motion.

Not seeing anything wrong with the request, she lifted her left hand and placed it into Spiro's warm palm. Their long fingers were adorned with a unique silver ring, and small white tattoos marked the spaces between each knuckle. Before she could study the intricate symbols further, she felt a strange vibration emanate from Spiro's hands. A soothing warmth spread up her arm toward her heart, and Mariana felt her anxiety slipping away. She met Spiro's eyes, recognizing the strange sensation;

it reminded her of Cybele's radiating power, an energy current thrumming beneath their skin.

When Spiro pulled their hands away, the sensation faded. "Your body is recovering smoothly."

"You're a healer," Mariana said in awe. "I didn't know any fae could do that."

Spiro's lips curved into a small smile. "My mother was a healer. I was fortunate enough to inherit her power. But I cannot heal everything."

Mariana hesitated, her voice faltering with trepidation. "Do you know what was done to me?"

Spiro sighed, their attention flickering to Kenna and Dax, who were quietly bickering with each other. Clearing their throat, they glanced over their shoulder at the two. "Can we have the room, please?"

Kenna nodded, pulling her black jacket tighter around her shoulders. She shot a glare at Dax before stepping out.

Grabbing his cloak, Dax motioned toward the door. "I'll be right outside if you need me."

Spiro tilted their head. "Perhaps you should go put on some dry clothes, hmm? Before you catch an illness even I cannot heal." The suggestion was more of a command than a request.

Dax bit the inside of his cheek, and Mariana had to hide her smile behind a cough. He hesitated, meeting her gaze.

She gave him a small nod.

Spiro waved a hand. "Go on. We'll be fine."

"Alright," Dax muttered, tugging his coat tighter as he left.

The door closed softly, leaving an unfamiliar stillness behind.

Spiro let out a heavy sigh, their smile faint and brittle. They reached out and gently squeezed Mariana's hand.

"It's a binding spell."

Mariana frowned. "A binding spell?"

Spiro nodded. "The spell took time to take root. Your body rejected it so fiercely, it nearly killed you. I was able to calm the resistance, to help your body relax, accept the transformation, and complete the spell."

Mariana's stomach dropped. "Why?"

"It was the only way to save your life. I can still feel your energy, the same way I can feel the forest's energy. It's as though the siren within you is caged—present, but hidden away."

The room suddenly felt smaller, like the walls were inching closer. Mariana clenched her fists against her lap as hope, fragile and dangerous, was kindled in her chest. Her voice cracked when she asked, "Can you undo it?"

Spiro hesitated. Their lips parted, but the words seemed to falter on their tongue. They took a slow, deliberate breath before answering. "It's an ancient spell, an extremely powerful one. It would have gravely impacted the caster just as much as it did you. May I ask who did this to you?"

Mariana released a shuddering sigh and lowered herself onto the edge of the bed. Her hands gripped the blankets beneath her. "My mother."

Spiro's head tilted slightly, expression unreadable. They pulled a nearby stool closer, sitting across from her with calm precision. "Queen Cybele?"

Mariana's head snapped up, surprise flaring in her wide eyes. "Yes. How did you know?"

"You remind me of her—strong, brave, determined." Spiro studied her carefully, their gaze both calm and piercing. "Your mother is incredibly skilled and a master of her power. She would have known the consequences of a spell like this on both of you. And yet, she did it anyway." The question hung in the air, unspoken but impossible to ignore: *Why?*

Mariana's expression darkened, her jaw tightening as anger churned beneath the surface. "She betrayed me."

Spiro leaned forward, their arms resting on their knees. "Why would she do that?"

Mariana averted her gaze, her eyes fixed on the floor. The anger in her chest tangled with something raw and aching. Her voice was a whisper when it finally came. "I don't know." She blinked hard, fighting back the sting of tears. "It doesn't make sense. She ... she broke something in me."

The words hung between them, brittle and sharp as shattered glass. Spiro didn't push. They waited.

After a long silence, they asked, "Why did you leave the safety of the sea, Mariana?"

The question hit her like a wave, and for a moment, all she could do was stare at them. The answer felt too heavy, too complicated, and yet it burned at the back of her throat, desperate to escape. She swallowed hard, her gaze flickering to the faint light filtering through the curtained window.

"What was so important," Spiro continued gently, "that you risked your life to come here? Because as far as I know, sirens are still banned from these lands—"

"I had no choice," Mariana interrupted, her voice breaking. She could so easily blame Dax for dragging her out here, but the truth was more complicated. Even if Dax hadn't taken her, she would have come anyway. She knew that.

Spiro's steady patience seemed to draw the words out of her. "It's because we're banned from the fae realm that my sister, Astra, is out here. She wanted to restore peace with the king, and when she didn't come back ..." Mariana's voice wavered, but she forced herself to continue. "I knew something was wrong. I just wanted to bring her back."

"You make it sound like you've given up," Spiro said carefully.

Mariana let out a bitter laugh, throwing her hands up in frustration. "Look at me! I'm a siren trapped in a fae body with no power and no way home. I can't save my sister like this! My own mother threw me out into this realm with nothing but my armor. That's it! How am I supposed to keep going? There's no use fighting the truth."

Spiro regarded her for a long moment, their gaze unwavering. "If you give up now, what will your sister do?"

The question cut deeper than she expected, settling over her like a suffocating weight. She shook her head slowly, burying her face in her hands. "I was stupid to think I could do this. I have no idea what I'm doing. I'm so ... lost."

The silence that followed felt heavy, but not unkind. A warm hand landed gently on her shoulder, and Mariana looked up through the tangle of her hair to find Spiro's steady gaze.

"We all get lost sometimes, Mariana," they said softly. "It's part of life." They stood slowly, their movements deliberate. "May I show you something?"

Mariana hesitated for a moment, her mind a mess of fear, doubt, and the faintest spark of curiosity. Slowly, she brushed the hair from her face and nodded. "Alright."

Spiro's lips curved into a small, reassuring smile. "Get dressed and meet me outside."

Mariana blinked in surprise. "Where are we going?"

Spiro stopped at the door, their hand resting lightly on the handle. They glanced over their shoulder.

"Somewhere that's safe for the lost to be found."

With that, they slipped through the door, leaving Mariana alone with the lingering echo of their words.

CHAPTER 25

Dax took a deep breath of the fresh spring air, releasing it slowly as he walked toward his cabin across the bridge. As it came into view, he stopped to stare at the A-frame cabin he had built with his own hands. Memories of the years of hard work it took crossed his mind.

In Kythera, every juvenile had to build their own cabin as a rite of passage into adulthood. He remembered contemplating the design and layout for weeks before starting the project. With how many centuries that had passed since the construction, he was amazed that the cabin was still standing after all this time.

Closing his eyes, he tilted his head toward the sky and felt the first few raindrops kiss his face. The droplets cooled his heated skin. The smell of the forest wafting through the air, filling his lungs, was rejuvenating.

A shoulder bumped into his as someone sidled up beside him. He knew who it was just based on the scent. Shifting his gaze, he eyed his sister's mischievous look.

She leaned on the railing beside him and winked one of her kohl-lined eyes. "Need a knife to shave your head and face?"

A corner of Dax's mouth lifted, and he considered it as he ran a hand through his black hair. The motion was strangely familiar. He tried recalling a vague, blurry memory of a soft, calming touch as fingers gently stroked the longer hair on the top of his head. But just as quickly, the memory faded. He shook his head. Suddenly, he had no desire to shave.

"I'll take care of it once we get to Aurelia."

Kenna lifted an eyebrow at him. "You've always kept it so short, you look weird with hair."

Dax tilted his head at her. "I think you're just jealous of my gorgeous black locks," he teased, knowing how much Kenna wished she hadn't inherited the white streaks in her hair like Spiro.

She punched him in the shoulder and chuckled. "You're such a jerk. I can't stand you."

"There's a whole forest to be elsewhere, why don't you find a branch to swing from or a hole to jump into?"

Their serious gazes met before they both began to chuckle.

As children, they had been the epitome of stupid. Running through the forest, jumping off boulders, swinging through the trees, even venturing into a giant snake's den once in an attempt to steal an egg.

"Remember that time you climbed the Natura Nexus to find an eagle?" Kenna laughed. "Spiro was so mad at you."

"Mad enough to ban me from leaving my cabin for weeks."

Natura Nexus was the largest redwood in the center of their village, their Mother Tree. Blessed by General Cornelia herself to bring prosperity to Kythera. And climbing it as a child? Highly frowned upon.

"Ahhh, those were the times. Kinda hard to remember now, though," Kenna said with a tilt of her head.

"It's true, you are getting old."

This time, Kenna pushed him, calling him all sorts of names before stepping away from the railing. "Hey, there's someone who's been dying to see you."

Dax turned to look at her. "Who?"

"You'll see. C'mon," she said with a small grin and started walking down the staircase that would lead them to the other levels of the village and eventually the ground.

Dax bit the inside of his cheek, glancing back toward the clinic. Mari was with the person he trusted most in this world; she'd be fine.

With that in mind, he followed Kenna down the winding staircase to the ground level, where she led him to a large wooden barn near the stables.

Kenna unlocked it and swung the barn doors wide open. It was pitch-black inside until she turned a light on, and a soft glow illuminated the giant black and white creature within.

"Leo? Look who it is!" Kenna mewed, and Dax couldn't believe it when the creature turned to face him.

"You kept him all this time," Dax said in awe, hands on his hips, standing by the door. Leo's bright, sunshine eyes stared at him, not as though Dax was the next meal, but instead like they were a shy child scared to approach.

"Of course I did. He's a magnificent hunter." Kenna scratched his spotted ears, then moved to his mane, earning a loud purr. "Remember when you found him?"

Dax stepped forward, then sat down on his haunches to get a closer look. "Yeah, he was so small back then." The rare leomagnus cub used to fit into the nook of Dax's elbow, sleeping soundly after a full meal of deer meat.

Dax had found Leo half-starved and desperate, alone, crying out in the forest. There was no way Dax could've left the cub out there on its own. Of course, Spiro strongly objected to keeping the cub, especially since Dax would have to leave it to return to Aurelia. That had been nearly three years ago.

Now, Leo was the size of a large horse, with paws twice the size of Kenna's head.

"He's grown up to be a strong, sweet, handsome boy, haven't you, Leo?" Kenna placed a loud kiss on Leo's cheek before ushering him toward Dax.

"How did you convince Spiro to let you keep him?" Dax asked as Leo slowly approached him, his head extended to sniff Dax's hands.

"Well, I kinda gave them no choice," Kenna replied with a closed-lip, guilty smile. "By the time Leo was large enough to hunt on his own, he was domesticated. Now we're stuck with him." The way she said it and the soft glow in her cheeks as she stroked Leo's soft fur made Dax realize how much he missed seeing his family happy. She lifted her eyes to his. "You know, he's yours. You found him."

Dax shook his head but smiled softly when the creature allowed Dax to pet his head. Leo laid down and stared up at him fondly. "He belongs to you now. Besides, Aurelia isn't a place for a leomagnus."

"I meant you don't have to go back. You can stay here, Dax. Even Mari is welcome."

"Kenna ..." Dax cautioned, instantly irritated.

"No, listen to me," she ordered firmly. "Spiro and I have been talking. I'll go with you to Aurelia and work out a deal so you can come home. It isn't right that you're trapped under the royal family's rotten thumb—"

"Stop this, please," he begged quietly.

"I can't. You know that. You're my brother, I can't just stand by and let you sacrifice yourself for us."

Dax stood, and Kenna did the same. Leo lifted his head to glance between them, probably sensing the tension.

"Let me come with you to Aurelia," Kenna urged, but Dax shook his head, growing more and more irritated. "You belong here with your people, Daxon—"

"I belong nowhere!" he shouted.

They both winced, especially when Leo retreated a few steps into his barn.

Dax sighed. "Sorry. I just ... You can't come with me. Mari has to go to Aurelia, and I have to be the one to take her there."

"Why does she have to go?"

"She's trying to find her sister." Dax looked away, hoping to indicate that nothing was left to discuss regarding the siren.

"Dax ... *please*. Let me go with you."

He shook his head. "There's nothing but darkness in Aurelia," he murmured. "Trust me."

"And who's going to pull you from that darkness, huh? If you won't let us, then who?"

For reasons he couldn't understand, he thought of Mari. The pull he felt toward her was unlike anything he could describe. But her future didn't have him anywhere in it. That much was certain.

"I don't need anyone to help me, Kenna. I've survived this long on my own. I'm fine."

He gave Leo one last stroke on the head, and as he turned away, he heard his sister softly say, "And that's what scares me."

CHAPTER 26

MARIANA FOLLOWED THE VILLAGE leader down a spiraling wooden staircase that wrapped around the trunk of a colossal tree. The staircase creaked softly underfoot; its wood worn smooth by countless steps. The boots Spiro had given her pinched her toes, and the ache in her feet made every step feel longer. At least the sweater and leather jacket they'd provided were warm, warding off the crisp morning air.

As they descended, Spiro exchanged greetings with several villagers passing by. All of them had the same stone-gray skin. Their movements were unhurried but purposeful, their simple leather coats and fitted pants blending into the earthy tones of the massive tree's bark. Their boots were nearly silent against the damp wood, a sharp contrast to Mariana's uneven steps.

No one gave her so much as a second glance. They seemed entirely focused on their errands, barely acknowledging her presence. Mariana wasn't sure whether she felt relieved or unsettled, but their indifference gave her time to take in the beauty of her surroundings.

The early rays of morning sunlight pierced the towering canopy above, scattering golden light that made every droplet of dew glisten on the leaves and vines. Clusters of moss swayed gently in the breeze, and small, glowing insects flitted between the branches like tiny lanterns. Despite the sweater's warmth, a chill settled into her bones as she realized just how far above the ground they were. Her stomach flipped every time her gaze strayed toward the edge of the staircase, where the forest floor stretched impossibly far below.

Back home in the depths of the sea, she'd been surrounded by shadows, the press of water, and the steady heartbeat of the ocean. Up here, the open air felt foreign. The unfamiliar height made her palms sweat despite the bite of the cool morning air, and she clutched the railing tighter to steady herself.

Spiro slowed as they reached a small cabin nestled against the tree's massive trunk. Moss draped over the edges of its sloping, a-frame roof, dripping raindrops. The doors were open wide, spilling warm, golden light onto the damp wooden platform outside. A faint smell of fragrant wood drifted from within, inviting and calming.

Spiro motioned her forward, and Mariana stopped before a standing plaque that read: "*History is only forgotten by those who have lost their culture. May we never forget our past and those who lived it.*"

Those words echoed through her mind as she stepped into the warmth and gazed at the walls.

"Wow." Mariana could hardly believe her eyes. Every wall was lined with floor-to-ceiling paintings framed in ornate red wood, each of them unique with bright colors.

"This is our historical gallery," Spiro said as they both approached the first painting on the left. The tiny plaque beside it said: "*The Ascension*."

Mariana lifted a hand to her mouth as she marveled at the artistic creation. Four figures glowed high above a war where chaos and destruction reigned. Mariana instantly knew those were the Four Generals. Each figure burned a different color, symbolizing the four magical elements.

For the sea, the figure named Tarquin glowed in various shades of azure. Next was Magnus, with the power of the sky, who shone as golden as the sun. To its right was Cornelia of earth, who glowed a brilliant array of mossy hues. And lastly, Minerva glowed the chilling bloodred of spirit.

Behind each of the Generals was a hazy, bright white figure with no distinguishable face or features. Those were the Gods.

The painting depicted the origin of the fae.

Mariana had heard the story from Astra when she was a youngling and quickly decided she preferred the story of Seraphina and the origin of sirens.

The Gods had first created humans to use as pawns in bloody battles. Eventually, they grew bored with how quickly the humans perished and created the fae: resilient, immortal beings that could endure generations of gruesome, entertaining wars.

This time in history was called the Blood Era.

The Four Generals each had their own battalion with thousands of expendable fae and took orders from their God or Goddess. The fae were ordered to fight each other, rebuild their populations, and then fight again.

The bloody cycle continued for thousands of years until one day, the Gods vanished. The Generals could no longer hear their orders, and the war ceased as confusion spread. However, peace was not what came next.

Mariana moved on to the next painting labeled: "*The Infernal Wars.*" It was a particularly gruesome masterpiece of a bloody battle in the middle of a forest.

The Infernal Wars occurred when the Generals began fighting to establish lands to build great kingdoms. For nearly three thousand brutal years, the fae realm had been ripped apart and united over and over again as, one by one, each of the Generals perished.

Slowly, the power bestowed only to the Generals began to spread as they mated, and dynasties were born with magic flowing through their veins.

Tarquin was the only General whose power did not spread, as he was the first to die, before reproducing. Supposedly, he had been murdered at the start of the Infernal Wars by his lover, who sided with General Minerva. Mariana had always found that fact interesting, as she wondered whether there would be fae with power like her own if Tarquin were never killed. There was no known record of how potent Tarquin's magic was due to how quickly his life had ended.

Mariana stepped up to the next painting, unsure about its story. The plaque read: "*Mocanus: Challenged to Rise Again.*" Confused, she took a step back to observe the entire painting. A lone warrior stood among a field of fallen, broken, bloody bodies surrounded by huge boulders and broken trees. Everyone had the same stone-colored skin as those who lived in Kythera.

The painting appeared to be of a dark and painful past. Mariana could practically feel the emotion radiating from the last warrior standing. It must've represented a gruesome battle that ravaged their people.

Taking a seat on the bench facing the painting, she contemplated what was happening in the scene. Who was the warrior left standing? The figure was blurry and had no distinct features, yet it felt so familiar ...

"Who painted all of these?" she asked. None of the artwork had a visible signature. Though sirens didn't paint underwater, all the records of paintings she'd seen stored in the Athenaeum had signatures on the bottom left or right corners. Even the sculptures around Salus had the artist's signature on them somewhere.

"I don't know that the artist ever wants to be known, unfortunately," Spiro replied, causing Mariana's expression to drop slightly.

"Are they still alive?" she asked softly.

Spiro nodded and stepped closer to the painting. "I imagine they don't want to talk about what's happened to them. Perhaps painting helped them begin to heal. I can't say for certain, of course. Although ..." They paused as their eyes locked on the lone warrior. "I feel this was their way of reminding all of us that our past cannot hold us hostage." Spiro cast their eyes toward Mariana, searching her face. For what, she didn't know. "We all deserve to keep moving forward."

Mariana looked back at the painting. She could see what Spiro was doing, trying to show her that she, too, had to keep moving forward. But what about the darkness that would follow her? Even the lone warrior in the field of dead bodies had to be haunted by what they'd experienced.

"What happened here? What story was the painter trying to tell?"

Spiro sighed. "A somber and unfortunate one." Pausing, the leader sat down on the bench beside her. "Do you know the story of the Mocanus tribe, Mariana?"

She shook her head.

"Mocanus means 'gray mountain people.' A name given to us by General Cornelia. She didn't know of our true origin—none of us do—but that didn't stop her from learning all there was to know about our culture. She was ... intrigued. And she found her place among the Mocanus. Her home. She lived here, in Kythera, until the day war showed up at our front door and took her away."

"Did you know Cornelia?"

"Yes, she was my mother," Spiro replied casually, and Mariana felt her throat close up.

"What?" she squeaked.

Spiro laughed at her shocked expression. "Yes, my mother was Cornelia. And I can tell you, she was no ordinary fae. From the short time I got to know her, she was strict, paranoid, and constantly talking about war. I'd never known someone so courageous yet so terrified of the world. I wish I could recall what she looked like. I only remember that she always had flowers and leaves in her white hair." Spiro curled a white loc between their long fingers before dropping it back into the mix of dark hair.

Mariana glanced at the painting of the Generals again, noticing how Cornelia's skin was almost as pale as Astra's, but she had a moonbeam glow about her. Whoever Spiro's father was must've been Mocanus for them to inherit the gray skin tone.

"Did you ever see her again?" Mariana asked with hesitation as she studied Spiro's distant expression.

They blinked a few times before shaking their head. "No, sadly, I never knew what became of her until news spread of her death. But the Mocanus were devastated by her disappearance. So was I. And when the time came to defend our land, we heeded the call. Minerva sent her legion of warriors to attack us in the hopes of conquering our land. During that battle, we realized that the Mocanus resisted Minerva's magic. We defeated them all." Spiro paused and looked down at their hands. "Minerva was killed shortly after by the son of Magnus, King Thaddeus, who was worshiped for killing his father's murderer and uniting Aurelia."

Mariana's brows tightened as she tried to remember her history lessons. King Thaddeus was the father of King Stavros.

"King Thaddeus was charming," Spiro continued. "He promised the Mocanus that, for their assistance in defeating an enemy legion, he would grant us protected lands that would prosper and remain peaceful. However, as the dynasties of the three other Generals began to rise and Aurelia began to split apart, King Thaddeus recruited the Mocanus people to be his 'killers of the night.'" Spiro shook their head sadly. "He used us as weapons to fight enemy units because they couldn't see us coming. Most of our people were dead by the end of the

Infernal Wars. King Thaddeus was killed, and as King Stavros was crowned, we hid away in the mountains once more."

Mariana considered Spiro's words. "Then why is Dax working for King Stavros?" she asked carefully, realizing after she said it that Spiro was unlikely to share anything about that with her.

Spiro studied the painting for a long moment, and Mariana regretted asking. "I'm sorry. I know that is none of my concern. I hope I didn't offend you."

The village leader turned to her, and with a sincere smile, they said, "You didn't offend me. You are always welcome to ask your questions. However, I can't answer this one as it is not my information to tell."

Mariana sighed and gave a brief nod before thinking of something else she had been dying to ask. "I have a personal question for you, then, if you're willing to answer it?" She couldn't keep the hesitance from her voice as she spoke.

"I'd love to hear it. I'll answer the best I can," Spiro replied. The anxiety that had taken root in Mariana's chest began to loosen as she stared at the leader's welcoming expression.

She took a deep breath. "Are you ... Dax and Kenna's mother or father?" The question slipped out easily enough, but Mariana couldn't help feeling like the world was about to collapse on top of her. It scared her to think how easily she could offend the wise leader.

Spiro chuckled. Mariana felt her cheeks warm and released a nervous smile.

"That is a valid question, not to worry," they said, patting her hand affectionately. "I gave birth to my children. But I am neither a mother nor a father."

Mariana considered this. "You're different from anyone I've ever met before."

"I take that as a compliment," Spiro replied with a generous smile, then glanced at their hands, covered in tattoos and rings. "Mariana, I've lived many lives within this same body. And after quite some time, I realized I could no longer identify as just female. Nor did I feel I was a male. I simply became ... Spiro. I freed myself from a prison I didn't truly understand, one I had chosen to live in for far too long. Now, everyone here understands that my seemingly endless life cannot be boiled down to a category I fell into the moment I was born."

The insightful words had Mariana contemplating the cultural norms of her people. The foreign concept that someone could identify as just *themselves* without considering the dividing line between male and female was ... enlightening.

"Your words have given me so much to think about. Sirens are all born female, and that's an important part of our culture. I don't know that any of us would understand what it means to erase the barrier between identifying as male or female. Though I'm certain a few of my sisters would appreciate the chance to." Mariana smiled at the wise fae. "Your courage and strength are honorable."

Spiro shook their head, unable to meet her eyes. "I don't know about that. Some would disagree and say it was cowardly. Although, all I did was stop trying to be all that I was expected to be," they replied with a shrug.

"It's a good thing I don't care how others view it," she chuckled. "I respect your choice and am grateful you shared this with me."

"You're welcome. Thank you for asking." The village leader smiled at her. "And thank you for coming down here with me."

Mariana glanced around the room, admiring the paintings. "I can see why you wanted to show me." She swallowed hard as she thought of her sister. "Astra would have loved it here."

"Perhaps one day, after you've found her, you can bring her here, show it to her."

Mariana turned her head toward the leader. "You'd allow me to come back?"

Spiro smiled down at her. "Of course. It's a bit of a challenge getting here, so you may want to request the help of a certain *Mocanus*, but I have a feeling he'd be willing to bring you back."

Mariana knew they meant Dax and began to wonder what he had told them while she was passed out. "He's a bit of an enigma. I never know what he's thinking," Mariana admitted.

"Well, I can say with certainty that he's never brought anyone here before. You are the first. And truthfully, I'm glad he did. If he hadn't ..." Spiro's words trailed off, and they sighed.

"I might not be alive."

Spiro gave her a short, sad nod. "And you might not have been given the chance to save your sister."

Mariana glanced down at her hands, remembering how Dax had made her form a fist.

Warriors were strong; no matter the bruises, the scars, the pain inflicted upon them, they always got back up. Even that lone warrior in the painting had found a way to keep going. Broken and alone, yet alive with purpose.

Mariana fisted her hands, remembering the words of her people: *From ruin, we rise.*

CHAPTER 27

Dax sighed as he approached the council room, the weight of his responsibilities pressing heavily on his shoulders. The moment he stepped inside, the spicy, warm scent of incense flooded his senses, reminding him of home and times long past.

"Daxon," Spiro greeted warmly and stepped toward him with open arms. He smiled as he approached, both their faces lighting up with genuine affection. The two embraced, one hand behind the other's head, bringing their foreheads together with their eyes closed. They stood together in silence for a brief moment, a wordless exchange of comfort and strength. Dax could feel the energy his parent radiated, a bright light chasing away the shadows within his soul.

When they stepped apart, the shadows embraced him once again, creeping back into the corners of his mind.

"How did it go with Mari?" he asked, his voice barely concealing his concern.

"Good. She took the news well and understands what's happened. I took her back to the clinic so she could rest. I'm glad you're both here, though I wish the circumstances were different."

Dax nodded in agreement, the corners of his mouth twitching into a small, sad smile. "Thank you for healing her and for your hospitality."

Spiro's face fell, their expression tinged with sadness. "You speak to me as though I'm a stranger. It's been too long since you've been home."

Dax held back his groan, feeling a pang of guilt. "I've already heard enough from Kenna. I don't need another lecture."

He stepped away to stare at one of the many stained glass windows. Each one depicted a small part of the earth element: lilies growing in a green field where the redwoods and blackwoods intermingled, not far from Kythera. The one in front of him showed the colorful, rocky cliffs on the far eastern side of the fae realm, where only those courageous enough to climb several mountain ranges could get a glimpse. Dax had seen them once when he was younger, eager, full of life and energy. Now, he felt like a husk of his former self.

"She had to try, Dax. Your sister cares about you. I care about you," Spiro said softly.

"Staying away keeps you all safe. You know that," Dax replied, his voice strained.

Spiro didn't speak for a long moment, but Dax could feel their eyes on him, heavy with unspoken words.

"Each year that passes where you don't come home, I grow fearful that I'll never see you again." Spiro's voice cracked, and Dax glanced at them over his shoulder. The tears in Spiro's eyes were too much.

Clearing his throat, he stared down at his boots. "What would you have me do? The risk is too great to make the trip more often. Someone could follow me and find this place."

"Excuses," Spiro spat out, making Dax meet their angry gaze. "You would never let that happen. This is your home. This is where you were born. You have been ignoring the Earth's blessing—"

"Stop—"

"You are forgetting who you are, Daxon!"

He bit his lip and struggled to keep his voice calm despite the instinct to yell right back. "Spiro." He took a deep breath, attempting to calm his nerves. "Protecting all of you is all I want to do. Just let me do that."

Spiro shook their head and released a heavy sigh. Taking a seat at the long table, they regarded him carefully. "What's the point of giving up your life if you don't even remember what you're trying to protect?"

Dax began to chuckle as he rubbed a hand over his face. Why were the idiotic gods punishing him?

"The past century has been all about keeping Kythera safe. To keep what's left of our tribe alive. That's worth every sacrifice I can make. And if it means giving up a life for myself, then so be it."

The look Spiro gave him made his heart clench. It was time to go.

"Mari has agreed to keep Kythera secret. You'll have nothing to worry about."

Spiro nodded. "I trust her."

"Storm's on the way. We'll leave tomorrow once it's passed."
He walked toward the door. Spiro's voice stopped him.

"What will happen to her when you get to Aurelia?"

Dax glanced over his shoulder and knew the moment Spiro saw the answer.

Without saying another word, he left the conference room, his fists tight as he walked back toward the clinic. The tension tightened his spine, making his shoulders and neck ache.

After everything he'd done, it was still not enough. He was always failing in some way. In their eyes, he should be home, embracing nature. Nature was not their shield; he was.

He didn't need his tribe's gratitude. He just needed them to understand and let him suffer without the extra burden of guilt.

As he stepped into the cabin, darkness greeted him. There was an empty plate on the table, the bed was empty, and Mari was nowhere to be seen. His gaze wandered to the slightly open door leading to the balcony at the back, and he spotted the siren sitting in one of the hanging chairs through the crack. She may look like a fae after what her mother did to her, but he knew that trapped beneath, she was still every bit a siren.

She was wrapped in a fur blanket, and her deep teal hair blew gently in the wind. The edge of the storm was nearing. He stepped out and sat down in the chair beside her.

She glanced at him, her face less swollen than when she'd been crying. "How are you feeling?" he asked gently.

She lifted a shoulder. "I have to accept what's happened and find a solution. Letting it fester like an infected wound won't help me."

"That's a good way of looking at it."

"It's the only way I know how."

They fell silent and remained on the balcony until the sun began to set. The sky reminded Dax of a painting. The mix of colors coated everything the light could touch in a soft orange and rose hue.

When Dax glanced over at Mari, he couldn't breathe. He couldn't think. All he saw was her. A pale gold light kissed her skin in the final moments before the sun dipped behind the mountains.

"Wanna take a walk?" he asked, praying she would say yes. He wasn't sure why he needed to be in her presence, but something about her calmed him.

"In the rain?" she asked, glancing toward the misty forest.

"Yes. It'll also be dark soon."

She stood up, leaving the blanket in the chair. "Absolutely."

CHAPTER 28

"You know, when you asked me if I wanted to take a walk in the rain and the dark, this wasn't what I was imagining," Mariana said as she struggled to get her feet out of the thick mud she was currently stuck in. The squelching sound of her boots echoed in the damp forest, blending with the steady patter of rain against the dense canopy above.

Water dripped over her forehead, down her nose, and onto her lips, leaving a cold, bitter taste. Her hair was soaked, plastered against her scalp, but at least her skin stayed relatively dry with the leather coat and pants she wore. The coat, a gift from Kenna, clung to her like a second skin, offering a small shield against the relentless elements.

Dax laughed, a deep, resonant sound that seemed to cut through the gloom. He walked over to her, his experienced steps avoiding the mud puddles with ease, and bent down to help her. The smell of wet earth filled the air, mingling with the scents of leather and rain.

She stumbled over a rock, her foot slipping in the mud and splashing it all over her pants.

"Shit!" Groaning up at the darkened sky, she shouted, "Why is gravity so awful!" Her frustration echoed through the trees, followed by the distant call of a night bird.

Dax smirked at her, his eyes twinkling with amusement. "Get on my back, I'll take you the rest of the way."

He bent down, and Mariana accepted the invitation enthusiastically, jumping onto his back without a second thought. She smiled as he grunted and stood up, the warmth of his body seeping into her own.

"Thank you," she whispered into his ear, her stomach fluttering when she saw his cheek lift into a closed-lip smile. The moment's intimacy made her heart race, each beat echoing in her ears.

Somehow, this fae could make her smile during the darkest part of her life. Resting her head against his shoulder as he carried her, she closed her eyes and savored the feeling of the rain against her cheek. Surprisingly, she wasn't as cold as she would've expected. Spring was close, the promise of renewal and new beginnings in the air.

She needed to focus on what would come when they arrived in Aurelia. After speaking to Spiro, she realized the amulet was her only hope of reversing the binding spell. She had to find it. Otherwise, she'd never go home. The weight of that reality pressed down on her, a constant reminder of what was at stake.

Astra would have known where to look; she was sure of it. Her sister had always been resourceful, a beacon of hope in Mariana's darkest hours.

"We're here," Dax said, pulling her from her thoughts. She opened her eyes and slid off his back to stare at a massive tree.

"Holy ... Goddess," she breathed. The tree was the width of a small house and so tall that she couldn't see the top of it as it disappeared into the fog. Standing torches glowed softly around them, their light diffused by the mist. They weren't lit by fire or electricity but by some fuzzy-looking substance she could only imagine was similar to the glowing algae they had in Salus.

"What is this?" she asked, slowly approaching the tree.

"Natura Nexus. Our Mother Tree." Dax lifted a hesitant hand to the trunk. Instead of placing his hand on it, he let his arm drop. "It was blessed by General Cornelia herself as a gift of prosperity to our tribe."

Mariana stared into its thick branches, the pine needles blocking off the rain and finally allowing them to dry. She could feel the power emanating from the tree, a subtle thrum that resonated through her body.

"Wow, it's a marvel. A monument." She chuckled, amazed at its absurd size and beauty. The tree seemed ancient, timeless, a living testament to the history of Dax's people.

Dax sat down, leaning his back against the tree and sighing as he rested his head. The soft glow of the torches cast shadows across his face, highlighting his strong jaw and the determined set of his mouth.

"Why did you bring me here?" She couldn't help but wonder; this seemed like a sacred place where outsiders wouldn't be welcome. The air felt charged with significance, each breath a connection to the past.

Dax shrugged, resting his arms against his bent knees. "I think everyone should see it, feel the power that grows from its roots."

Satisfied with the answer, she sat beside him, bringing her knees up to her chest and resting her hands on top. The ground was surprisingly dry beneath the tree, a small sanctuary from the dampness surrounding them.

"How did you come by a rune stone?" he asked, touching the blue star sapphire charm on her cord bracelet. His fingers were gentle, careful, as he touched the stone.

"A what?" She shifted closer to show him. The warmth of his body was comforting, and she ached to close the distance between them.

Dax lifted the stone and brushed his thumb over the smooth, domed top. "A rune stone. They're incredibly rare and supposed to have the essence of a god's magic. I've only ever seen one in red, not blue. It's beautiful," he murmured, and then met her eyes. His gaze was intense, filled with a mixture of curiosity and admiration.

"My mother gave it to me a long time ago."

Mentioning Cybele made her mouth pinch and her gut tighten. Anger at what her mother did to her still made her blood boil. But no matter how she felt about Cybele, she would follow through and find Astra. For Luna. Her sister was all that mattered now.

"I'll go with you, Dax," she said, pulling his gaze toward her. "To Aurelia. No fighting, no bindings—or drugs." She pointed at him, and he let out a low laugh. "Just, please, help me get my sister out safely. That's all I ask."

They stared at each other. Mariana's eyes pleaded for him to agree, while Dax's remained unreadable. Finally, he dragged his gaze away to stare up at the Mother Tree's branches.

"I'll do what I can," he murmured, and her heart began to dance. "But you have to understand something, Mari."

"What?" she asked, looking away. She hid her satisfied smile behind her hands and warmed her chilled cheeks.

"When we get there, you're still subject to the orders of the royal family. I can't do anything that would jeopardize my agreement with them." His words were a stark reminder of the complexities of their situation.

Her smile faded. "Because you want to keep your people safe," she finished for him, understanding the loyalty he felt to protecting his family. It was exactly what she was trying to do. Once she got to Aurelia and had Astra safe beside her, they would find a way out and, somehow, find the amulet together. And Dax ... well, she'd probably never see him again.

She shifted uncomfortably as the truth started to sink deep into the pit of her stomach. The thought of losing Dax—of never seeing him again—was a pain she hadn't anticipated.

"Will you come back here? After you take me to Aurelia?"

"No," he clipped. The finality of his answer hit her like a physical blow, a cold realization settling over her. Lifting her head to look at him as he stared off into the distance at the mist curling around the trees, she wondered why he was so quick to answer.

"Why not?" she asked, her voice barely above a whisper.

His frown deepened. "A slave doesn't get to go home."

CHAPTER 29

BY THE TIME THEY reached Dax's cabin, rain had soaked them to the bone, leaving them dripping and shivering as they stepped inside. He turned on a light in the corner of the room, illuminating the small cabin. Dax swept his eyes across the dark space. Everything was still right where he'd left it all those years ago—a large bed in the corner covered in furs, shelves lined with books, hunting gear stashed to the side, and a large, thickly woven blanket draped over the back of a leather couch—except it looked liked someone had dusted.

Mari hesitated near the door, hugging herself tightly as water dripped from her hair and clothes onto the wooden floor. Her teeth chattered, and she rubbed her arms briskly in an attempt to warm up.

"This isn't the clinic," she said, her voice sharp with suspicion as she glanced around.

"No," Dax replied, shrugging off his soaked coat and tossing it onto a nearby hook. "It's my cabin. You're staying here with me."

Mari's brow furrowed. "Why? Don't tell me it's because you're worried about me."

Dax crouched by the hearth, coaxing the embers to life. "In case someone else needs the clinic to heal."

Mari scoffed softly, folding her arms as she leaned against the door frame. "You're telling me no one else in the village has a spare room? Or is this just your excuse to keep me where you can see me?"

Dax glanced over his shoulder, the flickering firelight casting restless shadows over Mari's features. "Maybe I don't trust you to stay out of trouble."

Her mouth opened to retort, but the cold finally got the better of her, and she shivered hard. He stood and motioned her toward the fire.

"Stand here," he said, his voice soft but firm. "I'll get you something to wear."

Mari stared at him for a moment, her lips pressed into a thin line, before stepping closer to the hearth.

"Now would be a great time for my power to come back so I could expel all this water," she muttered under her breath, her voice tinged with frustration but softened by the slight tremor in her words.

Dax quickly grabbed a dry towel from the washroom, then a shirt and pants from his dresser before walking back to Mari.

"They'll be big on you, but they're dry—"

His words were cut off when he saw her standing shirtless in front of the fireplace, holding up her top toward the heat of the flames.

Her long, wet hair draped over her chest, barely concealing the shadowed curve beneath.

He swallowed hard. "What are you doing?" The words came out lower than he intended, his throat tight.

She glanced over at him, and his chest seized. *Gods, she is beautiful. Dangerous, but beautiful.*

Mari looked over her shoulder, her expression bemused. "Drying my top." She said it so matter-of-factly, as if this wasn't at all unusual. "It's freezing." Then she went back to staring at the top, willing it to dry faster.

Dax cursed under his breath and moved toward her, lifting the dark fabric of the shirt he brought like a curtain in front of her. "Put this on. Now."

Mari arched a brow but didn't argue. "You Fae are such prudes," she muttered, then stepped out of her wet boots and pants.

Turning down his gaze, he focused on his boots while trying hard to forget what he'd just seen. "We're not prudes, we're—" He juggled for the right word. "Respectful."

Mari snorted and put on the shirt. It hung just above her knees.

He held out the pants, but she only lifted an eyebrow at him.

"You're just as bad as mortals. I don't get what the big deal is. Our bodies are something to be proud of," she said, ignoring the pants. He dropped them on the couch.

Dax scrubbed a hand over his head and chuckled. "You're right, how could we ever think that being nude in the dead of winter would be a bad idea?"

He peered down at her. The firelight danced across her face, catching the faint blush on her cheeks. She opened her mouth to retort, but her breath hitched when he stepped closer, brushing a stray strand of hair away from her scarred temple. His fingers lingered for a moment too long, and he noticed how her breathing stilled.

"What are you doing?" she murmured.

The question lingered. What in the blazes was he doing? It was like his feet and hands had moved without his consent.

Taking a step back, he cleared his throat. "You take the bed—I'll sleep here." He collapsed onto the leather couch with a sigh.

The crackle of the fire and the steady rhythm of rain on the roof filled the silence between them. Dax let his eyes drift shut, exhaustion seeping into his bones. But he could feel her gaze on him, a warmth prickling his skin.

"How old are you?" Mari blurted.

Dax glanced at her through hooded eyes and saw her cheeks blush pink. A slow smile tugged at his lips before he could stop it. "How old do you think I am?"

"That's not an answer."

"No, but it's more fun this way," he said as he draped an arm over the back of the couch and smirked up at her.

She squinted, tapping her fingers against her lips as if in deep thought. "Hmm ... over a century?"

That startled a laugh out of him, deep and genuine. The innocence in her blush and the way she crossed her arms made him want to stand up and kiss her.

"Okay," she muttered, rolling her eyes. "So definitely older than me."

"Definitely," he said softly, and regarded her with an amused tilt of his head. "Why so curious?"

She shifted awkwardly. "I just wasn't sure if it would be, you know ... respectful to take the bed from someone so ..." She gestured vaguely. "Mature."

Dax's brows lifted, and he sat forward, resting his arms on his knees. "Mature? Really?"

Mari shrugged, biting back a smile. "I was trying to be polite."

He stood, shaking his head with an amused huff. "Look, I'm not ancient. And if I wanted the bed, I'd take it."

She gestured toward the inviting pile of blankets with a sweep of her hand. "Then take it. It's plenty big enough for the both of us. Besides, this is your cabin."

Dax's jaw tightened as he glanced at the bed, then back at her. His shirt hung loose around her frame, her hair still damp and curling at the ends. He could imagine the feel of her warmth beside him, her weight against his chest.

No. Absolutely not.

He cleared his throat, tearing his gaze away. "Not necessary," he said, his voice gruff. "You're my guest. Take the bed."

Mari opened her mouth to protest, but Dax rubbed at the ache in his neck, dismissing her. "Get some rest. We've got a long day ahead."

There was a moment of silence before she sighed and padded to the bed, slipping beneath the mound of blankets without another word.

Dax waited until she settled before removing his boots and lying on the couch. The cushions were lumpy, and his pants were still damp, but he didn't care. He stared at the ceiling, cursing himself.

A slave doesn't get to go home.

Why had he said that? He scrubbed his face, suppressing a groan of frustration when he heard something beyond the rain.

The sound of shifting blankets drew his attention. Mari kept shifting around, like she couldn't get comfortable.

"You okay over there?"

"It's so cold," her small voice answered in return.

The fire crackled steadily, but the heat hadn't yet reached the corners of the room, especially with the wind howling outside, freezing gusts seeping through the tiniest of cracks.

He sat up, rubbing his face with both hands. He couldn't ignore it—the soft whimpers, the way her teeth chattered like the wind rattling the windows. This was madness, but he stood anyway, crossing the room before he could talk himself out of it.

He pulled back the blankets to slide in beside her.

Mari stirred, her breath hitching when he wrapped an arm around her, pulling her close. Her body was like ice against his, and he exhaled softly, his lips brushing her damp hair.

"I'm only doing this so you don't freeze to death," he muttered, more to himself than to her.

Mari snuggled closer. "Whatever you say." Her voice was a sleepy murmur. "I knew you wanted the bed."

CHAPTER 30

As Mariana stepped out of the cabin, the crisp mountain air rushed into her lungs, sharp and invigorating. It carried the earthy scent of pine and rain-soaked soil, tinged with the faint sweetness of wildflowers. She closed her eyes, letting the freshness seep into her, chasing away the last traces of sleep.

The storm had passed overnight, leaving the world transformed. The forest glistened with droplets of rain, each leaf catching the sunlight and refracting it like tiny jewels. The sky was a vivid, endless blue, with streaks of soft white clouds drifting lazily above the peaks.

She'd slept better than she had in weeks, cocooned in the warmth of the fur-covered bed. Dax had been gone when she woke—no note, no word, just the lingering scent of pine and leather.

Mariana inhaled deeply again, trying to shake the odd hollowness in her chest. It wasn't like she needed him when he'd had things to do. Still, the space where his presence had been felt curiously empty, and she hated how aware she was of it.

She gazed at the towering waterfall beside the village, its grand roar echoing through the trees. At the base, partially concealed by the waterfall's mist, was a machine. Mariana could just barely make out spinning wheels and cords snaking across the river rocks, extending toward a large building. It must have been their source of electricity.

Sunlight filtered through the mist, and a rainbow of colors appeared, raining down into the brimming pool below.

Mariana swallowed the lump in her throat as she stared at the waves flowing downriver. She missed the water and its comforting embrace as she sank below the surface. She missed the taste of the sea and the rush of the current flowing through her hair. She missed her tail. Her sisters.

Lifting her hand, she placed it over her chest. Beneath the leather coat was her bone armor, crafted specifically for her by Aurora. Wearing it made her feel closer to her sister and gave her the hope she needed. She cleared her throat and blinked away the tears in her eyes.

Now isn't the time to wallow in self-pity, she scolded herself. Dropping her hand, she thought of Celeste's lesson about moving forward. Her friend had always believed in looking toward the future instead of wallowing in the past.

Every time she thought of Celeste, she didn't know what to feel. Revenge echoed in her ears, a part of her begging to inflict harm on those deserving. But there was another part that whispered, *It isn't worth it*. Her cursed sisters, including the Siren Witch, would never stop taking mortal lives unless they were ordered not to by their queen. And the only way that would happen was if Sirenia was restored.

Ultimately, that was her final mission, and she could see no other path that Celeste would be more proud of as a way to honor her fallen friend.

Letting go of the railing, Mariana turned on her heel to continue down the deck, unsure where she was going.

She descended a set of winding wooden stairs to the level below, where the familiar sounds of clashing metal caught her attention. Glancing over the railing, she spotted Dax and Kenna sparring in a large training area. A crowd of betting villagers formed around them. It was the first time she'd seen so many of Dax's tribe in one place. They seemed to be steering clear of the cabin she'd stayed in.

Mariana leaned against the rail, eyes trained on their fluid movements as the duel turned in Dax's favor. Although Kenna's moves were as graceful as a willow swaying in the breeze, Dax had a fierce strength that dominated every clash of their blades.

It appeared Dax was about to win, until Kenna swiftly rolled by him, followed by a kick to the back of his knee.

A weak spot, Mariana realized, watching him stumble forward. She smiled faintly, recalling how she did the same to him the first time they fought.

Seizing the opportunity, Kenna leaped onto his back, using his weight against him, and they crashed to the ground.

The crowd erupted in cheers as Kenna triumphantly raised her blade into the air, declaring her victory.

But then Dax bucked her over his head, and she rolled, landing on her back. They both burst out laughing as they dropped their blades and shook hands, still panting from the exertion.

Mariana's lips lifted. She released the railing and continued on the downward path toward them.

The stairs creaked under their weight, the sound melding with the distant rustle of leaves and the occasional chirp of birds. As they descended, the warm light from the village above dimmed, replaced by the cool, dappled shadows of the forest floor in the early morning light.

Mariana spotted Dax and Kenna standing with Spiro.

"Have everything you need?" Spiro asked him as she approached, their voice filled with quiet concern. Kenna handed Mariana a backpack with a small, reassuring smile. The backpack was well-worn, its fabric faded but clearly reliable.

"Yeah," he grunted, his voice rough around the edges, betraying the tension he tried to hide. His eyes, however, softened when they met Kenna's.

"You should take a couple of horses," Kenna offered, her eyes flicking to the stables. "You'll get there faster."

Dax shook his head firmly. "Can't risk the tracks. Besides, you'll use it as an excuse for me to return them."

Kenna grinned mischievously. "I mean, it would be the perfect excuse to come back." Dax shook his head and pulled her close. They hugged each other in a way Mariana had never seen before—one hand behind each other's head, the other on the back, eyes closed, and foreheads touching.

She averted her gaze, staring at the rays of sunshine breaking through the branches above them, feeling the bittersweet warmth on her skin. The sunlight filtered through the leaves, casting a mosaic of light and shadow onto the forest floor.

She missed her family but couldn't imagine how Dax felt, knowing he would have no choice but to go years without seeing them again. The thought of separation weighed heavily on her heart, each beat a reminder of the sacrifices they both had to make.

"Be safe. Come home when you can," Spiro told him, their voice carrying the weight of unspoken fears.

Dax gave them a solemn nod, his eyes shadowed with guilt.

"Mari, it was wonderful to meet you. I wish you luck on your journey and hope our paths cross again." Spiro took both her hands in theirs, a faint hum of energy coursing through her that instantly made her smile. The touch was comforting, a gentle reminder that she wasn't alone in her struggles.

"Thank you, Spiro. For everything," she said, her voice filled with genuine gratitude. The village leader gave her a warm smile and let go of her hands.

They watched Kenna and Spiro walk back up through the village's maze of intricately carved and weathered staircases until they disappeared.

Then Dax turned to Mariana, his expression hardening with resolve. "Alright, first things first. I need you to wrap this around your face." He handed her a long strip of brown fabric. She took it, pinching it between her thumb and forefinger. The texture was unpleasant, slightly rough, and thick.

She lifted an eyebrow at him. "Excuse me?"

As he led her out of Kythera, he pointed to a field of red flowers growing between the trees. The flowers, vibrant and otherworldly, swayed gently in the breeze, their petals glistening with dew. "Those flowers release a toxin into the air that causes hallucinations if anyone breathes it in. My people don't feel its effects, but you will. I don't need you running away and getting lost out here because you think ghosts are attacking you."

Mariana stared at the flowers, suddenly feeling the weight of the truth. Their beauty masked a deadly danger, a reminder of the deceptive nature of the world around her. "Did you take me through the flowers when you brought me here?"

Dax nodded, inspecting her downcast expression.

Celeste hadn't visited her in her dreams; it had all been a figment of her imagination. The realization hit her hard, a cold, bitter truth that tightened her throat and made her eyes sting.

She swallowed, her eyes blurring as she brought the rag up to her face and tied it behind her head, obscuring her vision and covering her nose and mouth. The fabric smelled faintly of earth and wood, a grounding scent amid her rising anxiety.

"I got you, just follow me," Dax said softly, taking her hand. He led them through the forest, his grip firm and reassuring.

The pungent, sweet smell of the flowers, accompanied by the harrowing moans and screeches of the ghosts in her mind, was difficult to ignore. Each step felt heavier, the weight of unseen eyes pressing down on her.

"*Mari?*" She heard the gentle, sweet voice call her name and began shaking her head. It was Celeste's voice, achingly familiar, pulling at her heartstrings.

It's not real, it's not real, it's not real—

"*Mari, please look at me. I'm right here!*" Celeste pleaded. The desperation in her voice was heart-wrenching, a cruel trick of her mind.

No, it wasn't Celeste, not really. And yet it sounded just like her. The conflict tore at her, a battle between reason and emotion.

Her heart raced. She struggled to keep calm, gripping Dax's hand tighter. Cold, soft touches skated over her skin despite her thick leather jacket. She shivered, her fear a palpable presence in the air. Her spine went rigid when, beyond Celeste's pleading voice, there was a song.

The song. The melody was haunting, a ghostly echo from her past.

Her feet stopped, and she listened. The voice was faint and difficult to hear over the screams, but it grew louder with each breath.

It can't be.

She didn't remember falling, but when Dax picked her up, holding her close to his chest, she buried her face in his cloak. Gripping his lapels, she tried desperately to memorize the haunting melody, until the sweet flower scent faded along with Celeste's voice and the song she used to hear when she was a youngling.

Dax set her down on a bed of pine needles and removed the fabric, tucking it into the bag on his back. "You okay?" His face tightened with worry, his eyes scanning her for signs of lasting distress.

She blinked away the sudden brightness and nodded, her mouth a thin line as she tried to forget the sounds still echoing in her ears. The brightness of the clearing was jarring, a harsh reminder of the reality she had just left behind. "I'm fine. Let's go," she said, her voice hoarse as though she were the one who'd been screaming, not the ghosts.

When she tried standing, her legs gave out, and she fell to her back.

"Just breathe deeply," Dax said, sitting down beside her. "You need to clear your lungs." His voice was calm, a steady anchor in the storm of her emotions.

Mariana shook her head and covered her eyes with her hands as tears began to trail down the sides of her face. "Those flowers are *awful*," she said harshly, her voice thick with sudden grief she hadn't felt in so long. She'd thought she was strong enough to push back the impending tidal wave of emotions, but when it broke free, it was like drowning all over again.

The sound of Dax chuckling made the water recede slightly, and she wiped her face. "I know, I've seen full-grown scouts with their heads between their knees crying like babies when they stumble upon the field. When I lived at home, I used to have the privilege of pulling them out before they went completely mad."

"I can see how someone would go mad." She sniffed and stared skyward. The clouds rolled in again, covering the beautiful sun and cloaking everything in a gray tint. The shifting weather mirrored the tumultuous state of her mind.

"I always wanted to ask them what they heard. What they saw." She heard the lingering question in his voice and sat up. She groaned. Her hair was an absolute mess. Shaking her head, she started pulling out pine needles from her braid. The task was methodical, distracting herself from the lingering fear. Dax pulled a leaf from her head, and they both laughed softly.

She cleared her throat. How was she supposed to explain what she had heard?

Rubbing her forehead, she sighed. "When Celeste died, I blamed myself. I felt like I should've somehow stopped it, like I had the power to. But I've realized I don't have the power to stop anything." Mariana lifted her eyes to his and murmured, "I heard her voice back there. And I wished it were real. But neither the flowers nor I have the power to bring her back." Turning away, she dragged her wrist under her nose and scoffed. "Just like I have no power to bring back the song," she quietly said to herself.

"What song?"

Shit. "Uh ..." *Might as well confess you're insane.*

"This is going to sound crazy," she admitted, "but from the day I was born, I could hear this ... song. My mother tried dismissing it as whales singing, but no one else could hear it. Just me. Then I discovered it was coming from the sky, and I had to know what it was saying. So—" She cleared her throat, heat rising to her cheeks—"I would leave the palace's protection and go to the surface to listen to it. I could never make out the words, but it was always there in the background. Until the day I came of age, and it stopped. I woke up on my birthday and haven't heard it since."

"Strange," he murmured, his eyes narrowing in thought.

"When I got too close to the sun and burned my face, I realized how careless and thoughtless I had been. I almost died. I asked Nyx, our tattooist, to cover it all up—well, except this one." She gestured to the scar on her temple. "I kept that one as a reminder."

"The sun did this to you?" he asked, touching her scar. His touch was gentle, his fingers tracing the outline of the scar with a tenderness that made her heart ache.

Her lungs struggled to operate with how close he'd gotten. "Yes," she whispered, and averted her gaze, her cheeks flushing with warmth. "The only way for a siren to be permanently scarred is by the sun. At the time, I didn't have full control of my power and ..." Mariana's voice trailed off as she recalled how angry her mother had been every time she came back with a new scar. She rubbed the nasty one on her right hand, wishing it would disappear just like she had when she first was burned, but at least it remained semi-hidden beneath the swirling wave tattoo. "Let's just say I'm not exactly proud of my scars," she confessed, then laughed sadly.

Dax took her hand gently, inspecting the scar there. Mariana suddenly felt laid bare, like he'd be able to see past all the tattoos to the ugly truth hidden beneath.

She almost pulled her hand free when he lifted it to his lips and placed a kiss over the scar. Her heart stopped dead in her chest, the simple gesture overwhelming her.

"Your scars are beautiful," he murmured, and their eyes met. Mariana couldn't breathe. His emerald gaze held hers, drawing her in, making her toes curl.

"How can you say that?" she asked, her voice barely audible, a mix of disbelief and vulnerability in her tone.

"We all have something we're ashamed of, Mari. Your scars shouldn't be one of them. They're a part of you," Dax replied, his eyes never leaving hers. "Your shield."

Mariana swallowed hard, feeling the weight of his words settle into her heart. "No one's ever seen them like that before."

"It's hard for us to see what makes us strong," he said softly, squeezing her hand. His touch was a lifeline, grounding her in the present.

In that moment, surrounded by the silence of understanding, Mariana felt a flicker of hope she hadn't known she needed. She released a small laugh and wiped her eyes. "Why is it so easy to tell you everything?" she asked softly.

He brushed her hair back as it fluttered in the breeze, then settled his warm hand on her cheek. Something deep inside her ached, and she couldn't stop herself from leaning toward him. His lips stopped close to hers, their mingling breath hot as they waited for the other to make the move.

"We shouldn't," he whispered darkly, his voice filled with regret.

As the wind grew in intensity, she shivered. Tilting her head, she whispered back, "Why not?" His eyes trailed from the base of her throat to her lips, lingering on her mouth.

"Your soul isn't full of shadows like mine is, Mari." His words were a confession, a glimpse into the darkness he carried within. He was a man of a thousand secrets, his past locked so tightly in darkness that she wondered how long he'd been its prisoner.

Hearing him say that made her settle her hand over his heart. "So let me chase them away," she whispered.

Dax rested his forehead against hers, keeping them from going any further. He swallowed and pulled away to stand.

Mariana blinked. Disappointment cut through her like a knife, the moment slipping away.

"Samos is a day's trek away," he said, clearing his throat while glancing toward the darkening trail as the clouds rolled in. The sky was a tumultuous sea of gray, promising more rain. "If we move quickly, we'll arrive by sundown."

Mariana nodded, trying to forget his lips. She hesitated before taking Dax's offered hand and stood. Releasing a deep breath, she swallowed her pride and followed him into the misty forest.

CHAPTER 31

SOAKED TO THE BONE, they sloshed through the rain into Samos long after they were supposed to. The town's lamps cast the darkened street in gloomy white light.

Dax took a deep breath and glanced over his shoulder at Mari, trailing behind, her eyes staring at the lights. *Gods, she's beautiful.* Even with half the forest trapped in her long hair, her bright, curious eyes made him want to step close to her.

Clearing his throat, he stared into the lights, burning his eyes and the ridiculous thoughts in his head. "Electricity," he said. "Samos is a mining town of lumen crystals. It's what gives the kingdom electricity."

Mari craned her head to look up at the tall lamppost. "Do all towns in the fae realm have electricity?"

"No, just a few. Some have hydro-power, though."

"Like—" Mari stopped herself from saying it aloud as two tired fae hobbled past, but he heard what she meant and nodded.

Kythera utilized the waterfall's energy to power their village. They didn't believe in ripping apart the earth for the luxury of eternal light.

Pulling Mari forward, he guided her toward an inn lit with soft-glowing windows.

"The buildings look so ... strange," she commented, staring at the curved stone doors, archways, and roofs darkened with rain.

Dax's mouth lifted. "Wait till you get inside."

They walked into the Wandering Wyrm Inn, and Dax watched Mari's eyes bulge from her skull.

Numerous metal lanterns hung from dark wooden beams along the ceiling, the glow from within each one revealing different types of dragons that used to exist long, long ago. Golden light beamed from within, casting shadows that mimicked the fierce forms of dragons in flight onto the polished stone walls. Some lanterns flickered so that it seemed flames licked from the dragons' mouths, giving them an eerie semblance of life.

Dax stepped across the thick, muddy rug that used to be an azure color toward the massive bar, where an ancient dwarf was refilling a mug with amber liquid. With a bushy gray beard that flowed down to his chest and thick curling eyebrows that seemed to possess a life of their own, Rufus Bonewyrm embodied the inn's rich history and enduring spirit. His eyes, sharp and gleaming like the finest gems, held countless stories of the past, each as captivating as the tales depicted in the shadows cast by the lanterns above.

Resting his hands along the smooth, dark mahogany bar top, Dax waited for Rufus to notice him. He used the time to inspect the wall of bottled spirits, many of which Dax knew were so potent, they were illegal. He knew Rufus mislabeled the bottles so he could hide them in plain sight.

Dax heard Mari gasp from behind him. He turned to see her staring across the wooden tables and chairs filled with patrons at the massive fireplace dominating the other side of the space. The corner of Dax's mouth lifted in amusement at her complete enthrallment. He had to admit it was a wonder to behold.

The fireplace had a mantle and hearth crafted from ancient dragon scales that retained a subtle iridescence even after all this time. Above the fireplace was a grand tapestry depicting the legendary battle between the last of the great dragons and a legion of fae under General Magnus, the one who had ordered all dragons to be eradicated—a tragic genocide fueled by fear of dominance and power.

"Well, I'll be damned," Rufus said slowly from behind him. Dax turned in time to see the old dwarf grip his bulging belly and laugh with his deep, gritty voice. "Daxon fuckin' Ironclad!"

Dax laughed at the last name Rufus had bestowed upon him the time he showed up dying on the inn's doorstep. He tried to push the memory back into the dark crevices of his mind as he gripped the dwarf's thick, leathery hand.

The last names of those who were *Blessed* weren't necessary since they could reveal which General they were descended from. But for Rufus, last names were the lifeblood of his ancestors. He chose Ironclad for Dax since he had returned from the brink of death—on more than one occasion.

"Still dodging death, I see."

"Hah! You know me, old as shit and short as shit." Rufus let out a hearty bellow and slammed a fist against the bar top. "I'm too ornery to go down. I'd kick the sand too much, wake my neighbors from their eternal slumber." He continued laughing.

Dax glanced over the counter at the wooden platform hidden behind the barkeep, making Rufus appear taller.

"How's the leg?"

Rufus lifted his wooden left leg and slammed it down on the platform with a mighty grin. "I've only had to replace it twice! The last one was a boating accident—don't ask." He shook his head like it was a hell of a story, and Dax was tempted to pester him for it. "Who's the little lass?" Rufus gestured toward Mari, who was inspecting the fireplace up close, running her long fingers along the dragon scales.

"I'm helping her get to Aurelia. We need a place to stay. Got any rooms?"

Rufus shook his head. "Nah, just the cellar. But it's got *a bed.*" He giggled with a wicked gleam in his eye and held up a key.

Ignoring what he was implying, Dax groaned. "Great! We get your sour, smelly bed. What a treat." Dax made to grab the key—knowing very well that the cellar was where the old fart usually slept off his famous benders—but Rufus held it just out of reach.

He chuckled, a deep, gravelly sound, waggling the key teasingly. "There are fresh sheets on it, I swear. And"—he leaned in conspiratorially—"there might be some leftover whiskey under the bed. Just mind the spiders—they're the friendly sort." He finally let Dax snatch the key, his grin never faltering. "You watch over that lass, now. Aurelia's no place for the faint-hearted."

"Already on it." Dax tipped his head to the old dwarf and walked over to Mari.

"This is amazing. The craftsmanship is ..." She covered her mouth with a hand and shook her head. "I can't get over it. I've never seen anything like it."

"Rufus did it all himself. Spent years collecting the scales from old battlefields when they were finally safe to walk on." Dragon flame was known for its undying burn. Even after all that had perished, there were some places where the ground still smoked.

"It's amazing he's even still around. How old do you think he is?" Mari asked in amazement.

"Who knows."

Dax had no idea how the dwarf had survived this long. Before the Infernal Wars, after the dragons were declared a threat to the General, the dwarves rebelled. But it was a battle they'd never win. Rufus watched his whole family die and still walked the land where they fought till their dying breaths. It haunted him, though, beating him with every breath he took. When the grief ran wild, the dwarf would fall into a drunken depression, drinking enough illegal liquor to kill a horse. He could've traveled up through the Varasova Mountains, where many surviving dwarves had established their own towns. Still, Rufus stayed close to where his family was buried. To remember them. Something Dax greatly respected.

"Can you imagine all the stories he could tell? All the tales of glory and dragons flying through the sky ..." Mari said wistfully.

"We can stay up here and have a drink, if you like. Rufus will gladly talk your ear off."

Mari opened her mouth just as someone stepped up behind Dax.

The room went unnaturally quiet. Tension filled the air like a noxious fog. Everyone seemed to hold their breath as Dax slowly looked over his shoulder.

Standing within punching distance stood the blond male from the Crossing.

He smiled. "Surprise."

The chilling sound of claws scraping metal followed. Then, chaos erupted.

CHAPTER 32

THE METAL TABLE BESIDE them burst upward, slamming into Dax. He landed on his back with a grunt onto the dirty stone floor.

Mariana's heart seized as everyone around them ran screaming.

She reached for the bone dagger at her hip—

What felt like claws reached up behind her and gripped her arm, stopping her.

A creature made of swirling darkness with bright red eyes slithered out. It pulled Mariana forward with a force she didn't expect, wrapping its dark tendrils around her neck in silent warning.

"What is this thing?" she gasped, raising her hands to rip it apart, but her fingers only clawed at the air. There was nothing she could do to make it stop.

The blond male shrugged, still smiling.

"A gift from the Matriarch," he said as Dax stood up, seething with anger. The stranger's eyes slid over to Mari. "To find and transport you to Aurelia. *Now.*"

"She's not going anywhere with you," Dax ground out, unsheathing the long blade strapped across his back that he'd brought from Kythera. The polished steel glinted under the light, promising a swift death for those who met its sharp edge.

"The Matriarch has grown tired of waiting. She wants her," he said, pointing at Mariana, "transported to Aurelia by tomorrow morning."

"Thanks for the reminder, now back off and get out of here," Dax ordered darkly.

The fae shook his head like he had sad news. "I have my orders. Don't make this any more difficult than it needs to be."

Dax glanced between the fae and Mariana. She could see it then, the way he struggled.

"Who's the Matriarch?" she asked Dax in a low voice.

The male stepped toward her and looked down at her with the grayest eyes she'd ever seen. They were completely devoid of color.

"She's someone you never want to disobey. My name is Cyrus." He held out a sun-kissed hand as though he expected her to shake it. When her glare never left his face, he dropped his hand with a ghost of a smile.

She turned back toward Dax, who seemed torn with indecision.

"Daxon?" She heard Rufus call out from the bar, but instead of answering him, Dax tightened his grip on his weapon like he desperately wanted to use it. But something held him back. Something he wasn't telling her.

"You know what will happen if you don't come with me. I have horses ready," Cyrus said, leaning a hip against the fireplace. With a smirk, he added, "Or we can do it the fun way: tied up and dragged behind. Your choice."

Dax growled. His brows were low over his rage-filled eyes.

Mariana didn't understand why he wasn't acting on that rage.

"Dax?" she whispered. When his gaze slid to hers, she gave him a pleading stare. His jaw tightened. He slowly exhaled before sheathing his weapon.

Her chest tightened at the sound.

"Fine," Dax relented, "we'll go with you. But she stays close to me. Let her go."

Cyrus lifted himself from his lax position. "I don't think that—"

"Now!" Dax shouted, making her jump.

Cyrus begrudgingly flicked a hand, and the shadowy creature disappeared.

Dax marched over to her and lifted her face to his. "You okay?"

"What are you keeping from me?" she asked softly, and when he averted his gaze, her stomach squeezed.

"This is all very touching, but we need to get moving." Cyrus gestured for them to follow. Dax took Mariana's hand and apologetically pulled her toward the door leading outside.

Rufus lifted an eyebrow at Dax, who just tipped his head toward him and placed the cellar key on the bar.

They left the inn and approached two horses secured to a post.

"We'll follow you. She rides with me," Dax stated, his mouth set in a firm line.

Cyrus smirked, glancing between the two of them. "Fine, but don't be surprised when she stabs you in the back—or in the balls." He lifted himself onto his horse with ease.

Dax lifted Mariana by the waist and placed her on the horse before climbing to sit behind her. As he settled in, his chest pressed against her back, and his hips fit snugly against her. Mariana struggled to steady her heartbeat. She wasn't sure if it was from how close he was or that he wouldn't answer her question on who he was working for.

"What in the burning stars is happening?" Mariana whispered harshly to him as he guided their horse to follow Cyrus.

"Nothing has changed," he replied quietly against her ear. "You're still going to the royal family."

"Then, *who* is the Matriarch?"

"It's just a name," he breathed. "She won't hurt you."

The fact that he even needed to say that made her scared. She tried stomping on that fear, telling herself that no matter what, they were on their way to Aurelia, where her sister was imprisoned. She should've been elated to know she was getting there faster, and by sunrise, she'd be hugging Astra.

She held onto that hope like a lifeline as they traveled through the dense, dark forest. Having never been on a horse before, she fidgeted and was uncomfortable within the first few hours. Dax kept telling her to calm down and eventually settled a reassuring arm around her stomach. Trapped—she should've felt trapped. Instead, she pulled it closer around her. Dax leaned his head against hers, keeping a tight grip on the reins, and held onto her until pale light brightened the sky into a deep violet hue.

Wait—

It wasn't dawn lighting up the sky. It was the fae palace.

Her breath caught at its magnificence.

Its walls were illuminated from the ground up, making it appear taller and more massive. In contrast to the darkness, its presence was striking. Eminence and power radiated from it like it was made to house the gods. Perhaps it was a tribute built for them, a temple, in case they ever decided to visit the world they'd left behind.

Astra was in there. It was still far, so far away. And yet Mariana felt the impending force of what was to come strike the breath from her lungs.

She tried focusing on her sister. She could already feel Astra's willowy arms wrapping around her, embracing her in love.

Mariana's throat tightened, and she couldn't fight the few tears that escaped her closed eyes. She missed Astra more than she could ever explain, and all she wanted was to make sure her sister got to hold her daughter again. Luna would be over the moon; her smile would brighten their dark world. That was all Mariana wanted. But it was only the first step.

Seraphina's amulet had to be found and kept safe from the fae king. There was no way Prince Helios could return; war would destroy the last of her sisters, and with so few left, she feared their existence would be wiped from the world. As soon as the amulet was hidden within the walls of Salus, Mariana could breathe, and the council could form a plan.

The impressive fortress imprisoning her beloved sister beckoned, its impenetrable white walls and guarded towers taunting her. She gazed at the spires that reached so high into the sky that the tips brushed the dark clouds. She stared at the massive illuminated dam separating the palace from the city. It was difficult to gauge how tall it was, but she assumed it was more than a ten-story drop to the canal below that fed into the sea. Two massive sewer drains spewed water waste into the waves where the sea met the cliffs. Mariana shook her head at the disrespectful contamination.

"You alright?" Dax asked from behind her.

She swallowed and nodded, keeping her gaze steady on the palace until it disappeared behind the forest as they descended a hill.

"One hundred and twenty-two," she whispered. She licked her chapped lips, her voice was strained when she said, "That's how many sirens are left in the world. More than half of them cursed murderers." She lifted a shoulder. "But they're all my sisters. They're all I have left."

Dax must've known how difficult this was for her, for he stayed silent behind her, listening intently rather than interrupting her thoughts.

"I don't even know if there will be anyone left by the time I'm supposed to—" Her voice cracked, and she gulped down the fear attached to the words she'd almost spoken.

—by the time I'm supposed to become their queen.

"There hasn't been a youngling born in Salus since I was born." She shook her head at the absurdity of that statement. She was the youngest siren alive.

And it was her destiny to save them all.

"I have to save her," she murmured. "I have to save Astra and bring her home."

Dax tightened his arm around her, and she held onto it as she rested her head against his shoulder. Her eyes closed, accepting the weight of exhaustion and stress.

Dax stayed silent. He just pulled her closer and didn't let go.

CHAPTER 33

AURORA SQUEEZED THE SPONGE into a jar, and she watched the gray, shimmering oil drip to the bottom of the glass. She pulled her hand out of the thick, kelp top that trapped the oil in the jar. The sponge immediately refilled with saltwater, and Aurora went back to wiping the queen's forehead. With each wipe, more oil appeared, beading along her mother's face.

Aurora sighed, the sound mingling with the soft clink of her gold bracelets as she worked.

It appeared to be tainted magic leaking from the queen's pores, but Aurora had no idea why. What had her mother done to suffer such a heavy backlash of fallout? She'd have asked Cybele herself, but the queen had remained unconscious since whatever had happened.

She repeated her movements. Swipe, squeeze, swipe ... But nothing she did made it any better. Tainted magic was toxic to those who breathed it in. It had to be constantly maintained until the fallout receded.

Three sirens entered the queen's chambers, and Aurora handed the task to Malea before noting the other two in the room.

Aurora glanced between the Siren Witch and Luna. Both claimed to have no idea what had happened to Cybele, which Aurora hardly believed. It wasn't that she didn't trust them; it was that their family loved keeping secrets like they were diamonds to hoard.

"How is she?" the witch asked softly, her posture stiff and hands clasped tightly together as she gazed at the queen's still form. She looked worried, an emotion Aurora hadn't realized the witch even possessed.

Clearing her throat, Aurora crossed her arms. "Still hasn't woken up. *Whatever* happened to her is taking its toll," she said with an insinuating lift of her brow, which the witch ignored.

"Will she survive?" Luna asked with her arms wrapped around herself.

"She will, if by some miracle, we can secure the amulet. We must hope that wherever Mariana is now, she brings it back to us." The witch approached Cybele and squeezed her wrist tightly before moving back toward the door. "Keep me updated," she said to Aurora over her shoulder, then left.

Aurora scrubbed her face with her hands, frustrated with ... well, everything.

"My mother told me about the amulet before she left," Luna said in her sweet, gentle voice. It sounded so much like Astra's. "What it can do." Aurora uncovered her eyes to look at her niece. "Mariana knows what's at stake. And yet she's still not back with my mother or the amulet." Her tone took a turn toward venomous.

"What are you talking about, Luna?" Aurora asked darkly. "Mari was taken against her will." They'd confirmed it with a village boy in Egan Village, who claimed to have seen it happen. *A hooded boogeyman snatched her right up!* he'd said in a squeaky voice. Aurora had to clarify who or what he was referring to with the boy's parents. Turned out to be a mortal superstition. Still, Aurora listened to how the boy described this "boogeyman," and it sounded like a fae was responsible for taking Mari. "Besides," she added, "she's only been gone for a week."

Aurora had fought with the queen tooth and nail about going after her sister, finding her, and getting her back immediately. The queen wouldn't have it and had said Mariana now had the chance to prove herself like she had been begging for. Aurora still couldn't stomach their mother's refusal to rescue *any* of her daughters.

Luna shrugged. "I heard she escaped, and the queen forced her to go back to her captor. That it was the only chance of saving my mother."

Aurora's eyebrows lowered. "Where did you hear that, Luna?"

Luna didn't answer her. Instead, she moved toward the door before stopping. She glanced back at Aurora.

"If Mari doesn't come back with my mother and the fae get ahold of that amulet, she'll be a traitor. And you know what happens to traitors of the crown."

They were fed to the vile beasts lurking in the darkest parts of the sea. And from the warning glinting in Luna's moon-like eyes, Aurora could see she was hungry for blood. Luna didn't understand that Mariana was already willing to die trying to save them all.

But Aurora would never let that happen.

"Be careful what you say, Luna. Like calls to like, and if you let that darkness consume you, there will be no coming back."

"There's no *darkness* in my soul," she spat. "Only the light of the moon. And *she* sees everything." She left with the whip of her tail, and Aurora shook her head.

The Goddess Selene was the "*she*" Luna referred to, whom Luna was named after. Sirens didn't pray to her like they did to Amphitrite—other than most of the cursed. Before the Scourge became a necessary evil, very few had even recognized her as a goddess. Something about that had always bothered Luna. She and many cursed sisters fully embraced what it meant to be one of Selene's Midnight Daughters—sirens who never wore armor enchanted by Cybele so they could bask in the sunshine, instead they chose the darkness of the sea under the full moon.

Even though Astra didn't understand Luna's fascination with the unpopular goddess, she had always accepted it. Told her daughter she could pray to whomever she heard in her heart. Aurora thought all of it was the craziest shit she'd ever heard. Who wouldn't want to feel the sun's warmth on their skin? See their scales glitter under the sunshine? Who would want to only see the world under the cover of darkness?

Luna would shout at her that she would always have the moonlight to guide her through the world, but that wasn't true. A new moon was always swallowed between the folds of the midnight sky. Something Luna seemed to forget, along with the fact that Astra had named her daughter Luna, not because she wanted her to become a Midnight Daughter, but because she was a celestial light of the heavens that brought hope to those trapped in darkness.

Aurora glanced down at the queen and sat on the other side of her bed, watching Malea repeatedly wipe Cybele's forehead. She wondered if what Luna had said was true.

Had Mari returned to Salus, and had Cybele somehow forced her heir back into the wild to fend for herself? It was difficult to believe, but Aurora knew deep down that Luna spoke what she thought was true.

"She's changed," Malea observed softly, glancing at the door Luna had exited through before her eyes landed on Aurora. "I know it isn't my place—"

Aurora held up her hand. "It's fine, Malea. You know it's fine. Please, continue."

As Queen Cybele's lady-in-waiting, Malea heard more than any other siren in the whole palace. She always refused to reveal a single hidden truth, but Aurora could see how she struggled.

"Malea," Aurora said gently. "Tell me."

Malea sighed. "The way Luna is behaving—it worries me. I always liked Astra, and you know I'd die for Princess Mariana, so if somehow Luna knows what's happened, then clearly, it's not being kept a secret."

Aurora went still.

Swallowing, Malea murmured, "Mariana came back through a portal the witch opened for her when she reached out for help. I didn't see what happened, but I heard Mariana say she thought a trap was waiting for her in Aurelia."

Aurora's stomach tightened, her mouth pressing into a thin, grim line. "The queen didn't listen to her," she added, knowing the answer.

Malea sadly shook her head. "The queen asked me to fetch Mariana's armor." Malea closed her eyes briefly, like the next part hurt her. "Then she told Mariana to go back to her captor. He'd lead her to Astra. And then I—" Malea averted her eyes briefly, biting her lip. "I heard gasping, like Mariana was in distress. I heard the witch say, 'You know what you have to do,' and said something like Mariana had to go back or she'd die. I still don't understand what she meant." Malea shook her head and continued wiping the queen's forehead. "I don't know, but the queen was on the floor the next moment, the princess was gone, and the witch was telling me not to say a word."

And yet Luna knew everything. There was only one other siren who could've told her.

"Thank you for sharing this with me, Malea. Your loyalty to Mariana doesn't go unnoticed."

Malea gave her a small smile, making Aurora's heart constrict with an old memory of when they had been courting each other. But that was a long time ago, before the Banishment.

Lifting her mother's limp, pale hand to her face, she kissed the top and got up from her seat.

Cybele's hand suddenly gripped her own. And what she mumbled loud enough for Aurora and Malea to hear made the room fall still.

CHAPTER 34

FOG DRIFTED AROUND MARIANA'S legs, the fine mist coating her exposed skin. She expected to shiver, but the sensation never came. She wrapped her arms around herself and noticed she was still wearing her long-sleeved top, chest armor, and leather pants, but her coat was missing. What had happened? Where was she? Where was Dax?

Mariana frowned. She was surrounded by a dark forest, with a pond that shimmer before her.

She stepped forward, realizing her boots were gone. The mud squished between her toes as she approached the pond. Something swirled beneath the water, sending gentle ripples across the surface. Kneeling, she gasped as her reflection stared back at her.

She was a siren again—

Her fingers brushed along her throat for the gills she could see in the reflection, but she felt nothing there. Glancing down at her hand, she saw that her skin wasn't the pale blue color the reflection showed; it was a beige color.

Disappointment flooded through her as she glared down at the pond. It was a trick.

A splash distracted her, but before she could see what caused it, her world swirled, and she was falling. Then, a bright light blinded her, and she felt grass beneath her hands.

She squinted, blinking as she tried to understand where she was.

Sunshine beamed down at her, warming her skin. A cool breeze swept through the trees, brushing along the skirt of her long white cotton dress. Wait—a dress?

She didn't recognize the gown at all. The gold thread woven at the edge of her sleeves looked like twinkling stars. The front had a celestial design of the sun emerging from behind clouds at the top, with the moon's rays of light shining out from below. The fabric stopped just above her ankles but flowed long behind her. It was the softest fabric she'd ever felt, and it clung to her every curve as if it had been made just for her.

A bird chirped overhead, drawing her attention high above to see a snow-covered mountain. She peered at the mountain's magnificence momentarily before wispy clouds edged in golden light covered it up. She let her eyes drift down to see a large lake. Boulders and fallen trees blocked off the edge of it. What leaked out from the confines of the dam flowed downward past her feet and over the edge of a cliff into the mist below. The trickle of water was like music to her ears, soothing and freeing, like the sound could carry her away.

Perhaps it already has, she thought distantly. This world felt as natural as the moss beneath her feet, yet she had the odd sensation that she was far from reality.

She couldn't remember anything from before this moment. Where was she? Glancing around her, she didn't recognize the trees with white trunks billowing around her. Slender, leafy branches swayed in the breeze as they reached up toward the sky. Tiny indigo flowers sprouted from the grass before her, beckoning her forward.

Mariana reached down to touch one of the petals, being as tender as possible, as she feared breaking the delicate flora. That was when a song whispered in her ears, riding the wind.

Standing, she glanced around, expecting to see someone nearby, but no one was there.

She knew the song. Her breath caught in her chest as she listened. There was a subtle waver as if dancing along the breeze and swirling around her in an enchanting hug.

Then ... the song stopped.

Her smile slowly faded. What happened?

Moments ticked by, and Mariana felt her hope slipping away. Then, a crisp breeze swept her dress and hair back from her face, again bringing along the enchanting melody. This time, she walked in the direction it was coming from.

Mariana smiled. Tears glistened in her eyes, and her feet obediently followed the sound.

She still couldn't make out the words, even as the song grew louder. She wished to understand what it was saying. As the tempo sped up, her footsteps quickened.

She cleared the mass of trees, and the music stopped.

Mariana stared at a shimmering wall. It sparkled and glimmered like a million stars sewn together into a massive mural that spanned as far as she could see.

What in the world could it be? And why had the song led her to it?

She took a few tentative steps toward the wall. It shimmered as if her presence was affecting it somehow, and when she was only an arm's length away, she stopped.

Unsure of what to do next, she had begun to lift a shaky hand toward the wall when a soft voice spoke from behind her.

"*Listen.*"

Mariana spun around, her heart racing against her ribs. But there was nothing.

She huffed a breath and brushed her hair away from her face. As she turned back toward the wall, she heard it again.

"*Wilted hearts spring anew when the stars sing their song over the sea. Listen,*" the ethereal voice whispered beside her, though she knew nothing was there. The words were perplexing. What did it mean?

"Who are you?" she asked breathlessly.

"*High tides wash away scarlet tears staining the forgotten. The crimson sea roars, glittering and gasping as it retreats. Luminaries sing bright like the sun under the cunning moon, guiding the way. Follow carefully.*"

Mariana shook her head in confusion. "Follow it where?"

"*Salvation,*" the voice whispered hot against her ear. Then everything dropped out from under her.

CHAPTER 35

DAX CALLED MARI'S NAME again for the fifth time, and she gasped awake.

"Finally." He chuckled. "You were stuck so far in your dream, I thought I might have to drag you out."

Mari shook her head and cleared her throat. "Are we almost there?" she asked, glancing around. Dawn had finally graced the sky.

"Yeah, we're here."

Mari groaned, gripping her hips.

"Sore?"

She nodded, then let out a soft gasp as Aurelia's glinting gates came into view.

The gates were magnificent. The copper and gold motif depicted a large sun shining from high above the mountains, shrouded in swirling clouds. A single person holding a sword pointed straight toward the heavens, with a billowing cape in the center. Just below, three figures knelt before the fae with the sword.

General Magnus. Pronouncing his victory over the fae realm when he established the kingdom of Aurelia. The other three kneeling figures must've been the other Generals.

Dax didn't pay much attention to it, whereas Mari peered at it in amazement. Instead, he met the curious eyes of all the fae guards opening the gates for them.

Cyrus held his head high as he entered first, then glanced back at Dax with a smug grin. "Keep up, Dax. I'd hate for you to get lost without me to guide you."

Dax was tempted to throw one of his daggers at the male's cocky face. Gods, he wanted to kill him. But knew what would happen if he did. Gripping the reins tighter, he guided the horse through the cobblestone streets.

People dressed in colorful clothing and adorned with jewelry haggled with the merchants or chatted away as they sipped morning spirits at eateries with enticing, delicious smells.

They passed the city center, where a prominent statue, three or four stories tall and carved from a single piece of marble, stood. It depicted a male with long hair shouting up at the sky. The robes along his form seemed to ripple in an imaginary wind.

"Who is that?" Mari asked him.

Dax shrugged. "It's not clear. Some believe it to be a symbol of contempt for the gods who left. Others believe the gods cursed this male to stare up at them forever."

No one knew who made it, but it felt God-given, especially after it had withstood the Infernal Wars. Thus, General Magnus declared the capital city of Aurelia to be built around it.

"Why are they praying to it if they have no idea who it is?"

"Everyone needs someone to pray to," he murmured, watching the few Aurelians placing their hands on the statue's base as they whispered their greatest fears, wishes, and dreams. They believed someone was listening.

"Even you?"

The question startled him. When he glanced down at Mari, who had turned slightly to glance sidelong at him over her shoulder, he saw the underlying curiosity swirling in her ocean eyes.

Dax shook his head. The gods wouldn't listen. They never had, and they never would.

Mari didn't say anything, but her eyes told him she had questions. He was thankful when she turned back to stare ahead.

"Wow," he heard Mari breathe, and a corner of his mouth lifted. He followed her gaze to the mansions lining this side of the city. Some of the large buildings had sculpted marble columns carved with depictions of the Gods and Generals of war. Stunning motifs glowed with lights along the walls of several establishments as the wealthy flaunted their prosperity.

They crossed the long stone bridge leading to another gate—this one a solid piece of pure white crystal, enchanted with deadly spells for those who tried to climb it unbidden.

Mari's breath hitched, head tilted to gaze up at the dominating height of the palace.

Dax took a steadying breath as the gate opened to a large, manicured courtyard with a glittering fountain. He'd stared into that mosaic fountain before, wondering what in the Seven Seas he was doing with his life.

And now he was thinking the same as the approaching guards ordered him and Mari off the horse.

Dax held Mari's arm as she struggled to stand straight after being on the horse for so long. But when she glanced up, he heard her murmur, "*Beautiful*."

He had to admit, it was true. The grounds surrounding the palace were meticulously maintained, with paths winding through beds of vibrant winter flowers that thrived in the cold morning air. Statues of mythical creatures and legendary figures spread around the landscape, adding to the sense of wonder.

"Ahh, friends! This is where I leave you," Cyrus called from atop his horse, making Dax grit his teeth. "It was *not* a pleasure escorting you. However, I have a feeling we'll see each other again. Perhaps next time, it *will* be a pleasure!" He smiled down at them, but Mari promptly ignored him, absorbed in the serene landscaping, while Dax glared up at him.

"Perhaps next time, I'll get the chance to punch those pearly whites into your skull."

Cyrus winced and *tsked*. "You're very violent. You really should talk to someone about that," he said nonchalantly, making Dax growl.

Cyrus glanced down at Mari, who finally met his serious gaze. "Be careful around this one," he said in a low voice before nudging his horse and galloping toward the royal stables.

Mari turned and glanced between Dax's tight fists and the angry look on his face. "Wow, he really got to you, huh?"

Ignoring the question, he nudged her toward the tall bronze doors. Six guards trailed behind them, and three more guided the way.

"What a welcoming party," Mari muttered, and Dax felt his eyebrows lift briefly in agreement.

The doors opened inward. Two sentinels dressed in gleaming, spotless armor stepped aside to hold the massive doors. Their entourage of guards led them into the garden. Somehow, it was even more extravagant than the courtyard.

Spring was just beginning to whisper its presence, and the garden responded with an almost ethereal beauty. Closed, colorful flower buds dotted the edge of a pond, awaiting the breath of warmth to reveal their hidden beauty. The pond rippled slightly, and Dax's eyes caught on the vibrant hues of colorful fish darting beneath. Fish that enjoyed eating warm flesh. He kept that little fact to himself as Mari gazed around in wonder.

The garden was a marvel, a sanctuary amidst the stone and grandeur, where every flower, every statue, and every path seemed to whisper secrets of beauty and power. But Dax knew those whispers were laced with danger.

"I'm glad to see you finally made it," a songbird voice called from the second-story balcony. Dax gritted his teeth as he dragged his eyes up. There, high above the rest, stood the princess in all her golden fucking glory.

CHAPTER 36

A BRIGHT LIGHT SHONE through the opening behind the princess, revealing her silhouette.

Halia descended a set of stone stairs and approached them. She was even more striking than Mariana had imagined. Tight onyx curls spilled over one shoulder to her waist from where a crown of woven emeralds and diamonds nestled on her head, glinting in the light. Thick black eyelashes surrounded her slightly upturned, warm, maple eyes, accented by a line of sharp black ink. The dark brown skin on her high cheekbones was dusted with gold, and her plump magenta-painted lips must've attracted admirers from around the world.

"It is truly wonderful to meet you, Mariana. I'm Halia, princess and heir to the Kingdom of Aurelia," she declared, her arrogance on display. The intricate gold-painted designs on her hands shimmered like the glittering dress she wore as she extended them to either side, before folding them gracefully in front of her.

Was *she* the Matriarch?

"Where's my sister?" Mariana asked, knowing her tone was far more severe than she'd intended. But that was who she truly wanted to see.

Halia's mouth lifted into a small smile that didn't reach her eyes. "You've had a long journey. Why don't we show you to your room before we discuss—"

"You wanted me here by morning. Here I am. I don't need rest, I need to see my sister. Where's Astra?"

Halia dropped her smile. "Hand over your weapons and follow me," she ordered.

Mari reluctantly handed Dax her dagger, trusting him to keep it safe.

Halia flipped her hair over her shoulder and led them into the palace. Dax held Mari's arm lightly. The trail of guards formed a circle around them the moment they all passed through the gleaming wooden doors held open by sentries standing tall in their impeccable white uniforms.

The morning light streamed through the entryway, casting long shadows onto the tiled marble floor. Warm air greeted Mariana, soothing the spring chill outside. The sound of their steps filled the ample space, but Mariana tuned it all out at what she saw.

A tropical paradise filled with lush greenery and blooming flowers lined their path. Tall palm trees shot up toward the domed glass roof, revealing the pale sky still waking from its slumber. The sound of water trickling caught her attention as they rounded a bend in the path, revealing a creek flowing through the palace. It was beautiful. An ethereal wonder that anything like this even existed—especially through the harsh winters Mariana had heard so much about.

The path diverged into several routes, some through carved white stone archways, and others leading down curving stairwells.

"This way," Halia called, breaking the spell. She began walking up a wide staircase with sparkly white veins running through the sandstone. The click of her heels was like the steady drip of water before a dam broke. It reverberated through Mariana's head, killing the soothing sounds of the paradise surrounding them.

Dax gave her a sad smile and pulled her up the staircase. Their muddy boots left a trail behind that someone was already wiping away.

They walked down a hallway full of paintings. Some were landscapes, others of people enjoying parties, dancing, and scandalous debauchery—some of which made Mariana blush and turn her face toward the polished floor. She could see herself in its reflection and wondered if she'd just walked straight into the den of the beast.

After what felt like years of walking, Halia finally approached a set of arched double doors. Mariana inspected the details carved around it as Halia unlocked the doors. Her head tilted at the sight of sirens swimming, elements of the sea surrounding their tiny forms. Why would a fae palace have any reference to her people?

Halia pushed the doors open wide and stepped into the darkness within.

Mariana held her breath as they all followed. Dax dropped his hand, and Mariana found herself missing the contact.

Light suddenly spilled into the room, temporarily blinding Mariana, as curtains on the far side were pulled open. Halia turned, hands clasped together, and walked back over to them through the beam of light. The touch of a cruel smile graced her face.

"How does it feel to be in your mother's wing of the palace, princess?"

Mariana squinted at her. "What are you talking about?" she murmured. Then, her eyes caught on a large painting hanging high above a dusty fireplace, and everything came crashing down.

She couldn't breathe.

Within the ornate gold frame was the startling image of Queen Cybele and King Stavros, sitting side by side and holding hands.

Her hands shot up to her mouth, her stomach instantly nauseous.

"Interesting, isn't it?" Halia began taking slow, steady steps toward her. "The person your mother was in love with is the same one who banished your people. Killed *thousands* with a single order." She held up a manicured finger before dropping it back down. "Tore down your beloved queendom into the pile of rubble it is today, burying the corpses of your dead sisters." Halia stopped in front of her, close enough that Mariana was tempted to slap her for even daring to speak of her people. "And yet he built an entire wing of the palace just for her." Halia lifted her hands and gazed around the gloomy, forgotten space.

"This—" Mariana's fisted hands shook with building rage. "It can't be true. This is an illusion. A lie!"

Halia *tsked,* shaking her head. "You know, you can yell like a child, but it won't change anything. This is all very, *very* real."

Mariana instantly hated her. Hated the way she smelled of gardenias and honey. Hated the way her skin shimmered and gleamed. Hated the way every hair on her head seemed perfectly in place. She especially hated the stupid smile on her face, like this was exactly the reaction she'd hoped for.

"Where's my sister? Where's Astra?" she ground out.

Halia straightened and stared down her stupid, perfect nose at Mariana from the few inches of height her heels granted her. "She's gone. And you're going to find out where she went."

Astra is ... gone.

Mariana's wide eyes snapped to Dax, who wouldn't meet her gaze. *Did he know this whole time?*

She shook her head and glanced back at the princess. "No, you're lying."

Halia tilted her head. "You know I'm not. You're smart, Mariana. So was your sister." She turned on her heels and walked to a white desk covered in old parchment. "Astra came here to strike a deal with the king. She wanted to bargain for the sirens' claim on their fallen queendom. Luckily, I found her first."

Wait—"The king doesn't know about Astra?"

Halia let out a short laugh and shook her head. "I couldn't let your sister meet with my father, considering she was willing to help him bring back my brother—his *precious son.*" Halia spat, rested her hip against the desk, picked up a book covered in delicate gold leaf designs, and flipped through it. "Astra told me she was a scholar. And that she knew that within her mother's library, there were texts that held the location of an amulet." She slammed the book with a loud *bang* and met Mariana's eyes. "Seraphina's amulet. Heard of it?"

Mariana's gaze never wavered, revealing nothing. Though her heart was pounding so hard beneath her ribs, she could hardly breathe.

Slowly, a smile spread over Halia's face. "Yes, I believe you have." She set the book down and rested her hands on the desk behind her, clinking the gold rings adorning every finger. "The amulet is said to have the power to bring back someone from the Eternal Sands. Its powers beyond that are a mystery, but one thing is certain. You, my dear Mariana, are the only one who can activate it."

What? Mariana's brows furrowed in confusion as what the princess said washed over her. "What are you talking about?"

Ignoring her question, Halia continued. "I arranged for you to be brought here after I discovered that Astra had gone missing and took a valuable piece of information with her." Halia stood at full height and slowly walked toward her. "You came all this way to save your sweet sister. And you still can. All you have to do is find out where she went."

Astra knew where the amulet was and didn't want it getting into Halia's hands.

"What do you plan on doing with the amulet?" Mariana asked, though she knew the answer was simple. It was all about power. Something it seemed Halia had always wanted.

Halia smiled down at her. "Don't worry about that. For now, get some rest. I'll have some food delivered, and feel free to request anything you desire. Once you find the amulet's location, we'll find your sister." The way Halia said the last part had Mariana grinding her teeth.

Conniving snake.

Halia exited the desolate chambers shrouded in secrets and sorrow with her guards close behind her. The only one who remained was Dax. He hesitated as if there was more he wanted to say.

"Did you know?" Mariana asked in a low tone. She knew the answer but needed to hear him say it.

Dax sighed heavily, his shoulders sagging, and rubbed his forehead. "Yes." Dropping his hand, he met her stare and held it steady. "I had to do everything I could to get you here alive and well."

Mariana scoffed and gave him a closed-lip smile with a shake of her head. "Mission accomplished." Then she clocked him right in the jaw.

Dax grunted and held his face before working his jaw.

"Get out," she muttered.

He met her eyes, and something within her snapped.

"GET OUT!" she screamed.

Dax took a startled step back.

Mariana's eyes flooded with tears. She shook with rage and quickly turned, refusing to let him see her cry. She wrapped her arms around herself, listening as his hesitant footsteps faded.

As the door shut and the deadbolt locked her into her mother's abandoned chambers, Mariana dropped to her knees and screamed. The sun's pale light shimmered from behind retreating clouds, casting ghostly shadows around her broken soul.

CHAPTER 37

DAX LISTENED TO MARIANA'S rage from outside the door. Bangs and crashes soon followed as he listened to the pain he caused her. When her screams turned to sobs, he stayed until he couldn't take it anymore and quickly walked away.

He headed for his living quarters on the other side of the palace, where all the palace servants stayed.

As soon as the door shut behind him, he looked around the space he hadn't seen for weeks and sighed heavily. All he wanted to do was go back to Mari and explain himself, but nothing he could say would do any good.

Dax gripped his neck and walked toward the modest leather couch on the far side of the room before sitting down.

Big windows let in the sunshine that couldn't mask the life-less feeling in the brick-walled, tidy living room. Dax had all the basics he could need: a desk stacked with paperwork, a bookshelf sparsely filled with books, a small kitchenette he never used, and a sitting area he hardly relaxed in. Dax's eyes traveled to the two doors on the other side of the room. One led to his bedroom with a small attached bathroom. And the other ... He eyed the padlock still attached to the door handle. He didn't have an inkling of desire to open that one. He couldn't even remember the last time he'd entered that room.

Though it was nice to be back in his own space, nothing about his residence made him feel at home. It was a place to escape and sleep. That was it.

Gripping his hands together, he leaned his elbows on his knees and thought of Kythera. He missed it already. The peaceful, serene forest. The calm silence—

His door flew open.

"I heard you were back! About time!" Kosta shouted as he walked in with an outrageous swagger that everyone loved. Dax shook his head and stood up, one side of his mouth lifting at his obnoxious friend.

Kosta's informality was reserved for only when the aristocrats were absent. Otherwise, he was a stern Lieutenant of the Royal Guard. By the look of the steel helmet in his hand, his short, dark brown hair dripping sweat at the curling ends, and the smear of dirt on his tan face, Dax knew he'd just come from training.

Kosta was as dedicated as they came. He always worked hard to ensure the palace stayed safe. He was an excellent fighter and had the intuition of a thousand-year-old monk. Honestly, Kosta would've made a fine captain if he wasn't so fiercely protective of his younger sister, Ophelia, who also lived in the palace. Unfortunately, Dax knew what his friend would do if it came down to either saving her life or the royal family's. Thankfully, wherever Halia went, Ophelia seemed to be close behind.

Dax clapped Kosta's outstretched hand and gripped it tightly before slumping back on the couch. Kosta took the opposite seat with a smug grin on his face. Dax lifted an eyebrow.

"So," Kosta drawled. "What's the siren like? You took longer to get back than I expected."

Dax snorted. "You lost a bet, didn't you?"

"Hell yeah, I did!"

They laughed, but Kosta's eyes told Dax he wouldn't let it go.

Truthfully, Dax didn't want to talk about Mari at all, to anyone. He was trying to protect her, to keep curious eyes and minds as far away as possible.

Protective and possessive are two different things.

Clearing his throat, Dax shrugged and replied, "There were a few roadblocks along the way."

"Well, I can't wait to read that report."

Dax couldn't help grinding his teeth as he gave a tight-lipped smile.

"Agreed," a melodic, feminine voice purred from the door, and both males stood up straight as Halia waltzed in. "Although, we don't want any prying eyes to acquire such information. Perhaps we shall have a verbal debrief instead, Dax?"

Dax inclined his head. "Of course, Your Highness."

Halia's maple eyes shifted between them, making them both unsteady.

"Now that the siren is here, I want to make it very clear that this is to be kept strictly confidential." When they both agreed, Halia smiled. "Good. Please excuse us, lieutenant. Dax, come with me."

Dax threw Kosta a look that said, *See you later, if I survive this*, and followed Halia to the door.

He kept his gaze straight ahead and not on the sensual sway of Halia's hips, like he knew she'd hoped. He wasn't surprised by the act; Halia had made it clear over the years that she would've taken him into her bed whenever he liked. Unfortunately for her, arrogance was a turn-off. And despite her efforts to hide the truth, Dax knew who her heart truly belonged to.

Each click of her heels on the polished floor made him want to flee, but he continued following her to her study. Once inside, Halia shut the door with a soft click.

Although Halia gave off the impression that she craved Dax's desire, the only person she truly cared about was the female dressed in white sitting in a burgundy velvet chair across the room.

Ophelia was a Seer and one of the last known descendants of General Minerva. Though she reigned from House Spirit, she knew very little of her abilities other than the few things mentioned in ancient texts, since no one alive could teach her. She mostly listened to spirits that told her the secrets locked behind closed doors or conjured the occasional spirit shadow, like the one Cyrus had said was a gift from the Matriarch, which had been pulled from the Veil by Ophelia.

She did anything and everything the princess asked of her.

Halia sat down at her grand, pale oak desk, detailed with gold lines, and regarded them with a scrutinizing stare. She gestured for Dax to sit beside Ophelia, and he reluctantly obliged.

"I want the amulet secured as fast as possible. And I want you two to get Mariana to find out exactly where her sister went."

Dax held back a scoff. "Do you honestly think Astra would've kept anything that revealed the location here in the palace for just *anyone* to find?"

Halia shook her head and lightly threaded her fingers together in front of her. "Not just anyone. Mariana. She knew I was going to have her sister brought here, and I'm willing to bet she left her some indication about where the amulet is."

"There has to be something in the library," Ophelia noted softly. "That's where Astra was searching before ..." She let the rest of her words hang in the air. Then she cleared her throat, and her eyes shifted with uncertainty between Halia and Dax. "I'll bring Mariana some food and get it started." She stood.

"Wait," Dax blurted, and averted his gaze. "Just ... make sure you don't give her any meat."

Ophelia gave him a small smile and a nod before quietly leaving the study with soft steps.

When they were alone, Halia stood and walked over to a tall mirror hanging above a burning marble fireplace. She ran her fingers through her hair as she glanced at him in the reflection.

"Speak freely."

Dax heard it. The shift in her voice revealed that she was the cold-blooded Matriarch beneath her pretty golden exterior.

Whether that title had been given to her by her cohorts, her victims, or she'd bestowed it upon herself didn't matter. Halia was proud when she heard it whispered under people's breath in the dead of night, like a prayer, or under the bright sun like a curse. And it kept her illicit schemes secret from her father.

Two summers ago, when a diplomat was found murdered in his home, the Matriarch had been the primary suspect. King

Stavros ordered his spies to identify the culprit, but nothing was found. The Matriarch was just a phantom in the wind and a slice to the throat when no one was looking. Despite Halia's claim that she wasn't involved in the diplomat's death when Dax asked her, he knew there had been a quarrel between the two before the incident. Like everything the Matriarch got involved in, the truth was washed away along with the blood she hired someone to spill.

Dax bit the inside of his cheek. "Why did you send Cyrus and those goons after us?"

"You know why," she said, keeping her eyes steady on herself as she reapplied her lipstick.

"One of them had widow toxin coating his blade. It almost killed me."

Smacking her lips together, she placed the lipstick on the white mantel and finally met his eyes. "But it didn't." Spinning, she walked over to him and touched his shoulder. She tilted her head down to look at him from under heavy lashes. "You know I'd never let anything happen to you," she said sweetly.

Dax's jaw tightened. "How much does Cyrus know?"

"As much as I want him to know." She stepped away from him to look out at the glittering sea from a row of windows. "You see, Daxon, I go to great lengths to ensure my trust is given to those who deserve it. And when I can sense that someone's loyalties are not as strong as they should be, I'm required to test them."

She turned. The sly glint in her eye made Dax shift in his seat and avert his gaze. He knew what she was getting at, and all he could think was how to prove he was still loyal to her. Or had he already? The question hung heavy in the air, and Dax's eyebrows lowered as what she said settled in.

He landed furious eyes on her. "You sent me to abduct Mariana as a *test?*"

Halia walked over to him with the grace of a panther stalking its prey. Each step of her gold and black stilettos *clicked* against the hardwood floor, reverberating in his eardrums. "I sent you to *retrieve* Mariana. After my other precious siren escaped so *unexpectedly*, I took a closer look at all those who claimed to be loyal to me."

She knew what had happened. She knew what Dax had done and chose to punish him by capturing Mari.

Dax held his ground. He knew his importance to her. Otherwise, she would've just had him killed.

"You completed the mission, and for that, I commend you. However." Halia sat on her desk in front of him. When her dress parted, her exposed, long legs brushed his, and as she leaned in, her exotic floral perfume wafted toward him. "I've learned that a wolf can follow its handler's orders just as well as it can bite them the moment they turn their back." Halia licked her plump lips and fluttered her thick lashes like he'd seen her do countless times before. "Tell me, Daxon, are you a wolf? Are you *my* wolf?" she whispered seductively.

He knew it was all an act, and she expected him to play his part.

He pushed himself off the chair and stood tall above her. Leaning in close, Dax tilted her chin with his fingers, and watched her painted lips part. "Don't keep me in the dark, Matriarch. Otherwise, this partnership ends."

Dropping his hand from her chin, Dax marched toward the door, determined to leave.

Halia started cackling, making the hair on the back of his neck rise.

"You say that like you have the choice."

Her words stopped him in his tracks. He stared at the door, wishing he could tell her to fuck off. But he couldn't.

"Daxon," Halia crooned. He reluctantly turned around, eyeing her where she lounged on the desk, her skirts still open, but at least she crossed her legs. "Don't forget why you're here. You're *mine* for as long as you want to keep your little village safe and sound." Her eyes glinted with the underlying meaning of her words: *Obey or lose everything*.

CHAPTER 38

WHEN MARIANA'S THROAT TURNED raw, and the fury in her heart simmered down, she opened her eyes and gasped. The crystal chandelier above her rattled. Papers that had been on the desk were floating back to the ground. The wide-open drapes still billowed in a dying breeze.

"What the ..." she murmured in confusion.

She stood on shaky legs and searched for an open door or any other source of the sudden gust of wind, but found none.

Weird.

Clearing her throat, she diverted her attention from the strange wind to thinking of Astra. How would she have found the amulet? Would she have left a clue? Something for Mariana to find? Did she even know Mariana would come after she'd escaped?

Scrubbing her face with her hands, she huffed and glanced around the disheveled space.

She shook her head, ignoring the familiar buzz fading under her skin. She was exhausted, but she had to start searching.

She flipped off the confusing painting of King Stavros, who looked at her mother like she was his whole world, then scanned the papers littering the ground.

When the foyer yielded nothing, she went upstairs, searching for any sign of her sister. Instead, she found traces of her mother's past life, before the Banishment. It was like opening a door to a world she'd never imagined. It felt like a haunted tomb.

The second floor had four bedchambers; the first two were adequately furnished, and the third one was completely empty. Mariana paused at the fourth door at the end of the hall. It was her mother's old bedchamber. She could feel it.

Every instinct yelled at her to turn around, that she had no right to enter without permission. But a small part of her nudged her forward, whispering that Cybele would've wanted her to go in. Taking a deep breath, she stepped silently onto the plush ivory carpet and entered the forbidden space.

Though the queen was far away within Salus, Mariana hesitated to touch anything, fearing she'd disturb the priceless relics. The armoire beckoned her forward. It was likely filled with colorful dresses sewn with the finest thread by the best seamstresses.

She had never been allowed in her mother's chambers in Salus without explicit permission—which she'd never received. She had no idea what it looked like. This part of her mother's life felt strangely intimate, a part of Cybele's past that had never been revealed to Mariana or Aurora.

Wait ...

Were the other bedchambers meant for her and her sisters? Had Cybele planned for a part of their future to be in Aurelia?

Mariana hadn't been born yet, so Cybele would have been trying to have another child. One bedchamber for each daughter … the empty one meant for her heir.

Not sure what to think, she kept exploring. On the vanity, the makeup bottles, brushes, and jars were neatly organized. Colorful glass perfume bottles lined a shelf below a gold-rimmed mirror.

Cybele wore perfume? The idea was strange since sirens didn't wear scents. Mariana wondered what they smelled like, wondered what her mother had worn around her lover, but her hands remained firmly by her sides. She had no right to touch her mother's personal items and feared disturbing the way they had been left a century ago.

Then, it occurred to her that someone must have been cleaning the wing occasionally. Otherwise, it would've been in worse condition.

After leaving the bedroom, she made her way downstairs through a curved doorway into a study. The musty smell from the lack of fresh air tickled her nose. Dust coated every surface except the desk, the few pages and books lying about, and the lonely pen, sticky with ink that had bled dry from its tip. It could've been a sign her sister was here, but she had no way of knowing for sure.

With a groan of frustration, she began inspecting the desk. Her eyes caught on a book with blue swirls and foreign letters on the cover. She didn't recognize the language. Picking up the book, she was surprised by its weight. She'd never held a book before, considering all siren knowledge was stored within the orbs inside the Athenaeum beneath Salus.

Staring at the book, she opened it and flipped through, surprised at how much she enjoyed the smell of the paper and the sound of the pages brushing against each other. It reminded her of when she and Astra had daydreamed about restoring Sirenia. She wanted to open up her own public library. And somehow, Mariana had to find her and allow her to do just that. Setting the book down, she took a deep breath.

A closed door across the room beckoned her. She walked toward the door, then slowly turned the ornate brass handle, unsure of what she would find on the other side, and swung it open.

Her jaw dropped.

The famous library.

Taking a few hesitant steps forward, she glanced around the space, overwhelmed by its sheer size. Two stories of books taunted her with their hidden knowledge.

Her lungs seized, and she speared her fingers through her hair, pulling it back from her eyes. Gazing around the lifeless room housing silk sofas, she scanned the painted walls lined with bookshelves. Cream-colored velvet drapes hung heavy over the windows, keeping most of the light out.

Fear coated her insides like oil. Defeat loomed in the distance with a darkness that threatened to swallow her whole.

How was she supposed to find anything in this immense place? How was she supposed to find her sister or the amulet? It was insane.

She sat down on the polished hardwood floor in the middle of the library. Leaning her head back, she inspected the room. Her eyes wandered over a large antique mirror and colorful paintings of the sea, settling on the murals along the walls. The north, east, and west walls all depicted a forest with white birds flying by, and the southern wall, the only one with windows instead of bookshelves, presented a glittering horizon over the sea.

Mariana recognized the white-barked trees, the slender leaves sprouting from them, the indigo flowers blooming near the white baseboards, the white-feathered birds, and the mountain in the distance.

Standing up, she slowly turned in a circle as her mind reeled. Her heart pounded, filling her ears with its beating rhythm.

She'd seen the place in the mural before—in her strange dream.

Was it near Sirenia? Had the person in her dream been showing her where Astra was? Or was it merely a coincidence that the painted walls of her mother's library matched her vision?

"Mariana?" a light and soft feminine voice called out distantly. It didn't sound like Halia.

Mariana quickly moved into the study. Glancing around, she grabbed a candle holder and tested its weight as she silently approached the foyer.

An elegant, dainty fae wrapped in an ivory hooded dress stood in the middle of the room holding a silver tray. Tight golden curls highlighted with lilac streaks spilled from beneath the hood. When the fae glanced up, she spotted Mariana, and her eyes widened.

Mariana kept the candle holder clutched tightly in front of her as she took a few steps forward. Standing by the door behind the female was an attractive but menacing fae male. His attention was focused solely on Mariana, and she couldn't help it when her face heated under his steely gaze. He appeared every bit the terrifying warrior, ready to kill. Tousled, short dark hair, a sharp jaw locked tight and covered in stubble. The hours of training he endured under a blazing sun were evident from his tanned skin and the large muscles straining beneath his polished armor.

"Hi," the female squeaked and carefully stepped forward, lifting the tray with her gloved hands. "I brought you some food. Can I set it down somewhere?"

Mariana stepped back, not saying anything. She wasn't sure what the female had been sent here to do, but she didn't look like any ordinary servant. Her clothing looked soft and silky, leather sandals buckled with gold. Even her makeup appeared skillfully applied. And the guard behind her looked ready to defend if necessary.

"Who are you?" Mariana was surprised the female didn't wince at her fierce tone. Instead, her freckled cheeks turned a bright shade of pink as she walked over to the fireplace.

She set the tray down on a small, round table between two dusty chairs and lifted the covering. "My name is Ophelia. That's Kosta brooding by the door. He won't hurt you." She set the lid down and presented the steaming food on the plate to Mariana. "And I certainly am not here to hurt you either. Care to eat?"

Mariana's eyes shifted between Kosta and Ophelia, desperately trying to keep her stomach from grumbling at the delicious smell drifting from the tray.

Ophelia gave her a hesitant smile and poured a glass of water from a silver pitcher. "I can't imagine what you've been through. I would be frightened too if I were you. I mean, honestly, I probably would be dead by now." She chuckled, and Kosta shot Ophelia a dark look from the corner of his eye.

Interesting.

Mariana noted all the weapons on the guard, then shifted her gaze to the female now sitting in one of the plush velvet chairs in front of the fireplace. Mariana then noticed the female's legs were also covered in tight white leggings that stopped just short of her ankles. The female's face and feet were the only parts of her where her pale skin was visible.

"Kosta, is there any chance you can request the fireplace to be lit? It's chilly in here," Ophelia said to the guard, rubbing her hands over her arms.

Kosta glared at Mariana for a long moment before slightly opening one of the double doors and whispering to the person outside. A few silent minutes later, a servant arrived, quickly built a fire, then disappeared again.

Mariana grew irritated by the guard's hateful gaze. His eyes were like molten silver. She set down the candle holder before cautiously approaching the tray, where Ophelia sat patiently.

She believed the fae wasn't here to hurt her, considering she appeared and sounded harmless. Keeping her breathing steady, Mariana sat in the chair across from Ophelia, who smiled brightly.

"Dax let me know what you would enjoy. I hope it's to your liking," Ophelia said as she gestured to the plate filled with different types of roasted vegetables and fresh fruit.

Flavor exploded over Mariana's tongue, and she had to stop herself from moaning.

Once the plate was empty, Ophelia again covered the tray with a satisfied grin.

"There, I'm sure that will make the search easier. Want some help?"

Mariana stared at the female in confusion as she wiped her mouth with a cloth napkin. "Help?"

"Yes, with finding out where your sister went."

"Why?"

Ophelia shrugged. "I've got nothing better to do at the moment, and I enjoy a good mystery."

Mariana shook her head. "No, why would I want you to help me?"

"I imagine you want to find her quickly, and in that case, you need help." The female stood and strode with purpose toward the study, leaving Mariana gaping after her.

The guard's dark eyes never left Mariana, who suddenly wanted to follow the strange female.

"Looks like you've already searched the study. Let's look in the library." Ophelia turned from the messy desk. Mariana trailed behind her.

"This library is amazing!" Ophelia shouted up toward the arched two-story ceiling of painted clouds. "It always takes my breath away when I walk in."

"You've been allowed in here before?"

Ophelia averted her gaze and tugged on a loose curl. "No one is *supposed* to be in here, but ..." She swung her arms out and spun in a circle, "Look at all this! How anyone can keep this locked away for no one to enjoy is beyond me."

Mariana glanced around the room and wondered the same. "I can only imagine the king hates this place. I'm surprised he didn't have it destroyed."

"Oh, he would *never*." Ophelia scoffed, but her eyes widened. She peeked an eye at Kosta quickly before turning away and strolling down the length of the library toward the impressive windows at the end.

Mariana stared after her. Was she not supposed to have said that? Why wouldn't the king want it destroyed? Didn't he hate sirens and Cybele?

With furrowed brows and eyes watching every detail, Mariana studied how Ophelia easily navigated the library. She knew this place well. Clearly, she had an ulterior motive for being here, and Mariana had a feeling it was because Halia had sent her in to find the amulet's location.

"So, your sister was very intrigued by siren history and always seemed to be in this section here." Ophelia stopped in front of a bookshelf that had a wooden ladder directly beside it. Mariana approached her and stared at the books.

"How do you know?"

"Because I was helping with her research," she replied, setting her hands on her hips and inspecting the shelves. "Huh, that's odd. Everything is out of place. None of the books on these shelves are where they should be. They're all out of order."

If Mariana knew anything about Astra, it was that she hated disorder. She loved organizing so much that she had the habit of straightening up all of her sisters' rooms, despite their protesting. If what Ophelia said was true, then this was a sign her sister wanted her to find something.

"Uh—Ophelia," Mariana started, and the fae turned to her with a hesitant smile. "I'd like to search on my own, please. I appreciate the help, but—"

Ophelia lifted her hands. "Say no more. I'm happy to let you have your time alone. If you ever need me, though, just say my name out loud, and I'll hear you." Mariana squinted and tilted her head, unsure how she would just *hear* her. But before she could ask, Ophelia gave her a little wave and walked out, Kosta following her.

As soon as they were gone, Mariana took a deep breath and began pulling books from the shelf that she hoped held the answers she so desperately needed.

CHAPTER 39

THE SILENCE THAT GREETED Dax the moment he entered the med bay was peaceful, and he welcomed its calming effect on him. He spotted the white-robed female holding the hands of a crying male and could barely hear her soft words.

Ophelia's eyes were black, starry orbs. Her heart-shaped lips uttered soft words to the distressed male. She was deep in the spirit realm.

"She's at peace and pain-free," Ophelia murmured. "She says to take care of the children. Watch them grow up, she says, and enjoy every moment you can, and know that she'll be right there the entire time. She loves you."

The male's head dipped, his dark hair falling over his wrinkled eyes. "Oh, Celia," he sobbed, his body shaking with grief. Ophelia winced as her eyes turned back to their pale rose hue, and she put a gentle hand on his shoulder, staying with him until the tears stopped.

Dax recognized the servant, though he'd never spoken to him. He considered how fortunate the palace workers were to have access to the royal med bay and that Ophelia offered her services to those grieving. Despite the minor pains it caused her.

"Thank you, Seer. What you've done for me ... I cannot thank you enough. My dear Celia never deserved to suffer. The cancer consumed her before we had any chance to stop it. I was so angry, and now, I see that she's in a much better place." The male sniffed and wiped his eyes with the tissue she handed him.

"She is," Ophelia assured with a small smile. "And one day, when your time comes, you will be reunited once again. Until then, enjoy being with your children. Do as Celia asked and watch over them."

They both stood, and Ophelia kept a steadying hand on his arm as they walked to the entrance, passing Dax, who kept his head down.

"Seer." The male paused and gazed at Ophelia with hope. "Is it true that Celia's spirit will be with us? If I speak to her, will she hear me?"

Ophelia nodded. "Yes, the spirit world is kind. For those who wish to remain close to their loved ones, the Eternal Sands holds their place for them in the desert until they are ready to rest. Your Celia will remain close to you within the Veil for as long as you and your children need her." Ophelia squeezed the male's hands and gave him a reassuring smile.

He sniffed, thanked her with a relieved smile, and exited the med bay.

Ophelia turned to Dax and clasped her hands in front of her.

"Strange seeing you here. I thought you hated the clinic," she said with a lifted brow and a curious smile.

"On the contrary, it's the doctors I don't like. I prefer the healers outside the palace."

"Ahh," she said and crossed her arms. "So why are you here, then?"

Dax rubbed his neck and stared at the floor for a moment. "Have you seen her?" He hesitantly lifted his eyes to see Ophelia's amused gaze.

"Yes, I have." She took the seat beside him. "She's strong, brave. I like her." Her gaze turned curious as she inspected him. "You should go see her."

Dax bit the inside of his cheek. "If Halia wants the location, then it's best that I stay out of Ma—" He cleared his throat, just barely stopping himself from mentioning Mari's name in a public space. "It's best I leave her be."

The Seer hesitated, like she wanted to ask him to spill everything on his mind, but to his surprise, she didn't. Instead, she nodded.

"I understand. It's easier to run away into the night than face the challenges that dawn brings to light."

Dax's brows dipped. Did she just call him a coward? "I'm not running from anything." He cared about Mari—far more than he should have. If anything, he was saving her by staying away. He couldn't have the darkness infecting him tainting her life.

Ophelia placed a gloved hand on his arm, her eyes going soft. "Maybe not, Dax. But sometimes, we don't realize we're running until we're out of breath. The hardest paths often lead to the most worthwhile destinations. Trust yourself to face the dawn."

~

He repeated Ophelia's words over and over in his mind as he walked down the hall toward the forbidden wing. Not even the king visited the place. Queen Cybele had resided in her private wing whenever she visited the kingdom. That was before Dax worked for the royal family, before he became their servant—their dog to order around.

He nodded to the guards stationed at the door, then took a deep breath. He placed his hand on the knob and had to work up the courage to step inside.

Darkness greeted him, the only light coming from the fire burning in the ornate hearth. Did Mari not know how to turn on the lights?

Closing the door softly behind him, he glanced around for any signs of Mari, but found none.

He reached a hand up toward the switch that would turn the lumen chandelier on, just as Mari said from the darkness, "You shouldn't have come here."

Dax dropped his hand and exhaled slowly, turning to face her. She stood by the fire. The flickering light danced along her features, casting shadows that sharpened her frown.

"I know," he murmured and stepped toward her.

"Stay where you are." Her voice was as cold as an ice storm ready to tear him apart.

"I just wanted you to have this." Slowly, he placed her bone dagger on the table beside him next to a vase of dead, shriveled-up flowers. He was surprised they hadn't dissolved into dust.

"My dagger," she breathed. As she stepped forward, her scent filled his lungs as though he was finally breathing fresh air.

Lifting it into her hands, she inspected the weapon with fond eyes.

"And I wanted to say I'm sorry," he said, his voice catching unexpectedly.

Face the dawn.

Mariana didn't look at him as she sheathed the dagger in its place against her hip.

"I couldn't tell you your sister was gone and risk everything."

Finally, she lifted her glare to him. He saw the violent storm surging within her deep turquoise eyes and held himself still, preparing for her wrath to be unleashed.

"Why are you so devoted to her?" she asked, her gaze unwavering.

Dax reached up and squeezed his tightening neck. "I have no choice."

She sighed and closed her eyes. He took that moment to look her over. Her mouth was tight, and the skin around her eyes was puffy with exhaustion. She blinked but kept her gaze averted. With drooped shoulders, she wrapped her arms around herself as though searching for comfort. Something he found himself wishing he could provide her.

"After I saved your life from that toxin, I kept asking myself why I'd done it." She spoke softly, as though she was talking more to herself than to him. "Why did I save the same fae's life that took me away from my home? It would've been so easy to leave you there to die. Then something happened."

She stepped toward the fire and stared into the flames with glassy eyes. "Something inside me said that I couldn't let you die. For some reason, I wanted to trust you. And yet, when we were in that river together, I knew ..." She peered over at him, and his heart constricted at the pain evident in her gaze. "I knew you couldn't be trusted. So, I tried to go home, but my mother—" she sniffed and looked away. "She shoved me back through that portal after sealing my fate as a fae, and I landed in your arms. And for some reason, I felt safe."

"Because I will always keep you safe, Mari. I never lied to you about that."

She scoffed and looked away. "It was foolish of me to think I could trust you. Especially when I have no reason to trust anyone."

He opened his mouth to object but stopped himself when he realized she was right. She couldn't trust him. He'd lie to her in a heartbeat if it meant protecting his family. Yet he'd risked everything to save her life, taking her to the only place he knew she would survive.

"When I carried you to my home and showed you everything and everyone I care about. *That* was my deepest truth. And now, you hold the power to burn it all to the ground, just as Halia does."

"And you think that's enough for me just to forgive you?" Mariana scoffed. "I shouldn't have to worry about what else you're keeping from me, Dax! I shouldn't have to fear that everything I've ever felt for you was built on lies!"

"Fine! Yes, I lied, okay. I get it. But I never meant to hurt you!" he yelled back, then winced. This was not going the way he thought it would.

"You didn't just hurt me—you betrayed me," she said with a threatening darkness in her eyes. She turned, but he couldn't let her just walk away. He reached out to grab her hand.

"No!" she shouted, and a blast of air slammed him backward. Dax hit the wall with a grunt, barely catching himself from falling over.

Her hands shot up to her mouth, eyes going wide.

Dax stared at her. Had *she* just done that?

"That was sky magic," he muttered.

"It wasn't anything," she said with a tremble in her voice.

Dax studied her. "When did that start, Mari?" he asked softly.

She didn't say anything, instead just staring at her hands in disbelief.

"Mari?"

"You need to leave now," she ordered, her voice hollow.

"We shouldn't end things like this. Talk to me."

She brought her eyes up to meet his, and he saw the warning stirring within them. "You betrayed me and made a fool out of me. And for that, I will never forgive you." Turning, she began walking into the darkness beyond an open door. "Leave, Dax. And don't come back."

As he watched her disappear, he resisted the urge to go after her.

With his hands clenched at his sides, he looked up at the vaulted ceiling, shrouded in the dust and shadows of the neglected palace wing.

"Godsdammit," he muttered.

He was trapped. Neck-deep in the quicksand of his life. And the one person he thought could pull him free had just walked away, her footsteps a fading echo in the cold, dark corridors.

CHAPTER 40

THE LIBRARY WAS QUIET, the stillness broken only by the soft *thud* of a book being closed. Ophelia rested the thick tome in her lap and stretched in the chair she was sitting in, her legs hanging over one of the armrests. Her gaze drifted across the room to Mariana, who sat at a wide oak table near the fireplace.

The siren's teal braid cascaded over her shoulder, shifting slightly as she bent over the stack of books in front of her. Her long fingers moved quickly, flipping through pages with an intensity that spoke of urgency. Every now and then, she jotted something in the margins of a loose sheet of parchment, her brow furrowed in concentration.

Ophelia tilted her head, intrigued. "Find anything interesting?"

Mariana didn't look up.

Ophelia chewed on the inside of her cheek and glanced across the room at Kosta, who was leaning against the doorframe, staring off into the distance. She wished he'd listened to her plea to stay outside. It was hard enough getting the siren to talk to her. Shifting her gaze back to Mariana, she noticed she didn't have any gills like Astra had on her neck.

Planting her feet on the ground, she cleared her throat. "Hey, I noticed you don't have any gills. Is that something you can make disappear like your tail or—" The words died on her lips as Mariana shot her an icy glare that sent a shiver down her spine.

"I'm sorry," she apologized softly, averting her gaze. "I just wasn't sure—"

Mariana shut the book with a *bang*, startling Ophelia. Their eyes met, and immediately she could see the pain deep within, hiding beneath the dark glare.

Kosta straightened and glanced seriously between them but didn't move from his position.

Gripping the book tightly, Ophelia asked, "What happened?" Her words were small, quiet, but she knew Mariana heard her by the way her eyes closed as she sighed.

A moment passed as Mariana clearly struggled with whatever was consuming her thoughts. Her brow was still furrowed, mouth tight. When she finally opened her eyes, she looked ... heartbroken.

"My mother cast a binding spell on me. I'm no longer a siren."

Ophelia let out a soft gasp, hands darting up to her mouth.

Mariana shrugged, like she was trying to pretend the issue was behind her, yet it clearly bothered her. "For now, at least. I think the amulet might be able to remove the spell."

Ophelia's hands drifted down to her lap, eyes widening. "That's why you look so much like a fae. Because you are one now, aren't you?"

The look Mariana gave her answered her question, but it appeared almost too painful for her to say out loud.

Why would Mariana's mother do that to her?

Glancing down at the siren book she clutched in her hands, she began to wonder something.

Clearing her throat again, she lifted her head to find Mariana staring into the fire with glassy eyes.

"What's it like living underwater?" she asked, hoping the change of subject might help.

Mariana looked over at her but didn't say anything. Instead, she studied her.

Ophelia shifted in her seat. "I only ask because I look at all these books"—she gestured to the library—"that couldn't survive underwater. So, how do your people keep their history?"

Sitting back in her chair, Mariana crossed her arms. Her voice was calm and clipped when she answered. "Why does that matter to you?"

"It's fascinating, that's all," Ophelia said, shrugging. "A culture without written records—it must be difficult, preserving your history over centuries."

"We keep our knowledge to ourselves." Her tone left no room for anymore inquiries.

Not knowing what else to say, Ophelia simply nodded and stared down at the swirly lettering of the book in her lap.

It was one of her favorites. The romantic tale of two lonely sirens who were split up during the infernal wars only to find their way back to each other by the end. Any time she had the chance to sneak into the siren library, she'd find it and reread it for hours. At least until a spirit decided to pester her with gossip.

"You know, I admire your people's ability to tell amazing stories." Ophelia lifted her head to gaze lovingly at the shelves of books surrounding them. "They're so beautiful. It's heartbreaking that they're locked away in here with no one to read them."

"Is that why you're here?" Mariana said with a lifted eyebrow. "To read books?"

Ophelia sighed as she stood up to put the book back. "I'm here as a friend," she answered honestly, then faced Mariana, who scrutinized her from where she sat. "I want to help you search if you need it, that's all."

"That's all?" Mariana asked, her monotone voice clearly conveying her disbelief.

"Yes. The faster we find out where the amulet is, the faster we can go get it and keep it safe." She quickly lifted a hand toward Mariana. "Keep your people safe too. Helios cannot be allowed to return."

Mariana's mouth lifted like she was amused. "Let's get one thing straight. You're here to keep an eye on me and report back to your mistress that I'm behaving and not hiding any information I find. That's why you want to help so badly, and we both know it."

Ophelia lifted her head and pursed her lips. "Honesty and trust are appreciated, but Princess Halia—"

Mariana cackled. "*Honesty and trust?* Are you joking?"

Ophelia only stared at her, unable to think of what to say.

Mariana waved a hand through the air. "The princess wants the amulet, so her father doesn't use it, ensuring she stays the heir to the throne. I get it. Doesn't change the fact that she's a downright evil bitch for not only holding my sister hostage but sending someone to abduct me and drag me all the way here just to do it all over again."

Ophelia's eyes widened as she stared in horror at what Mariana just said. "The princess is not—" She shook her head, unable to even whisper the words. "Listen, it's true that her methods are ... a bit extreme, and I will say that I do not agree with the way she handled the situation with your sister, nor do I condone what she's done to you, but she has done admirable things for this kingdom since taking over as regent for King Stavros."

Mariana crossed her arms and squinted up at her. "Like?"

"Like—" Ophelia stuttered, flustered when the words escaped her just as jumbled spirit voices began whispering vehemently into her ears. "Sorry," she muttered as she closed her eyes, willing the spirits to calm so she could speak.

"What's happening?" Mariana asked, her voice distant and muted behind the cacophony of voices.

Grinding her teeth, Ophelia forced the voices to quiet. She took a deep breath the moment her ears only heard the crackle of the fireplace, then opened her eyes to find Mariana staring at her with a confused expression.

"I apologize, the spirits were a little loud. As I was saying—"

"Spirits?" Mariana asked, then her eyes widened. "You're from House Spirit. You're a Seer."

Ophelia nodded, holding her gloved hands in front of her. "Yes I am."

Lifting a hand to her mouth, Mariana gazed at her with a stupefied look.

Irritation tightened her fists, and she quickly sat in the chair across from Mariana. "Look, I want to be your friend, I'm not lying about that. I really liked Astra. She was kind, and though, she, too, didn't like to tell me anything, I could tell how much she missed her family."

"Hmm, I wonder why," Mariana muttered.

Ophelia ignored her. "I understand that feeling, deeply," she admitted, thinking of her parents. Sadness gripped her throat, and she tried shoving the feeling back as she recalled why she had even brought it up. "I would do anything for my family, and I know you would too. Princess Halia saved me. She offered me a way to escape poverty and has done the same for so many. She works day and night to make sure this kingdom has everything it could need to thrive because everyone who lives in Aurelia is her family."

Mariana's eyes lifted to the painted ceiling like she wanted to roll them but had to hold herself back.

Realizing she wasn't going to win this battle, Ophelia stood and waited for Mariana to look her in the eye. "I'm so sorry you're trapped here. It's not right. But know that I am here for you if you need anything. I don't want you to feel alone." Striding toward the doors, she said over her shoulder, "I'll be back later with dinner."

She headed over to where Kosta waited for her, but when she heard her name, she glanced back.

Mariana was chewing on her lip when she met her conflicted gaze.

"I hate eating alone. Bring something for yourself too."

Ophelia's chest lifted. It was true she may have had orders to keep an eye on Mariana, but the idea of having a friend that wasn't her brother lit her up inside, even if it was for a short time.

She lifted a thumbs-up before leaving the library, thinking of how to tell Halia she wouldn't be dining with her that evening.

CHAPTER 41

MARIANA TUCKED HER HAIR behind her pointed ears before taking a bite of an apple and grabbing another book from the never-ending bookcase. Two days of searching every book in the area Ophelia mentioned with nothing to show for it—yet. She just had to keep looking.

Ophelia continued bringing her meals and ate with her, chatting about nothing important in that carefree, lighthearted way she had about her. She even started bringing her chamomile tea when Mariana let it slip that it was her favorite.

Eventually, Mariana began enjoying the disrupted silence that came with Ophelia's visits. She hadn't asked to assist with the search since the first time; instead, she just sat in the library until Mariana politely asked her to leave. It wasn't that Mariana wouldn't have appreciated the help. She just couldn't risk the information getting into Halia's clutches. And Mariana knew that if Ophelia found something, she would report it back to Halia—whether or not she wanted to be her friend, it was clear who would always come first.

Dax heeded her warning and didn't come by again. A part of her, deep down, secretly missed him.

Her stress had created a viper's grip in her chest, and with each passing hour that she found nothing, it tightened its coil a little more around her heart. There had to be something here—a note, a letter, or a phrase circled in a book.

She sat down on the cold floor, set her apple down, and opened a black, velvet-lined book with the moon phases etched in gold foil on the cover. She ran her fingers over the book, marveling. She wondered if it was the type Astra dreamed of storing in her Sirenia library.

Staring at the book, she sighed. As she opened it up, the sound of paper slipping through pages had her sucking in a breath.

She reached for the letter that had fallen on the floor. The bundle of pages shook in her clammy hands, and she found herself hesitant to open it. Could this be what Astra wanted her to find?

Slowly, she opened the letter and couldn't stop the tears that slipped down her cheeks as she began to read.

My dearest sister,

Please forgive me. I never intended for you to get caught up in this. Your safety has always been my top priority, and yet, here we are. My youngest sister, reading a letter I wrote, in the hopes of her finding it, while most likely trapped by the same fae that trapped me. It's sad how laughable it is, isn't it?

Mariana, I first want to say that I love you, and I am so proud of you. You being here, reading this, means you were able to escape the darkness imprisoning us within Salus. There is so much I must tell you, and know that I wouldn't say anything unless I were certain it was all true.

Mariana's eyes caught on the next sentence, and she shook her head. Her breathing turned shallow as her brows furrowed.

I've discovered secrets that will most likely get me killed. Secrets that I have to share with you so that the stars will align in our favor, giving you a fighting chance to save our people.

While in Salus, I discovered a connection between the day of your birth and the date of the Banishment: You were born only eight months after that tragic day. At first, I found it odd that the dates aligned so perfectly, and yet no one ever discussed it. Then, I realized it was to keep you safe and the siren throne secured.

Cybele was pregnant at the time of the Banishment, and as I'm sure you've already found out, our mother and Stavros were in love. She kept her relationship with the fae king quiet after the Banishment for fear of retaliation from our people and the fae. The news shocked me. I never would have guessed Cybele felt any affection for the fae king, considering her hatred for him after Sirenia fell by his order. And it got me curious. Everyone who knew about Cybele's relationship with the fae king kept quiet about it. Why?

That was when I made the connection. They were trying to keep you, the heir to the throne, safe. King Stavros is your father, Mari.

Mariana's heart stopped as she stared at those words. It couldn't be true. How could Astra possibly know this for sure?

While I was doing research in the Athenaeum, I found a record of Cybele and her Guardians going undercover into the fae realm with the hopes of finding a fae male to mate with. And as you know, successful siren pregnancies are just as rare as fae pregnan-

cies. It took Cybele nearly four centuries to give birth to Aurora and myself, and yet she got pregnant the very first time she tried after the Banishment? It was nearly impossible. I had difficulty with accepting her "luck" and the link between your birth date and the Banishment. That was when I went to the Siren Witch for answers.

The witch told me Cybele discovered she was pregnant with you after the Banishment, and she knew you would never be safe if her people found out you were the descendant of King Stavros. To keep the truth of your birth father hidden, the witch helped Cybele devise a story to tell her people: she would travel to the fae realm in secret with a Guardian to find a fae male to mate with, in the hopes of birthing an heir.

Of course, if Cybele had actually traveled to the fae realm, it would've put her life and yours at risk. Instead, she made the guardian accompanying her take a vow of silence, and together, they disappeared. When they came back, Cybele announced her pregnancy, bringing joy to all of Salus despite everyone being unaware of the truth.

They said you were born early, though you were perfectly healthy and showed no signs of physical stress. And now we know why.

This means you are a princess of both Aurelia and Sirenia. And an heir to the fae throne. You can never tell Halia about this, Mari. She will do anything for power. You cannot trust her. She will never let you live if she knows the truth.

The only one you can trust is King Stavros. I expected to hate him, but when he found me in this library, I could see just how heartbroken he is, even after all this time. He truly loved our mother, and I believe with his help, we can restore Sirenia to its former glory. Stavros doesn't want to see us suffer anymore. He only wants his son back. And he wants to meet you. His daughter shared with his lost love.

Something I found interesting that Stavros revealed to me was that Helios had been courting Zafiria before he died. I asked the king if he truly believed that Cybele killed his only son, for even I don't believe it, and I only saw the remorse in his eyes. After so many years contemplating the past, the king believes Zafiria was truly the one who killed Helios, and Cybele took the blame. I cannot understand why Zafiria would have killed him. Maybe a lover's quarrel? But I know for certain that there is more going on than they're telling us.

This leads me to my next secret, the one Halia discovered, which was what forced you here.

Halia approached me one day, demanding to know the identity of "the daughter of the sea and the sky," claiming they were the only siren who could unlock the amulet. I knew instantly she meant you, but I tried to stay quiet. I have no idea where she got that information from, but there are spies everywhere. Someone must have been listening to me ramble—you know I have a tendency to read out loud.

Within the book where you found this letter is information about Seraphina's amulet. It reveals how Seraphina was birthed from the heavens and reborn within the sea. Thus, only a daughter of both the sea and sky can activate or silence the amulet's power. That's you, Mariana. Your father is from House Sky, and you are a daughter of the sea. Halia was furious when she found out I kept information from her. I thought I was strong enough

*to keep silent, but when Halia threatened Luna's life, I felt
your name spill from my lips. I'm ashamed, and I'm so sorry.
I knew she would send someone after you, and I knew I had to
escape her prison as quickly as possible.*

*I suspected that you would have already been advocating
for my rescue when my Guardians arrived back home without
me. Yet I knew our mother would not send help. Before I left
for Aurelia, I made her swear to me she would not send anyone
to rescue me if anything went wrong. I never wanted you or
any of our sisters near this place, but the moment I said your
name to Halia, I knew I had failed you. That is my burden
to bear.*

*And now that I have the location of the amulet, I can only
pray that the Goddess will guide you to this letter. The secrets
I've held can save your life. Consider the information wisely.
And dispose of this letter the moment you read it.*

*I wish I had more time, but the king has a plan to get me
out of here and to Sirenia so I can secure the amulet for you.
That is where I'm headed and where you must go next. If what
this book says is correct, then the amulet was hidden by our
ancestors within Seraphina's statue at the center of Sirenia.
When you arrive, I'll have the amulet ready for you, and we
can reunite amongst the ashes of our fallen sisters. Together,
we will light the way to a bright future for our people.*

Be safe on your journey, sister. I love you.

Astra

Mariana read Astra's letter three times before throwing it into
one of the many fireplaces Ophelia had requested to remain lit.
It had probably been to keep an eye on her, but Mariana never

saw the servants who kept adding wood to the fires. They came and went like ghosts.

She watched the pages burn into ash within seconds, and her heart finally felt free. Then the hair on the back of her neck stood up, and she knew someone was watching her. Turning quickly, she found the same turquoise eyes as her own staring at her. Eyes that belonged to none other than King Stavros.

CHAPTER 42

"It's you," Mariana whispered.

King Stavros stood tall, his rich brown skin contrasted by an open white fur-lined surcoat, revealing a cobalt tunic embellished with gold thread. His long black hair stopped at his broad shoulders, where it was brushed back beneath a gold crown that glinted under the chandeliers.

He was every bit as intimidating as Mariana could've imagined. And yet, as she continued to stare at him with wide eyes, she noticed he was doing the same. He hadn't expected to find her here.

"I—uh—" She stumbled over her words until she cleared her throat. "How did you do that? I didn't hear you come in at all."

The question seemed to pull Stavros from his confused stupor, and he regarded her carefully. "I can manipulate the air around me, making myself as silent as a mouse when I want to go somewhere in peace without watchful eyes," he stated softly, his voice deep and soothing.

His words rippled through her as she considered what Astra had said in her letter.

Your father is from House Sky, and you are a daughter of the sea.

Mariana took a steady breath, realizing she was standing in front of her father and that there was the possibility that she had more magic than she even knew about. She thought of the incident with the papers floating to the floor, the curtains billowing from an imaginary wind after her meltdown. Had she done that?

The questions began to build in her mind, swirling and threatening to spill over.

"Are you alright?" Stavros asked, stepping forward and reaching out a hand to steady her. She hadn't noticed the ground tilting toward her.

Mariana shook her head to clear her troubled mind, then glanced at the hand on her arm, following it up to the eyes she'd known her whole life, though they belonged to someone else.

"You look unwell, child. Let's sit." The king guided her toward the seating area at the back of the library. Mariana sat on an ivory silk sofa while he took the chair beside it, staring at his hands. She wondered what he saw.

He glanced up. "You are Mariana?" he asked with a hint of wonder.

Nodding, she averted her gaze, trying and failing to come up with the right thing to say. In the awkward silence, she said, "You look different than you did in the painting."

King Stavros's brows lowered in confusion, and she realized he had no idea what she was referring to.

"The painting of you and my mother in the foyer," she supplied.

The king's lips twitched. "How did I look?"

"Happy," she said before she could stop herself. But it was true. The king—though he appeared just as young as he was when the painting must've first been commissioned—had grief forever lining his eyes. The haunting pain in his face was unmistakable.

Astra was right. He was heartbroken. "And your hair is much longer," she blurted, her cheeks growing warm.

Stavros smiled tightly before nodding. "You're right, I was happy back then. And I am due for a haircut." He chuckled.

Mariana held back a smile as it dawned on her that *"back then"* was when he had ordered the death of her people. She shouldn't be smiling or laughing with him. He deserved none of it.

She sat up straight and glared at him. "Yes, 'back then' was a very different time, wasn't it?"

King Stavros only stared at her, and when the sadness in his eyes became too much to bear, she stood up and crossed her arms.

"Do you know how much pain you've caused my family? How many of my sisters you slaughtered during the Banishment?" Her voice wavered at the end, and she gritted her teeth.

Stavros opened and closed his mouth, as if struggling to find words. Then he stood and walked over to a glass display case housing several siren artifacts and gazed at them in silence.

Mariana was tempted to ask what he was staring at when he finally spoke, his words laced with pain. "The day you lost Sirenia was the day I lost my son. Back then, I believed it to be just. But that is no excuse. I regret what I did, Mariana, and I am sorry."

Her eyes went wide as he spoke her name like a prayer. "Well, apologies don't mean anything when my people are still dying. Every day, more of us fall victim to the Scourge just to keep our population steady. The cruelty you've inflicted upon us for a *century* is cause for more than just an *apology*." She spat the last word like it was acid on her tongue.

"You're right," he whispered and turned to face her. "That's why I want to help you and Astra restore Sirenia."

Mariana stared at him in shock. She'd read what her sister said about the king wanting to help them, but she never imagined she would hear it from him.

"How?" she asked harshly, attempting to keep hope from her voice. "By us handing over the amulet? Bringing your son back and dooming us all once again?"

Stavros shook his head. "Helios would not bring war upon you, I assure you."

"What makes you so certain?"

The king paused, staring at her with such intensity, she had to fight to keep from looking away.

"Astra told me she would be writing you a letter. Was that what I saw you burn in the fire?"

Mariana gave a curt nod.

"What did she say?"

"She said that I should trust you. That you think Cybele isn't to blame for Helios's murder, that it was the Siren Witch."

"And do you believe her?"

"I believe that Cybele took the blame for killing Helios. Trusting you? Not so much."

His lips twitched. He began walking slowly through the library, his black boots echoing through the vast room. Mariana followed on hesitant feet.

"Her name at the time was Zafiria, and I believe my son was secretly courting her. Their relationship was inappropriate, and I'm sure they both knew it. I believe they quarreled, and Zafiria killed Helios."

"I would've suspected he could easily survive an attack by a siren scholar."

"Helios could hold his own in a fight, but he loved fine liquor. She poisoned his cup. His heart gave out. And Cybele found him." The king stopped in front of the draped windows, a crack of light shining on his face. "My son was a great male, but he was vengeful. Had been since he was young. I can remember the time he discovered his favorite toy warhorse had gone missing, only to find it was another child that had taken it. The boy's mother claimed it was by mistake. Helios pretended it was fine, grateful to have the toy back.

"However, I knew my little rebel had something up his sleeve. And just a few days later, a different child was crying that all of his toys were broken. Come to find out, Helios discovered it was not the first child who had taken the warhorse but another, and he punished him the way he saw fit."

Mariana didn't know what to make of the story, though it reaffirmed that Helios was trouble.

Mariana had a difficult time believing the witch had poisoned Helios. Why would she? Were they truly in a relationship?

Maybe the situation was flipped, and Helios was going to hurt her, so she defended herself. Either way, Mariana didn't believe for a moment that her mentor killed Helios intentionally, if at all.

"My point," the king continued, "is that my son is brilliant. *Was* brilliant," he corrected, then cleared his throat before turning around to face her. "He will know who truly killed him and seek vengeance on only the one responsible. As is right."

Helios would go after the Siren Witch. A part of her heart lurched at the thought of anyone harming one of her own, especially someone she cared about.

"And what if I try to stop him?"

The king gave her a tight-lipped smile. "I'm assuming Astra's letter also told you that I am your father." The expression on her face must have confirmed it. "Then you should know I will never allow harm to come to you." His brows scrunched, and he gave her a sad smile she hoped wasn't supposed to be reassuring. "Well, I should say, I will do everything in my power to keep you safe."

"Did you—" Mariana hesitated and bit her lip before sighing, "Did you know about me?"

He shook his head and looked away. "No, though I wish I had."

"Why? Would it have changed anything?"

Stavros stared at the floor for a moment. "I'd like to think so." He continued to study the marble beneath their feet until he finally met her eyes. "I come here when I miss her."

Mariana knew instantly who he meant by *her*.

"That's why you haven't torn this place apart. You still love her."

The king glanced around the room and gave her a solemn nod. "This was my love letter to her. I envisioned our lives here. She and I. Our children. I'd like to walk, will you join me?"

He held out an elbow for her, and she hesitated before accepting the invitation. Giving her a small smile, the king walked her from the library into the main hall.

"See this long stretch of wall here? I planned on having paintings done of her daughters and displaying them."

Mariana glanced at the wall, imagining for a moment Astra's and Aurora's portraits hanging there, then her own at the end. As she blinked back the vision, Stavros pulled his elbow from her hand.

"Pardon me, I just want to clean this up quickly." The king bent down to gather all the loose parchment littering the floor from the wind that had manifested from *nowhere* during her strike of anger earlier.

"Why?" she asked, bewildered by his impulse to clean when no one was around.

Stavros paused, then neatly shuffled the pages he'd collected. "I ask myself that very question frequently. And do you know what I tell myself?"

Mariana shook her head.

He gave her a sad smile. "I'm still allowed to dream."

After placing the stacked pages on the desk nearby, he lifted his elbow again. "Shall we?"

Mariana took his offering, and together, they walked up the steps to the second floor.

"These were bedchambers made for all of you," he admitted softly, staring at each of the four doors.

"If you didn't know about me, how did you know you'd need to build a fourth room?"

Stavros gazed down at her and smiled. "I had hoped we would have a child together."

Mariana couldn't handle the emotion in his eyes and looked away, her throat growing tight.

He led her into each room, explaining the different colors he'd had in mind and how he would've liked to add a saltwater bath to each of them, then a tunnel on the first floor that would've led out to the ocean so they could all come and go as they pleased.

As he spoke, Mariana realized how much the king had thought about them being a family. And he was still dreaming they could be.

She blinked back tears, pushing away thoughts of what could've been. Then he turned to Cybele's bedchamber and seemed to pause by the door.

"This, I admit, is the hardest room for me to enter," he said softly, a slight blush gracing his high cheekbones. "You see," he started, his voice cracking slightly, "I always wished this could become a second home for all of you. A peaceful place to escape, or a path for adventure. I see now that, perhaps, it was a nonsensical dream."

Mariana couldn't stop herself. In a moment of weakness, she leaned her head against his shoulder, smelling the fresh scent of mint wafting off his surcoat as they stared at her mother's door.

"I don't think so," she whispered, holding back the emotion brewing deep in her chest.

They stayed that way for a long moment before venturing back downstairs, neither of them strong enough to enter her mother's room.

They sat down on two velvet armchairs in a drawing room beside the foyer, and Mariana regarded him carefully.

"Was my mother ..." She paused as she struggled to find the right words. "What was she like when you knew her?" She bit the inside of her cheeks, slightly embarrassed for asking, but she wanted to know more about the siren she had been before the Banishment, before Mariana was born.

Stavros got a glimmer in his eye. "I'd say she was magical. The moment she entered a room, she commanded it. All eyes were on her, and she knew the power she held." He averted his gaze, peering down at his clasped hands. "I fell in love before I knew what love was. My first wife died soon after Halia was born, and though she deserved to be loved, I couldn't give it to her. I tried ... but that feeling was not even comparable to how much I love Cybele." Speaking her name seemed to affect him, as he grew silent and appeared contemplative.

Mariana felt the urge to speak but had no words to say. The waves of pain coming from the king were enough to make her unbearably sad.

Eventually, he cleared his throat and glanced up at her. "Although, I hear she is not the same siren I fell in love with."

"No, she isn't," she muttered.

She could feel his studying eyes on her, but she refused to meet them.

He sighed. "When I discovered Astra in here, I knew she was one of Cybele's daughters. It was in the way she held herself, the way she demanded answers, much like you have." He smiled softly at the memory. "She was a force of nature. And when we talked, she told me there was an amulet that could bring back my son, and I began to hope. Something I hadn't felt for a very long time. And when she told me I had another daughter, I was elated. It was then I realized I had been living in darkness for so long, I hardly recognized true light."

Mariana felt her lips tug upward at the thought of Astra bringing light back into someone's life. "That sounds like Astra. She has that effect on everyone."

"Indeed, she does." The king smiled then, truly smiled, and Mariana swallowed down the urge to smile back. "And then she made a deal with me. One that I hope we can also make."

Mariana instantly grew tense as she awaited his proposal despite knowing exactly what he was going to say.

"Mariana, if you can bring my son back to me, I will do everything I can to help bring prosperity to Sirenia. Please, help me make things right again."

They stared at each other, the king expecting her to agree, while Mariana silently weighed the possibilities. In the end, she stood.

"That's the deal you made with Astra. I trust my sister, but I'm sorry, I can't trust you. Not yet."

The king seemed to visibly shrink as her words sank in. He swallowed and gave her a nod before standing. "I understand. The only thing I ask is, please do not trust Halia. I love my daughter, but I'm afraid our goals do not align. She fears that if her brother returns, she will not become queen. That is why I've given her almost full reign over Aurelia, so she can do the good she hopes for our glorious kingdom now while she can. She will be a fine ruler, but she was not meant to be the ruler of Aurelia."

Mariana considered his words. "I would never trust her. She had me abducted and has imprisoned me here, after all."

"Yes, well ..." The king glanced around the room before settling once again on her. "I can help with that, if you wish."

Something about his offer didn't sit well with her. She didn't want anyone saving her, not anymore. But she couldn't throw out the option.

"I'd appreciate that. But not yet. I haven't finished searching, and I want to make sure there isn't anything I've missed."

"Well, I'll check on you soon. It is best that Halia doesn't find out I was here. I'd prefer her to think I'm oblivious to all her clandestine affairs."

Mariana nodded and watched the king begin to walk away without making a sound. How did he do that? A trick she had to learn. He stopped near the door to the foyer and looked back at her. "Mari, I hope one day to build that trust with you, if you'd allow me the opportunity."

Her heart skipped as she stared at the fae she could easily call her father. And yet the more she stared, the more she only saw a stranger. But if the tugging in her chest told her anything, it was that she had room in her heart to forgive him, and possibly get to know him.

"I think I'd allow that, one day," she murmured with a small smile that he returned before continuing on his way.

When he disappeared, she released a heavy sigh and hung her head.

"Finally," a female voice said from behind her. "I thought he'd never leave."

CHAPTER 43

"'SHE WILL BE A fine ruler, but she was not meant to be the ruler of Aurelia.'" Ophelia's entire body was shaking; her voice trembled as she recited what the spirits had whispered into her ears. The darkness of the spirit realm shrouded her mind, making her blind to everything but the ethereal messages. The familiar chill of the realm seeped into her bones, amplifying her determination.

"The king went on to tell Mariana he could help her escape, but she turned him down," she continued, her voice tinged with confusion. Clearing her throat, she added, "He wishes for her to keep their meeting secret from you. And then he leaves." Ophelia took a deep, steadying breath, grateful the whispers had ceased. She braced herself for what came next.

Surging forward, she pushed her soul back into the living realm, as if stepping out of water fully clothed. The weight of the world smothered her, while a familiar pain twisted and crippled her muscles. She released her breath slowly, easing herself through the agony until it dispersed into nothingness. A new scar would mark the journey, she was certain. Already, she felt its gnarled fingers sinking deep into her right shoulder. Lifting a white linen-glove hand, the fabric covering the discolored, mutilated flesh beneath, she rubbed the spot. Years of entering the spirit realm had left their mark on every part of her body except her face—the price she paid for wielding her power.

It was unknown why the Generals' descendants suffered consequences, called fallout, from using the power coursing through their veins. The Generals themselves weren't documented to have received any punishment. Not even Minerva, the General of House Spirit, was ever reported to have been riddled with scars from her magic. So why were her descendants?

Some believed it was because the Gods never intended for the Generals to reproduce, and thus, their power required balance. Others argued that the Generals' power was so potent that they could reverse the effects of fallout. The scholars of Aurelia had debated this endlessly, their theories filling volumes of books that lined the palace library.

Ophelia could live with the pain as long as her spirits had something important to report back. Her role was crucial, and the sacrifices she made were for the greater good. Each scar was a testament to her dedication and the heavy burden she bore for the kingdom.

The room she returned to was dimly lit; the only source of light came from the setting sun, casting long, golden shadows across the floor. Rich tapestries adorned the stone walls, depicting the history of Aurelia's noble line, while heavy, dark wooden furniture added a sense of weight and permanence. The air smelled faintly of aged parchment and books, a comforting scent that reminded Ophelia of the countless hours she had spent here advising Halia.

As she blinked in bright sunlight streaming through the windows, her vision returned to normal. She saw Halia, her beautiful princess, staring blankly out at the horizon, rays of light illuminating her stunning features. Halia stood on the balcony, the gentle breeze playing with her dark, flowing hair, her regal posture a stark contrast to the turmoil Ophelia knew raged within her.

Ophelia stayed seated in the leather chair, silently scanning Halia's tense body and crossed arms, waiting patiently for her to process what she had reported about the conversation between Mariana and King Stavros.

It didn't feel right telling Halia everything. She was already invading their privacy enough as it was, so she had chosen what to repeat carefully. She knew the king's words hurt Halia more than she would ever admit. Her princess wanted to be the greatest queen this realm had ever known, yet her father failed to see her potential. The bloody fool.

Halia deserved to be queen. She had acted as regent, running the entire kingdom for the last several decades, because her father was a failure. The king had become unreasonable and indifferent since the siren banishment. Aurelia's crime rate had risen, merchants were desperate for more trade goods, and citizens struggled to make the wages needed to feed their families, especially in the outer towns. The kingdom had been descending into chaos due to his lack of concern and discipline.

Then Halia stepped up, and everything changed. The Kingdom of Aurelia began to prosper again, while the king wallowed in self-pity, oblivious to every sacrifice and difficult decision Halia made to keep the kingdom she loved from crumbling. She restored trade routes, negotiated peace treaties, and implemented reforms that brought prosperity and stability. Her compassion and intelligence won the hearts of the people, who saw her as their true leader.

Now, here he was, making Halia doubt her self-worth, doubt her ability to rule, when she deserved only praise and the crown he was unfit to wear. The frustration and sadness in Halia's eyes made Ophelia's heart ache. She wished she could ease her princess's burdens, but knew that all she could do was offer her unwavering support.

Ophelia had vowed never to keep anything important from Halia, but there were moments like this when she wished she had. The truth, while necessary, was often a heavy burden.

"I don't believe for a second that Mariana isn't planning a way to escape. We know she learned information from the letter Astra left her. Information that undoubtedly included the location of the amulet." Halia turned and faced Ophelia, her head held high, determination replacing the doubt in her eyes.

Ophelia's heart brightened at the sight. Halia wouldn't let the king's words get to her. The fire in her eyes was a reminder of the strength and resilience that had always defined her.

Clearing her throat, she said, "Why don't you just tell Mari the truth? Maybe if you explain to her why it's so vital that Helios doesn't come back, she'll work with you to find the amulet and keep it somewhere safe, away from the king."

Halia shook her head. "I cannot. Sirens like her are not to be trusted. I tried trusting Astra and look where that got me."

Ophelia bit her lip to keep from pointing out that Halia had *imprisoned* Astra and forced her to look for the amulet's location instead of *trusting* her ...

Halia approached, the soft rustle of her gown the only sound in the room, and Ophelia quickly stood.

"Tell Kosta and Dax to bring her to me, will you?" Halia reached up and twirled one of Ophelia's curls between her fingers. Ophelia held back from kissing them. They were alone, but that didn't always mean Halia welcomed the affection. Instead, Ophelia stared up into the eyes of the female she loved with her whole heart and smiled before bowing her head. "Of course, Your Highness."

As Ophelia turned to leave, she couldn't help but glance back at Halia. The princess stood tall, a beacon of hope and strength. The kingdom needed her. But more importantly, Ophelia needed her.

CHAPTER 44

MARIANA LEAPT INTO HER sister's arms, smiling wide.

"Rora! What are you doing here? How did you get in?"

"No fortress could keep me from getting to you," Aurora mumbled into Mariana's hair. "Besides," she said as she pulled back, both of them gripping each other, "after centuries of sneaking into the palace, I knew my way in." Aurora winked at her, and Mariana squeezed her arms covered in black silky fabric.

"Did Cybele tell you where to find me?"

Aurora's bright eyes dimmed, and her smile faded. She shook her head, her braid falling forward from her hood. "No, the witch finally told me what happened," she said. "I can't believe they made you go back. And that Cybele bound you in fae form. It's just ... cruel."

Mariana wanted to agree. Wanted to condemn her mother for doing anything so awful to someone she claimed to love and care about. Instead, after everything Astra had revealed in her letter, she found herself saying, "I think I understand why she did it."

Taking a deep breath, she glanced at the bookcase she'd been searching through before she found Astra's letter.

"Astra's gone," she said softly.

"What?" Aurora's face was scrunched in disbelief. "How? Where is she?"

"I think you know where," Mariana offered softly. Aurora nodded in understanding. "Astra left me a letter. I already burned it, but it said—" She took a deep, steadying breath and met her sister's golden eyes. "It said my father is King Stavros."

Aurora blinked, her jaw dropping slightly. "That explains so much ..." she muttered, pulling her hands from Mariana to cross her arms. She began to pace.

"Did you know Cybele and Stavros were lovers before the banishment?"

Aurora tilted her head. "I mean ... When this place was built," she said, gesturing to the whole wing the king had built for her—for them, "I suspected so, but I never saw them together. They usually regarded each other like they hardly knew one another. Now I realize it was all an act."

"Yeah," Mariana muttered, wrapping her arms around herself. She told Aurora the rest of what Astra's letter had revealed.

Finally, Aurora stopped pacing. "So, Halia *and* the king want the amulet?"

"Yes."

"Then we need to leave—now. You know where Astra went, and we can keep it from them—"

Mariana held up her hands. "Wait, it's not that easy anymore. I can't swim anywhere, I have no tail!"

Aurora shook her head. "We'll find a way. We have to get to Astra. Hopefully, she's found the amulet and we can get it back to Salus before—" She stopped, her eyes falling as her lips thinned into a grim line.

Mariana's eyebrows lowered. "Before what? Rora?"

"Before Cybele dies."

The way she spoke sent chills down Mariana's body.

"The fallout is killing her," Mariana murmured, releasing a heavy sigh.

Her sister nodded. "The witch says the only way to save her is with the amulet's power. But we have to move fast, she doesn't have much time left, and Luna—" Aurora sighed and shook her head.

Mariana's chest tightened. "What about Luna?"

Aurora swallowed, unable to meet her eyes. "She's not the same. She's ... changing." Her gaze lifted toward Mariana, who inspected the way her brows were tight, her mouth taut. "I don't know what's going on with her. She's acting out, talking about revenge if you don't bring Astra back or the amulet. She's even been staying in the caves with the cursed."

Mariana released a shaky breath. "She's probably seeking solace from the only place that can give it."

"Maybe." Aurora bit her lip. "With how close she's gotten to the witch, I fear what she might do."

Lifting her hands, Mariana scrubbed her face and sighed deeply. This wasn't good. None of it was good. Astra would never have let Luna take part in the Scourge, but now that her mother was missing, she was scared, alone. Luna had struggled to find her place in Salus, always believing it was beside her mother, but now that she didn't have Astra anymore, there was a hole in her life. One she was desperate to fill, no doubt. Without the positive influence of Cybele, Aurora, or Mariana in her life, the only person she would feel comfortable turning to was the Siren Witch.

"There's one more thing I have to tell you," Aurora said softly, making Mariana go still, halting her hurricane of thoughts. "Cybele declared—"

"Put your hands up! Now!" a deep male voice shouted.

Mariana and Aurora both turned to see Kosta pointing a loaded crossbow at her sister. Dax stood behind him, staring at Aurora in shock.

In the blink of an eye, Aurora slid across the polished floor and tripped Kosta. His back hit the floor. Lifting the crossbow into her hands, she pointed the loaded weapon at his throat. She grinned down at him, her knee resting on his chest.

He sneered up at her and tried lunging for the crossbow, but she kept it just out of reach.

Aurora *tsked* and shook her head. "Sorry, hot stuff, I always have to be on top."

In the chaos, Dax slipped over to Mariana.

"Are you okay?" he asked, placing his hands on her cheeks. She was so shocked—and strangely relieved—to see him, it took her a moment to pull away.

Aurora pointed the crossbow at Dax. "Step away from my queen!"

Mariana's head whipped toward her sister.

What did she just say?

Her throat closed, and her vision wavered.

Cybele had declared Mariana queen.

Chapter 45

Dax and Mariana exchanged glances, their shock evident, before turning to the red-haired siren.

Mariana was the new Siren Queen.

If there hadn't been a crossbow pointed at him, Dax would have stepped close to Mari and asked what had happened. Did that mean Cybele was dead?

"Aurora," Mari cautioned.

Suddenly, it clicked: The red-haired siren was Mari's sister, the one who made armor and weapons from basilisk bone. Dax recognized her then as the Scarlet Serpent.

In a sudden flurry of movement, Kosta bucked, throwing Aurora off balance and tackling her. They wrestled for the crossbow until Aurora punched him so hard in the jaw that Dax winced at the cracking sound. Kosta fell off her, and Aurora stood with the crossbow in hand. She took a few steps back as Kosta rose, clutching his jaw with fury in his eyes.

Shaking her head, she gave him a smug grin. "Dumb pricks like you really shouldn't play with weapons."

"By the order of Princess Halia, I demand you to throw down the weapon. You both are coming with us!" Kosta's deep voice boomed with authority.

Aurora laughed, the melodic sound echoing through the library. She tried to speak but snorted instead, continuing to laugh at Kosta's look of pure annoyance.

Kosta's eyes shifted to Dax, glancing at the daggers still sheathed at his hips, then back to his eyes in question. Dax shook his head grimly. He'd never pull his weapon on Mari, not anymore.

Aurora must've noticed Kosta's gaze because her piercing stare landed on Dax, her laughter dying down. "Hand your weapons over," she demanded, gesturing for Mari to take them.

"He won't hurt me," Mari assured, but when Aurora gave her a look that said *Do it*, Mari reluctantly pulled the daggers free from Dax's belt.

"We can't go with you," Mari said, meeting his gaze before stepping back. "Halia and the king cannot get ahold of the amulet. We need it to save my mother's life."

He couldn't read the look on her face. It was as if she struggled with their relationship as much as he did.

"The princess would never stand for this!" Kosta shouted, ever the loyal soldier.

"We could just kill them," Aurora said with a shrug, staring at Kosta like he was a bug to crush. "That would send a message to that sleazy bitch."

"No," Mari stated firmly. "We can't kill them, we need their help."

"We are not helping you," Kosta spat.

Aurora aimed the crossbow between his eyebrows, and Dax waited with bated breath, the world seeming to slow. "Yes, you are," she warned. "Because if you don't, this arrow will end up in your skull. I haven't spilled any blood in a very, very long time, *fae*. But I won't hesitate now." She gently rested her finger against the trigger. "Care to test me?"

"Stop!" Mari shouted, jolting Dax. Her hand was lifted toward her sister. "No bloodshed. I *refuse* to start my reign that way."

"Then what do we do?" Aurora asked, not lowering the weapon.

Mari bit her lip, an apology visible in her eyes. "We take them with us. They would know how to secure a boat."

Fear continued to grow inside Dax's chest as he thought about what would happen if he and Kosta simply disappeared. If they disobeyed orders.

"I'll go," he said to Mari. "I'll take you wherever you want, but leave Kosta here." At least then, Kosta could tell Halia what had happened. Dax couldn't let her think he'd betrayed her, not at the risk of what she would do to his family.

Aurora shook her head, a wicked gleam in her eyes. "No, the pretty boy comes with us too, just in case we need a sacrifice for the kraken," she taunted.

"Dax," Mari said softly, drawing his attention. "This is the only way I can save my sister and my mother's life. Please don't make this difficult."

"He might not, but I will," Kosta sneered, and Aurora smiled.

"I'm hoping you do," she purred.

Ignoring them, Dax gripped his neck, eyes cast down at the dusty floor. "Halia will harm our families if she thinks we betrayed her," he said, already knowing he'd be going with them whether he refused or not.

Aurora snorted. "I know how to remedy that."

As they prepared to depart through the hidden tunnel Aurora had used to enter the private wing, Mariana's eyes fell upon the note they'd left in the center of the library. Dax waited at the tunnel entrance, watching Mariana smile down at the words that would surely make Halia explode with rage.

Halia,

I'm borrowing your boy toys for a while. They put up a good fight, I'll give them that. Hope you don't mind. Kisses!

The Scarlet Serpent

P.S. Touch my sisters again, and I'll slit your throat.

CHAPTER 46

Home, Mariana thought as she gazed out at the midday glitter of the sea.

The breeze billowed the sails, flowing through every tendril of her hair, and filled her lungs with its comforting, salty scent.

They were on their way to Sirenia. They would find Astra, secure the amulet, go back home, and save their mother. *Finally*, the tide was turning in their favor.

"You're not tying that correctly," Kosta sternly stated. "It won't be tight enough!"

Aurora huffed. "How about I tie it around your neck, and you can find out for yourself how tight my knots are!"

Mariana's lips twitched. The bickering and threatening between the two hadn't stopped since the moment they entered the tunnel out of the palace.

Whereas Mariana and Dax hadn't spoken a word to each other.

Glancing down at her hands gripping the wooden railing, she could still feel the searing touch of Dax pulling her into an alcove with him as two patrolling guards strolled by the docks.

In that moment, Mariana didn't want to leave. She met his eyes and felt that instinctive pull she'd tried so hard to forget. Even now, she was desperate to forget that connection.

Her eyes slid over to where Dax stood, one arm on the railing, the other on a rope connected to the sails. He scanned the waves, the horizon, the ships nearby. He was always doing that, inspecting his surroundings.

Mariana knew Dax was on the verge of figuring out who her father was, if he hadn't already. She couldn't risk leaving him behind and letting him tell Halia the truth. If Halia knew they were sisters, she would see Mariana as an even bigger threat, someone who could take the crown she so desperately desired. And though a small part of her believed Dax would never put her in danger like that, she told herself she couldn't take the chance. She had to bring him along. Or at least ... she tried to convince herself that was the only reason.

Before he could notice her staring, she looked away and took a deep breath. He'd been willing to come with them and barely argued with her despite the obvious risks involved. It was like he wanted to be here, with her, close to her. Or was that just her imagination?

His boss was Princess Halia—*the Matriarch*. He was probably just following Mariana to get the amulet. Take it back to Halia, who'd make him into a knight or something stupid.

Her fists tightened on the railing. There was no bloody way she was going to let Halia or Stavros get ahold of Seraphina's amulet.

"If you don't let go of that wheel, I'm going to stab you," Aurora threatened.

Kosta growled, "Just tell me where in the blazes we're going, and I will steer us in the right direction!"

"Move out of the way, *fae*, I will steer!"

Mariana shook her head, hiding her smile. They were like two bitter eels zapping each other over and over again to prove who could handle the sting the longest.

When they were still on the dock, scanning the various boats and ships bobbing in the water, they had hidden behind a cluster of wine barrels. A group of distracted, chattering guards was walking by, and Kosta looked like he was ready to shout for help. Aurora, who was crouched behind him, pointing a dagger into his side, leaned toward him and whispered something that made Kosta go deathly still. Whatever Aurora had said to him must've made all thoughts of shouting for help flee his mind, since he secured the boat as fast as possible. However, it only amplified the visible rage inside him.

Kosta wanted something to control, that much was obvious. He was most likely someone who enjoyed being in charge. And his nemesis was the spitfire siren trying to take away any semblance of that control.

"Let go of the wheel!" Aurora shouted.

"I have experience sailing a ship. Just tell me where we're going!" Kosta roared right back.

"Sirenia," Mariana stated loudly over them as she turned. Kosta and Aurora were still as they stared at her, both their hands on the wheel as though they were in the middle of grappling for control. "We're going to Sirenia. Rora, let him steer, it'll give you the chance to shoot him with your fancy new crossbow if he changes course."

Aurora smiled. "Gladly," she said, then let go of the wheel. Picking up Kosta's crossbow she'd discarded off to the side, she took a seat on a barrel across from where Kosta stood brooding. She winked at him, earning a growl. Aurora snickered.

Mariana walked down the short staircase to the second level of the small boat and took a deep breath. There was a single, tiny cabin and a galley with just enough provisions for the journey. With a selection of boats to pick from on the dock, they aimed for a boat named *Zena*, as it had just finished being loaded with supplies. Then, when it was empty and the path was clear, they slipped aboard. Only when the boat was leaving the dock did the owner notice and begin shouting for help, but it was too late. They were already sailing into the horizon.

"Think they'll ever get along?" Dax said behind her. She whirled toward him, her heart racing.

Swallowing, she glanced around the tiny space, realizing how close they were.

"What do you mean?" she asked. "They're practically married."

A smile broke through, and Dax laughed, the sound making her stomach flutter.

"I just hope they don't kill each other," he said.

The way he was looking at her made her whole body warm. Averting her eyes, she shook her head, rubbing her hands together nervously.

"Aurora vowed never to take a life again unless she had no choice. I doubt she'll believe Kosta's life is worth the burden she'd bear if she broke the vow."

"She's the Scarlet Serpent," Dax murmured.

Mariana's eyes speared him. "Don't call her that."

Lifting his hands, he said, "My apologies."

Turning from him, she grabbed a ladle and sipped fresh water from the barrel beside her. It tasted faintly of the wood it was stored in. She hoped Dax would just go back up top, leave her alone with her confusing emotions.

"I really think we should talk," he murmured.

Hanging the ladle on its hook, she plopped the lid over the water. "There's nothing to discuss."

"I think there is."

"No," she said and tried to move past him, but he put a gentle hand on her waist, stopping her.

The contact made her body hum, like something inside her was awakening.

Her heart sped up, as did her breath.

"Mari, there's so much I want to say, please just listen," he pleaded.

"Stop," she whispered, suddenly afraid.

"If we're stuck on this boat together, I think we should at least clear the air—"

Mariana pulled herself roughly away from his touch. "Stop, Dax. There's nothing that will fix this. I can't—" She stopped, a heartbeat away from crying. Spearing her hands through her hair, she gripped her head and closed her eyes, willing her body to calm down. Sighing, she whispered, "Nothing we say, nothing we do, is going to change the truth, Dax."

She finally opened her eyes. If there were ever a moment for Mariana to suddenly go blind, this was it. The pain in Dax's eyes was almost unbearable. But she didn't turn away. Instead, when he stepped in front of her, she craned her neck to meet his gaze.

The air between them was thick, crackling with energy. An invisible hurricane ready to destroy them both. The perfect disaster.

"All I want to do is apologize." He spoke in a low tone that caressed her skin. She held back a shiver. "I know that anything I say won't fix what I did, but I had to. If I betrayed Halia and told you your sister was on her way to Sirenia, then my family—"

"Wait," she murmured, her eyes searching. "You knew my sister was on her way to Sirenia? How?"

Dax rubbed the back of his neck and closed his eyes with a long sigh. "Because the king asked me to help her escape safely." His green eyes opened to look at her. "So, I did."

Mariana wrapped her arms around herself, remembering what her sister had said in her letter ... *the king has a plan to get me out of here and to Sirenia so I can secure the amulet for you ...*

It all clicked into place. Dax was the plan. And Halia had ordered him to capture Mari because of it.

"You work for Stavros *and* for Halia?"

"Yes."

She thought about everything he'd done for them. He essentially worked for and against both Halia and the king, a tug of war between the monarchy. How did he live like that?

"I don't understand. Why do you do it? Why work for them?" she asked quietly.

He swallowed, his face tightening as though thinking about the *whys* hurt him.

"I know she's holding the safety of your family over you," she continued. "But you do not belong to her, Dax. And you don't belong to the king. You are not their slave."

Dax shook his head, his expression defeated. "You don't understand."

"Then tell me. Help me understand," she pleaded.

Standing tall, hands on his hips, Dax regarded her carefully. "After I silenced my power, I didn't have a way to defend my family anymore. We'd been hidden for so long, but after an Aurelian scout discovered our location and somehow escaped us, I realized I had no way to protect them.

"My people were weaponized and oppressed for so long during the Infernal Wars that we longed for peace; we longed to hide from the world. But that wouldn't be possible anymore if word spread that we still existed. That we didn't all die out in the war. So..."

He sighed. "I approached the royal family. The king saw my military background as a benefit, but Halia saw something else. And the scout? He belonged to her. She made a deal with me to protect the location of Kythera while I worked for her under the guise of working for the king, and my servitude began."

Mariana shifted on her feet, suddenly unsteady with all the information. "How long ago was this?"

"Too long."

Irritation spiked through her, but she brushed it off.

"Why did you silence your power?" She shuddered at the thought.

He shook his head, as though just thinking about it was too much. "That's a story for another time."

The defeated look in his eyes told her it was a sensitive subject.

"I just wish—" He sighed deeply. "I wish I could show you how sorry I truly am—for everything. I never wanted to hurt you, and when I told you I'd protect you, I meant it."

"Dax," she started, her voice wavering. He'd given up years of his life to protect his family. Everything he did was for them. They were more alike than she'd thought. And she could see in his pleading gaze that he was telling the truth.

"Where do we go from here?" Her voice was small, weak, like she was desperate for an answer to an impossible question.

Dax worked for the royal family that would stop at nothing to get what she needed to save her mother's life. If he risked leaving Halia's clutches, he'd get caught in her claws and torn up in the wreckage. Kythera would be at her mercy.

Mariana couldn't imagine that beautiful village being burnt to the ground, the Mother Tree in ashes. Her heart ached at the idea of their people losing their home the same way her sisters had. She couldn't let that happen.

Dax didn't say a word, like he knew as well that there was no answer. There was nothing left to say. So, she closed the space between them. Lifting herself onto her toes, she wrapped her arms around his neck and hugged him.

When she felt his arms embrace her, sealing their bodies together, she felt it again. That instinctive pull toward him, the same way the sea pulled her close. Burying her face in his neck, she felt tears prick her eyes.

He was the home she'd never get to have.

"Let me help you with your power," he whispered into her hair.

Mariana's brows pulled together. "How?" she asked, her lips moving against his skin. She stopped herself from kissing that spot.

"I can show you how to control it." He pulled back so he could see her face. "I want you to be able to defend yourself properly. If you know how to control your sky power, none of them will stand a chance against you." Dax stared into her eyes like he was making a vow, and she felt how deeply he wanted her to be safe, even if that meant protecting herself when he wasn't there.

Her heart cracked. He wouldn't always be there, and she needed to learn how to control whatever was building up inside her.

"Okay," she finally said.

Dax made to let her go, but she pulled him back to her, hugging him again.

"Can we just stay here for a second?" she asked softly. "Just for a second."

He released a low chuckle and held her close. "Always."

CHAPTER 47

ASTRA MOVED SLOWLY THROUGH the muck of the old siren temple, her every step deliberate, as if she could feel the weight of the past pressing down on her. The journey to find these ruins had been grueling, taking days of tireless searching. The entrance had been buried under layers of debris and bones, relics of a forgotten time when the temple was alive with the songs of her sisters.

So many sisters had died on the day of the Banishment. The memories flooded Astra's mind, almost impossible to believe even now. The air was thick with the scent of decay, and the eerie silence was broken only by the distant dripping of water.

Astra's hands dragged across the cracked stone walls, the rough surface covered in slimy algae that left a trail of green on her fingertips. The texture of the algae contrasted sharply with the cold, unyielding stone beneath.

Pushing away a broken stone door, Astra stifled a gasp as she stumbled upon the skeletal remains of the priestesses. Their bones were entwined, a silent testament to their vow never to leave the temple undefended. They had remained true to their word, even in death. Moving around them, Astra continued through the murky, placid water that lapped against her legs and then rose to swallow her form entirely.

Sirens were born to see through the dark, but as she tried to navigate the cloudy depths, her vision faltered. She struggled to make out what lay ahead; her eyesight was not what it once was. Her once lustrous pearl-white hair had started to turn a cloudy gray, and the skin on her hands was wrinkling, revealing the truth she could no longer ignore: She was aging rapidly. And death was beckoning with a bony finger.

Astra's hands tightened into fists. She refused to be intimidated by the fear of death. She transformed into her tail, then continued through the temple with blind purpose until a slight glow from beneath the rubble caught Astra's eye. She pried the glow torch free, the algae trapped inside the sphere at the top swirling within. Holding it in front of her, she swam slowly through the murky corridor. The light chased away the shadows, causing crustaceans to skitter into dark crevices. As she entered the sanctuary, the torchlight flickered off the octagonal stone walls, which were adorned with ancient carvings.

Astra swam toward the nearest wall and began deciphering the inscriptions. The ancient language told of Seraphina's story and the amulet's creation. As she read, the deeper, darker history of the amulet began to reveal itself. The more she deciphered, the more her eyebrows furrowed, and her body grew taut with tension.

Astra stopped in front of a carving of a siren with claws growing from her fingers and beasts rising from the depths beneath her. The details were intricate, the depiction almost lifelike.

"Siren Queen Vasiliki, great-great-granddaughter of Seraphina, exploited the amulet's power," Astra read aloud, her voice echoing in the stillness. "Her corrupted beliefs and tainted nature cultivated death and destruction across the Seven Seas. With the amulet, she summoned Poseidon's Reapers." Astra covered her mouth with her hands, her eyes widening in terror.

Poseidon's Reapers were legendary beasts, feared throughout the ages. Capable of devouring entire cities, they left nothing but rubble and ash in their wake. After they killed their master—Amphitrite's lover—she imprisoned them beneath the sea. Alone and heartbroken, Amphitrite birthed her only daughter, her angel, Seraphina, and together, they created a new life high in the heavens.

"Riddled with power, the queen's soul turned to rot, and her body began to decay. Desperate for a cure to the fallout, Queen Vasiliki used the amulet's power to create the Scourge." Astra's voice dropped to a whisper, her mouth hanging open in disbelief. The origin of the Scourge had always been shrouded in mystery. "After the amulet's power killed Queen Vasiliki, her daughter, Queen Aikaterini, used the amulet to imprison her mother's beasts once more. She demanded the priestesses hide the amulet and never speak of Vasiliki's corruption."

Astra read the last of the passage and stared at the carving, her mind reeling. Without any of the priestesses to preserve it, the paint detailing the hand-carved images had begun to chip away, a tragedy that mirrored the fading memory of their sacrifices.

With tentative fingers, Astra traced the clawed hands reaching into the sky. The cold stone seemed to pulse under her touch, as if the ancient magic still lingered. "She wants the amulet," Astra breathed, her voice barely more than a whisper. Her touch moved down to the beasts rising from the trench, and she snatched her hand back, wrapping her arms around herself. "It's all about revenge."

A clang echoed behind her, breaking the silence. With a gasp, Astra whirled around, dropping the torch. It landed on the rubble beneath them without a sound, its light flickering as shadows danced on the walls.

The temple seemed to hold its breath, the weight of history pressing down on Astra as she froze, the darkness closing in around her.

CHAPTER 48

MARIANA AND DAX STAYED close to each other as the days blended together. They spoke little, but their small shared touches said everything. The occasional brush of their fingers, the gentle placement of his warm hand on her lower back, or the way he brushed a loose strand of hair away from her face. Mariana and Dax sought out these moments whenever they could—but only when Kosta and Aurora were preoccupied with not killing each other.

And yet, that's all they were—silent touches of what could have been if everything were different. If they weren't on opposite sides. If they lived in different worlds. If Mariana wasn't the Siren Queen and Dax wasn't a servant of Aurelia. Every time she looked into his eyes, she felt a growing love that tore at her heart, knowing they could never truly be together.

Mariana had to admit she still didn't fully trust what he would do if he were cornered. If he *had* to choose. And what if he did choose her? What if he defied Halia and fought to protect Mariana? She would have no way to protect Dax's family, to defend Kythera against any sort of retaliation.

It wasn't a matter of Dax choosing her over his family. Honestly, she'd lose all respect for him if he *didn't* choose his family. No. It was a matter of trust. Could she trust him to work for the enemy while believing his heart belonged to her?

One looming, daunting question hung in the air between them: What would happen if Halia ever ordered Dax to kill Mariana?

She didn't want to consider what would happen, and yet she still had to take it seriously. Which was why she had to become stronger.

The first thing she wanted was to learn how to control her sky power. It was chaos beneath her skin—lightning, thunder, and wind all rising within. She had no idea how to tame it, but Dax knew how. She didn't want Kosta to know about it in case he put the pieces together that Stavros was her father. Thus, they only practiced when it was Kosta's time to rest below deck.

Aurora would steer the boat, and Dax would instruct Mariana on how to treat her power like it was a living thing above, beneath, and all around her.

"The Generals had a different kind of power than what you had as a siren," he said. "You were born with your power of the sea, whereas the Generals' power was given by the elements they belonged to." Dax held her hands, palms up against his, and her heart quickened at his touch. "Instead of being the source of power like you were before, you are now a conduit. You can channel the power from the sky and cast it."

Letting go of her hands, he asked her to blow over the empty glass bottle in front of her. It took what felt like hours of groaning, bottles crashing violently, and frustrated sighs to do as he asked. *Control the power and cast it*, she kept chanting in her head, until finally, the bottle clanged against the wooden deck and fell gently with the wind she brought forth. She released a gleeful cheer, quickly smothered when Kosta came up top, asking what was so exciting.

"We found the stick you use to jam up your ass, and we thought you might like it back," Aurora sneered with a saccharine smile. "You're welcome."

After Kosta walked back down below, grumbling about jumping off the ship, Aurora winked at Mariana. She always knew what to say to distract him, and Mariana began to wonder if her sister enjoyed getting under his skin.

She saw a glimpse of pride in Dax's face and felt a bitter-sweet pang.

"Thank you," she whispered, and he gave her a small smile.

~

Two days later, Mariana stepped onto the upper deck and breathed in the salty scent. After sleeping nearly ten hours, she'd awoken. Using her power took immeasurable concentration and energy she wasn't used to. Her siren power to control water had essentially come from within her siren soul, which had been far easier to wield than this newfound power from the sky.

For a while, it felt like she was grasping the clouds and getting nothing but rain. Once she understood how to listen to the call of her power and act as a conduit to channel it, everything changed.

"I want to do something bigger," Mariana told Dax as he steered the ship. "No more blowing down bottles."

Aurora had just gone below to get some sleep, despite grumbling about Kosta snoring like a pig, leaving Mariana and Dax to watch the sunny horizon. They were getting closer to Sirenia; she could feel it in her bones.

The sunshine warmed her face as she watched the white sails undulate in the calm wind.

"Like?" The way he looked at her made her bite her cheek to keep from smiling. She'd missed this, this feeling of happiness and warmth when they looked at each other. She cleared her throat and walked over to him before glancing up.

"Think I can fill those sails on my own?"

Dax followed her gaze for a moment before meeting her eyes. "I know you can."

Everything seemed to slow as he stared at her.

"Show me how," she murmured.

He held out his hand, and she took his warm grip. As he pulled her close, he turned her so her back was against his chest, his arms trapping her as he steered the boat.

"Feel the wind. Though it may be soft, it's still there, present, waiting for your control," Dax whispered into her ear.

She tilted her head back to rest on his shoulder and closed her eyes.

"Feel it brush over your skin, through your hair." His lips brushed the shell of her ear in a gentle kiss, then he rested his prickly chin beside it. "Imagine it rippling the ocean's surface, moving the clouds ..."

Listening to his words, she began to concentrate. She had realized that anytime she tried using her sky power, it was like a door she needed to open, releasing the energy trapped within.

She heard the sails billow and whip around.

"Concentrate," Dax urged gently.

Taking a deep breath, she told the wind to do as she commanded and felt it brush against her face in answer. The boat surged.

"You're doing it," Dax said into her ear, and she opened her eyes to see the sails billowing out in full, the wind pushing them forward.

Mariana smiled. Turning her face to look at Dax, she found his eyes already on her.

"You're incredible," he whispered like he couldn't help himself.

Her body melted into his as her tongue licked her parched lips. Dax watched the movement.

"I want to kiss you," he admitted, and her body begged *yes*.

"That's the second time you've said that to me."

The corners of his mouth lifted slightly, light rippling off the waves brightening his eyes. "Keeping track, are you?"

She lifted a shoulder. "If you keep saying it without the follow-through, then you'll force me to make a list."

He laughed; the smile she loved so much spreading across his face.

Loved? Had she really just thought that?

Mariana's heart pounded, the words hanging in the air between them, heavy with unspoken promises.

"Well, it sounds like I should save you the trouble." His head came down close to hers.

He's a distraction, some hidden voice in her head whispered.

Before his lips could close the distance, Mariana pulled out of his arms. A sharp pang of guilt twisted in her chest, breaking the spell. "I ... I have to stay focused," she murmured, more to herself than him. "If we lose control now ..."

She met his sad gaze, searching for something to hold onto—some way to balance the desire that swirled between them with the harsh reality of their situation. She wanted to believe him, to believe that they could steal a moment from the chaos that surrounded them. The fear of what might come next was a dark cloud, threatening violence.

"The moment we give in," she whispered, her voice barely audible over the creaking of the ship and the rustle of the sails, "everything changes."

Dax reached out and pulled her closer by the waist, one hand on the wheel, the other firm on her lower back.

"I'm not afraid of change. I'm afraid of losing you. I can't stay away any longer." His free hand left her waist to cup the back of her head. "And nothing is going to stop me from finally kissing you."

Before she could say another word, Dax dipped his head, and their lips met. Electricity coursed through her at the connection, lighting her up.

Home, she thought as she wrapped her arms around his neck, deepening the kiss.

His tongue danced with hers, and her body began to hum with energy.

Dax lifted her into his arms, and she wrapped her legs around his waist as he leaned her gently against the wheel. The wind swirled around them, cooling their heated skin.

Mariana couldn't help moving her lips down his jaw, tasting his neck.

"What are you doing to me?" she heard him whisper, and her lips tilted up, kissing his neck again before biting gently. "You keep doing that, and we're going to have a lot more explaining to do if we're caught," he said, pulling her face toward him and kissing her again, making her smile brightly.

"Who says we're going to get caught?" she teased, pushing her hips into his.

"I do," a male voice drawled lazily. Mariana dropped to her feet as Dax swung his head around to find a yawning Kosta.

"If you two are done fondling each other, I'd like to get back to steering duty. Assuming the wheel is clean ..."

Mariana did her best to hide her blush, pulling away from Dax, who had a smug grin.

"It's as clean as your hands are," Dax replied, clapping his friend's shoulder.

Mariana gripped the railing tight as Dax came up behind her, trapping her with his body. She internally groaned and bit her lip to keep from turning around and kissing him again.

"I'm going to go distract myself by grabbing some food, want anything?" he asked against her ear.

"Mm-mm," she hummed, trying to keep herself calm and collected.

"You okay?" His hand ran up her arm. She'd taken off her long-sleeve shirt earlier as the sun began to heat the boat, but now she wished she'd kept it on. His touch did something to her, something she couldn't explain.

"Go downstairs," she ordered, pushing him away as she tried—and failed—to hide her smile.

Dax chuckled, walking away to say something to Kosta. Whatever the male replied made Dax bark out a laugh, but Mariana didn't hear any of it. She was too focused on getting her body to stop humming.

Her magic was pulsing beneath her skin, begging for a release far more powerful than filling sails. And it scared the shit out of her.

She had to find a way to let it out, safely—glancing over her shoulder, she saw Kosta scanning the waves, humming softly—and without him noticing.

Turning her head back to the horizon, she wondered if she could control the clouds rolling above them. Would it be enough to calm her down?

Closing her eyes, she felt her power expand around them and then shoot into the sky. Without having any idea what she was capable of, she started out small, using the air to churn the clouds.

Glancing up, she watched the puffy clouds swirl over the blue sky.

By the goddess ... I'm doing it!

Smiling softly, she closed her eyes again and began concentrating on the clouds, churning them faster, condensing them, feeling her power surge up through her—

"Storm's coming in hot!" Kosta shouted, and she opened her eyes to find the clouds above had darkened, threatening rain.

The boat rocked, and Mariana quickly realized what she'd done. Stepping back from the railing, she feigned obliviousness and sat down at the table.

"Nah, it'll pass over us in a moment," she said to Kosta, who gave her an unsure glance.

Just as his eyes trailed back up, the sky had already begun to lighten.

"See? I grew up watching storms, that was nothing." She waved a hand, then leaned her head against her fist, appearing bored despite her thundering heart.

Kosta only frowned up at the sky, and for a moment, Mariana grew uneasy, worried he was going to suspect it was her. But as the blue sky began to peek out again, he shrugged. "Hmm, weird."

She slowly released a sigh.

CHAPTER 49

Aurora turned in her cot restlessly. Her mind was spinning, torturing her by flashing images of scenes she'd thought were long forgotten.

Bloody water. Broken bones. Broken glass. Shards of it sticking out of—

"*Stop!*" she shouted, bolting upright and clutching her head.

Dax, who'd been putting together something to eat in the galley, poked his head into the ridiculously small room with two bunks wedged inside.

"Hey," he called softly. "You alright?"

Her breath came out in short pants, but she managed to nod.

Brushing her hair back, she sighed. "Yeah." Swallowing the bitter taste in her mouth, she nodded again, not meeting his eyes. "I'm fine, just ..." She couldn't find the words. Her mind was a tangled mess of thorny vines she didn't dare reach her hand into.

"I get it," he murmured, staring out the porthole letting in rays of the setting sun. His eyes caught hers. An unspoken understanding passed between them.

In all her time as the Scarlet Serpent, traveling all over the fae realm doing her mother's dirty work, Aurora had only seen Dax once—passed by, more like. But she knew who he was. Back then, his legion of midnight warriors were legendary, battling armies twice their size under the cover of darkness. They would infiltrate enemy encampments, leaving them completely decimated. Not a soul was left to talk about the *killers of the night*. They were King Thaddeus's most honored legion during the Infernal Wars.

Dax was a trained warrior, and she a trained killer. Yet the blood on their hands stained the same.

"You hungry?" he asked.

"Uh, yeah, I'm starving." She pulled herself from the cot and stumbled into the galley—if one could even call it that. It was a stove, a shelf, and a pantry all crammed into a corner.

Dax handed her a wooden bowl of boiled potatoes and onions.

She held back her grimace and forced a smile as she took the bowl.

He laughed at her expression. "I know, it's not ideal, but at least it's better than this overly salted jerky Kosta and I gotta eat."

"Sounds yummy," she drawled, staring down at her potatoes.

Dax had turned toward the stairs carrying two bowls of heaping brown ... *yuck* when she put a hand on his arm, stopping him.

"Listen, I ..." she sighed, unable to believe what she was about to say. Dax seemed like a decent fae who clearly had some shit to sort out. But he had also protected Mari when Aurora couldn't.

She owed him this. "I see how you look at her, and how she looks at you. Be careful." Dax opened his mouth, brows drawn together in a tight line, but she continued before he could speak. "They say never fall in love with a siren for a reason, Dax. Her love can either save you or destroy you. Just ... remember that."

Aurora averted her gaze and pulled her hand back, suddenly uncomfortable.

He stood in place for a moment, seemingly absorbing what she'd said before giving her a wordless nod and walking slowly up the stairs.

Aurora released a deep, bottomless sigh and trudged up the stairs after him.

Dax handed a bowl to Kosta, who thanked him from where he stood at the wheel.

Kosta sniffed the food, frowning. "Are we sure this is even meat?"

Dax shrugged, sitting next to Mari at a sun-bleached wooden table with a rickety leg. "You get used to it." He turned to Mari, who was idly braiding her hair. "Are you sure you're not hungry?"

Mari shook her head and gave him a grateful smile. She looked tired, Aurora noted, the dark circles forming beneath her eyes a clear indication she needed rest.

"You should try this," Kosta said, holding out his bowl. "It's got just the right *overly salty* taste. Basically it tastes like it came straight out of the ocean. You'll love it."

"We don't eat meat, idiot," Aurora sneered, chewing her potatoes.

Kosta retracted his hand. "How was I supposed to know that?"

"Not sure. If you had a brain, I suspect you'd have figured it out from day one on this damn boat when I said we would not be eating any of that vile, salty-ass meat."

"I thought you were being picky," he muttered, and Aurora squinted at him.

"Excuse me?" she asked in a deadly tone.

"Have you ever tasted meat, Rora?" Mari asked curiously.

Aurora shrugged. "Once." She eyed the suspicious meat Dax was picking at from his own bowl.

"What was it like?" Mari stared at the meat too, her lips pulled together and her nose slightly wrinkled, as though the scent of it was making her nauseous.

"Exactly how you'd imagine. I was sick for days. The fae bastard that gave it to me claimed it was the best roasted duck he'd ever cooked and I *wasted* it." She shook her head, lips tugged up slightly at the drunken memory.

Mari grimaced. "It looks disgusting."

Dax chuckled. "It tastes like it looks."

"It's not that bad," Kosta said, chewing. "I've had worse."

"Like what?" Dax asked, an amused grin on his face.

Aurora groaned. "Why would you ask him that?"

Kosta's thick lips opened and closed as if he was considering what snarky comment he'd say back, but Aurora held up her hand to stop him. "Don't make me throw you overboard."

He scoffed. "I'd like to see you try!"

In a flash, Aurora had unsheathed her dagger and was holding it against his jugular, the vein pulsing in fear. Kosta stilled, the silver depths of his eyes staring into her own, and despite the urge to look away, she kept her gaze firm and unflinching.

"You know," she breathed against his lips, "it really is such a shame that such beauty was given to a complete idiot."

Something shifted in his eyes, a heat that made her step back immediately and turn away from him.

At least it got him to shut up.

Needing to be as far from him as possible, Aurora walked over to the railing close to where Mari still sat, Kosta's eyes trailing her. Little snorts came from her sister as she tried holding back her laughter, making Aurora fight the urge to smile.

Mari stood and bumped Aurora's hip as she took up the spot next to her. Happiness shone in her eyes that were like bright pools of water glinting against the setting sun. "Ready for tomorrow?"

Aurora gripped her bowl tight, punching back the images of broken glass, broken bones—

"Are you?" she asked, her voice thick and strained. She cleared her throat, and glanced sidelong at her sister, who had no idea what their homeland looked like. No idea about the pain and suffering their people had experienced.

"I'm ready to finally have Astra back. To know she's safe with us." Mari shrugged. "And ... maybe there's a part of myself that's looking forward to stepping foot on the land everyone always talked about. Finally seeing it for myself."

The wistful look in her sister's expression made Aurora's heart squeeze painfully tight.

"Mari," she started, but closed her eyes. She had to tell her the truth. Setting down the bowl on the table, she ignored the way Dax's cautious gaze shot up to hers and regarded her sister carefully. Taking her hand, she said gently, "Sirenia is ... It's going to look very different from the way history described it. Because of the Banishment."

Mari stood up, giving her a nod that said *duh*. "Of course it is, the king ordered it to be destroyed. I know it's not going to be ... *pretty*, but still—"

"I just—" Aurora sighed and met her eyes. "I just want you to be prepared for what you're about to see." Because truthfully, Aurora wasn't. The day she'd chosen to visit Sirenia after the Banishment, ignoring their mother's orders never to return, was a day that changed her life forever.

She hadn't been expecting the apocalyptic intensity of witnessing all that had been done to their people. Sisters lying dead in pools of bloody water everywhere. The ash burned her lungs, making it impossible to breathe. The glass, the columns, the walls—everything was destroyed. The water was tainted, foul, choking her when she tried to swim upstream. Eventually, she'd had to turn back and swim away from it all.

It took her months to stop waking up screaming for help. Years to finally stop seeing it in her nightmares.

There was a part of her that felt guilty for all of it. She wasn't in Sirenia when it happened. She was on a job for the queen, far from it all. When word spread, she had no idea what to do. It was a miracle she even heard the message her mother kept sending through the sea over and over, begging for any lost sisters to join them in Salus. But Aurora arrived alone. The only siren who'd heard the message and lived long enough to get to safety.

Mari placed a warm hand on Aurora's shoulder, yanking her back from her thoughts.

"Rora, I can handle it." She gave her sister's shoulder a squeeze. "I'm going to get some rest now, okay?"

Aurora nodded numbly and watched her step toward the stairs. Glancing between her and Kosta, Mari said, "You two play nice."

Rolling her eyes, Aurora tried to hide her smirk as her sister descended the steps and disappeared from view.

Her gaze slid to Kosta's and narrowed as his glare locked onto hers. She blew him a kiss, earning a scowl, before turning her face toward the darkened horizon.

Gritting her teeth, she gripped the railing tight. She had to prepare herself for all that was to come. Not just seeing their broken homeland but for what came next.

Inhaling deep, she closed her eyes. The wind blowing through her hair had a certain ... taste to it.

Lifting her face, she studied it.

It was slightly bitter, tainted, almost impossible to notice amidst the salty air unless one was paying close attention. Something so familiar and yet foreign that she studied it long into the night as the stars soared overhead.

By dawn, she realized what it was. A foreboding message that soured her stomach and laid an icy hand on her heart.

You know what's coming, the wind seemed to whisper to her.

Death. And they were sailing directly toward it.

CHAPTER 50

MARIANA STARED AHEAD AT the looming foggy land of Sirenia on the horizon and thought about what would come after. After she brought Astra home. After the amulet was safe. After her sisters were safe.

King Stavros had pleaded with her to bring his son back with the amulet; he assured her that he only wanted peace between their people. But how could she take the chance? Bringing back Helios would be a disaster. Though she didn't completely trust the Siren Witch, Mariana knew she would never hurt her. If she killed Helios, then Mariana would essentially have aided in the witch's death. The witch had been there for her all her life. Could she turn her back on her after everything?

Mariana pulled her hand up to fiddle with the tiny black shell dangling from her bracelet, the same charm the Siren Witch had given her right before she left Salus. It had been a birthday gift. The witch was hardly affectionate, but when she wanted to, she had ways of showing she cared about her family.

No, Mariana couldn't help the king.

When she returned to Salus with the amulet, she and her sisters would discuss their options with the council. Together, they would come up with a plan to restore Sirenia without risking the witch's life. And Mariana would have a very long and hard conversation with her and Cybele. They had kept too many secrets, and it was time to release them.

Mariana swallowed and dropped her hand again, praying that once she had the amulet in her hands, she could reverse the binding spell her mother had placed on her, and she would be free to swim again.

"What is that?" Aurora's question was laced with fear, making Mariana's heart stutter as she turned around. Her gaze trailed to where Aurora was staring behind the boat. Her stomach tightened.

"How?" she breathed in horror.

Kosta and Dax finally realized what was happening and saw what was on the horizon. A royal ship. Sailing with Aurelia's colors, directly toward them. Toward Sirenia.

As quick as a whip, Kosta jerked Aurora close and held a knife against her throat. "This ends here," he said darkly while glaring at Mariana.

Aurora started laughing, a deep cackle that raised the hair on Mariana's arms. "I knew it. I knew one of you would find a way to lead that snake to us. We should've killed you," she said, staring at Dax.

Mariana's eyes shifted to him, seeing the look of rage on his face. "Dax wouldn't do this." She focused on Kosta, determination in his cold, hard gaze.

"You selfish, arrogant bastard," Dax growled.

Mariana touched his arm. Dax turned to her, setting his hands on her cheeks. "You have to leave now," he blurted. "Get off the ship. I'll distract them so you can get away."

Kosta shouted, "Surrender now! There's no escaping—"

A flash of dark, silvery scales launched up from the sea, and teeth sank deep into Kosta's neck.

CHAPTER 51

Kosta's guttural scream sent chills down Dax's spine. Aurora slipped from Kosta's grasp as they all stared at the ghastly serpent holding onto his neck.

It released him with a sickly slurp and turned its eyes on Mariana.

In a slithering, creepy voice, the serpent said through a mouth not meant for words, "*Go get the amulet, little one.*"

Mariana gasped. Indecision clouded her eyes, but Dax knew she had to leave. Otherwise, Halia would catch up with them, and it would have all been for nothing.

Pulling her close by her hand, he met her stare and kissed her. Her mouth instantly melted into his, her hands coming up around his neck, holding him tight. He never wanted to let her go, and his heart twisted painfully. Fear that this was the last time he'd get to hold her close sliced through him like a knife, nearly choking him.

He pulled back just enough to whisper against her lips, "Go, please. Save your sister."

Nodding, Mariana swallowed hard as he kissed her knuckles and let her go.

"Keep her safe," he said to Aurora, who nodded and grabbed Mariana's hand.

Aurora glanced over her shoulder at Kosta and sneered, "If I see you again, I'll kill you." Then they jumped off the ship, splashing into the waves.

Aurora transformed and pulled Mariana along toward their forsaken homeland.

Gritting his teeth, Dax closed his eyes. His soul yearned to go with her, as he felt her getting farther and farther away from him. He fought every instinct, every muscle twitch that begged to jump into that water after them. But this wasn't his journey; it was hers. And he wouldn't hold her back.

Shaking his head, Dax opened his eyes and turned toward Kosta, his body shaking with rage.

Leaning on one arm against the deck to keep himself upright, Kosta held his other hand to his neck. Blood leaked through his fingers, his breath coming out in harsh pants through gritted teeth. His neck was healing—slowly. It was only a matter of time before they found out whether the wound would seal before he lost too much blood.

"How did you do it?" Dax asked grimly.

Kosta winced as he lifted the arm he was leaning on and stuck his hand into his pocket. He pulled out a polished piece of rose quartz with runes engraved all over it.

"Locus stone," he panted. "Ophelia has the other one."

Dax hissed a slow curse. Of course, the siblings would have tracking stones. Scrubbing his face with his hands, Dax released a shout of fury. "Do you realize what you've done!"

Kosta's gaze swept past him for a moment, his mouth a thin line. "The moment I saw the way you looked at her, I knew you wouldn't stop them." His jaw tightened. When his eyes traveled back to Dax, his frown deepened. "You're in love with her."

Dax straightened, his chest flipping uncomfortably. "No, I'm not," he stated softly.

Kosta rolled his clearing eyes and shook his head. His neck was still bleeding, but the blood was dripping slower from his fingers. "I knew I had to come with you, but I also knew that there was no way I was about to seal our fates with Halia's wrath. She has my sister—"

"She loves your sister—"

"It doesn't matter!" Kosta's mouth tightened. "Halia doesn't know what real love is. She'd punish Ophelia just for being related to me—a betrayer! I couldn't let that happen," he confessed. His throat bobbed.

Dax sighed, recognizing the scared look on his friend's face.

"Let's hope you made the right choice."

Kosta's mouth lifted, his sad eyes wandering back toward Sirenia. "Let's hope you did too."

CHAPTER 52

WAVES CRASHED OVER HER head, the relentless current pushing Mariana toward the beckoning shore. Salt stung her eyes, and the roar of the ocean filled her ears, making it hard to hear anything else.

"Come on, Mari, swim!" Aurora shouted, her voice piercing through the chaos as she pulled her sister forward with determined strength.

Mariana's skin was numb, and her muscles ached painfully against the churning waves that tried to drag her under. Each stroke felt like lifting lead weights, but she focused on keeping her breathing as steady as possible, allowing the sea to guide her home.

The moment she felt sand beneath her feet, she pushed against the weight of gravity and the water that threatened to pull her down. She trudged up the shore, each step an arduous battle. Stopping on her hands and knees to catch her breath, she lifted her head, scanning the fog-drenched beach with weary eyes.

Aurora, having transformed, walked up beside her, her breath coming in sharp, ragged gasps.

"It's so much worse than I thought," Mariana panted, her voice trembling with fear and exhaustion.

Rotten wood, broken stones, and years of overgrowth littered the area that had once been a bustling harbor. The fog obscured their view beyond a few yards, but the devastation was clear. She prayed this was the worst of the damage, yet she knew that was false hope.

"We have to move," Mariana said between breaths, glancing at her sister. Aurora gave her a grim nod, fully aware of the danger that pursued them.

Aurora offered her hand, and Mariana took it, grateful for the strength in her sister's grip. Together, they disappeared into the blanket of fog, their footsteps muffled by the dense, eerie silence.

Time seemed to slow as they moved. Keeping a steady eye on the ground, they navigated the ruins, jumping over fallen columns and dodging broken buildings. Mariana had no idea where they were going, yet it was as if her feet knew the path by instinct.

The deeper the sisters ventured, the more evident the destruction became, even with their limited visibility. Mariana splashed through a puddle, cursing the misstep before realizing how quiet it was. The dense fog made navigating the area more difficult, but at least it muffled the sounds of their movements, offering a semblance of protection.

The sound of trickling water in the distance caught her attention, and she pulled Aurora forward. When a massive cliff came into view, their steps came to a halt. Staring at the wall of mossy bedrock, Mariana trailed her eyes up the leaking water that went higher and higher until she could barely see the top through the gloom.

"The waterfall," Aurora whispered. "It's dammed. That's why there's no water flowing through to the sea."

Fallen trees and boulders precariously obstructed the river that had once cascaded down the mountainside. Mariana could make out the distorted flow, but with how faint the sound was, she imagined it had to be far away.

Following the path of the escaped stream, she turned and choked at what she found. Her eyes instantly filled with tears, and she covered her mouth in horror. Aurora stepped up beside her, a horrified sob escaping her lips.

It was the beloved glass dome, shattered. Thick broken glass and twisted metal filled the depths of the dome that had once brimmed with life. Amongst the countless vines growing around the debris, thousands of siren bones lay scattered.

Mariana's blurry eyes beheld the bleached bones of tails, skulls, ribs, and femurs strewn within the remains of the dome Astra had spoken of. The enchanted glass, designed to protect them and provide sanctuary, was now a symbol of hatred, violence, and death inflicted by the fae.

No—the king had done this. *Her father* had done this. The male with sad eyes and a broken soul.

He turned Sirenia into a burial site.

Mariana's heart cracked as she fell to her knees, imagining the terror and pain of watching the glass crash down, slicing and killing everyone beneath it. The water would have turned red with the blood of her dead sisters, their lives flowing into the sea where they belonged.

"Wait," she whispered, swallowing down the pain as understanding dawned on her. *High tides wash away scarlet tears staining the forgotten. The crimson sea roars, glittering and gasping as it retreats*, she recalled.

"The voice from my dream ..." she breathed.

Aurora sniffed, staring down at her with tear-filled eyes. "What?"

"My dream. It spoke of the Banishment."

Aurora didn't respond, but Mariana felt her sister's hand on her shoulder, offering the support she desperately needed.

"I had a dream just before I entered Aurelia," she said, clearing her tight throat. "It said things I didn't understand at the time, but now I get it. Whoever it was, they were leading me here. To Sirenia."

"You don't think ..." Aurora's small voice trailed off, and Mariana lifted her eyes to meet her sister's gaze.

"Astra," she whispered. Was she dead? Had she been the one leading Mariana to the amulet all along? Had something gone wrong after she escaped Aurelia?

Mariana covered her face, shaking her head. *No. No, that can't be true.*

She stood up, wiping her eyes, refusing to believe it. "No, Astra is here somewhere, and we need to find her." She took a deep breath and gave Aurora a determined nod. "C'mon."

As they continued navigating the rubble, Mariana asked, "Where do you think the amulet would be?"

Aurora shrugged. "I'd guess the temple. It was over here."

Her sister led her to a massive pile of large boulders and stones with faint carvings worn down over centuries of erosion. "How do we—"

Then they both heard it; the faintest sound of a female voice calling for help. Mariana whipped her head around, her heart tugging her forward.

Astra.

As fast as her feet could carry her, Mariana raced toward the sound of Astra's cries. The urgency in her sister's voice propelled her forward, her heart pounding in her chest like a war drum.

"Here!" Aurora shouted from between the remnants of a broken stone archway. The ancient language carved into the weathered stone revealed it was the entrance to Seraphina's temple, a place of legend and mystery.

Mariana ran over to her, gasping as she reached the edge of a deep chasm. Aurora grabbed her arm just in time to keep them both from toppling over. Astra lay on the ground far below, at least two stories down, amidst the crushed stone and collapsed marble pillars, reaching a weak hand up at them.

Panting, Mariana asked, "How do we get down there?"

Aurora glanced around, scanning the area for any possible descent route. Without the water that once filled the temple, making it possible to swim toward the bottom, how were they supposed to get to her? The temple, now drained and desolate, offered no easy path.

"The vines," Aurora murmured, her voice a mix of hope and determination. She approached a thick cluster of vines that snaked their way down into the depths. "We have to climb down."

The sisters descended into the ruins, their fingers gripping the vines tightly. Aurora landed first, crouching beside Astra and lifting her head gently into her lap.

"Rora," Astra murmured through chapped lips, as pale as the bones scattered amongst the rubble.

Mariana quickly finished the climb and joined her sisters. Sitting down, she grasped Astra's cold hand, trying to warm it with her own. The touch sent a shiver through her; Astra's skin was as cold as the stone surrounding them.

"Mari, I'm so glad you made it." Astra's voice was strained, as if it took all her strength to speak. "You found my letter?"

"You mean the novel?" Mariana joked, trying to ignore the unnaturally dark veins running up Astra's neck through her ashen skin. The attempt at humor felt hollow in the grim surroundings.

Astra managed a guilty smile, but it faded quickly. Her lips thinned, her expression turning serious.

"There's still so much to tell you," Astra whispered, her voice barely audible.

Mariana had to push back tears as she inspected Astra. Her normally pale blue eyes were muted, dull, rapidly blinking as though she were fighting tears too.

Gripping her frail hand tighter, she said, "We'll have time to speak later, but we have to get you out of here—"

"No," Astra stated firmly, shaking her head with surprising force.

"We have to get you back home, to Luna," Aurora tried, but Astra just kept shaking her head, squeezing her eyes shut as she began to cry. The sobs were obviously not just from sadness but also from pain, deep and relentless.

"Astra, what happened to you?" Mariana asked softly, noticing the bruises all along her sister's body. She still wore the delicate, soft robes she'd donned when she first left Aurelia, now tattered and stained. Her enchanted armor was gone, but the fog seemed to protect her from the sun's harmful rays.

"Attack," Astra gasped between sobs. "I was attacked."

"By whom?" Aurora demanded in a stern voice, contrasting the gentle movements of her hand against Astra's now gray hair.

Astra shook her head again, keeping her eyes shut. It was almost as though she couldn't believe it herself, couldn't bring herself to say the name aloud.

"We have to get her out of here," Mariana said to Aurora, who gave her a grim nod.

Something was terribly wrong with Astra, and if the person who attacked her was still around, they needed to act fast.

Mariana and Aurora began to stand, lifting Astra, when she gasped, her eyes wide with pain. She let out a scream, causing her sisters to quickly and gently set her back down.

"Stop! I can't, I can't—" Astra sobbed. Squeezing Mariana's hand, she looked up at her with so much heartbreak in her eyes that Mariana felt like her whole body was drowning in quicksand, a never-ending feeling of hopelessness and fear.

"Mari, you have to get the amulet," Astra said in a breathy whisper. "You have to protect it."

"Astra, I think it's best if it stays where it is. We have to get you help—" *You're dying*, Mariana almost said. Clearing her throat, she tried to smile. "Don't you want to see Luna?"

"The amulet," Astra muttered, her eyes fluttering as she fought to stay conscious. "You have to keep it away from her." She must've been talking about Halia, who was already on her way here.

The pleading look in her sister's eyes made Mariana release a long sigh. She felt the amulet was better off where it was but knew it might be the only way to save Astra and Cybele.

"Okay," she said softly. "Where is it?"

Astra lifted a shaky hand and pointed a bony finger at a dark tunnel across the ruined temple. "With Seraphina."

Mariana stood up and glanced at Aurora. "I'll be right back."

"Be safe," Aurora replied, her voice heavy with worry.

After giving her sister a small nod, Mariana approached the tunnel. A gentle breeze greeted her, carrying the musty scent of age and decay, welcoming her into the abyss.

Taking a deep breath, she descended into the pitch-black passageway. She dragged her fingers along the wall to steady herself, to keep from tripping over vines and rubble. As she moved deeper, a pale light came into view. The tunnel opened into a massive room with a half-empty pool at its center. Peeking over the ledge, she could see half the stone ceiling lying in shambles at the bottom of the crystal-clear water. She couldn't fathom how it managed to stay clean, but as her gaze lifted, she caught sight of a statue at the center of the pool. A statue of Seraphina.

"Wilted hearts spring anew when the stars sing their song over the sea. Listen." Mariana's eyes widened. It was not a statue.

"High tides wash away scarlet tears staining the forgotten. The crimson sea roars, glittering and gasping as it retreats." The ethereal sound of the voice was so familiar that Mariana's jaw dropped as she recognized the words.

"Luminaries sing bright like the sun under the cunning moon, guiding the way. Follow carefully," Mariana murmured, finishing the riddle. "It was you," she breathed, staring into the eyes of Seraphina.

CHAPTER 53

SERAPHINA SMILED AND DIPPED her head in agreement. "Come here, my dear."

Mariana glanced at the pool before she sat down at the ledge, pulled the dreadful boots off her feet, and plunged into the cold water. It was deeper than she expected. Surfacing, she pushed her hair back from her face and began climbing the short altar. As she reached the top, she stood and stared at the spirit of the first siren.

Seraphina smiled at her. "I know you have many questions. Please, ask them."

"You were the one in my dreams, you led me here, to Sirenia." She could hardly believe it. An angel, the first siren, was leading her to the amulet.

"Yes."

"Why couldn't you simply tell me where to go?"

"If I did, you wouldn't have gone on the journey you were meant to travel and find those you were destined to meet. I cannot interfere with fate, though I do like to think I can help others guide you along the way to where you must go."

"And were you the one who sang to me when I was a youngling? Were you the voice coming from the sky?"

The spirit shook her head. "No, your power called to you until it seemed you would not accept it. The day you became an adult, it ceased. Your mother helped you find it once again."

"That's one way to put it," Mariana drawled.

"Without her binding spell, you never would have harnessed your power of the sky," Seraphina declared. "In order to behold the amulet, you had to become the daughter of both *sea and sky*. Cybele knew your destiny had finally revealed itself, and she knew it was time."

"You're saying my mother knew about my hidden power?"

"Indeed, she was worried it would get you both killed. And like any loving mother would, she did everything she could to protect you."

Mariana bit her cheek and squeezed her fists.

"You disagree. What you believe is manifested from what you experienced. The truth is buried within your heart."

"What she's done is inexcusable."

"And yet not unforgivable."

Mariana swallowed and had to fight not to look away. This was Seraphina, her ancestor, the first siren, an angel. And she knew she spoke only the truth. Despite it being the hardest truth to accept.

"I brought you here, my dear one, so you can save our sisters."

Seraphina stepped close and lifted Mariana's hand. Hers was cold and airy, as though her body were made of clouds. Mariana held her breath as Seraphina draped the amulet over her head and around her neck.

The amulet, always described as pure golden light, fit in the palm of her hand. She lifted it, examining it closely. The circular gold piece was heavy and warm against her skin. Carved on the front were birds mid-flight, waves churning out at sea, and flowers and vines swirling toward the center that seemed to be missing something.

She placed her thumb over the divot, feeling the impression.

"How do I activate it?" she asked.

"You've always had the key." Seraphina gestured to the bracelet on her wrist. Mariana glanced at the star sapphire that glowed softly. "Generations of Siren Queens have kept the key safe, awaiting the moment a daughter was born destined to wield the amulet."

Mariana pulled the sapphire free and held it over the amulet. It would fit perfectly. And yet, she found herself hesitating. The moment she placed the gem inside the amulet, everything she'd been told she was destined to do would become real.

Her breathing turned shallow, and her hands began to shake.

Would she be able to save her people? Could she restore Sirenia without dooming them all? Was she the right person to face everything that was to come?

A pale hand touched hers, and she glanced up at the angel, who stared at her with love in her eyes.

"Don't be frightened, Mariana," she said gently as she tucked a strand of Mariana's hair behind her ear. "Your fear shows how much you care. That's how I know you are the only one who deserves to wear the amulet."

Seraphina smiled, and the weight bearing down on Mariana's chest began to ease. She smiled back and took a deep breath before placing the sapphire where it belonged.

The amulet brightened within her palm and hummed, as though it was pleased to be back the way it was, before Mariana felt her whole body light up.

She gasped as a door within her was unlocked, and her heart began to sing. Her skin turned back to aqua, her scales shimmering under the pale light from above. The warrior inside her shouted and cheered as her nails and canines sharpened. Her body ached to be in the water. Accepting the call, she let herself fall backward, diving off the altar. She splashed into the pool. Her tail emerged with a powerful force, and her gills opened on her neck.

Mariana laughed and cried out with joy at the amazing feeling of the water flowing over her as she raced around the ruins of the temple. It was like she had been trapped, choking in a fae body that wasn't her own, and finally, she could breathe.

With a grin, she shot out of the water in a tall arc, diving back down into the depths. She could hear Seraphina laughing from where she stood at the altar, and Mariana surfaced to gaze up at her.

She gripped the amulet tightly in her hand. "Thank you, Seraphina."

The angel bowed her head. "That amulet can do a great many things. I know your heart is pure, Mariana. Remember: death is only the next step in life. Something I never learned." The haunted look in Seraphina's eyes made Mariana's smile dip.

"Accept what is to come, and you will see the light of a new dawn."

Mariana shook her head. "What do you mean?"

Seraphina glanced at the amulet hanging around her neck. "Astra's next step is only a moment away. Best you be with her when she departs."

"I—" Mariana's throat tightened. "I can't save her?"

"The amulet's purpose wasn't to bring back life, nor was it to save life. It was to bring sunlight where darkness abounded."

Mariana's heart squeezed painfully. She shook her head, unable to accept the truth. "No—No. Astra doesn't deserve to die. You saved Erasmus, why can't I save Astra?"

Seraphina gave her a sad smile, one that slowly chipped away at Mariana's anger. "The amulet was not used to save Erasmus," she confessed, her voice a hollow whisper with so much heartache. "It was used to save our *baby*, to give my daughter a chance at life. I wanted to create a safe place for her to thrive, to survive, and to live." Mariana stared at her, completely and utterly dumbfounded. Seraphina sighed, sadness tightening her eyes. "Revisions of the amulet's story have been told over generations. I fear the story you are familiar with is not the truth."

The truth. It stung as sharp as a jellyfish, numbing her from the inside out. She could hardly believe it. Everyone knew the story; everyone believed the amulet could bring back life. *Save* a life. And yet ... it never did.

"This is only the beginning, Mariana," Seraphina said. "You have the power to save everyone. Bring our sisters home."

Mariana bowed her head at the angel. Then she swam to the edge of the pool, lifted her transformed legs out of the water, and shoved her boots on with haste, then shot down the dark corridor back to her sisters.

CHAPTER 54

MARIANA SKIDDED TO A halt, the light of day blinding her.

"*Queen* Mariana, what a delight to see you again," said an arrogant, feminine voice.

Mariana blinked in the brightness and looked up. Halia stood high above on the edge, five guards flanking her on either side, armed to the teeth.

Mariana's eyes widened when she saw Aurora and Astra floating above her, invisible restraints keeping them from moving.

Halia's hands twitched and moved in slow, small patterns, keeping her sisters trapped in the air she manipulated.

"Join us up top, won't you? We have much to discuss." Halia stepped back out of sight, pulling Astra and Aurora along with her until they were no longer dangling two stories above. Astra had passed out, but Aurora's eyes locked onto Mariana. Fear, dread, and rage were all present in that golden gaze.

Her sisters disappeared from view, and Mariana raced to climb up the vine, the amulet bouncing against her chest.

As she made it to the top, strong hands gripped her. Two guards pulled her along toward Halia. Mariana sneered at her smug expression.

They stopped her within spitting distance of the princess.

"You can't do this! She is a queen!" Aurora shouted, her voice muffled and strained as the sound barely made it through the invisible shield she was locked within.

Halia laughed, and Mariana's fists tightened.

"Don't you see where we are? Look around you! You are a queen of NOTHING!" Halia practically screamed. The sound reverberated up and down Mariana's spine. Those words lodging themselves in her heart.

"However, I will be a queen of *everything*." Halia smiled and extended a graceful hand. "The amulet," she demanded.

Mariana only stared at her, not daring to move a muscle.

"Give me the amulet now, or I will take it."

The threat loomed, and yet Mariana wanted to shake her head and roll her eyes. This was a princess who always got what she wanted, threw a tantrum when she didn't, and judging by the way everyone feared her other name—the Matriarch—she also killed whenever she pleased.

Aurora shifted, straining, desperate to be free of her restraints. Mariana glanced at her sisters, then back at Halia, who was becoming more and more irritated with each passing second.

"What will you do with it?" she asked. "Only a siren can wield it. It's useless to you."

Halia's mouth lifted. "Holding a power like that is *never* useless," she said with a quiet menace that made every muscle in Mariana's body tighten.

"It can't bring back the dead," she said, almost pleading. "It was never made for that. Seraphina herself told me." Mariana had hoped the truth would change Halia's mind, but it was clearly wishful thinking.

Halia shook her head slowly. "I'd rather not take any chances." She snapped her manicured fingers. "Hand it over."

"Let my sisters go first."

Halia groaned. "I will let them go once the amulet is safely in my possession."

Mariana's skin began to hum, her power reaching out toward the air, keeping her sisters trapped. She ran imaginary hands over it, testing it for cracks.

"In fact," Halia added, "once I have it, I will let you all go to do what you wish. Crawl back to that underwater city of yours or stay here, I don't care. Just give it to me."

Invisible tendrils of air found a tiny seam in the magic, and Mariana gave Halia a small smile.

"No, I think I'll keep it."

With a flick of her wrist, her magic speared through that crack.

Halia shouted as Astra collapsed to the ground, and Aurora grabbed her bone daggers from her waist.

"I warned you what would happen if you touched my sisters again," Aurora sneered, a wicked grin on her face.

"Restrain her!" Halia ordered.

The guards sprang into action, releasing Mariana. Aurora's daggers whirled, slicing through the air with lethal precision. Two guards fell instantly, clutching their throats. The remaining three hesitated, casting nervous glances at each other.

Mariana took the opportunity to sprint toward Astra, her heart pounding with desperation. She knelt beside her unconscious sister, her hands trembling as she checked for a pulse. It was faint, barely there. Mariana's breath hitched.

"Go!" Aurora shouted at her just as she flung one of her daggers into a guard's stomach before yanking it back out to swipe at another.

While her sister kept the guards distracted, Mariana lifted Astra's frail body into her arms. She wasn't sure how Halia had magically lifted both her sisters into the air so easily, but Mariana worried she'd drop Astra, injuring her further, if she tried. Instead, she gritted her teeth against her straining muscles as she ran into the fog.

"Stop!" she heard Halia scream behind her, but she kept going, ignoring the grunts of pain and clash of metal against bone. Aurora was a superior warrior to those guards; she could handle them.

Mariana's arms and legs barked at her to release Astra. Panting, she set her sister down, leaning her back against a boulder.

"Astra, please wake up," she said in a pleading whisper, gently shaking her shoulder and patting her cheeks. They were freezing to her touch.

Astra groaned, her eyes fluttering. "The amulet," she murmured, pressing a shaky finger to the blue stone that glowed gently at her touch.

Mariana's eyes blurred with tears as she watched her sister's heavy eyes lift to her face.

"Get out of here. Protect it," she whispered.

Mariana shook her head, her heart clenching at the thought. "I'm not leaving you here—"

"Step away from her," a cold voice sounded above her, and Mariana glanced up toward the point of the blade Halia was holding.

Slowly, Mariana stood from where she'd crouched and took a small step back.

"Why are you doing this, Halia?"

Where is Aurora? Mariana glanced past the princess toward the fog.

The princess rolled her eyes. "You know why. The fate of my kingdom depends on who possesses the amulet. I will not allow my brother to be resurrected and ruin all I've done. Now, drop your dagger and hand over the amulet."

Mariana swallowed. "Astra has done nothing wrong. Please, just let her go, and we can work out an agreement. I don't want to see Helios return either."

"Nonsense! I know the deal *she* made with my father! The moment she gets her hands on it, she will fulfill their agreement. And I can't let that happen."

"So what's your plan, then? Destroy the amulet? It's powerless in your hands."

"Exactly. Although, I do not wish to destroy it. Instead, I will deprive all of you of the chance of ever using it against me. It's safest with me. Hand it over, or your sister dies."

Halia stepped toward Astra and pointed the blade at her. Mariana glanced down at her sister, who was growing paler and paler with each breath. Her limbs were shaking with the effort to stay upright.

"Don't let her take it," Astra forced out with an effort that made her close her eyes and release a heavy breath.

Mariana took a step back. She needed to redirect Halia's attention away from Astra.

"You want the amulet? Come get it."

Turning quickly, she bolted for the broken glass dome just as she felt airy vines yank at her feet. She slammed to the ground just as she reached the edge, her breath rushing out of her lungs.

Gasping, she stared down into the destruction, the bones, the *water*. Mariana's body hummed with the familiar pull. The water below was connected to the sea.

Glancing behind her, she saw Halia slowly stalking toward her, the blade's tip dragging along the ground. She was smiling, like she thought she'd won.

Shoving her hands beneath her, Mariana stood. She glared at Halia, teeth gritting and fists clenched tight enough to hurt.

Allowing Halia to possess the amulet was not an option. Neither was accepting her sister's death. Mariana's hands began to shake.

"This is your last chance," she warned Halia, who released a sharp laugh.

"Doubtful. I have all the power here, *sister*."

Mariana's eyes widened. *What did she just say?*

Halia released a vicious scream along with a hurricane of wind at Mariana, throwing her into a fallen column. Her breath shot from her lungs upon impact.

The water trapped at the bottom of the broken dome behind her beckoned with the promise of chaos, and Mariana answered the call. As she lifted herself to stand, she pulled the water up from the depths, feeling it surge behind her in a mighty wave. The bones of her dead sisters swirled within the churning water.

Power sang beneath her skin. The rush of ecstasy after so long without using her magic had her laughing like mad. She smiled at Halia.

"Surrender!" she shouted at the princess.

Halia briefly turned her scowl behind her at where Astra hid, before giving Mariana a villainous grin.

"Never."

Halia lifted her arms, one aimed at Mariana, the other at Astra, who floated from the ground with her hands clawing at her throat as though there were an invisible pair of hands choking her.

Rage burned bright through Mariana's veins, numbing her to the point that she didn't feel the amulet lifting from her neck.

Mariana watched in delight as Halia's eyes widened the moment she released the unforgiving wave. Water swallowed everything in its wake and violently slammed into the dam above.

Mariana's heart seized as she realized her fatal mistake. Her power broke the dam, the waterfall breaking free with a devastating roar. She screamed, watching helplessly as trees, boulders, and debris descended upon her sister.

Astra's pale, teary eyes were the last thing she saw before water crashed down, consuming them all.

CHAPTER 55

Salt. The taste—the feeling—flooded Mariana's gills, stroked her hair, and held her close like a loving mother's hug, welcoming her home the moment she was spat out into the sea. But that comforting feeling faded quickly as the pain in her body and heart became all-consuming.

Flashes of memory ripped her mind apart. The fear in Astra's pale eyes. The roar of the water bursting free from its restraints, crashing down with a vengeance. Waves from the savage onslaught she'd caused pounded, beat, sliced, and threw her body around like a shell caught in its snare.

She had done this. Her beloved sister ... was dead. All from one stupid, reckless swipe of her hand.

When the river spat Mariana's body out into the sea, she didn't transform her legs into her tail. She didn't call for help. She floated, staring lifelessly up as the sun dipped below the horizon and darkness swallowed the world. The deeper she sank, the more she begged the Goddess to let her forget. Just one last mercy, that was all she asked for.

The mercy to forget that she had failed.

When her body landed gently atop a bed of coral, thousands of fish burst from hidden crevices, fleeing her invasion. She jolted and blinked to clear the haze. Beams of moonlight high above illuminated the rolling waves, making them glow and glitter from below. Blobs of darkness trimmed with light caught her eye. She blinked again, willing the floating blobs to focus. Her eyes went wide, her heart coming to a halt.

They were bodies.

Aurora.

Within seconds, she transformed, her tail whipping for the surface. Her head burst through the water. Wiping her eyes, she grabbed the nearest body. Turning the head toward her, she saw one of Halia's guards staring back at her with dead eyes. She said a silent prayer and released the body.

"Aurora?" she shouted over the roaring waves and wiped her eyes. The stars glinted from the sky as she shouted her name at them, but no reply came. She let out a whimper, imagining herself falling deeper and deeper into her own nightmare. She had to find her, unable to bear the thought of losing someone else she loved.

The truth spurred her forward, and she grabbed the next nearest body.

Face after face, and none of them was the one she begged to see. Finally, floating near the beach, caught in a wave, she found her.

"Rora!"

Her eyes were closed, her skin chilled, and her body limp. "*No, no, no.*"

Quickly, she pulled her sister toward the shore and willed the waves to wash them up the sandbank. The water retreated, and Mariana put her fingers to her sister's throat. Steady heartbeats.

"Rora, wake up!" she shouted, shaking her sister's shoulders until her eyes finally opened.

Aurora groaned, clutching her head. "Did I drown?"

Mariana wanted to laugh at the ridiculous question, but the weight of all that had just happened pushed it away.

"That's a little impossible, don't you think?"

Dropping her hands, Aurora stared up at the night sky. "Anything seems possible these days. Like those powers of yours." Her eyes slid over to Mariana.

Grief tightened her face. She wanted to cry, but felt like she had no energy left to shed a single tear.

"She's dead, Rora," Mariana confessed, staring at her hands. "Because of me."

Aurora gently took one of Mariana's hands in her own and squeezed it. She sat up with a wince, then regarded her sister carefully. "Listen to me. Whatever happened was not your fault—"

"Yes, it was," she admitted in a deadly whisper. Tears leaked from the corners of her closed eyes. "Halia attacked and I—" She released a ragged breath. "Astra was crushed under the debris from the dam breaking. There was nothing I could do—" Her voice cracked, and she began to sob. It felt like an old wound had been ripped open. Mariana had just gotten her sister back when she thought she was dead, and now ...

It wasn't fair. All she wanted was her sister. To hold Astra and grip her close, wrap her arms around her, and never let go. She missed her sister so terribly that the thought of never seeing her again ... Her body shook, racking sobs tearing her chest apart.

Aurora pulled Mariana close, directing her head into the crook of Aurora's neck.

It was a motherly touch, one so familiar to her. Celeste used to hold her like this when she had been a youngling, after her mother said something vile and cruel to her, when the cursed would tease her, or when she was simply upset over nothing at all. She missed her.

Mariana's crying slowed, her enervated body still clutching Aurora tight, refusing to believe she'd ever lose her too.

"I thought ..." Mariana sniffed. "I thought the amulet could stop whatever was happening to her, but Seraphina said—" The words died on her tongue.

"What?" Aurora asked gently, stroking Mariana's knotted hair. "What did she say?"

Mariana swallowed, throat tight. "She said the amulet wasn't meant to bring back life or save it. Astra was already dying. Someone attacked her to the point—" She choked on her words.

"That she couldn't be saved," Aurora finished for her.

Mariana shook her head, squeezing her eyes shut.

"There's only one thing left we can do." Aurora pulled back, and Mariana lifted her gaze into her sister's raw, heartbroken face. "Let us pray for her safe journey to peace," Aurora suggested softly and gripped Mariana's hands. They closed their eyes and silently prayed to Amphitrite.

Mariana clenched her teeth tight to keep from sobbing again, but the tears still ran down her heated cheeks.

With every moment that passed, every word she whispered under her breath, she could feel Astra's soul lifting, listening to their prayers.

"Astra," she breathed. Then, what felt like a cold kiss was placed on her forehead. *Goodbye*, it silently whispered.

When Mariana could breathe again, she opened her eyes the same moment Aurora did. She squeezed her hands again.

"We have to be careful how we tell Luna. With how she was behaving when I left ... I just don't think we can predict what she might do when she finds out."

"Okay," Mariana whispered.

"At least we have the am—" Aurora's eyes went wide as she glanced down at Mariana's chest.

"What?" She glanced down too. It was gone. The amulet was gone.

Her heart tripped, frantically skipping as she looked around the sand.

"Where is it?" she shouted frantically.

"I have a feeling I know where it is ..." Aurora muttered, looking out at the darkened sea.

Mariana's eyes turned in that direction, and she cursed. Lights flickered on the midnight horizon.

"Halia has it," Aurora said grimly. "If she didn't, I doubt she'd be sailing away on her grand ship."

Mariana held back a scream. She vaguely recalled the faint sensation of the amulet lifting right before ...

"Godsdammit!" she shouted. "Astra begged us not to let her have it. She was the one person!"

"I'm not so sure about that," Aurora said, making Mariana turn her questioning gaze toward her sister.

"What do you mean?"

"I don't know," Aurora said, gazing off into the distance. "But something in the way Astra said it ... You have to keep it away from *her*, remember? It just—" Aurora shook her head. "I don't know, it just didn't seem like she was talking about Halia."

"But Halia *is* the one who has it."

Her sister stayed silent beside her, and Mariana began to realize they had to come up with a plan. And quickly.

"Without that amulet, will Cybele die?" Mariana asked quietly, lifting grim eyes to her sister's.

"I'm not sure. The witch seemed adamant that the only way to save Cybele was with the amulet."

Mariana tilted her head. "Something Seraphina told me was that the amulet's purpose was to bring light where there was only darkness. Would fallout be considered darkness?"

"I don't know that it's just the fallout killing Cybele," Aurora said carefully. "Did you see the way Astra's veins looked? It was like squid ink was flowing through her body. It's the same way Cybele's veins looked before I left."

Confusion swept over Mariana in a tidal wave of dread. "So ... whoever attacked Astra might also be poisoning Cybele?"

Aurora bit her lip and nodded. "I think so. Someone in Salus is killing her."

Mariana released a deep sigh. "We don't know for sure, but whatever is plaguing Cybele, maybe the witch knows it can still be reversed with the amulet."

"If anyone truly knew and understood what the amulet is capable of, it would be the witch," Aurora pointed out. "She was the only scholar allowed inside Seraphina's temple to record data before the Banishment. Usually, only the priestesses were allowed inside, but they made an exception for her once we started using orbs to record all our history."

"So, the witch is probably right, then. Which means we have to get that amulet back from Halia."

"We can swim to her ship, take it back from her," Aurora suggested, but Mariana shook her head.

"It's too risky. Too many guards on board could stop us before we reached it. Besides, we have no idea where it is. And if Halia really wanted to, she could consider it an act of war." Mariana bit her lip, trying to think of a solution, but there was only one that she kept circling around, not wanting to accept it.

"Well, we have to come up with something."

The two fell silent, ideas swirling between them in the midnight air, until finally, Mariana sighed, sagging.

"I know what to do," she admitted heavily. She let her eyes close, wishing there was another way. But there wasn't. She was the queen now, and queens made difficult choices when it meant saving their people. "She'll want power in exchange for power."

Opening her eyes, she studied Aurora, who reached out to hold her hand. It gave her the courage she needed to share her idea with her sister. Her voice was so thick with grief, she could hardly speak, but when she finally got it all out, Aurora's mouth was pinched tight, her eyes on the sand.

"Think it will work?"

Mariana glanced out at the sea as dawn began lighting up the sky. "We have no choice. It has to work."

CHAPTER 56

DAX WATCHED HALIA STARE at the amulet, as if it were a fascinating trinket, from where he and Kosta were shackled to the railing.

After they had been transported off their small boat onto the massive ship, Halia didn't trust them not to try to escape, despite Kosta assuring her he would never turn on the crown. Dax had stayed silent. Halia never took her eyes off him, searching for the truth he hid well beneath his stoic gaze.

Even now, he held his tongue despite every instinct, every urge to ask what had happened to Mari. To ask if she was alive. Or if she was ...

No, he couldn't consider that a possibility.

"Can we please let them go now?" Ophelia asked anxiously. Halia glanced up at her, then back at Dax and Kosta. All of Halia's once-immaculate makeup had been washed away. Her lavish dress stuck to her like a second skin, thin gold thread unraveling the intricate design it once had. Even her usually perfect hair was a mess of frizzy braids clinging to her neck. None of the ten royal guards Halia had departed with had returned with her.

She stood tall, like a lone wolf, ready to bite, claw, and snarl at anyone who stepped too close to her prize.

Dax held Halia's stare until she nodded to the guard standing beside them to unlock the shackles. As soon as they were free, Kosta swept Ophelia into a hug.

Halia's amber eyes continued scrutinizing Dax, then she motioned for him to follow her below deck. Dax followed reluctantly but kept his head high while reminding himself to remain calm.

What Kosta had said to him back on their small boat stuck with him—that he was in love with Mari. Despite the ache in his chest shouting the truth, he had to keep up the facade that there was no love. Not a chance of it ever existing. For the sake of his people.

Halia had threatened his family in the past when Dax refused to do something she'd asked, such as the time she ordered him to slit a servant's throat for stealing one of Halia's heirloom necklaces. He'd told her no, that it went far beyond their deal. He was not an assassin; he was a warrior. Halia's response was simple: She wanted proof of his loyalty to her and handed him a dagger with a royal seal. Then proceeded to tell him that if he didn't follow through, then he was holding the very weapon that would kill Kenna.

Dax felt his hands begin to shake as he recalled the memory of standing over that poor female as she cowered before him, begging him not to hurt her.

When he brought the blade up and cut his forearm, allowing the blood to splatter and drip across the servant's small room, she stared up at him in confusion.

"Leave. Disappear and never come back. Because if she discovers you're still alive, then it's both our heads," Dax had ordered, and the young servant obeyed. She gathered what little she owned and escaped that night. He never knew what became of her, but when Halia heard about the blood all over the missing servant's room, no body—or necklace—to be found, she questioned him. All he told her was that investigations led to questions that shouldn't be asked. It was better if the court believed it to be a confusing mystery than a solvable one. Dax wasn't sure Halia had believed his answer, but that didn't matter. She had no proof of him disobeying her. Even now, with her staring up at him from where she sat with her glass of wine that swirled with movement from the ship, she had no proof he was disloyal.

"Tell me, how did that siren coerce two of my top operatives into following her onto a boat and sailing all the way out to this Gods-forsaken land?" she asked, staring at her wine.

Dax clasped his hands behind his back. "Does it matter? It all led to you taking possession of the amulet. The thing you wanted most."

Halia's eyes slid to his and latched on.

"Are you curious to know how I got it?"

Dax shrugged, despite his stomach churning with possibilities. "Not particularly."

She tilted her head. "I sense a change in you."

He sighed. "How so?"

Halia studied him. "You're not looking at me like you hate me. That, I was used to. No, I sense ... acceptance. Like a worm that knows its destiny is to be eaten by the bird."

Dax swallowed, unsure what to say.

Setting down her glass, she stood and approached him slowly. "You know, Dax, if I didn't know any better, I'd say you and the siren had gotten terribly close."

He shrugged. "It's better that she thinks of me as a friend."

"Why's that?"

"Intel," he blurted, internally wincing at his haste to explain. "I heard Ophelia was doing the same, so I followed her lead."

Halia's lips twitched. "I see." She tapped her hips with her fingers that were missing rings that he had no doubt she could easily replace. "I suppose it doesn't matter now." Turning, the princess shrugged as she sat back down. "I doubt she survived the dam crashing. Her sister certainly didn't."

Dax blinked, thinking of Aurora. "The Scarlet Serpent is dead?" he asked, his chest constricting.

Halia took a sip of her wine. "Astra," she corrected. "The last I saw of the other one, she was battling three of my guards. I doubt she made it through without a blade in her stomach."

His hands began to shake. He squeezed them tight behind his back.

Lifting the amulet in her hand, she peered down at it. "Beautiful," she breathed. "So much blood spilled over something so small." Her gaze flew up to his. "Tragic, don't you think?"

Careful to keep his jaw from clenching, he nodded. "What do you plan to do with it?"

Halia paused, her gaze lingering on the amulet before meeting Dax's eyes again. "I originally planned to destroy it. But now"—she sighed, her expression softening ever so slightly—"it feels like a waste. Too much has been lost for it."

Dax watched her carefully, his mind racing. This was the first time he'd seen any sign of doubt in Halia. "And what of the sirens? With this, you could give them back Sirenia. Keep them in line, enforce peace—"

Halia chuckled dryly. "Peace? You think, after everything, *peace* is still an option? No, this amulet ... it might just be my ticket to something else. A way to rewrite the rules, perhaps even the throne itself."

"The throne?" Dax repeated, the words tasting bitter in his mouth.

"Yes." Halia stepped closer, her voice dropping to a whisper. "You see, Dax, power isn't just about maintaining order; it's about rewriting it. With this"—she held up the amulet—"I can challenge anyone, even the king."

Dax's heart thudded in his chest. This was more ambition than he had ever heard her express. The king was his ally, but if he ever chose to give Halia the throne ... "And where does that leave people like us? Those who have bled for your cause?"

Halia's face hardened. "Loyal soldiers are always rewarded, Dax. But traitors ..." She let the word hang ominously in the air. "They find that my grudges crush windpipes and spike heads."

Dax's brows lowered, understanding the unspoken threat. "I am no traitor, Halia."

"I know," she replied, her voice softening again. "Which is why I am offering you a choice. Stand with me, truly stand with me, and I assure you the rewards will be beyond your imagination. For you and your people."

Dax considered her words, the weight of his next decision pressing down on him. Here was a crossroads, one that could change everything. "And if I refuse?"

Halia smiled, cold and calculating. "Then I suggest you pray that your beloved Mari could forgive you for what would come next."

CHAPTER 57

"*OH, HOW THE WAVES roll in, faster than the setting sun, faster than the rising moon*—Gahhh!"

The old male shouted as Mariana pulled herself up out of the sea and onto Aurelia's dock.

Standing up straight, she gave him a sheepish smile. "Sorry to startle you," she panted. "Lovely singing voice, though!"

Leaving the gaping sailor behind, Mariana quickly ran the length of the harbor, wet hair flying behind her, lungs and limbs shouting for a break. But there was no time for a break. No time to breathe as she sprinted toward the shimmering gates of the Aurelian palace.

It had been two days since she and Aurora left Sirenia's shore. By now, her sister would've returned to Salus, ready to protect their mother. They had no idea who was hurting Cybele, but if the same assailant had truly attacked Astra, then Cybele had to be protected. Aurora and Mariana had vowed on that forsaken beach that they would do everything they could to save her.

That all started with securing the amulet and protecting Cybele from further harm.

"I am Queen Mariana! Let me in!" she shouted up at the gates, then breathed a sigh of relief when they opened a moment later.

Using her power, she expelled the remaining water clinging to her skin, clothes, and hair, leaving a small puddle behind her as she entered the immaculate courtyard.

The fountain glittered, spewing water gently into the pool below. The sound was soothing, and Mariana took a deep breath, calming her heart.

The peace was broken by the clacking sound of shoes over the stone path.

A short, round-faced servant quickly approached her and bowed, his lips pursed distastefully at her outfit.

Mariana resisted the urge to slap the look right off his face.

"Queen Mariana. Please do accept our humble apologies, but now is not the time for any visitors."

"I need to speak with Princess Halia. It's urgent."

The servant shook his head, the tuft of graying hair atop his head moving with the breeze. He clasped his white-gloved hands and gave her a pointed look. "That's simply not possible. Princess Halia is preparing for the funeral. She is very busy."

Mariana's eyebrows furrowed as she stared at him. "Pardon me, whose funeral?"

He blinked at her. "King Stavros, may he rest in peace." He said it with a slight bow of his head.

Mariana felt her jaw drop along with her stomach. All she could hear was the erratic beat of her heart drumming loudly in her ears.

Her mind couldn't process what he'd just said. "The king ... is dead?" she breathed.

She lifted a shaky hand to her lips.

Stavros. The king who had destroyed Sirenia. The male who had loved Cybele and sired Mariana. The father who died dreaming of what could've been.

She could hardly believe it.

"No," she whispered.

"Yes, it is a tragedy," the servant commented. "It was so sudden, and unfortunately, the medics do not know the cause of death." He sighed dramatically, almost wistfully, as if knowing the cause of death would solve everything. Then he turned on his heel. "Please follow me; I will take you to your room."

His curt behavior pulled her from her foggy stupor. "Wait," she blurted, and the servant turned to look at her. "What's your name?"

He lifted his head proudly, a slight smug look in his blue eyes. "Rupert, Your Highness."

Mariana took a step toward him. "Rupert, I need you to pass a message along to the princess. Tell her I must speak with the council at their *earliest* convenience. Do you understand?"

Rupert seemed to hold back a retort, his lips pinching. "Of course, I shall pass along the message." He eyed her up and down before turning on his polished shoes again. "Please follow me."

Stepping into the inner courtyard, Mariana swallowed. She was still reeling from the news when a voice shouted, "Mariana!"

Turning, Mariana saw Ophelia practically running toward her from the other side of the fountain. Her ivory robes billowed in the breeze, and yet her hood somehow stayed atop her curly blonde hair.

Ophelia slowed as she neared, her bright eyes shimmering with delight. "Rupert, I have it from here. You're excused," she said to the servant without looking at him.

Rupert's eyebrows scrunched together. "Madam, I do believe I should be the one to escort—"

Ophelia finally glanced at him, eyes narrowed. "Thank you, but I will escort her royal highness into the palace. You are *excused*."

Rupert huffed, then turned and dramatically marched away.

Ophelia bit her cheek to keep from laughing, causing Mariana to do the same.

"I'm so glad you're okay, after everything that's happened. And that letter your sister left for Princess Halia in the library." Ophelia's eyes widened before she giggled. "I've never seen her so angry in my life."

Any hint of amusement Mariana felt faded away into grim sadness. Kosta had been caught in the crossfire of all of this, and so had the Seer. "Ophelia, I want to apologize."

"For what?" Ophelia asked, concern in her gaze.

"I overheard that Kosta is your brother. I'm sorry my sister and I—That we—"

Ophelia shook her head and placed a steady hand on Mariana's arm. "There's nothing to be sorry for. Kosta is so uptight all the time. He tries to hide it with his bad *humor*, but really, he needed to get away from the palace."

"But the way we did it—he could've died—" Mariana stumbled over her words, trying to find the right thing to say when Ophelia suddenly pulled her in for a hug.

The Seer was slightly taller than her and tightly wrapped her arms around her shoulders. "I forgive you, Mari. Please, it's okay. I promise," she said gently.

Mariana hugged her back, grateful.

Pulling back, Ophelia squeezed Mariana's hands gently. "I know things have been messy between us. But ... I'd really like to be your friend, if that's something you're okay with? If not, that's totally fine! I just—I hope we can find some common ground, or—"

Mariana bit back a laugh as she gave Ophelia's arms a reassuring squeeze. "Ophelia, I'd like to be your friend too."

Ophelia let out a small, relieved laugh. "*Good.*" Her eyes roamed Mariana's face and neck, probably taking in the fact that her skin was now pale blue. "I'm happy to see your gills are back! I'm so glad you found her."

Astra. Mariana swallowed, her smile strained. She opened her mouth to respond when movement across the courtyard caught her eye. High up on the second story, Dax was walking across the short bridge between buildings. His face turned, and he stilled. Their eyes met for a second. All Mariana wanted to do was run to him, leap into his arms, and hold him close.

The shock on his face shifted into haunted sorrow. His head dipped, looking away from her, as though he couldn't meet her gaze any longer. Clenching his jaw, he forced himself to keep going. He never looked back.

Mariana felt tears well up in her eyes as she watched him cross through a doorway. Whether it was from stress, fatigue, or heartbreak, she couldn't tell. And she didn't want to. She had no idea where she and Dax stood, but clearly, he didn't want to see her.

Ophelia had apparently seen what happened and took Mariana's hand, giving it a reassuring squeeze.

"He's been distant since we returned and discovered the king had passed."

"Dax and the king helped Astra escape," Mariana admitted softly.

The Seer dipped her eyes. "I know. He chose to help her despite the repercussions that would come if Halia found out."

Mariana didn't miss the guilt in those words. "And did she?"

Ophelia swallowed, lifting her gaze to Mariana's. An unspoken truth passed between them as the Seer gave her a small, sad smile.

"Come on, let's get you to your rooms."

Ophelia graciously pulled her along, away from the storm and into the hurricane.

CHAPTER 58

THE DAY CAME AND went like the tide. The bright, unforgiving sun was a glaring beacon over Aurelia, as though it was screaming that something terrible had happened there. And that evening, the whole city went quiet.

King Stavros was dead. And there was no explanation as to how.

Watching from high above in her bedchamber, sitting on the window ledge, Mariana witnessed thousands of fae gathering to honor their dead king. From the palace to the city, Halia led the parade behind the king's grand golden coffin, using her power to hold and guide it gently down the bridge with the wind. The gold paint glinted against the setting sun as the hands of young, old, wealthy, and poor brushed along the coffin, sweeping the slightest bit of gold dust onto their fingers.

When Mariana asked Ophelia to explain their ritual, she said the gold dust would cling to the skin for weeks. It was a sign of respect, symbolizing how many lives the king had touched with his compassion and strength as a ruler. If the king were respected by his subjects, his coffin would be brushed free of gold before being buried in their royal cemetery on the other side of the city. And from what Mariana could tell based on the silent hands touching the coffin as it moved along, the king would not be disgraced from where he awaited his transition from the Veil to the Eternal Sands.

Mariana had heard of the Veil before, the ethereal land where souls wandered before they were buried in the Eternal Sands.

Sirens feared it. They were daughters of the sea. Their souls weren't meant to be buried underground. This was why their cremation ceremonies were held so quickly after death, in order to ensure Amphitrite could lead their dead sister's soul to peace within the sea.

A twinge of guilt coursed through Mariana. She would have no gold on her fingers. She didn't know Stavros as her king or as a father. She had no respect to give.

Her chest throbbed as she imagined the life he had envisioned with her mother, the life he'd hoped for until the moment he took his last breath. The memory of them together, weaving through the abandoned rooms full of hope, was all she would have of him. As they'd stared at her mother's closed door, Mariana's hand in the crook of his elbow and her head against his arm, she knew he had been imagining Cybele opening that door with a bright smile on her face. Instead, they would never see each other again. They were lovers destined to become enemies. And that made her want to cry.

Gripping her arms, she stared down at the sea of bodies weaving together, trying to get close to the coffin, and wondered if Dax was among them.

She missed him. Seeing him when she arrived had pushed all the hidden emotions she felt back up to the surface. She had neither the time nor the mindset to process her emotions. But she was certain that if given the choice, he would be down there paying his respects. Somewhere, awaiting his moment to feel the gold cling to his skin. She imagined for a moment being down there beside him, their hands touching as they said farewell to a father Mariana had never really known and a king Dax had known all too well. Choosing not to partake in the fae ritual was customary if one had no relationship with the deceased, as she had been told by Halia in a terribly stoic letter while planning their father's funeral. But the simple excuse for Mariana not to get involved felt more like a request than a suggestion.

Mariana still had no idea how Halia knew they were sisters, unless Stavros had decided to tell her sometime before they all traveled to Sirenia, though that made little sense. Perhaps he'd thought it would bring them closer together? She shook her head at the absurd thought. Did he know he was going to die, and that's why he'd told her?

When she asked Ophelia how the king died, she said no one knew. His heart simply gave out. He had silently died in his study with thousands of books as witnesses. A few hours later, a servant went in to check on him, only to find the lifeless king staring out the window, gazing at the magnificent city he had cherished. Or had failed, in Halia's eyes.

It was strange how similar it was to the way Helios had died. Everyone in the palace whispered about it. Theories that Cybele might have been seeking revenge against the king and hired a mercenary, or even the Scarlet Serpent, to kill him quietly swirled around the palace. But Mariana knew it hadn't been her mother. And it certainly hadn't been Aurora. No, a different person came to mind as she contemplated how Stavros had died.

Astra and Stavros both believed that the Siren Witch killed Helios and let Cybele take the blame. Why would she have done any of that? And would she have tried to kill the king?

Aurora had warned Mariana repeatedly about Luna's behavior. Would she have found a way to kill the person she thought took her mother? It seemed unlikely. Luna was so ... timid, certainly not the killing type. So, who was behind all this? She certainly didn't believe that Stavros dying the same way that his own son had was all coincidence.

And yet, something kept snagging Mariana's thoughts.

Everything centered around the amulet. Someone desperately wanted it.

Halia would've been keeping it close. No doubt she had it around her neck at that very moment, making it nearly impossible to steal without her noticing.

Scrubbing her face with her hands, Mariana sighed. Her mind was tired, and her body was aching. She'd hardly slept over the last week.

Tomorrow morning, after Halia was officially Queen of Aurelia, Mariana would have a meeting with her and the council to discuss the future of Sirenia—and the possession of the amulet.

Glancing back at the gold coffin before it disappeared into the throng of fae, Mariana said a silent goodbye to the father she had never really known and walked away from the window.

As she lay in bed that night, all she could think of was the moment when she hugged her sister goodbye on the beach. They had a plan.

Aurora would protect their mother, and Mariana would return home with the amulet.

There was only one way to get it back.

Tears leaked from Mariana's eyes, staining the silk pillow as she thought of all that they were about to lose.

CHAPTER 59

BREATHE. JUST BREATHE. MARIANA stared at the council, sweat rolling down her spine beneath the stifling dress that had been given to her. It was the color of the sea, and it squeezed her waist so tight, she was sure her ribs were visible through the fabric.

The council room was enormous, at least three times the size of the council room in Salus. It had tall, arching beams of pearly white stone running from the center to the marble walls, all carved with scenes of prosperity and war, as though the two reflected one another.

Halia's eyes narrowed as she waited.

Mariana cleared her throat. "Council, I come to you today not as the Queen of Sirenia, not as the Queen of the Leruna Sea, but as Mariana, the daughter of Queen Cybele and King Stavros."

Shocked gasps whispered across the chamber, and Halia sat up straighter in her chair, never taking her searing eyes off Mariana.

"Can she prove that?" she heard one of the council members ask.

"King Stavros was courting Queen Cybele, don't you remember?" another counselor said in a dramatic whisper that may as well have been a shout.

"Let's skip over the dramatics, shall we?" Halia interrupted the clamorous crowd and stood, her large gold crown glittering with untamed power. "Queen Mariana, I made precious time in my very busy schedule for you today. Please tell me why that wasn't a mistake." Her words were laced with a venomous undertone.

Dropping all pleasantries, Mariana glared at her. "I want my amulet back. The one you *stole* from me. It is an heirloom that belongs to the people of Sirenia. *My* people." The council erupted with whispers again, and Mariana raised her voice, keeping her eyes solely on Halia. "I could consider that an act of war. It doesn't belong to you, and I am willing to make sacrifices to see it returned safely to me."

"Sacrifices?" Halia chuckled, and the council laughed alongside her.

"Why are we even listening to this *naiad?*" a male with a particularly large nose asked suddenly, and Mariana felt her blood begin to boil.

"I am not a naiad. Call me that again, sir, and I will show you exactly what a *siren* can do," she spat out.

"She threatened me! She threatened me!" he shouted hysterically.

Halia rolled her eyes and sat back down. "Oh, hush, Silvester, there isn't a day that goes by where you aren't threatened.

Queen Mariana, what exactly are you willing to sacrifice for the amulet?"

Standing straighter with her hands firmly locked behind her back to keep from strangling Silvester, Mariana said, "My right to the Aurelian throne and ..." She took a steadying breath. "Sirenia's independence."

The chamber went silent.

Halia leaned forward. "Excuse me. I must've misheard you, Queen Mariana, but are you saying you wish to abdicate to Aurelia?"

Mariana felt every muscle in her body grow taut as the corner of Halia's mouth lifted.

"In exchange for the amulet, Sirenia will merge with Aurelia, growing it into an empire, and you will become Empress Halia."

As the council began discussing the proposal's logistics among themselves, Halia and Mariana stared each other down. The air felt suddenly sticky and warm. The cold spring breeze drifting in through the massive open windows did little to cool the heat radiating from the two queens.

"Council," Halia interrupted the babbling members so suddenly that they were all startled. "You are all excused."

Swiftly and without a single word, the council shuffled out of the room, leaving only Mariana and Halia.

"You realize what you're giving up, don't you?"

Mariana sighed. "Unfortunately, yes, but I also know what I'm gaining. I want to maintain my rule as Queen of Sirenia, but under the sovereignty of the Empire of Aurelia. Your protection, access to trade routes, and aid in rebuilding would all be possible if—" Mariana stopped, realizing how quickly she was about to ask for help. Swallowing her pride, she lifted her head. "Queen Halia, the century of hostility between our people can be laid to rest. The war King Stavros started ended with his death. My sisters deserve to have their home back. I know there was a time when sirens and fae lived peacefully side by side, and that's all I want to give them. I've seen how much you love this kingdom. With Sirenia as an ally, both our regions will prosper again. Please."

Mariana's throat tightened as she thought of all they'd lost. All her sisters, including the cursed, deserved to enjoy their lives basking under the sunshine or the moonlight, not hiding in the darkness of the sea. Mariana met Halia's eyes. "Please help both our people understand what it means to be alive again."

The silence that followed was daunting. Halia's impassive face inspected Mariana's like there were secrets hidden beneath, but when she saw there was nothing left, she lifted her hand and snapped her fingers. Immediately, a lankly male servant entered silently and bowed his head to Halia.

"Your Majesty?"

"Give Queen Mariana an invitation to tonight's Spring Solstice Celebration," she said firmly as she stood and walked down the steps of her throne toward them.

The servant handed Mariana a gold-foiled invitation, and she took it carefully from his gloved hand.

"My council and I will have a copy of the treaty ready for you to review before the festivities. If everything is acceptable," Halia said, standing in front of Mariana and looking down at her from tall heels and an even taller crown, "then tonight, we shall make history."

CHAPTER 60

"COME WEARING *ART,*" MARIANA said with a frown.

After a brief description of the celebration of Queen Halia's coronation and the Spring Solstice Ball, the curly writing stated the expected attire without any further explanation.

"Confusing," she muttered.

She inspected the words like they would pop up from the parchment and put her out of her misery of guessing.

True to her word, Halia had a copy of the treaty sent over to Mariana's bedchamber with plenty of time for her to review it. After working over the document, making adjustments to tributes, military obligations, and clarifying Mariana's rights as queen, the final treaty was being prepared for signatures at the ball. But as Mariana contemplated what *wearing art* meant, she realized she was completely out of her depth.

A knock at the door drew her attention, and she dropped the invitation on the desk before getting up and opening the door.

Ophelia stood on the other side, a bright white box in hand and a smile on her face.

"Hello, may I come in?"

"Of course." Mariana welcomed her inside. "What's inside the box?"

Ophelia laid the package down on the bed and opened it with a silly grin. "I found a dress for you to wear tonight!" she exclaimed and pulled out a glimmering bundle of teal fabric. "It reminded me of the ocean, and I thought you might like it," Ophelia said as she held up the two-piece gown.

"It's beautiful." Mariana gazed in wonder at the shimmering fabric. "Is this what Halia considers art?"

Ophelia laughed. "Queen Halia loves fashion. Although, she makes everything she wears look stunning." Her cheeks turned pink, and her eyes went wide as she realized how exposed her heart was on her sleeve. "I mean ... how can she not! She's already beautiful all the time; fashion just *adds* to her beauty." Ophelia closed her eyes briefly, clearly embarrassed, as Mariana gave her a knowing smile.

"How long have you been in love with her?"

Ophelia released a hesitant chuckle and shook her head. "I'm not *in* love with her. I mean, of course, I *care* about her. How could I not! She's done so much for me and my family, and she's amazing and—"

Mariana continued to stare at her friend as she rambled, the raised eyebrow and small knowing smile a metaphorical *and* ...

When Ophelia patted her cheeks and continued chuckling like a nervous hen, Mariana placed a steadying hand on her shoulder. "Does she know?" she asked softly.

The tiny, hesitant nod Ophelia gave her was so sweet that Mariana wrapped an arm around her shoulders, hoping to encourage her.

Ophelia sighed in a way that made Mariana's heart squeeze. "I've loved her since the moment I set eyes on her." She shrugged. "I'm helpless. No matter the storms we navigate together, no matter the scars we bear together, I'm hers. And I wish so badly that she could be mine."

Mariana's brows pinched. "Why can't she be?"

"She's now the queen of the largest fae kingdom on this side of the world." Ophelia offered the excuse like it validated everything, and yet Mariana found herself utterly confused.

"I don't see why that should keep you two from being together. If she loves you too, then she should fight for you. Fight to be with you. That's true love, Ophelia. And you should accept nothing less."

Ophelia gave her a shy but appreciative smile. "So should you," she said, lifting an eyebrow.

Mariana had to look away, unable to admit to what she was implying.

"So, where is that fiery sister of yours?" Ophelia's eyes twinkled mischievously. "Kosta hasn't stopped *complaining* about her. I'd say she did a number on him."

Mariana released a sighing chuckle. "Yeah, they really enjoyed stepping on each other's toes. Aurora went back to Sirenia." She rubbed her hands together, curiosity getting the best of her when she asked, "How did you and Kosta both end up working at the palace?"

Ophelia sat down beside her, pushing the gown box over. "Kosta was hired as a royal guard some time ago. I would visit him during his breaks and ... well ... one day, I had an *altercation* with a spirit that left me in the medical bay. Basically, I passed out, and Kosta rushed me to the medics. It was a whole dramatic thing, which Halia heard about, so she approached me. Asked me to live in the palace and be her right hand. I agreed instantly."

"Because you fell in love with her the moment you saw her?" Mariana gave her a teasing smile.

Ophelia rolled her eyes. "I mean ... It wasn't the *only* reason." Her smile dipped slightly. "No, I was desperate to find a place to belong. Our parents were dead; our home was a shack on the outskirts of the city. I had no one except my brother, who lived in the palace and sent me all his earnings just to keep me alive." She shook her head, shame clouding her expression. "I hated every moment of my life back then. Now, here in the palace, I have purpose. A home."

Mariana nodded. She understood the spiraling turmoil of not knowing where you belonged or why you were even born. It used to bother her daily when she felt like she couldn't do anything to help her people.

"Helplessness and hopelessness make the best of friends when you're left alone with them in the dark."

Ophelia lifted her eyes to Mariana's and gave her a forced smile. "All we can do is keep going, right?"

Mariana swallowed. "I don't know. Lately, I've felt like everything has been falling apart. I lost my sister. My mother is dying. And the fate of my people rests on my shoulders."

Ophelia's eyes dimmed. "I'm so sorry."

"Sometimes, I don't know how to keep going," she admitted. "I wish I could crawl into a cave and hide from it all."

"Unfortunately, I don't think that's possible." Ophelia sighed. "All I know is that things happen for reasons we have no right to understand. But we were destined to be here. Especially in this moment."

Mariana scoffed and crossed her arms. "Now you can see the future?"

"No." The Seer shook her head. "But sometimes, I think my spirits can."

Mariana couldn't tell if she was being serious.

"I have a hard time understanding them sometimes," Ophelia explained. "Their words often overlap and confuse me. Sometimes, they're even in other languages—which has caused me a lot of headaches over the years. I've learned to speak twelve languages, *all* in an attempt to understand them." She kept her eyes down and shook her head in disdain as Mariana's brows lifted with admiration. "Even then, I still struggle." Ophelia sighed and looked down at her hands. "All I know is that the moment I heard your name from Astra, it turned the spirit world upside down. But then it quieted again, and ..." She struggled to grasp the right words and shook her head. "It was like a storm had passed over the Veil, and when it was over, the words were clear."

Mariana had no idea what to make of Ophelia's confession. She made it sound like it was important. "What does it mean?"

Ophelia shrugged. "My guess is that the spirits know you're important enough to keep safe, and they're trying to help you by having me guide you. They know more than we'll ever know. Secrets that we may never hear."

"Help me with what, exactly?"

"Well, first I'm going to help you into this dress," she said in a cheerful tone, holding up the gown. "Then we can figure out the rest." Ophelia gave her a wink. "Let's turn you into a *queen*."

Mariana rolled her eyes.

Ophelia helped her into the first layer. It was a deep teal color, mimicking the shade of Mariana's hair. Its layers swirled softly around her ankles before pooling at her feet. She gazed at herself in the mirror as Ophelia busied herself with getting the second layer ready.

The dress did remind her of the sea. The top was a deep V exposing her cleavage, which she guessed was to be covered up by the second layer. Her back was completely exposed, revealing the scales she was proud to show off. The silky material faded into soft shades of white with each ruffle, as though Mariana was wearing a hundred waves cresting along her body. Her hips were exposed through large cut-outs, sparingly laced together with a shimmering ribbon.

Mariana couldn't help herself. She spun, amazed at how the waves came alive, rippling in the light. Ophelia smiled at her in the mirror and then told her to hold still. She laid a semi-transparent, shimmering fabric over Mariana's shoulders, securing the sheer material with the string at her hips. Mariana ran her fingers over the pearls sewn into the edges and marveled over the softness of the beautiful gown.

"Here are the sandals that match." Ophelia helped Mariana put on the pearl-white shoes with low heels, despite mild protesting and a few choice words.

Then she felt something heavy being placed on her head and lifted her eyes to the mirror.

"Hold still," Ophelia ordered as she secured the pearl and gold wire crown, then arranged her long, wavy hair before meeting Mariana's shocked eyes.

"There." Ophelia clapped her hands with pride. "Now you look like a queen."

Mariana touched the small crown on her head, wondering why Ophelia would have given her one. "You didn't have to do this."

Ophelia waved her hand. "Nonsense, I wouldn't let my friend walk out there wearing anything less than something spectacular."

"Will she be angry that you helped me?" Mariana knew Ophelia understood who she meant, but the Seer only shrugged.

"Let me deal with that. You deserve that crown just as much as she does," Ophelia said with a wink, then began adjusting the ruffles before noticing how quiet Mariana had become. Glancing at her reflection in the mirror, she tilted her head. "What's wrong?"

Mariana didn't know how to explain it, but she felt like an imposter. She didn't want to be queen, at least not right now. Her stomach tightened painfully as she stared at the crown pinned to her head. Her fingers began to fidget with the gown's ruffles and pearls. So many pearls.

"Mariana?" Ophelia turned her around by her shoulders. "What's wrong?"

"I, uh ..." She struggled to find the right words, but there was only one person she wanted to speak to at that moment. And he wasn't here. "I need to ..."

Ophelia gave her a soft look as though she could read her mind. "Go to him. I'll cover for you as long as you need."

They shared a small smile, and Mariana gave her hand a grateful squeeze before turning to leave.

Ophelia murmured softly, "His heart is scarred beyond recognition, and yet it still beats strong and true. His soul may be shadowed, but that changed the moment he saw you."

CHAPTER 61

TAKING A STEADY BREATH, Mariana walked down the ornate hallway, her heart skipping, her hands shaking. Anxiety was choking her, the weight of everything she had to do smothering her. She could barely breathe.

"Queen Mariana," a flat male voice rang down the hallway. She turned to find a servant holding a silver tray in their hand with an envelope on top.

As he approached, he said, "Apologies for the abruptness, Your Majesty. I was instructed to deliver this to you immediately." He held the tray out toward her, the envelope beckoning.

Mariana's brows furrowed as she picked it up and opened it. "Who's it from?"

She barely heard the name as she began to read. The words tightened her chest as they seemed to lift from the page, staining her vision. Squeezing her eyes shut, she crushed the letter in her hand.

Glancing up at the lanky male, she firmly asked, "Where is he?"

As soon as he told her, Mariana marched through the palace until she found the right door and began knocking furiously. The sound of her fist hitting the wood echoed down the empty, bland hall of the servants' quarters.

A moment later, the door swung open. Mariana threw the crumpled paper ball at Dax, hitting him in the chest.

"You bastard!" She shoved him backward and slammed the door shut behind her. "How dare you! A goodbye letter? After everything we've been through!"

His shock dripped away into sadness as he stared at the crumpled parchment inked with heartache.

Dax sighed, his hands settling on his hips. "You don't understand," he whispered.

Mariana's eyes filled with tears. "Then explain it to me. Explain to me why in that letter you told me that all you wanted was to belong to me, and yet at the end, all it said was goodbye." When he didn't say anything, she shook her head. "How could you do that to me?"

"We both know this can't go on anymore. You're a queen. After everything that's happened—"

"Lies!" she shouted.

Dax shook his head. "I didn't lie to you, Mari."

"Then what is that?" she yelled, her voice cracking as she gestured toward the balled-up letter. She stepped toward him. "All this time, I thought what we had between us was special. You're now telling me that all of it was for nothing?"

Finally, his eyes shot up to hers. "No," he said firmly. "I'm telling you that you're better off without me. Destruction is all I leave behind, and I have been fighting to keep that from happening to you."

Mariana scoffed. "Oh, sure, like you have an almighty power to reign down chaos at any given moment. You're not that powerful, Dax! That's only an excuse—"

"You are *everything* to me! Don't you get it!" Dax shouted. His hands gripped her shoulders, then eased away as he stepped back. Mariana stared at him in shock as he scrubbed his face with his hands before swiping them over his short hair and resting them on his neck.

"You are everything to me," he repeated softly, the words trembling with restraint. His gaze lifted to meet hers, slow and deliberate. "But Halia gave me a warning. My divided loyalties threaten her—and she has the power to destroy me. To destroy my family." He swallowed hard, his voice dropping even lower. "And now, you." He looked away, jaw tightening. "I've lost everything before. I can't let that happen again."

The pain on his face made her chest feel like it was caving in, and all she wanted to do was make it better. The fire in her heart died down to a smoldering pile of ash. Gathering her strength, she took a hesitant step toward him. "Halia doesn't scare me," she said softly, taking another step. "What scares me is losing you." When she tilted her head to look up at him, she rested a hand on his cheek. "Tell me what's going on in that mind of yours."

"You don't want to know," he whispered darkly, trying to pull away, but she settled both her hands on his face and held firm.

"Yes, I do. Don't think you can make decisions for me. You can't."

With a sigh, Dax rested his hands on her hips, one corner of his mouth tilting up. "That's right, you're a queen now," he said, glancing at the crown nestled into her hair.

"Yes, I am. And you have to do as I say." She smirked up at him and wiped her thumb over his paint-stained cheek. "To start, you're going to show me what you were up to in that room and why you're covered in paint."

With a heavy sigh and a glimmer of anticipation, Dax took her by the hand and pulled her toward the open door behind him.

Mariana's jaw dropped as she peered inside.

Small jars of every color imaginable lined the back of the room. Light spilled in from the large window on the left, glinting off the glass jars like a radiant rainbow. Easels and canvases were stacked on the right beside a desk covered in so much paint that it was impossible to know what type of wood it was made of. And in the center, resting on an easel, was a painting of her.

Mariana touched her lips as she stared at the artwork in awe. The image was from when she had been in Kythera. She was sitting on the balcony, wrapped in the fur blanket, her hair off to the side, exposing the column of her neck. Her face was painted in every shade of the sunset they'd witnessed that evening. It was angled in a way that indicated he had painted it the way he remembered as he sat beside her.

"I've never seen myself look like that before," she breathed. Her eyes scanned every stroke of paint, every detail from her tattooed shoulder to the subtle hint of the scar on her face.

"Look like what?"

Mariana blinked back tears as she realized how he made her feel. "Like someone who just emerged from a storm. Strong, brave ... beautiful." Her voice cracked, and she couldn't recall the last time someone had made her feel this way.

Dax lifted her hand and placed a gentle kiss on it. "I remember that moment so vividly. I couldn't get it out of my head, so I put it down on canvas, thinking it would help me in some way. Looking at you while the setting sun lit up your face ... that was the moment I knew."

Mariana pulled her eyes away from the easel and gazed at him. "Knew what?"

He swallowed hard, his voice dropping to a near whisper. "Without you, there's no light in my world."

If a heart could sing, Mariana's would have been lost in a serenade of melodies beyond her control.

She took a step toward him and pulled his head to hers, resting their foreheads together. His strong arms slid around her waist.

"Never write a goodbye letter to me ever again," she whispered in quiet demand.

"Never."

With that word written in ink on her soul, she gently brought her lips to his. Breathing him in, she began washing away the contents of the heartbreaking letter from her mind. She'd never forget the way she felt when she read his confession of caring too much for her, that he couldn't risk his darkness infecting all the light she reflected.

Pulling back from their kiss, Dax dragged a finger under the strap of her dress, which had been revealed when the shimmering cover fell off one shoulder.

"Why are you wearing something a fae would wear?" His words were low, caressing every curve and making her breath uneven.

"It was given to me for the party tonight," she breathed. Her skin shivered as his finger began dragging the strap down. "The invite said, 'come wearing art.'"

Dax's lips lifted. "Mari, you don't need any of this. You're already a masterpiece."

The shimmering layer fell to the floor.

"Dressing like a fae won't change that," he whispered against her neck.

The other strap slipped down her shoulder, and her breath hitched.

"I wouldn't want to cause a scene," she gasped when his tongue caressed the sensitive spot below her jaw. He chuckled lightly before pulling back to meet her eyes.

"Your very presence causes a scene. A devastatingly beautiful scene. I'll show you."

Cool air swept over her skin as the rest of the dress fell away, pooling at her feet.

Mariana gasped when Dax lifted her into his arms, her legs wrapped around his waist.

He set her down on the edge of a desk splattered with old, dried paint and kept her knees tight to his hips. His eyes roamed every inch of her as though he was marveling at her beauty.

The strangest sensation rippled over her body. She blushed, suddenly hyperaware of how exposed her body was to him, the brush of her hair against her breasts, and the crown sitting heavy on her head.

The truth of what the crown represented still weighed heavily upon her. She reached up to pull it off, but Dax stopped her.

"Leave it. You're a queen, and I'll only treat you as such."

Her breath lodged in her throat as they locked eyes.

This was the moment, she realized, when a siren found her fae. Her mate. And she would do anything to protect him. The weight she'd felt before lifted. Like a hand pulling her to safety from a rogue wave, Mariana realized how much his words, his presence, calmed the storm inside her. She was so in love with him, he'd never understand. And it terrified her.

Dax dragged his hands down her hips, over her legs, to her ankles, then stopped. He frowned and glanced down at the sandals on her feet.

"What have they done to you?" he exclaimed softly, making her laugh.

He released the straps and pulled the sandals off.

She breathed a sigh of relief when she felt cool air on her dangling feet.

"Thank you, I thought I'd never be free of them," she confessed. Then Dax shoved her knees farther apart, and her smile dipped. It was then that she felt a different sort of storm building within her. The kind of storm that was pure anticipation and longing. The kind she could never deny.

She found the edge of his shirt and lifted it over his head, revealing the smooth, rippled muscle of his stomach. Mariana lightly touched his chest, her hand settling over his heart. It was beating hard, and she slowly lifted her eyes to his. He was so close she could see the flecks of copper in his irises and remembered the first time they had been this close. Back when she was his captive, she wanted nothing more than to be released. Now, all she craved was to be trapped in his arms. To be pressed against him again.

He slid his hands up her hips, up the sides of her waist, until they grazed the curves of her breasts. Lifting them higher still, he settled them on either side of her jaw, his thumbs caressing her cheeks.

"Don't stop," she breathed.

His eyes darkened, and their lips collided.

CHAPTER 62

A TICKLING SENSATION ON her stomach woke Mariana. Soft sheets shifted as she stretched her arms. Blinking through her blurry vision, she looked down her naked body to find Dax before her on his elbows, painting her stomach.

Her mouth lifted, and she giggled, "What are you doing?"

His gaze remained focused on the paint when he replied, "Painting you."

"Why?"

When his gaze met hers, she saw something there she'd never seen before: happiness. Pure, radiant happiness.

"Because you're the perfect canvas."

She released a laugh, her head falling back onto the pillow. "I've never heard you say anything like that before."

"Well," he said, dipping the paintbrush into one of the several little colorful jars on a rolling cart beside the bed. "It's not the last you'll hear." The wink he gave her made her toes curl. She sighed as he went back to the masterpiece he was creating on her skin.

She savored the soreness throughout her body. His touch set her on fire. She never thought she'd ever feel like this.

Glancing down at him, she ran a hand over his head, loving the prickly feeling of his short hair but missing the soft length it was at before.

"Why did you cut your hair?"

He shrugged. "I usually keep it this way, safer in battle. Why? Like it longer, Little Tempest?" He smirked at her.

She rolled her eyes and did her best to hide her smile with her hand. "I mean, if you're not planning to be in battle anytime soon, then ..." she lifted a shoulder. "Maybe you can grow it back out."

Dax quietly chuckled and winked up at her. "I'll think about it," he said, then went back to painting her.

Her mind began to wander. Thoughts of his home and his family, Spiro and Kenna. She wondered why he had an art studio here, but she hadn't seen one anywhere near his cabin in Kythera. Then a fog inside her question-filled mind lifted, leaving clarity.

"Can I ask you something?"

"I suppose," he replied with a hint of amusement.

Mariana lifted herself up, resting on her elbows. "You mentioned losing everything," she said as her fingers fiddled with the blanket beneath her. "And seeing your art studio—it got me thinking." Finally lifting her gaze, she expected to find the guarded mask she was used to. Instead, she found a relaxed expression she had to hold back from kissing. Biting the inside of her cheek, she prayed that what she said next didn't rhuin everything. "Spiro showed me the historical gallery in Kythera."

The light in his eyes dimmed. Pulling his gaze away, Dax dipped the brush into more paint carefully, meticulously.

"Dax, are you the lone soldier in the painting?"

The silence that came next made it difficult to breathe.

Licking his lips, Dax cleared his throat while staring at the paintbrush. She couldn't tell if he was judging the amount of paint on the tip or if he would stare at it forever just to avoid answering her. He gave a slight nod without looking at her. "Yeah, that's me."

She finally exhaled. "Challenged to rise again."

He nodded and continued painting her stomach. His jaw flexed as though he was working up the courage to speak.

"At the end of the Infernal Wars, I was in command of the last Mocanus regiment still alive. Word spreading that an enemy outpost was hidden in the Varasova Mountains, gathering forces. King Thaddeus ordered us to clear it out. A simple task, he'd said, considering it should be no more than a few hundred untrained soldiers." Dax scoffed and shook his head. "The only reason I agreed was that intel told me it was close to Kythera—too close. At that point, Kythera was barely a village, and only villagers who had no idea how to fight lived there. So, we had to go, and by the time we reached this supposed outpost, it was empty. It had been a trap."

Dax set the paintbrush down and sighed heavily. Mariana could tell this was difficult for him to talk about. Hoping to ease his anxiety, she ran a hand over his head and tilted his chin up to look at her.

"It's okay, you don't have to say any more. I know this is hard for you."

Dax shook his head. "I need to say it out loud. I haven't spoken a word of it to anyone other than Spiro since it happened." He pinched the bridge of his nose, then dropped his hand and stared at the paint on her skin. "It turned out, Minerva's three daughters and an alleged son of Magnus—who believed it was his right to be king—had joined forces and gathered twice the number of soldiers we'd predicted." Dax's eyes seemed to glaze over, like he had transported himself back to the battlefield. "They knew we were coming. Cornered us in a valley. And we were unprepared for the attack. It was pitch black, the moon hidden behind clouds, and all I could hear were screams coming from everyone around me. It was then I realized these were my people. Not my soldiers. And they were all about to die."

Mariana stayed perfectly still as she watched him, her heart squeezing painfully, knowing he was reliving the moment.

"I knew the enemy had to go down. If I didn't defeat them, they would attack Kythera and Aurelia. I couldn't let anything happen to them. And my soldiers knew there was a risk of never seeing their loved ones again by joining my regiment. Yet they did anyway, because they believed in fighting for their families."

"And they believed in you," Mariana whispered.

Dax squeezed his eyes shut. "All I remember is the ground shaking beneath my feet, and the mountains that surrounded us cracking. Then it all came down. It was a miracle I woke up, but when I did … everyone was dead." He opened his eyes and gave Mariana a heartbroken stare. "That's why I vowed never to use my power again."

"You're stronger because of it." Mariana gripped his hand and gave him a sad smile. "Challenged to rise again."

His mouth lifted slightly. "Challenged to keep living."

The statement made her chest cave in. She knew he didn't want to talk about it anymore, so she glanced at the paintbrush on the cart beside them and said, "Painting helps you relax?"

"Painting helps me forget—usually. You are the exception, it seems." A corner of his mouth lifted before pulling her from the bed. "Thank you for listening," he said quietly, holding her close but not close enough to smudge the drying paint on her stomach.

"You're welcome. Thank you for telling me."

The kiss he placed on her lips was full of so much emotion, Mariana could practically feel her heart growing wings.

Pulling back, he kissed her scar on her temple, making her realize he didn't know the true story of how she got it.

"Would you like me to share a story too?"

"Always." He dipped his brush again, swirling it in white. "I enjoy listening to you," he replied with a grin.

She shifted her left shoulder toward him so he could see the tattoo inked there.

"I got that tattoo to remember a couple of friends. Xena and Titus." She pulled her hair over one shoulder and began braiding it as she spoke. "When I was a youngling, I used to get into a lot of trouble," she admitted with an edge of regret. "Guardian Xena found me hanging around a fishing boat in the daylight. I was very young and curious, so..." Mariana took a breath. "I got too close, and a net caught me. I was fortunate, actually. The fisherman aboard saw me and let go of the net before he could completely pull me out of the water. If he had ... I wouldn't be here today."

"That had to be terrifying," he murmured.

She nodded, her face tight, remembering the pain. And all that happened afterward.

"Why do I get the feeling there's more to the story?" Dax asked, and Mariana met his curious gaze.

"Because there is."

"Tell me?" He placed a gentle kiss on the inside of her wrist before he continued painting, now on her hips.

"Xena rescued me from the net and pulled the fisherman down. She wanted him to pay for what he'd done and decided it was best to let Cybele decide his punishment." She shuddered as she remembered. "While he was a prisoner, I brought him food and water. He was kind to me. Even when the food I brought him wasn't edible, and the water wasn't drinkable for a mortal, he still thanked me every time. I was scared they weren't feeding him enough. Anyway, I learned his name was Titus, and he was from the Andros Islands. He said he wanted to speak with the Guardian who rescued me so he could thank her. I was confused, and Xena was skeptical when I asked her, but when he told her how grateful he was that she had saved me from his net, something happened between them—a mutual understanding." Mariana smiled softly.

She glanced down at the tattoo on her shoulder. "Xena vouched for Titus and asked Cybele to release him, but"—her voice cracked slightly—"Titus asked Cybele if he could stay. He wanted to learn more about us and ... I think he was in love with Xena. Cybele, of course, didn't want the mortal to stay, especially since we had no idea how to keep him alive down there. But then Xena offered to go with him for a short time."

Her throat tightened as she stared at the ceiling. Shame at what happened after gripped her stomach.

"Did she go with him?" Dax was looking at her when she glanced down at him.

She nodded. "My mother used the opportunity to spread a lie across the Andros Islands that sirens were *goddesses*. Xena might have loved Titus, I don't know ... but when Celeste first told me the story, I cried. The story of a *sea goddess* named Xena who loved a mortal man named Titus, and it all came crashing down on me that I had helped spread a lie."

Dax frowned. "I don't think you did anything wrong, Mari. Whether the story was true or not, it was Cybele's choice."

"Astra always said that," she commented, staring off into the distance.

"Did you find her?" Dax asked softly, drawing her gaze back toward him.

"Yes," she admitted. "But she didn't make it out during the ..." Her voice trailed off as her breathing turned ragged. She swallowed, taking a deep breath.

"Hey." Dax moved closer, brushing her hair away from her forehead and placing a hand on her trembling cheek as she fought back tears.

She was so tired of crying.

"I'm so sorry she's gone. But with everything that's to come ... Don't let the past consume you."

"Keep moving forward," she whispered.

Dax gave her a solemn nod. "Whether it's on legs or with a tail," he said with so much seriousness that she shook her head and gave him a closed-lip smile, surprised she was able to hold back from rolling her eyes.

He smiled and kissed her hands. "I mean it, though," he said, setting her hands down and staring at them. "You have to push through. These are the moments that define you, define what type of ruler you'll become. And I know you, Mari. You're going to change everything."

In the darkness of her mind, Mariana heard a voice whisper to her, "*I believe in you. Your destiny was written in the stars of the sky and the waves of the sea, the moment you were born. You'll save your people, I know it.*"

She smiled, wiping her eyes as she recognized Seraphina's voice. The Goddess believed in her, and so did everyone she loved. She had to move forward, as Dax said. She couldn't allow the past to hold her hostage or her guilt to consume her. Nothing good would come of it.

A sudden knock on the front door had Dax grumbling.

"Get lost!" he shouted, and just as he was lowering his head to kiss her, the sound of paper sliding under his door drew their attention.

With a groan, Dax stood and snatched up the letter.

"Who's it from?" Mariana called through the open door of his bedchamber into the living space where he stood.

His eyes quickly scanned the page before dropping it on a nearby table, before walking back toward her.

"It's from my family." He leaned over her and kissed her deeply. "They just want to check in, make sure I didn't lose you in the forest," he said with a grin, and then kissed her again before sitting up. "C'mon. Let me finish you up."

"What are you painting anyway?" she asked, glancing down at herself as he pulled her up by the hand and toward his painting studio.

"Patience." He winked. "You'll find out soon enough."

CHAPTER 63

MARIANA FELT BEAUTIFUL. JUST like she had when she saw her portrait. His love was evident in the designs and details he put into the artwork covering her body.

The stars and clouds covering her chest merged with beautiful, flowering vines that twisted around her arms. Her stomach and hips appeared like they were wrapped in the sea's comforting embrace. Swirling waves descended her thighs, leaving her knees bare. He left her scales and a few of her tattoos on display.

Fearing she would be too exposed under the watchful and judging aristocratic gazes of the fae that would be attending the ball, she donned the shimmering cover-up from her discarded dress on the floor. It covered her bare shoulders and was secure at the waist, where it billowed around her hips down to her calves.

"Ophelia will be sad I didn't wear the dress she picked out," Mariana mentioned.

Dax shrugged. "You wore half of it." His fingers glided along the edge of the cover-up, barely touching the skin on her neck. She shivered, a smile playing on her lips.

She laughed when he picked up her hand and spun her around. Then their lips touched, molding together. The heated kiss he gave her had her on the verge of begging for more, but he pulled back with a groan.

"The ball started almost an hour ago. You need to get going. You have a treaty to sign and your people to save."

Mariana swallowed, her muscles tightening as anxiety reared its glaring head. The crown she wore felt heavier than ever.

"Come with me," she whispered. "Please."

"I shouldn't ..." he started. "I wasn't invited."

She shrugged, a hint of a mischievous smile pulling her lips. "You're my guest. You're coming with me."

Dax smiled and gave her a sweet peck on her lips. "As you command, Your Majesty."

He dressed quickly in his finest outfit, made up of a black collared, long-sleeved shirt beneath a black and silver vest, black pants, and polished shoes. Then he took her hand and led her out of his rooms and through the palace.

Mariana struggled to breathe right, not paying any attention to the few looks the passing servants gave them as they approached the entrance to the Spring Solstice Ball.

"I'm nervous," she whispered as she stared ahead.

The white granite staircase leading into the heart of the palace was practically endless. Daunting. It could lead her to make the best choice for her people or doom them all.

"You can do this," Dax replied with a squeeze of his hand and began to lead her up the staircase.

Each step Mariana took felt like one step closer to sealing the fate of her sisters. Gravity pulled her muscles, every step straining her, urging her to turn around. But there was no other choice. She had to get the amulet back. For Astra. For Celeste. For Cybele.

Chattering voices and melodic music began filling the space between her heart and her head. Taking a deep breath, she took the final step and entered the fray.

The ballroom smelled of fresh flowers and citrus. Stunning, vibrant petals covered the floor, soft beneath Mariana's bare feet. The ceiling had glowing bulbs and colorful flowers hanging across it in a complicated pattern that highlighted the bright, sparkling chandelier in the center. Then there were the guests, sauntering around each other like flaunting birds trying to prove who wore it best. At least ... until they noticed her standing there. With Dax by her side.

The crowd gawked, parting a path for them as they began walking through the flock. Eyes roamed over her body like it truly was a masterpiece—or a scandalous statement.

Mariana paid them no mind. Instead, she focused on the small crowd at the back and made her way toward the sound of opulent privilege and egotistical laughter.

Halia's *queenliness* was on full display. Gold seemed to encase her, as though she was a gilded doll. The long, flowing gown she wore was literally leaving gold flakes behind as she walked. Perhaps a tribute to her lost father. Her diamond cape glittered down from her shoulders to the floor, making her sparkle so bright that the massive chandelier above her appeared dim. The high slit in her dress exposed her thighs all the way to her tall heels in a regal ensemble. And lastly, the final piece that established Halia's royalty was the shining crown on her head. The same crown that had lived atop the king's head.

Mariana watched in amusement as Halia's dramatic smile disappeared upon seeing her. She sneered when her eyes landed on Mariana's bare feet.

"I see you took my instructions quite *literally*. Could you be wearing any less?" The fae crowd around her giggled.

Mariana tilted her head. "In my culture, clothing means nothing. Instead, our bodies are to be cherished. My body *is* art. You're just lucky Dax painted it." She glanced at Dax, who stood beside her, stoic and unwavering.

Halia bristled, her eyes flitting between the two of them.

"I see," she said slowly, a hint of the venom she loved so much grazing the edge of her words. "Well." She cleared her throat, straightening. "Do try to keep the paint to yourself until our business is completed. I'd hate for any of the pristine furniture to be stained by your ... presence." Halia turned on her heel and began walking away with her nose high and posture stiff. "Come along," she commanded over her shoulder with a quick wave of her hand.

Mariana glared in her direction, then felt someone come up next to her.

"You look amazing, Queen Mariana," Ophelia exclaimed, and Mariana gave her a small, thankful smile. "Dax did all this?" Ophelia wiggled her eyebrows at Dax, who only chuckled and looked away. "Wow, he knows his stuff, huh?" she whispered to Mariana with a wink, linking their arms together.

Mariana couldn't help the blush that crept over her cheeks.

"Yes, he does."

"I'll lead her to the drawing room, if that's okay?" Ophelia asked Dax. He gave Mariana a questioning look, to which she responded with a small smile and a nod before letting go of his hand.

Ophelia led her forward excitedly, Dax a few steps behind them. They followed the trail of gold flakes Halia had left behind as she walked through her parting, gawking guests.

Mariana tipped her head toward Ophelia. "I'm sorry I didn't wear your dress."

The Seer shook her head. "Are you kidding? This is so much better. Besides, I just can't wait to hear about how he convinced you to *lose* the dress." She winked. Mariana laughed softly.

As they made their way through the crowd, Mariana had the chance to admire the incredible finery around her. Every guest wore something unique. A gown that appeared to have been spun of pure starlight. A dress suit that reminded her of a kaleidoscope of rippling glass. Robes made from roses, filling the air with their sweet fragrance. Even one of absolute, swirling darkness. That was the one that caught Mariana's eye the longest. It was incredibly difficult to fathom how the dress had been created, let alone made it to the ball filled with so much light. But perhaps that was why it stood out—shadows were at their darkest when light was at its brightest.

They made it to an open door where Halia stood waiting. Ophelia let go of Mariana's arm and gave her a reassuring smile before walking back into the crowd.

Halia eyed Dax. "You can stay out here like a good dog and guard the door."

Dax scowled.

As she was about to close the doors, Mariana made eye contact with Dax. The moment their gazes locked, his expression turned gentle. It seemed to say, *I'll be right here.* Then the doors closed with a resounding *click,* and Halia and Mariana were alone in the drawing room.

"Ready to become part of the fae realm again, Queen Mariana?" Halia asked as she rounded a grand desk where the treaty lay in wait.

"Let's drop the formalities, they're pointless here."

Halia smirked, pulling out a pen. "Don't like your new title? Well, I'd say the title of queen suits *me* rather well."

"I agree." Mariana's approval made Halia's eyes flash in confusion. "You were already running the kingdom. It only made sense that you finally got the title you deserved," she added as she scanned the treaty once more. "Though the circumstances upon which you received it are unfortunate." Her eyes lifted to Halia's, a question lingering in her gaze. Halia only stared at her, impassive and unperturbed.

"It is truly unfortunate. I will miss my dearly departed father with my every breath. May he rest in peace." Her face said otherwise.

Mariana quirked an eyebrow. "You're taking this quite well."

Halia sneered and took a step toward her. "You want to drop the formalities? Fine. Let me make something very clear. You are in *my* territory. That means the ground you're stepping on, the air you're breathing, and even the male you're sleeping with are *mine*." Halia stood up straight, peering down her nose at her. "Do I make myself clear?"

Mariana's fist tightened, holding back from throwing it right in Halia's pristine face. *Gods, I hate her.*

Clearing her throat, she cooled her features, masking her hatred with apathy. "It's clear you're having fun flashing around your new authority."

Halia cackled. "Oh, there's no mistaking the power I have. Now, sign the treaty, and let's get this over with. I have a party to host."

Mariana's brows dipped at the sudden urgency. Opening her senses, she searched for the amulet's power singing to her, but found nothing. Her stomach tightened.

"Where's the amulet?" she demanded, and Halia seemed to stop herself from rolling her eyes.

"It's safe. I wasn't about to bring it to a party with thousands of people. That sort of power must be protected. Now, sign the treaty so we can continue our evening. You'll have it soon." Halia's voice was firm, and Mariana tried to detect any signs of deceit.

Finding none, she sighed heavily and swallowed the lump in her throat. Without allowing herself any more time to delay, she picked up the heavy pen and signed the treaty.

Her breath left her the moment her swirly signature stained the page.

It was done.

Every siren remaining could now enter the fae realm without repercussion. They could live without fear of being hunted for bounty. They could rebuild Sirenia and watch younglings grow up in a safe place. They could grow old without fear of having to choose to fall victim to the Scourge's deceptive promise of eternal life.

She had done it. She was under Halia's thumb, but at least her people were free. And yet, she couldn't shake off the shivers running down her spine, indicating that something was wrong.

A gust of foul wind blew by, and her eyes landed on a swirl of light forming on the other side of the room. Loose parchment flew off the table before Halia lifted a hand to halt the wind.

The dread Mariana had been ignoring all night raged its mighty fist upon her as she watched a portal open.

A foot the color of pure darkness stepped through, and Mariana's heart seized.

The Siren Witch smiled at her. The amulet, glowing with power, hung around her ashen neck.

"Hello, little one."

CHAPTER 64

AURORA SWAM CAUTIOUSLY THROUGH the palace, her eyes wary of every sister she passed. Could one of them have poisoned Astra? Could one of them have done something to Cybele?

With the amulet now in Halia's clutches, Aurora had no idea if Mariana's plan to get it back would work. Regardless of what happened next, Aurora would defend their mother.

Cora, their healer, came into view, having just come out of Cybele's chamber.

"Aurora?" Cora called out, coral-pink brows drawn together. "Where have you been? Are you alright?"

"I'm fine. Is my mother getting better?"

Cora's bright gaze dipped. "No changes. I'm sorry."

It's not your fault, Aurora almost said, but she bit her tongue before she could. If someone truly had done something to both Astra and Cybele, the last thing Aurora wanted to do was give away that she knew. She needed to find out who was doing this and why they were after the amulet.

"Don't apologize, you've done everything you can for her." Aurora was about to continue when a cursed siren passed by, bumping her shoulder hard.

Sneering, Aurora eyed the cursed siren. "Watch it," she snapped.

They hissed at her, licking their crusty lips before moving along.

"What was that?" Cora asked, frowning as she watched the ghostly siren swim away with her bony, colorless tail.

"I don't know." Turning, she stared past Cora at the group of cursed sirens down the hall, who were eyeing her like she was a sack of mortal flesh they wanted to chew on. "But stay on alert. And let me know if you notice anything strange going on."

"Stranger than how the cursed are behaving?" She scoffed, shaking her head. "It's like they're waiting for something."

Aurora's eyes darted to her. The healer's words clanged through her head. "I have to go. Remember what I said."

Cora nodded. "I will."

Approaching the door leading into her mother's chamber, Aurora nodded to the two guards at the front. The cursed sirens didn't nod back; they stared at her without emotion. Unfeeling darkness swirled within their pitch-black gazes. Usually, they would at least acknowledge her with some form of respect. Their sudden indifference unnerved her.

Ignoring them, she pushed the door open and swam into the room, spotting Malea tending to the pale queen.

When Malea looked up, her eyes widened a fraction.

"Hey, thank you for keeping an eye on my mother for me while I've been gone," Aurora said quickly, approaching them.

"You're welcome," Malea replied hesitantly, seeming tense and unlike herself.

Aurora's brows pulled tight. "Are you—"

Malea shook her head slightly, her gaze burning holes into the cursed guards by the open doorway, who were not looking at them but down the hallway, as though waiting for something.

Aurora's stomach soured.

Keeping her gaze steady on Malea, she began slowly reaching down for the daggers at her hips.

Malea shouted, "Behind you!"

Aurora turned just in time to see a club coming down at her head.

CHAPTER 65

Mariana stared at her former teacher, friend, and kin with dread. The Siren Witch's long legs faded from pale white to midnight black, as though her feet were made of pure darkness. Her scales shimmered like black diamonds under the lights, where her silky dress exposed her knees and arms. The sleeves billowed out from her elbows like claws dragging along the marble floor. She was as thin as a skeleton, with skin as fresh as a newborn but with the beauty of a black rose.

The air around her stirred with a sinister energy.

The Siren Witch smiled at her, revealing two rows of sharp teeth. "Mariana, my dear. Oh, how I've missed you," she said with welcoming arms spread wide as though she expected her to step close for a hug. Instead, Mariana instinctively stepped back. The witch's arms drooped slightly. "Come now, there's nothing to be frightened of. It's time to come home."

"Home?" Mariana murmured hesitantly, her heart drumming in her ears.

"Yes." The witch gave her the look of a proud mother.

Mariana's gaze lingered on the beautiful, glowing amulet resting against her pale chest, then her eyes drifted to the fae beside her. Halia had the nerve to appear ambivalent beneath her stone-cold façade.

"You did this." Her words were so soft, she could barely fathom how Halia heard her.

The queen cleared her throat and looked away. "I did what had to be done—"

"What had to be *done?*" she shouted. Halia blinked at her in shock. "You hired the witch to kill your father just to take the throne, am I right?"

"Keep your voice down," Halia replied in a deadly tone, her expression tightening.

"I know it's true. Your people know it's true. And you tricked me into signing Sirenia's independence away when you had already given the amulet to the witch!" Mariana's pulse began to race as her rage boiled within her.

"My people will rejoice when they hear of what I've accomplished. They will parade in the streets when they hear that I made this righteous kingdom into an empire! I will live on forever as the savior of our people because I did what only a great ruler would do!"

"You're blind if you think the choice you made, *that* choice," she said, pointing at the amulet around the witch's neck, "was an accomplishment, because she's going to come after all of you."

Halia's eyes grew wary and darted to the witch, who released an exasperated sigh.

"She's hysterical. I have no intention of coming after the fae."

Mariana shook her head. "You manipulated Astra and me just to get that amulet. Are you seriously expecting me to believe that you're not going to use that power for revenge?"

"What revenge? Mari, calm down," the witch crooned gently from where she stood. Mariana still couldn't believe she had legs. "We can discuss everything once we're back in Salus. Come with me." It wasn't a request.

Mariana glared at her and shook her head. "I'm not going anywhere with you. For all I know, you're going to kill me the moment I walk through that portal."

The witch's head tilted, brow furrowed, and she gave Mariana a look unlike anything she'd seen on her face before. Sadness. "Now, why would I do that, little one? I've always protected you, and I will continue to do so. You're my family, and I want you by my side."

Mariana's heart tugged involuntarily, but she shook her head again. "You're lying."

The witch stood straighter. "I am not."

"What would you possibly want with me?"

The witch's voice grew firm. "I want you there when we restore Sirenia, when we bring our sisters back home to their rightful place. I want you there when we bring glory to our queendom once again."

Knocking sounded from the door leading back to the party. "Mari?" she heard Dax call out.

Her head whipped between the door and the witch. "And what about my sisters? My mother? Did you kill Cybele?"

"Cybele is alive," she said, the irritation clear in her tone. "If you want to see her again and say your goodbyes, you'll come with me."

"What did you do to her?"

"It's not what I did to her, but what she did to herself. The moment she turned you into a fae, she began to die. The fallout was too great."

"Mari!" Dax shouted again behind the door, the handle rattling.

"I'm getting sick of your vile lies," Mariana sneered at the witch.

"And I'm getting sick of your defiance."

Two figures stepped through the portal behind her, and Mariana's eyes widened in horror.

A creature unlike anything she'd ever seen stared her down, dripping saltwater. Its eyes were droplets of blood, its mouth a circle of razor-sharp teeth designed for tearing, and its body a motley of corals and seaweed woven tightly together.

"What are you—" Before Mariana could finish, the beast lashed out a long, octopus-like arm, wrapping it around her face and body. She thrashed violently as it choked her. Dax's shouting behind the closed door faded. Her vision grew hazy. She stared at the witch, who was looking down at her with pity.

"I missed you," she heard the witch whisper.

Mariana's eyes drifted shut. The sensation of the witch's fingers stroking her head gently was the last thing she felt before everything was swallowed by darkness.

CHAPTER 66

"Aurora! Aurora!"

She heard her name being shouted over and over. Small hands gripped her shoulders, shaking them. Aurora lifted a hand to wave them away, wanting to go back to sleep.

"Aurora, you have to wake up! Wake up!" Luna's voice became clear, as did the urgency with which she spoke. It stirred Aurora from her slumber, and she opened a hesitant eye.

"Luna?"

"Thank the Goddess!" Luna dived toward her, wrapping her lanky arms around Aurora's neck and rocking her back and forth.

"Stop," Aurora grunted, pulling from her embrace. She sat up, clutching her throbbing head. "What happened?"

"The cursed have taken over Salus. They threw us in here. I don't know where the others are."

The last thing Aurora remembered was the fear in Malea's gaze, the sound of her shouting to look behind her, and then ...

Aurora groaned, rubbing the sensitive spot on the back of her head where the club had landed its heavy blow. "Why didn't they just kill me?"

Luna wrapped her arms around herself and shrugged. "They killed Malea," she whispered, and Aurora's eyes snapped to hers.

"What did you just say?"

Luna's eyes were rimmed with red. "They killed her. She grabbed your dagger and—" She shook her head, covering her face with her hands. "It was awful," she said, muffled. "How could they do that to her?"

Aurora's heart was pounding so hard in her ears she could barely think. Lifting a hand, she gently rubbed Luna's back as she gathered her thoughts. Malea was dead. Cybele—

"What about the queen?"

Luna's hands dropped to her lap, and she shrugged. "I think they took her somewhere. I don't know."

"Shit," she muttered and scrubbed her face. As she dropped her hands, she glanced around. They were in the windowless pantry of the kitchens. Great.

"What are we going to do?" Luna whispered, sniffing.

Pulling herself up, Aurora glanced along the shelves. "I'm not sure yet."

Think, Godsdammit, think! How are you going to get out of this?

"Has anyone been by to check on us?"

"Just once," Luna replied, her fingers tracing the lines in the stone floor.

"When?"

She shrugged. "Maybe a half hour ago?"

Nodding, Aurora put her hands on her hips, instantly noticing her weapons were gone, but her armor was still locked in place around her chest.

"Okay, when they come back again, we're going to—"

The door swung open, revealing a scraggly cursed with vein-riddled skin.

Jocasta.

Without hesitation, Aurora slammed her forehead into Jocasta's, knocking her back.

Luna gasped behind her. Aurora wrestled Jocasta for dominance.

Grabbing Jocasta by her hair, she slammed the cursed siren's face into the wall. Hearing the crunch of bone and listening to Jocasta scream filled Aurora with unmistakable satisfaction. Jocasta reached her hands back, digging her razor-sharp claws into Aurora's skin as liquid darkness spilled from the cursed siren's nose, mixing with the water.

Aurora roared in fury and launched Jocasta through the door and into the kitchen. Her head banged against the table, causing bowls of ingredients scattered across the large preparation table to *cling*. Dinner must have been in the midst of being prepared when the cursed decided to attack, claiming Salus for themselves. Aurora's chest grew hot with rage as she approached the still siren. As Aurora pulled her up by the back of the neck, Jocasta moaned in protest, her eyes rolling to the back of her head, and Aurora growled at her. Dropping her into a chair, Aurora made eye contact with a very pale Luna.

"Get me rope from that cabinet," she demanded. When Luna didn't move, she shouted, "Quickly!" Luna jumped before wordlessly nodding. She grabbed the rope and handed it to Aurora, who made quick work of tying the unconscious siren to the chair.

"Lock the doors." Luna rushed to lock it before coming to her side.

"What are we going to do now?" Luna asked in a soft, unsure voice.

Aurora gave her a grim look before pulling her close. She wrapped her arms around Luna, squeezing her niece, grateful she was alive. Her heart ached at the thought of telling Luna of her mother's fate, but she didn't have the courage to utter the words. She'd tell her later, once the rest of their family was together again.

After a silent vow to Astra to keep her daughter safe, she planted a quick kiss atop Luna's head and let go. She turned to a stone butcher block sitting on top of the kitchen counter and pulled out a knife; the sound of the blade sharpening glorious to her ears.

"Now, we get answers." Aurora slammed the knife into Jocasta's tail, earning a startled scream.

The taste of rotten blood swirled in the water around them. Aurora tried not to gag as she yanked the knife free, pulling a few scales along with it. They floated gently to the floor in a plume of black blood.

"Tell me where they're holding the queen! Now!"

Jocasta gritted her teeth and seethed, her eyes darting around. Aurora knew she was looking for a way out, a weapon, anything she could use to get free.

"No one is here to save you. Tell me where the queen is or I'll cut off your fins," Aurora promised menacingly, holding the knife against the bottom of her tail.

Jocasta's eyes shot up to hers. "You're going to die, all of you! The sea doesn't belong to you anymore. The sea will rise as the moon beckons her daughters of the night up from the depths. All of you will die!" She cackled hysterically, and Aurora punched her in the face.

"Enough!" She gripped the cursed siren's dull, stringy hair and pulled her head back, pushing the knife against her sickly pale throat. She sneered in her face, "You want to see the moon again? You want to murder another mortal, feel their energy upon your black soul? Then you'd better tell me exactly where you're keeping my family, or I will rip you apart!"

Jocasta smiled, black blood between her jagged teeth. "Aww, in front of the weakling hiding in the corner? I doubt she'd survive the shock of seeing you unleash your fury upon me, *Scarlet Serpent*. You've frightened the poor weak soul." Jocasta cackled, and Aurora slammed her elbow into the bitch's face, pulling a scream and a whimper from her thin, cracked lips.

Moving away, Aurora let out a frustrated groan and went to the shut window across the room. She rested her palms against the frame, wishing she could leave the window open to let in fresh seawater, but it was too risky. She'd spotted cursed sirens armed to the teeth patrolling.

Salus had fallen into a stygian blackness. Even the bioluminescent garden had darkened, quieted. Death contaminated the water with a sickening taste of decay and rot that wasn't just from Jocasta bleeding out.

Aurora shook her head. Where once the cursed had been hidden beneath, they'd now risen to claim their place above everyone else.

Luna shifted in the corner, catching Aurora's eye. Jocasta's words bothered her. She knew Luna was scared, could see it in the way she gripped her arms tightly around herself and kept her eyes shut.

"Luna," Aurora called softly, and her niece opened her eyes. Blatant, heart-wrenching fear stared back at her in the form of bright blue orbs.

She sighed. "Close your eyes, Luna. It'll all be over quickly."

Luna's eyes widened a fraction before she shut them again.

Tightening her grip on the knife, Aurora moved with purpose to the fidgeting cursed siren.

The look in her gaze must've scared Jocasta, for she shouted, "Wait!"

Aurora dug the tip of her blade into Jocasta's chest, ready to plunge it all the way through, but hesitated just long enough for her captive to shriek, "They're in the throne room!"

Black blood leaked from the wound, and she gave Jocasta a vicious smile. "Thank you," she said, before plunging the blade deep into her chest.

With a gurgle, Jocasta slumped forward. Having heard what happened, Luna rose from her curled position.

"You killed her! You told her you would let her live if she told you where they were!" Luna shouted at Aurora, her face screwed up and flushed.

Gripping her shoulders, Aurora shook Luna. "Stop! We are at war, Luna! Don't you see that? I don't make it a habit to torture anyone! It is what I have to do to keep us alive, and right now, I have to save our family and keep you safe. That's my *only* priority!"

"You didn't have to kill her. She was a sister!" she cried.

Aurora let her arms drop, and her brows furrowed. "None of the cursed are our sisters anymore, Luna. The moment they turned against us was the moment they deserved to get a blade through the heart. Your true sisters are out there somewhere, and it is up to us to save them. Are you going to help me?"

Luna sniffed and seemed to take a moment to collect herself. As she wiped away the salt collecting in her eyes and turned from a lifeless Jocasta, she met Aurora's gaze with a certain disdain that sent a chill over her body.

"Fine. But every life has meaning and purpose. No more killing."

Aurora recognized the words Astra used to say. She put out her hand, palm facing up, and nodded. "I will do my best."

Accepting the answer, Luna placed her palm on Aurora's, and together, they left the foul room.

CHAPTER 67

THE SCENT OF WARM honey, herbs, and dust woke Mariana.

Blinking back her bleary gaze, she realized she was inside Celeste's cabin. The familiar, cozy scent conflicted with the instant, twinging pain in her chest.

Lifting her head with a groan, she sat up in the bed and squinted through the darkness.

"What is this place?" the witch asked from the kitchen area, staring at the dried herbs hanging along the wall.

"What ..." Mariana started, her mind clouded. "How did we get here?"

With an amused smile, the witch inspected the cabin. "You had it in your mind."

Shaking her head, Mariana swung her legs down to the floor. "Wait ... my mind?"

"Yes," the witch said casually. "The amulet has a plethora of power. When you were unconscious, I could hear your mind calling out. When I saw this cabin in your mind, I brought you here. I wanted to understand what tethered you to this ... place."

Her fingers brushed along a dusty shelf, and she frowned in distaste. "And some mortal that doesn't seem to be here."

"Celeste," Mariana said softly, her throat tightening.

The witch sat down in Celeste's chair, the one she'd been sitting in the last time Mariana saw her ... before ...

"Strange that you would cling to something so beneath you, Mariana." The witch met her turbulent gaze. "Who was she?"

"Don't you dare speak about her like that. She was more of a mother to me than anyone." Her voice broke slightly, but she quickly regained her composure. "You—You killed her!"

"Killed her?" The Siren Witch scoffed lightly, her smile cold and condescending. "Don't be ridiculous, Mariana. This mortal's death wasn't my doing. You're letting your grief cloud your mind. She was nothing"—she waved her hand dismissively, her tone darkening—"but a mortal who coddled you, made you weak."

"You. Killed. Her." Mariana ground out each word through clenched teeth as she fought to stay calm.

The witch's eyes narrowed, sending chills down Mariana's spine. She sighed heavily. "I'm afraid you're mistaken, little one. I've never been here before. I've never seen this 'Celeste,' and I certainly have never sent any of my lovelies to this place. You have my word."

"Your word clearly means nothing."

"Oh, because I have this?" She lifted the amulet and gazed at it fondly. "I did what I had to do. With the amulet, we can save our people."

"And what about Astra?"

Letting the amulet go, the witch sighed as though she was bored. "Yes ... that was unfortunate."

"Un-unfortunate?" Mariana stuttered.

"She didn't want to work with me." The witch shrugged nonchalantly. "She never would, so I did what I had to do. But I know *we* will achieve greatness, Mari. You and I, together, we can change *everything*."

"There is no 'you and I.' You've manipulated me, lied to me, and hurt the people I care about most in this world! All so you could trick me into getting that damn amulet for you!"

The witch winced and shook her head. "No, I simply nudged you along the way to fulfilling your destiny, little one."

"Destiny?" Mariana released a harsh laugh.

"Yes." The witch gazed at her, her expression softening. "Your destiny was written in the waves of the sea and the stars of the sky, the moment you were born, Mariana. You were always going to find the amulet that would lead to our people's salvation."

"Astra found the amulet," Mariana spat out. "And you killed her for it."

The witch sighed heavily. "Everything I did was to help you."

"Help me?" She shook her head, unable to comprehend what she was hearing. "Poisoning Astra did not help me! She didn't deserve any of this. None of them did!" As the words spilled from her lips, she remembered something. "Did you ... Did you do something to Astra's guards?" The witch said nothing, and Mariana's fists tightened at her sides. "It wasn't sun poisoning. Cybele's power was still strong when she cast the protection enchantment on their armor. I watched her do it. It was you. You killed them, didn't you?"

A corner of the witch's mouth lifted. "I knew you were too smart to fall for that." She shrugged and picked at her claws. "Yes, I killed them. They were on their way back with information that I wanted to hear first. One of my followers intercepted them, called for me, and they told me Halia had taken Astra. When I kept pushing them for more information ... Let's just say, they had trouble believing my intentions were genuine."

"So, you murdered them," Mariana said in disgust.

The witch's mouth pinched. "I knew I could get you to go after it if I pushed you to save Astra."

"You figured out I was the only one who could unlock its power."

The witch smiled. "I knew the moment Cybele told me she had been impregnated by the fae king, the only male with the power to bring down the sky. The moment I saw you, held you in my arms, I knew you were special. It was only after the Scourge opened my eyes and showed me the way that I realized the true potential of the amulet that only you could unlock. That's why I encouraged your mother to give you the star sapphire." The witch tapped the center of the amulet, where the stone glowed. "I knew one day you would need it."

Mariana stared at it, thinking about how she'd had the key the whole time. She'd almost lost it once playing in a bed of seaweed. Her mother would've lost her mind; the witch ... might've killed her.

Then she realized something. Her eyes shot up to the witch's. "How did you convince Cybele to cast the binding spell on me?"

The witch released a chuckle. "I really should never underestimate you, little one. I'm impressed you figured it out. Honestly, it all came to me in the moment. When you were screaming, I believed that the sky power your mother convinced you to deny your whole life had finally overcome you. It was easy to convince her you had to go back to ensure you didn't die."

"You made it impossible for me not to find the amulet. It wasn't just about saving Astra anymore. It was about getting home, and I couldn't do that as a fae."

"Yes, and if you learned more about your heritage along the way, then so be it."

Mariana scrutinized her. "You expected me to meet my father?"

"I suspected you would encounter him while you were in the palace. I didn't realize how much he knew about his daughter's *clandestine affairs.*" The witch chuckled, and Mariana's jaw dropped a touch.

"How?"

The Siren Witch eyed her bracelet. "The shell I'd given you. I could hear you through it." Mariana lifted the bracelet and found the shell. "Clever trick I learned a while back. Had Luna give one to Astra too, told her it would keep her mother safe."

Mariana crushed the shell furiously in her hand. "You're a snake."

The witch *tsked*, shaking her head. "You're looking at this the wrong way, little one." Leaning forward, she rested her arms against the table where Mariana and Celeste used to make tea together. "Your destiny has always been entwined with mine. Everything I did, and everything I will do, is for you. For us. For our people to thrive and survive. Don't you see? The fae will never be able to harm us again with your power and my control of the amulet. We'll be unstoppable."

She was a monster. A lying, cheating monster.

"Did you enjoy killing Stavros?" Mariana asked in a near whisper.

The witch began to laugh. "How could I not? The male was a walking wraith. I put him out of his misery. That fae should be thanking me. In fact, *everyone* should be thanking me."

"So, you killed both son and father." The witch's smile faded. Mariana glared at her. "How does it feel? Just as you had hoped?"

The Siren Witch smirked. "I'd say, even better. Stavros had to die anyway. He served no purpose other than darkening those palace hallways."

Mariana glanced away. The witch was avoiding anything to do with Helios, and Mariana suspected she knew why. "Do you miss him?"

The witch's cold, black eyes narrowed on her. "Miss who?"

"Your lover, Prince Helios. If you listened to my conversation with King Stavros, then you're aware I know that you were having an affair with his son."

With a roll of her eyes, the witch stood, her hands curled into fists.

"Did you enjoy killing him too? Did you enjoy causing all of your sisters to be banished, causing our queendom to fall?" Mariana's voice rose in volume with each word until she was shouting at the witch. "You did this! You have so much blood on your hands, you're practically soaked in it!"

"And I LOVE IT!"

Breathing heavily, the witch chuckled and gave her a smile that didn't reach her eyes. "You know, whatever this place is to you, whoever this Celeste was, I think it's time you finally let her go. Be free of all this ... *emotion*." She spat the word out like it burned her tongue.

"What? Like you think you're free of your past?"

The witch gave her a pointed look. "I am, Mari. And I'll help you be free of the poison this place has inflicted upon you." The witch nodded toward a shadow in the corner, and suddenly, flames erupted in the kitchen.

Standing, Mariana watched the fire climb the sides of the cabin, scorching everything in its path. Her hands shot up to her mouth.

"What are you doing?" she breathed in horror.

"Helping you rid yourself of this toxic place." The witch grabbed Mariana's arm and roughly pulled her toward the cabin's front door.

"No! NO!" Mariana shouted, tears flooding her eyes as Celeste's prized plants began to burn, her homemade quilt catching fire along with all her books. "Stop! It's all I have left of her!"

"It won't stop, little one. Let it go."

The witch yanked Mariana out the door and wrapped her arms tightly around Mariana's chest, trapping her. Mariana kicked and screamed, but the stabbing pain in her chest just kept growing as the fire consumed Celeste's cabin. The place where she had always escaped to, the place she'd felt safe, loved, and appreciated.

Mariana's chest heaved. She could barely breathe through her sobbing.

"You need to let her go," the witch whispered into her ear, gripping her wrists tight.

"Stop!" Mariana begged. "Please! Please don't do this!"

But the flames never stopped, even as it began to rain. The sky rippled with dark clouds, and thunder growled through the air, followed by bright flashes of lightning. Mariana screamed for help, but it seemed the villagers knew to stay away. Through it all, the witch held on, not letting her go until the cabin was nothing but a pile of smoldering ash.

"There." The witch let her fall to the sand. "Now you're free. Free from the false sense of safety, free from the poisoned past. It's time to move forward, Mariana."

"You're a monster," Mariana whispered coldly, her eyes never straying from the ashes of her friend's home. "How could you do this?"

"Because I love you, little one. I'd do anything for you. That's why."

Mariana's teary eyes shot up to hers. "Love?" She shook her head. "You don't know what love is. The Scourge and its lies made sure of that when it sank its wicked teeth into your black heart."

"Lies? You mean truth." The witch stared at her in disbelief. "I am more powerful than I've ever been. I am more awake than I ever was before the Scourge opened my eyes. Don't you see? You'll be thanking me for what I did."

Mariana turned away, wiping her face.

"We'll start anew, you and me. Together, we'll rebuild what was lost in Sirenia. And you'll see, little one, that this is the only way," the Siren Witch said with so much hope, it made Mariana release a harsh laugh.

She stood on shaky legs. "No," she muttered. Tears she couldn't stop streamed down her face, but her voice was steady and filled with resolve. "I'll never follow you. I'd rather die."

The silence, followed by a dark, grim sigh from behind her, made fear coat her insides. She slowly glanced over her shoulder. The look in the witch's eyes sent chills down her spine.

CHAPTER 68

AURORA'S BODY WAS TAUT, waiting for the next attack as they rounded the corner. Glancing down the long hallway, she gripped the knife in one hand and Luna's hand in the other.

She had to get her niece out alive. Find Cybele and the others. Get to Mariana.

Simple, she assured herself. Then she scowled when doubt in the back of her mind whispered darkly, *Liar*.

Killing Jocasta had done something to her, made her feel things she hadn't felt since before the Banishment.

Fear. Dread. Hatred.

As her anxiety continued to spike, she struggled to keep herself calm, gripping Luna's hand so hard, she heard her gasp. Releasing the hand, Aurora gave her an apologetic glance before focusing on how to get into the throne room without being caught.

Strapped to her waist were several knives from the kitchen. If all went according to plan, she could get inside, disable the guards, and arm the rest of her sisters. Together, they could fight their way out.

If only she could get her hands to stop trembling.

Cora, their healer, explained that when she felt this way, it meant she was suffering from an anxiety disorder caused by traumatic events. The very idea that she was inducing self-punishment after all she did as the Scarlet Serpent made her want to laugh. She'd never felt regret for what she'd done. She'd followed her queen's orders, killed the target, then went on her way. That wasn't the cause for whatever was happening to her. It was ridiculous.

Calm down, she coaxed herself silently, as though that would help in some way. When that didn't work, she chose the only available route: she ignored it.

"Luna, I want you to take this," she said as she handed her a knife, doing her best to keep it from trembling.

Luna's eyes went wide, and she pulled her hand away. "No, no way."

"Luna," Aurora warned, and she watched her niece shake her head vehemently.

Fine.

Strapping the knife back to her waist, she gripped Luna's arm and stared her dead in the eyes. "You have to have my back, do you understand that? If someone comes up from behind, I need you to warn me."

Luna gulped, looking like a frightened youngling despite them being nearly the same age. They just lived very different lives. Astra had never believed in war, only peace, and refused to make her daughter a fighter. Aurora doubted Luna had ever held a weapon with the intention to use it, especially against fellow sirens, cursed or not.

"Okay," Luna whispered.

The deafening sound of Aurora's heartbeat made it difficult to hear her reply, but she had to trust her only ally. Without another word, they both swam as silently as possible through the darkened corridor that would lead them to the throne room.

As the stained glass double doors came into view, she heard two familiar, slithering, snake-like voices.

Aurora and Luna paused as they spotted the two serpents guarding the doors. Their beady red eyes had excellent vision, and their whirling, black and silver-scaled bodies were coated in an oily substance that made them extremely difficult to fight.

Originally deemed pests for eating the bioluminescent flora in their gardens, the serpents had proved a challenge for the sirens, who had tried in vain to repel the invasive creatures. However, a turning point arrived when the Siren Witch utilized her dark magic to communicate with the serpents. She'd discovered their true preference for bloody flesh, akin to the cursed sirens afflicted by the Scourge, who supposedly ate the mortals they stole souls from during the culling. This understanding formed an unlikely alliance between the beasts and the witch. She used that alliance to save the gardens and gained formidable companions, whom she called her pets.

As Aurora pushed past Luna to peer out a window overlooking the gardens, her heart sank at the sight of engulfing darkness, confirming her suspicions. The witch was indifferent to preserving the luminescent flora; her only interest lay in manipulating the serpents to fulfill her demands.

Cursing softly, Aurora tried thinking of a way to lure the serpents away from the doors without the glowing flora.

Her stomach churned as an idea came to her.

She turned to Luna. "I have a plan." She grimaced. "But you're going to hate it."

Luna winced. "Will it work?"

Aurora nodded reluctantly.

"Okay," she sighed. "Let's just get it over with."

Moving quickly, Aurora went back to the kitchens and tried not to gag as she picked up Jocasta's severed arm. She swam back toward Luna, who awaited her in the servant's hall next to the throne room doors.

"Oh my Goddess," Luna gasped, covering her mouth and turning away from the gore Aurora dropped beside them.

"Quiet," Aurora whispered. "Go wait over there," she ordered, pointing toward a hidden alcove.

Luna moved into position as Aurora dragged her knife across her arm. Scarlet blood leaked into the water, swirling gently along the current flowing through the palace halls. The cut sealed quickly, then she gripped the knife and turned her attention to the open door leading out to where the serpents lurked.

Unable to ignore the sultry taste of fresh blood in the water, she heard them hiss before the first one bolted in her direction.

Fast as lightning, she drove her knife into the serpent's head just as it sank its teeth into Jocasta's severed arm. The blade crunched through bone into its brain, killing it instantly.

She yanked the knife free just as the second serpent speared through the water at her, teeth bared and ready to strike. Instincts brought her knife up in time to catch the serpent's mouth, its teeth digging into her hand. She used the knife trapped in its throat to slam it to the ground. Trapping it with her body, she yanked the knife free, shredding her hand against the creature's sharp teeth, and sliced open its stomach.

It jerked, and its red eyes went wide before it fell still.

Breathing hard, Aurora pulled the blade from the slimy flesh and grimaced as her hand began to heal.

Luna rushed over to her. "Are you okay?"

Aurora nodded. "I'm fine. We have to go before more come."

Together, they made it to the throne room doors and peeked through the thick, colorful glass.

The Siren Witch, crowned in her signature headdress, stared ahead with a smile. The crowd gawked at whatever she was saying.

"We have to get in there," Aurora murmured and slowly pushed the doors open.

"You all are so important to me, and now that our dear Mariana and Cybele are no longer with us—"

What did she just say?

"No." Aurora shot forward, her chest caving in. "No!"

Before she could get close enough to slam her knife into the witch's black heart, two grotesque creatures snatched her arms, making it impossible for her to move.

The witch—she had betrayed them. She was the one who had poisoned Astra and Cybele.

"Ahh! Aurora, what a pleasure for you to join us." The witch swam closer, a devilish smile on her face. Aurora's eyes caught on the amulet hanging around her neck, its glow pulsing with energy. "I was just informing our sisters that Mariana and Cybele have met a very unfortunate end. But never fear, we shall remember them and honor their memory by restoring Sirenia. Together."

Aurora screamed in fury, thrashing violently as her soul cried out. "What did you do to them?!" she roared.

The witch gave her a sad smile. Aurora didn't buy it, seeing the cruel intention hidden beneath. "They're gone, Aurora. Mariana couldn't handle the guilt she felt at having killed Astra. I offered her a warrior's death as a way out. She took it willingly, and Cybele died in the battle, trying to stop her."

Aurora snarled, "Liar!"

"My mother ... My mother is dead?" Luna whimpered from her position near the doors. "Mariana killed her?"

The Siren Witch's expression morphed into pure grief, confusing Aurora. Swimming slowly to her side, the witch settled her clawed hands on Luna's shoulders.

"Yes, my dear. I'm so sorry. My heart breaks at the thought, but Mariana did the only thing she knew to be right. Which was to die after what she'd done."

Luna began to sob. Deep, racking sobs that made Aurora's throat tighten.

"She didn't mean to." Aurora's voice was thick; she was barely able to get the words out. "Mariana loved Astra. She wanted to bring her home to you, but the witch—"

"Did what had to be done to avenge Astra's death. It was the only way. Mariana knew it."

"No," Aurora stated firmly, glaring at the witch, who pulled Luna close to her, not sparing Aurora a glance. "You're twisting the truth. Luna, don't listen to her."

The witch gently hushed Luna's cries, rocking her back and forth, all while smiling smugly at Aurora. "You're alright, my dear. You'll be alright. We'll get through this together. In Sirenia."

"Sirenia?" Luna whispered, pulling back to look up at the witch.

"Yes," the witch crooned. "That's where we'll start a new life. One where no one can hurt us ever again." She brushed back Luna's unruly moonlight hair.

Aurora couldn't take it anymore. "Stop, just stop." She shook her head as the witch's eyes narrowed on her. "Everyone here knows you're full of shit."

"That is a very unkind thing to say, Aurora." The witch let go of Luna after caressing her cheek, then swam back to where Aurora was trapped between the revolting creatures that the witch must've summoned with the amulet.

"You know, it was heartbreaking to watch what Cybele did to you all those years as her *slave assassin*. To watch you slowly wither away into *this*, a sliver of your former self, dying with each kill until you were nothing but a husk of who you were. I remember who you were before. The sweet, golden child the queen so desperately wished had been born with the power of the sea. But alas, she couldn't make you her heir, so she exploited your skills to do her bidding. It was tragic, and I wished for it to be different."

The witch gripped Aurora's jaw tight. She gasped in pain as the tips of the witch's claws dug deep into her face. She could feel something leaking from them, slithering into her bloodstream.

Aurora struggled, trying desperately to break free as the sounds of her sisters screaming for her became muffle.

"I didn't want it to be this way, but after everything you've done, you will die a weak, incapable failure. As it should be."

The witch let her go, as did the creatures holding her. As she drifted to the floor, the world fading away, she couldn't help but think that everything the witch said was true.

And it broke her heart.

CHAPTER 69

"IT PAINS ME TO hear you say that, Mariana. I admit, the ways in which I went about acquiring the amulet were unsavory, but it had to be done. I don't regret it. And I want you to understand that." The witch turned away, heading back toward the dark, churning sea just as her two beasts rose from the waves holding—

"Mother!" Mariana shouted and ran toward Cybele as they threw her unconscious body onto the sand. Her crown rolled from her head, landing near the witch's feet.

Chuckling, the Siren Witch picked up the crown. She held it in her hands, staring at it for a long moment, while Mariana lifted her mother into her arms.

She was so pale. Dark veins sprawled from her chest, up her arms, into her face, causing Mariana to fear the worst. Settling a shaking hand against Cybele's throat, she felt a pulse. Weak, but there.

"You could be so much more than she ever was," the witch sighed. Mariana met her gaze, hatred radiating from her toward the one who had betrayed them. "I wish it didn't have to be this way, Mari. Please, don't make this mistake." She held the crown out toward Mariana, who flinched away, gripping Cybele harder.

"Take the crown, Mari. Take the crown, and let's change the fate of our sisters forever. Let's bring them home together."

Mariana shook her head, her wet hair whipping her neck against the raging wind and rain. "You'll never understand. *That* is not my crown. And you are not my family. I will never go anywhere with you because all you do is leave chaos and heartbreak behind wherever you go."

A corner of the witch's mouth tilted, and she let the crown drop from her fingers into the sand. "Well." She cleared her throat and straightened her dress before lightly clasping her hands before her. "I wish it didn't have to come to this, but you've given me no choice."

The amulet hanging at her chest began to glow a frightening shade of red, pulsing black and white. Mariana struggled to breathe as she watched waves on the beach start to thrash violently, as though some creature was surging up from within.

The witch gave her a remorseful stare, one that Mariana almost believed was real. Even the tears in the witch's eyes seemed genuine as she spoke. "I love you, little one. I have and always will. And because of that, I will give you the honor of a warrior's death. May your soul find peace with your choice in the end."

Without another word, the witch and her creatures walked into the water, disappearing beneath the waves.

Mariana stared ahead in complete shock. Something was coming. All the hair on her neck and arms stood on end. She had to move quickly. Grunting, Mariana pulled her mother up the beach.

"I'll protect you," she whispered before kissing her cold forehead.

The sound of someone gasping startled Mariana. Looking up, she saw a group of mortals glancing between her and the violent sea with wide, frightened eyes.

Then a roar gurgled up from the waves that was so loud, it shook the ground.

"What are you doing?! Run!" she shouted at the men and women standing there. They all quickly fled toward the center of the village just as something large and wet slammed onto the ground beside her.

Holding back a gasp, Mariana stared up into the hungry eyes of a beast that could have only come from nightmares.

"Oh, Gods," she breathed before it slammed a large fin into her side, sending her careening into the waves.

Gasping back the pain, she quickly stood and shoved the sea back, away from her.

The beast reared its head and let out a piercing scream through a jaw of razor-sharp teeth.

Mariana clutched her ears against the sound. Lightning flashed above them, revealing the beast in its entirety.

The dark shimmering scales rippled over a muscular body the size of a house. It stood on four legs that ended in long, sharp claws that dug into the sand. Its short but powerful tail swung back and forth behind it. And its eyes peered at her with such malicious hunger that Mariana couldn't stop herself from shaking.

Mariana barely had time to react as the beast lunged. She threw up a wall of water with a desperate wave of her hand, the waves crashing into the creature's snout with a force that sent it staggering back. But it was only momentarily dazed; it quickly recovered, shaking off the water like a dog shaking off rain, and fixed its piercing eyes on her again.

"Shit," she muttered and ran up the beach.

With a leap and a swipe of its claws, it slashed at her back, sending her falling face down into the sand with a scream.

Gasping and choking, she moaned against the pain, feeling blood leak down her back and her legs, mixing with the wet, dripping paint sticking to her skin.

Mariana's heart pounded in her chest, but she forced herself to stay calm. She couldn't let fear paralyze her—not now, not with her mother's life hanging by a thread.

The beast circled her, snarling, its claws sinking deep into the wet sand. It wanted her to run again, clearly enjoying the chase. The chase, she wouldn't let it have.

Summoning all the strength she could muster, Mariana stood, then raised her hands high above her head. Her body hummed with energy that sped up her heart, and she smiled as the sea answered her call.

A towering wave surged up from behind the beast, curling inward like the maw of a leviathan. Mariana clenched her fists, gritting her teeth as she sent the wave crashing down, slamming the beast into the sand with the weight of a mountain. For a moment, it seemed the creature would be crushed under the sheer force of the water, but then it rose from the deluge with a thunderous roar, eyes blazing with fury.

Mariana's breath caught in her throat. The beast was relent-less, its hunger insatiable, and it was clear that it wouldn't stop until she was dead. But she was not defenseless. Not now, not ever.

The creature lunged again, its jaws wide open, but Mariana was ready. With a sharp gesture, she called forth a current from the depths, wrapping it around the beast like a vice. The water coiled around its legs, pulling it off-balance, and Mariana used the momentum to shove the creature back toward the sea.

The beast resisted, claws digging furrows into the sand as it tried to keep its footing. But Mariana's determination was stronger. She poured every ounce of her will into the sea, com-manding it to reclaim the monster that had dared to defy her. With a final, desperate push, the beast was dragged back into the churning waves.

But it wasn't enough. Mariana knew she had to end this here, now, before the beast could break free again. As the creature struggled against the undertow, Mariana reached up toward the sky, calling on the storm that raged above. The clouds churned in response, dark and furious, and the air crackled with the promise of lightning.

She thrust her hand down toward the beast, and the sky answered with a bolt of lightning that split the heavens. The strike hit the water with a deafening crack, and for a moment, the world seemed to stand still. The sea glowed with an eerie light, and the beast let out one last anguished roar before it was engulfed in a vortex of lightning and waves.

The sea swallowed the creature whole, and then, as suddenly as it had begun, the storm began to dissipate. The clouds parted, and the first rays of dawn broke through, casting a golden light over the beach.

Breathing heavily, Mariana stumbled back onto the shore, her legs nearly giving out beneath her. But she forced herself to stay upright, her eyes fixed on the spot where the beast had been. The water calmed as if the battle had never taken place.

But it had. And she had won.

Mariana's gaze shifted to her mother's still form lying on the sand. With a cry, she rushed to Cybele's side, falling to her knees and gathering her mother into her arms.

"Mother," she whispered, her voice breaking. Cybele's skin was cold, her breathing shallow, and the dark veins still crawled across her body like a poison that refused to relent. Tears welled up in Mariana's eyes as she cradled her mother's head, brushing a damp strand of hair away from her face. "Please stay with me. I need you."

Cybele's eyes fluttered open, just barely. She looked up at Mariana with a weak but proud smile, lifting a trembling hand to touch her daughter's cheek. "My brave daughter," she murmured, her voice so soft, it was almost lost to the sound of the waves. "You've become everything I always knew you could be."

Mariana shook her head, tears streaming down her face. "We'll find a way to heal you. We'll—"

"I love you, Mari," Cybele whispered, her eyes bright with tears in the rising sun.

"I love you," Mariana whispered back, clutching her mother's head to her chest. "Please don't go. Please don't leave me," she whimpered. But Cybele's hand slipped from Mariana's face, her eyes closing as a peaceful expression settled over her features.

The last of her strength faded, and her body went still in Mariana's arms.

"No," Mariana choked out, holding her mother close as her shoulders shook with silent sobs. The sun continued its ascent, bathing the world in light, but all Mariana could feel was the darkness closing in around her.

"Come back. Please don't leave me," she croaked, feeling the pain of everyone she'd lost smother her, drowning her in grief.

She stayed there on the sand, crying, cradling her mother as the waves gently lapped at their feet, the sea now calm and serene.

"Amphitrite, hear my plea, hear my wish, and guide my mother safely to the end. Guide her to a peaceful place where she can be happy, where she can bask in the sun without fear." Mariana pulled back, brushing her mother's hair away from her face, and sniffed. "Let her soul be free to wander the sea and give me the courage to do what must be done."

A cold, ethereal hand caressed Mariana's face, and she closed her eyes, leaning into the gentle touch before it slowly disappeared.

Opening her eyes, Mariana stared out over the horizon at the Leruna Sea. The sun rose steadily into the sky, bright and unyielding, just as she would be.

With a deep breath, Mariana wiped her tears, kissed her mother's forehead one last time, and slowly rose to her feet. A glint of light caught her eye, and she glanced at the diamond-spiked crown still lying half-buried in the sand where the witch had dropped it. She slowly walked toward it and picked it up, feeling the weight of its history, its legacy, and the responsibility that it represented.

She hated it even more now. And yet, she couldn't get herself to destroy it. No. She knew where it belonged, and it wasn't on her head.

With one last look at the horizon, Mariana made a vow to her mother, to Astra, and to Celeste.

No matter what happened, no matter the cost, the witch would die by her hand.

Epilogue

"Do you hear it?" The whispers echoed through the thick mist, a chilling breeze carrying them like secrets.

Spiders skittered across the damp ground, their tiny legs tapping against the cracked stones. The old trees on the island loomed, ancient sentinels, their gnarled branches reaching out like skeletal fingers.

"Tell me," she said, her voice a tremulous whisper swallowed by the fog. Her breath merged with the mist that shrouded the silent village.

"Don't you hear it?" they asked again, voices mingling with the rustle of leaves.

"Hear what? Tell me," she ordered softly, a shiver running down her spine.

"She's coming," a hot breath whispered harshly into her ear, the words searing her consciousness. She gasped, her vision blurring as she pushed herself free from the spirit realm. The sensation was like being pulled through a veil of icy water, making her breaths shallow and rapid.

The wind blew the fog back into the quiet village, wrapping the cottages in an eerie embrace while clearing the view ahead of her. A smile spread across her lips as she stood in the cobblestone square. Anticipation flickered in her single eye, the other eternally shrouded in darkness as she watched lightning brighten the horizon.

She sighed. "Finally."

The story continues in book two of The Leruna Sea Series:

Keep up with S.L. DeBois and The Leruna Sea Series at
https://www.authorsldebois.com

you were all there for me. I will always cherish our memories together, no matter where this next step in life takes us.

To my Wicked Sirens Street Team and beta readers, I mean it wholeheartedly when I say that my sails could not have been lifted without you all pushing the winds in my favor. Each of you is incredible, compassionate, understanding, and supportive in ways I never dreamed of. Thank you for spreading the word about this book, telling your friends and family, and being there for me.

To my fantastic editors, Megan and Laura, you both are so wonderfully talented, and you transformed this story into the novel I am so proud of. Thank you from the bottom of my heart.

Acknowledgements

Where to even begin! Let me start by saying that this book would not have been at all possible without the love of my life, Zane. You pushed me to follow my dreams, lifted me from darkness into the light more times than I can count, and listened to me whenever I knew something was wrong with the storyline, helping me improve it. You're one in a million, and I'm so glad I found you.

To my family, your support and encouragement bestowed the confidence I needed to finish this book. Mom, Dad, Mike, I love you and will always be so grateful for you. Your undeniable pride in me has pushed me to accomplish my lifelong goal, and now I can finally say I've done it.

Jocelyn, my bestie who stayed up late with me on more than one occasion to talk about this book, who fought the demons in my head with the sword of truth, and who read the terrible first draft, thank you for being you. Thank you for being my friend and always having my back.

Shout out to Kari, Tessa, and my entire CJ family. Thank you for your unwavering, unconditional support of my writing journey. Whenever I felt overwhelmed, insecure, or a failure,

www.ingramcontent.com/pod-product-compliance
Lightning Source LLC
Chambersburg PA
CBHW021118260626
47169CB00005B/1332

About the author

S.L. DeBois had a lifelong dream to become a published author. Growing up in Hawaii, where storytelling held deep cultural significance, she developed a love for learning and imagination. That passion and her love for Halloween—her favorite magical holiday—shaped her aspirations as a writer.

As she grew older, anxiety became her greatest nemesis (because, let's be honest, adulthood is no easy feat). Once again, she found solace in crafting magical fantasy stories, creating worlds where adventure and wonder thrived.

Now, living with her husband and mischievous pets, S.L. DeBois remains on the lookout for the next great adventure—whether in the real world or hidden within the enchanting pages of a book.

https://www.authorsldebois.com
https://authorsldebois.substack.com